D0870438

Available in Norton Paperback Fiction

THE
WHISTLING
SONG

"During his reading hours, which were between one and five o'clock in the morning, but not every morning, he had come to the disconcerting conclusion that whistling was not an important theme in literature. There weren't many authors who made their characters whistle. Practically none of them did."

—Julio Cortázar, *Hopscotch*

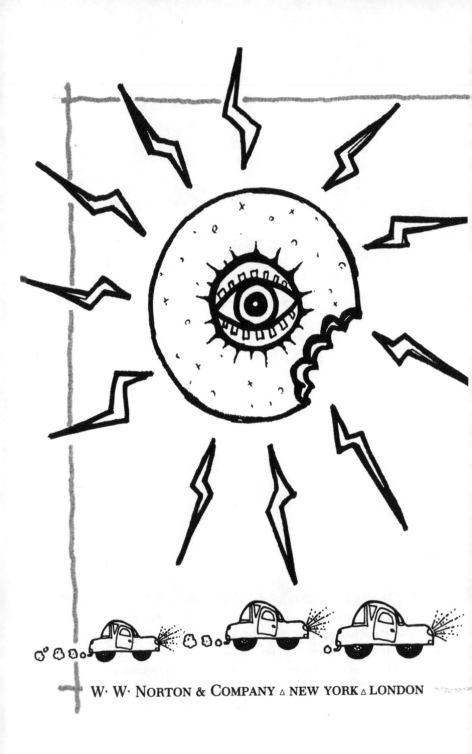

W· W· NORTON & COMPANY △ NEW YORK △ LONDON

THE WHISTLING SONG

A NOVEL

STEPHEN BEACHY

Printed in the United States of America

The text of this book is composed in Caledonia,
with the display set in Metropolis Bold.
Composition and manufacturing by
The Maple-Vail Book Manufacturing Group.
Book design by Michael Chesworth.
Title typography by Debra Morton Hoyt
Drawings by Curt Kirkwood
Lyrics from "The Whistling Song" reprinted by permission of Curt Kirk-
wood, *The Meat Puppets*.

Library of Congress Cataloging-in-Publication Data

Beachy, Stephen.
The whistling song : a novel / Stephen Beachy.
p.   cm.
I. Title.
PS3552.E128W4   1992
813'.54—dc20   92-31579

ISBN: 978-0-393-30949-2

W. W. Norton & Company, Inc.
500 Fifth Avenue, New York, N.Y. 10110
W. W. Norton & Company Ltd.
10 Coptic Street, London WC1A 1PU
1 2 3 4 5 6 7 8 9 0

CONTENTS

ACKNOWLEDGMENTS

The author wishes to thank the following for their encouragement and editorial assistance at various stages of this book: Frank Conroy, Allan Gurganus, James McPherson, Clark Blaise, Susan Daitch, Carol Houck Smith, Henry Dunow, Joshua Clover, Tracy Van Quaetham, Bruce Holbert and John Beckman.

Also, thanks to my family and friends, for everything.

And to James Michener and the Copernicus Society, grateful acknowledgment for their financial support.

Book One

It's the shadow in the dark
it's the silver in the park
it's the broken, faded bird
you've learned to call your heart . . .

it hovers in the living room
just above the door,
it whistles while it hangs there,
feathers drip from every pore
they show the spectacle of falling
and settle to the floor

—THE MEAT PUPPETS—
"The Whistling Song"

ONE

Δ

1

There was something powerful emanating from the bathtub, something magical churning there in the primordial Mr. Bubble sea. That's where everything began, laughter and dance steaming out of the seafoamy depths, life itself emerging joyful and slimy from below. Andalusia, the large, walnut-skinned woman who lived in the other half of our duplex, used to bathe me. The drowsy, unctuous feel of the bubbles, Andalusia's spicy aroma, nutmeg and cloves, little blobs of red and blue plastic bobbing in the water; it was heaven. The steamy, fertile heat, the feel of Andalusia's fingers, fleshy digits as slippery as birth. She soaped my little white belly, my little white toes, my little white kneecaps and my little white penis, an experience I particularly relished, prompting spasms of laughter with antediluvian glee. And she sang. Her swampy voice, a warm, oozing sensation, like wiggling naked toes in rich, gooey mud. She sang:

> "Alice, where are you going?
> Upstairs—to take a bath.
> Alice, you are so skinny,
> It almost makes me laugh.
> Alice, got in the bathtub
> Pulled, the stopper out.
> Oh my goodness, oh my soul!
> There goes Alice down the hole!"

The image of a tall, skinny white woman being sucked down the drain not only terrified and amused me, but also intrigued me. What would she find down there? As Andalusia leaned over me in her gaping, plum-colored dress, scrubbed behind my ears and sang, I plunged down the drain after Alice. The world was ancient and frothy down there, lush jungle foliage and bubbly orange vegetation slithered up and down, in and around the vast, hazy, aquatic landscape. Mushy trolls sat moaning low and smoking fragrant pipes, spearmint and cherry, luscious mermaids played the bongos, purple whales sent fountains cascading down over me, fresh ocean spray, and droned on in slippery voices: *The spiraling deception is the ritual journey of the soul in its mystic ascent; mysterium tremendum, cosmological speculation, ubiquitous maledictions, the shedding of blood . . .*

Alice, in the midst of it all, wandered frantically, whining, agitated, always looking for that elusive drain that would take her home, home, always searching for home, never realizing that she was already there. That bathtub was home; Mr. Bubble, the smiling pink god of love, watched over us from above, perched comfortably on top of the toilet tank. Me and Andalusia, we frolicked joyfully, as young lovers always do, could have stayed in that moist Eden forever. The most joyful times of my life were the evenings she baby-sat, in the tub with that huge woman, that fragrance, sweet and damp, earthy and clean all mixed together.

And then, the evenings that loomed ahead for the two of us. Card tricks on the dirty red carpet in front of the television, cards that vanished and reappeared right on cue, dancing jacks and queens and nines of diamonds. Melted colors of finger paintings; puppydog bicycles and three-headed spacemen, frozen maple syrup on a stick, frog meadows, enchanted chesspiece worlds. Andalusia loved to play chess, she taught me how. Pawns and rooks and stuffy bishops, beautiful, vibrant queens, passive, melancholy kings. Andalusia always took the white pieces, I took the black, in a reversal of the roles our chromosomes had dealt us. She could have won, easily, every time we ever played. She would gasp in astonishment as I cornered her king, declare, *Matt, you have done it again.*

Sometimes, on hot, breezy summer evenings, we did somersaults in newly mown grass under ominous, swirling clouds, ran wild, feeling the grass between our toes. Dark cumulus formations gathered overhead, protruding pillars of cloud, and hot, dusky winds. I loved tornado weather, it swept me away, flowed through me, all the stifled joy and rage of the billowing universe. Those winds, devil winds that whipped through my stringy hair, plunged down my throat, jangled my uvula and surged through my body with the scent of distant lands. I'd climb Mrs. Tyndall's maple tree during a storm to really feel it, the power, the magic, the wind. Rustling leaves and then overwhelming quiet, even in the midst of distant dogbarking, sirens and TV weathermen it was quiet, hushed with awe in the face of everything that is.

Mom would yell at me when I did that, climbed that tree. She said I'd be struck by lightning. Only Andalusia didn't mind, she knew that nothing could hurt me then. She even climbed up herself once, the whole tree shook with her weight, but she didn't fall. The wind swirled that plum-colored dress around, I could see pure possibility reflected in her eyes. I ran my hand up and down the trunk, felt the rough bark against my palm. We belonged there; the tree itself knew us.

She told me I was the only man she'd ever need. I'd always been with Andalusia, since before the dawn of time. On hot nights we'd lie together in front of the fan, me wet still from the bathtub, squeaky and pajama'd. Voices trembled and raved inside the fan, every sound the world could make, and Andalusia slept, her hand resting against my neck. I could feel the room breathing with her, the planet's shifting moods, Andalusia's quiet snoring. The world was most alive, fermenting and deep when sleeping.

Sleeping, dreaming, waking. Our living-room ceiling was plastered with adhesive glitters, stars that expanded the seemingly finite space into a universe. I leapt across infinity into

Andalusia's arms from the foamy, dilapidated sofa and rolled across the floor, waking the alligators who lived in our plumbing, shaking the world to its bubbly, molten, fish-eyed core. Globes and plastic astronauts, railroad tracks and the smell of Elmer's glue. *National Geographic*, zebras, tentacles, lips. The doomed journeys of crickets, the quiet explosions of earthworm excavations. Candles and masks, the Beach Boys and bones, the monstrous expanse of childhood time, lunatic time, anarchic and clumsy and tearing through fields, spilling pulp and confetti, overflowing the tub. Shattering hourglasses, sand on our toes.

Nights we'd watch the late movie, way past my bedtime. Andalusia made popcorn and we ate it out of a huge plastic bowl, licking the salt and grease from the bottom when there was nothing left but old maids, tossing the kernels into the air and catching them on our tongues. We watched in the dark, just the blue glow of the television, Clint Eastwood westerns with eerie, whistling soundtracks or *The Planet of the Apes*. But *Vanishing Point* was our favorite. It was a car-chase movie, an outlaw speeding down western highways, the last American hero, a snake charmer, faith healers, a naked woman on a motorcycle and the final scene: the final scene where it seemed like everything was lost, the law would catch him in his white Dodge Challenger, but he accelerated and the highway wavered and he kept on going and there he was, right there and *whooooooosh,* he vanished, vanished right into the air, into another dimension, out of sight, gone. I trembled and hoped someday I'd do that, too. *Whooooooosh,* vanish.

But Andalusia was the one who vanished. She moved away, as duplex dwellers are so prone to do. Duplexes are typically only stopping points on the way up: to single-family dwellings, penthouse condominiums and sprawling mansions guarded by gargoyles, perched and jeering on their cold steel gates. Or, for those in decline, a brief rest on the way down: to efficiency apartments, sleazy hotel rooms with semen-stained mattresses, correctional institutions of one sort or another. As a rule, duplexes don't serve as long-term housing. My own family was just exactly the exception to that rule.

Andalusia was gone. Who came in to fill the hole left by her absence? Some redhaired chickenwoman and her improbable husband, their silent baby that never cried and never smiled. That woman was always screaming in panic, screaming that it was dead, that crib death had slunk into our duplex and snatched her firstborn. But no, it lived on, always it was still breathing. Maybe it grew up to be mentally retarded. I can't say, I had no opportunity to observe the little bundle of blankets and face develop, for before long they, too, vanished into the blur of transient America.

There were others, countless others, people with tattoos and more babies and chain-smokers and people who watched TV loudly as I lay in my dark room, staring at the ceiling, traveling up and through into the stars beyond. Aliens with ludicrous, elliptical craniums drove spaceships shaped like banjos, interstellar unicorns whizzed past Pluto, and all the while crazed men shouted about slashing prices, clearing inventory, and swallowing live rodents from beyond the thin wall, violent and electric pleas to BUY, BUY, BUY. Their pleas merged with my dreams, my raw, bacony dreams of blowguns and mesmerists and, of course, Andalusia. I dreamed always of Andalusia. Nothing could erase her memory or ease the pain of separation, not shiny new toys or shiny new neighbors or Marcie Tyndall, my shiny new baby-sitter, the willowy daughter of Mrs. Tyndall in the house next door. Mrs. Tyndall was a dowdy woman, tough and grinning, the mother of several rowdy and delinquent youth. She used to spy me hanging out in the alley, digging through their garbage for hidden treasures or lurking furtively around their back porch.

"Well, look what's hanging about," she'd exclaim. "Careful, boy, somebody might mistake you for a mop and stick your head in a bucket of soapy water. Come to think of it," she'd add, after a brief, thoughtful pause, "my floor could use a good scrubbing har, har . . ." and she'd go so far as to pretend she was going to use me for just that purpose, picking me up by my feet and twirling me around their kitchen a bit. It was from this perspective that I observed that the Tyndall kitchen was, indeed, in need of a good disinfecting. I doubt a mere mopping would have really done the trick.

Marcie bore little resemblance to the sturdy loins from which she had sprung. Whenever Dad took Mom out for a night of tribal dancing around a blazing bonfire, to the pulsating rhythms of African drums, or when they went bowling sometimes, Marcie would come over and slouch on the sofa, leafing through magazines, oblivious to my existence. She was long-legged and fair-skinned, and I was too young yet to see what it was about her blue eyes and her apathy that drove all the neighborhood hoodlums into lust frenzies, squealing around corners in their pickup trucks, hurling beer bottles and shouting obscenities as Marcie sat barefoot on the porch on hot summer nights, sipping a beer. She said very little. She didn't do card tricks. By that time I was old enough to take baths by myself.

Eventually I didn't even need a baby-sitter. When I was ten I got my paper route. After the alarm clock shattered my dreams at three-thirty every morning it was silent and I was lord of all, a conquerer, a hero. They all slept innocently, Mom, Dad, the neighbors, unaware of the perils, the strange adventures that waited for me. Stealthily I would rise and slip into the night, prowl through the neighborhood beneath the dim stars or bright moon. Summer nights out there, brave and alone, were exquisite, dipped in green ink, a dark jungle calm. Lilacs smelled louder at night and the enigmatic smell of the river flew past, swampy and sweet if the wind blew from the north. Tuesday was trash day and my streets smelled like garbage, stray dogs terrorized my domain, but I spoke to them, carried sticks, and it was usually sublime. There was only darkness behind picture windows, tinkling wind chimes, the thud of the newspaper hitting the porch. I had the run of the territory, orbiting the silvery night. Mondays and Saturdays were best. Those were the light days. Wednesdays and Thursdays I was weighed down with advertising supplements. Afterward, free of all burdens and responsibility, if I didn't go straight home and collapse into bed, listen to the birds and the dawn, sometimes I'd walk from the end of my route, down a dark and frightening street, past a bro-

ken, hissing streetlight and a blue bugzapper that sent electric
shivers pulsing through the night, to the main drag and Donutland.

Donutland. Divine fragrance of freshly baked pastry wafted
through the air, early risers pondered their coffee and jovial
policemen chatted with the waitress, didn't even look at me. I
devoured honey-dipped donuts or apple crunch or banana frosted
with nuts. Orange juice, a skimpy glass of orange juice for sev-
enty-five cents, but tasty nonetheless. I watched the end of the
night merge with the beginning of the day, listened in on endless conversations about riding lawn mowers. All those policemen and waitresses and night sweepers and milkmen, all the
insomniacs and somnambulists and night clerks and dancers,
they were all saving up their money to buy riding lawn mowers.
Four-wheel drive, fifteen different attachments, vacuum suc-
tion, the planets were permanently aligned in their riding
lawn-mower phase, and nobody was willing to fight the forces
of destiny. Coffee was brewed, newspapers read. Old men shuf-
fled in and out, cigarettes burned forever, everything moved
slowly in Donutland. I could have stayed in Donutland forever,
would have gladly pledged my allegiance to the Donutland flag,
sworn to defend Donutland to the last drop of raspberry creme.
But sleepiness always swayed me and inevitably I trudged back
home, to bed, as daylight poured over my shining kingdom,
bringing on the sticky heat of the day and revealing the ugly
truths of a tired and sweaty neighborhood in Des Moines. I'd
pull my shades, crawl under the sheet, try to hide, but it never
worked. The daylight always found me.

When I was still tiny, Dad took me for rides on his red-and-
black Honda. Mom didn't want him to, she was afraid I might
die. Dad didn't think like that, so Saturday mornings when Mom
was out bowling with her league, off we'd go. Dad would kick-
start the engine, throw me on back and brrvrrmrvroooomm! Out
through the backyard, down the alley, so that nosy witch Wig-
gins across the street wouldn't rat on us. And wheee! Hanging
on to Dad's belt for dear life, shrieking in delight, the wind

blowing my greasy mop of hair every which way. Out, through the pothole-filled suburban streets, past other little kids playing in their yards. They'd watch with envy, miserable little urchins because they weren't lucky enough to be me on that bike. Out, past the tire factory and the interstate and into the countryside. Out, into the blue sky and that curvy highway, yowee, around those curves, past the big tank and the big swimming pool and on; trees and fields of corn and cars and sunshine, pure wild joy, exhausting exhilaration, speed. How very fast we moved, hurtling into the future, plunging into the welcoming, magic horizon of clouds, skies filled with whipped cream and maraschino cherries. We'd climb a steep hill at a zillion miles an hour, up, up, and just take off, zip past airplanes and hot-air balloons, spit on the birds, fly through donutholes in the sky, laugh and scream, faster, faster, whish, swish, then klunk, klunk, bounce down the alley, putter through the yard and home.

I'd be so worn out from ecstasy that I'd just wipe the cloud remnants off my body, so Mom wouldn't know, and lie there in the grass, in our little patch of backyard, too tired to move, watching the clouds drift by. White winds blowing white dragons, white unicorns and tragic white cow sorcerers gently by, against infinite blue, blue, the blue sounds of rustling blue flowers, blue smell of grass, enveloping blue. Dad would sit there at the table on the back porch, scribbling away at his elaborate theories: that subatomic particles exercised their free will; that psychic phenomena increased under reactionary governments; convoluted charts of ethical systems proving that dreaming, choosing and doodling were positive moral acts. Occasionally he'd glance up to admire me, his son, to fill himself with my traditionally childish presence, inspire himself with well-entrenched myths of innocence and joy.

Dad was a smart man, Mom always said, and someday he'd be rich and famous, although those things didn't really matter, especially the famous part. In the meantime he worked over at the mass-mailing factory, or sometimes at Jason's gas station, which he liked better, to make a little extra when things were tight. I liked to visit him there, to smell the gas on his hands.

Our side of the duplex was cluttered with mistakes from the presses, irregular magazines. UFOs, Boy Scouting, muscle men, cooking. Magazines aimed at housekeepers who liked to scuba dive, feminists who wore skimpy outfits, motorcyclists, chess players, gun nuts and fashion-conscious laborers. Dad showed me pictures in travel magazines, Greece or Tibet, and told me stories from his life: escaping a charging Komodo dragon, brunch with a tribe of cannibals, telepathic communication with a squirrel in Mount Vernon. Back before I was born he'd done a lot of exciting things. He'd even gone to college for a while.

Mom told me more stories than Dad did, but those were mostly out of books. She read me stuff out of the Bible, Noah and Jonah and the Garden of Eden, or Bible storybooks she brought home, filled with pictures of smiling, bearded men and women drawing water from the well. She was a pretty woman with a feathery voice. The way she read it, all that fratricide and apocalypse sounded harmless; mankind as a mischievous child and God, the loving disciplinarian. Flooding the planet, sending his people into the desert for years, swallowing Jonah in a whale. It was cartoon violence, like Bugs Bunny and the Roadrunner. Flattened, blown to smithereens, it all turned out okay in the end.

Mom always had a dreaminess about her, like she wasn't quite concentrating on the here and now. In the evenings she watched spiders spinning webs in our windows. She never cleaned them out. She hardly ever cleaned anything out, that was just her way. Empty milk cartons and peanut butter jars mated under our sink, breeding weird creatures that scurried about the kitchen all night while we slept. Life grew in the refrigerator, orgies of mold and crazed fermentation. Black things in yogurt cups, exuberant cheeses, zigzags of gelled bacon grease and troll embryos striped in colors in jars. Mom was a genetic engineer, creating amazing varieties of life through luck and sheer negligence. While biological anarchy evolved in her kitchen, she sat at the table, eating fried onions and crackers. She'd grown up on a farm, miles from anywhere, and if I listened hard enough I could hear the wind outside that dark farmhouse, late at night, my mother as a young girl at the window, waiting for unexpected visitors. I remember her in gardens, surrounded by weeds. I remember her at the sink, her wispy blond hair falling into her eyes as she washed a few dishes, wearing a ragged flowered apron and those baggy green pants. I remember her in rainfalls and tunnels and churches. Sunday mornings she always took me to church, although Dad didn't approve, in her pale frilly dress, her hair piled on her head.

"Organized religion is the most spiritually destructive force on earth," Dad said. "Spend the morning down at the river for Christ's sake."

"Well, hmm, yeah," said Mom. "But Matt needs some sort of moral training. Somebody has to teach him the difference between right and wrong."

Dad just grumbled into his Sunday paper and off we'd go, me in some obnoxiously hot, tortuous outfit, designed to punish me for my juvenile sins. Fat, buggy-eyed ministers or gaunt, quivering ostrich-men shouted at me about Gideon, and blaring trumpets and marching onward to Zion, repent, woe is me! Let the children come to me, you must be born again, saith the Lord, build your house on the solid rock, drink of the water of life, beware the mark of the beast. They shot lightning bolts straight into me as I fidgeted on the hellish wooden pews, trying to rouse me out of my boredom, but nothing could make those endless Sunday mornings bearable, not even a million volts of electricity running up and down my spine.

We moved around quite a bit, from church to church. Dad was happier that way, and even Mom got uncomfortable sometimes when old, blue-haired women from the front pews or mealy pastors in ashen suits would approach us after the service, ruffle my hair and try to get Mom to commit, to take a step for Christ, for the child's sake, at least think about the child's future. That was me. The child.

Occasionally, in between Catholics and Presbyterians, Mennonites and Unitarians, Lutherans, Baptists and the First Church of the Nazarene, occasionally we went to a Buddhist church. That was more fun. We sat on the floor and let everything stop. Dad even went along sometimes then, and would take us out for hamburgers afterward. My young mind had no trouble assimilating this strange variety of religious instruction and kneading it into a more holistic view of the nature of God and reality, including a rather schizophrenic image of Jesus, the suffering, Christ-eyed man with children on his knee who blessed the peacemakers while anticipating his fiery return to earth in the year 2000 to blow the shit out of the human race. The holy trinity was expanded into a super sevensome, including Buddha, Zeus, my dad and Underdog. Sunday-morning services, I was convinced, fit into God's scheme as a glimpse of what hell would be like for those of us who refused to eat our string beans and didn't brush before going to bed. Every Sunday, as the neighborhood creaked and groaned in the morning sunlight with its collective hangover, we'd putter along in our little green VW. I would stare groggily, Mom would hum along to *American Top 40* with Kasey Kasem and chew her nails.

"Here's a long-distance dedication going out to Gina Wunder," Kasey said in that Styrofoam voice of his, "from Bob, the young man she accidentally blinded in a high school science experiment. They were in love then, but circumstances tore them apart. Well, Gina, through the miracle of science Bob has his sight back. And most of all it's you he'd love to see. For Gina, from Bob, here's 'Muskrat Love.' "

As we pulled into church parking lots I'd always feel a nervous dread. I was a good kid, I knew, with nothing to fear from God, but the sulphurous odor of all that fire and brimstone made it difficult to breathe sometimes and we always sat behind men who sang loud and deranged. This enforced period of boredom had its benefits, however, became the impetus for creative action. Imagination wasn't just a luxury, but a necessary tool for survival. Usually I sat and drew pictures on notepads Dad brought home from the factory, dinosaurs and monsters and men with two heads. Sometimes I listened to the sermons, especially when the ministers started going on about the endtimes, when hundreds of thousands of good Christians would just vanish into the sky. Like *Vanishing Point*, I thought, and I drew pictures of people who'd vanished. I'd draw cars and houses and igloos and river rafts with squiggly lines, little wisps where the people had been, but weren't anymore. Mom always listened intently, refused to look at my drawings, even when I colored them in with crayons. Vermilion, magenta and aquamarine. I stuck the crayons in my nose sometimes to inhale their rich, waxy smell. I liked to smell Mom, too. She always smelled nice on Sunday mornings, dark red and yellow.

Dad usually smelled good, too, but it was a rough, mysterious smell. Alcohol and breath mints, cheap cologne, maybe, and old books. He used to rub his whiskers against my face when I was tiny and I would scream, scream, scream. Or he tickled me or rode me on his shoulders; my legs would fall asleep and I wondered as I reached up and touched the ceiling what it would be like to be so tall and so close to the ceiling all the time, so far from the ground. Now, I try to remember what it was like to be so close to the earth. I walk around on my knees sometimes.

Dad was a good-looking guy, dark and hairy and smart-looking, with glasses. His eyes were filled with visions, with original fire and sin. His teeth were yellow, he rarely brushed. There was something strong about him, a quiet, magic strength. Mom was good-looking, too, blue-eyed and gentle, but not so exotic. Good people, really, both of them, wonderful people. They gave me more than I can even fathom.

They were cordial and benevolent. They were a well-liked if somewhat misunderstood couple.

So, it was a grave disappointment not only to myself but to many of the neighbors as well when I had to wake up Mrs. Tyndall at five o'clock on a Wednesday morning to inform her that my parents were dead.

She had a black eye when my adamant doorbell ringing roused her from her slumber. Undoubtedly, it had been inflicted by Mr. Tyndall during one of their drunken poker-and-backgammon evenings. She wasn't especially pleased to see me.

"What do you want, you little sonofabitch?" she shrieked.

"I'm sorry to bother you," I said, "but my parents have been murdered."

I was always a polite, somewhat shy child. She shrieked once again, in disbelief, then thought better of it, grabbed my hand and marched me over to my house, a look of morbid curiosity plastered to her face.

My parents had been murdered. My parents had been repeatedly stabbed with a carving knife from our very own kitchen, blood spurting through Dad's once-dingy white T-shirt, his livid eyes glazing over, his head hanging limply to the side. Mom, too, stabbed right through her delicate pink nightie, her angelic sleep brought to an abrupt end by a knife thrust in her breast.

It was April.

My parents had been murdered. Mrs. Tyndall became quite hysterical. I remained calm, didn't even cry. I heard somebody say, through the mass of blaring sirens and shouting neighbors, that I must be in shock. I don't think so. If I was in shock then, I'm in shock now. The feeling hasn't really changed in these last ten tears. Just a quiet pain, like you have a little black ball, the consistency of warm tar, sitting there in your stomach, slowly, methodically eating away your innards, your kidney, your spleen. Occasionally acting up, threatening to explode and leave pus and blood splattered all over these railroad tracks, where I walk now, balancing on the rails, singing my own life to no one but myself.

My parents had been murdered. My silent night of soft, starry fragrances and thudding newspapers was shattered forever by flashing lights, prodding neighbors and bloody parental remains being wheeled around on carts. Words like *grisly, bizarre,* and *inexplicable* blared from neighborhood radios and televisions, newscasters with appropriately distressed expressions presented the shocking statistics that this made seven murders in Des Moines so far that year, up a whopping 57 percent from the year before. What did these figures mean? What were the implications for Des Moines? The citizens? The economy? Would potential industry be frightened away if this once safe and secure community melted into a bloodbath of senseless crime and violence? Would this psychopath strike again?

Neighbors darted and stared. Cars drove by, slowed, pasty faces peeked out to catch a glimpse of the strange carnival scene in my front yard. Uniformed men swarmed everywhere, poked through the rubbish for clues. The smell of Folgers instant filled the neighborhood, Mrs. Tyndall sobbed and wailed and poured herself a shot of Old Grand-Dad. Marcie sat on her front porch looking bored, teenage boys rushed up to impress her with the latest facts. The Pennels, the couple who lived in the other half of our duplex then, chewed their nails and vomited in the bushes. The Browns across the street sat on their porch and drank beer, I even caught a glimpse of Olivia Barnhouse, the evil woman across the street who summoned demons, watching from behind her black curtains. Donut-breathed men in blue questioned me relentlessly. People I'd never seen drank coffee or munched on granola bars, shook their heads and said, "There he is. Just look at him. The poor kid." Sirens wailed, dogs barked, sound warped itself into weird new variations. Finally an officer whisked me away, sat me on the front seat of his car and drove me off toward the station.

My parents had been murdered.

"You know, you're a very lucky little boy," the kind police officer informed me as he chewed his gum thoughtfully. "If you hadn't been out delivering the news, you'd of surely been stabbed, too."

He drove through a red light.

"Say," he said, "you got any uncles? A grandma, maybe? Who's your next of kin?"

I didn't say anything. I couldn't think of anybody. Everybody was dead.

"Don't worry," he said. "We'll get right on it, we'll find them, whoever they are. Everybody's got a next of kin."

He was wrong. Between a boating accident, two cerebral hemorrhages and a murder, I was it. The end of the line. Suddenly wholly alone, as if I'd been abandoned by space aliens in the middle of an Iowa cornfield. Disconnected, rootless, cut off from any life I had ever known. It isn't a pleasant thing to suddenly find yourself alone in the universe.

"Is there anybody?" they asked me. "Friends of the family? Anybody who might be able to take care of you?"

I thought hard.

"Andalusia," I said finally.

But they couldn't find her.

2

Little kids in a park in St. Louis stuck pieces of hot dog or chicken legs on a string and fished for crawdads in the scum-covered pond. The crawdads would hang there from the raw meat, clinging, leechlike. I sat and watched, spent entire afternoons doing that, back when Jimmy and me were living in the park, after we ran away from the orphanage. They'd throw the crawdads back in or stick them in peanut butter jars with holes punched in the lids so they could breathe and water in the bottom so they wouldn't dehydrate. The kids took them home as pets sometimes; they didn't boil the crawdads and serve them for dinner, at least none of the kids I talked to. It was late autumn, the nights were getting brisk, we were thinking about finding a good spot in an abandoned old building or maybe leaving for New York. An old bum wearing a dozen sweaters and carrying a scissors sat down next to me at the edge of the pond. Before I knew what was happening he cut the little boy's fishline and scurried off across the park with the raw drumstick he'd captured.

The little boy just watched after him, he didn't cry, his lips quivered a bit, but it might have just been the October wind. He walked over to where his little brother was fishing, grabbed his pole, took the hot dog that was hanging from the end and shoved his brother in the pond. His brother stood there, all dripping wet with slimy St. Louis pond water, paralyzed with grief and cold, and opened his mouth to cry. He stood for a long, long time with his mouth wide open, his face red and contorted, but no sound came out.

I stuck my hands in my pockets, walked off toward the street, stole a couple of bananas from the front of the corner grocery owned by that confused old Chinese woman and headed off toward the downtown to beg for spare change.

Δ

After the murder I was carted off to the orphanage in East Liberty. That first night we crossed the river on a ferry; the bridge had been knocked out by a tornado. It was a black, moonless night, mist rising from the river; the shrieks of the tornado dead pierced the rippling calm. A withered hand emerged from inky water, groped for a handhold on the boat. The ferryman crunched it with his boot. It slipped back into the water. I shivered. We hit ground and there I was. My new home.

At the orphanage I liked to spend my time curled up in dark closets. Father Larry opened the door once and found me there. The balding, middle-aged man studied me for a moment, just sitting there, twiddling my thumbs among the folded sheets and blankets, stood in silence, then clasped his hands together and gave his classic look of concern. Finally, he spoke.

"Is something troubling you, my son?"

More than any of the other fathers at our secular institution, Father Larry liked to fantasize that he was a Catholic priest.

"No," I said, looking straight at his shoes, "I just dropped my pencil."

"Oh," he said after a thoughtful pause, "I see. Well, come out, boy, and wash up. It's almost time for dinner."

I emerged, into the dull and constant light of the orphanage, a world of numerous knees and elbows and boyhood games involving the risk of concussion. I strove for a sort of transparency, moving slowly next to wallpaper, in gray corners, an invisibility in which I could hollow myself out, slowly die until I was blank enough that anything could rush in to fill up the space, any sort of language or even unspoken desire. The orphanage was all about unspoken desire, about isolation, conformity, thinly disguised threats of violence, oatmeal. Mostly it was about Father Larry, the planet about which we all moved in our pathetic orphan orbits. Father Larry was raw meat, instant mashed potatoes. Father Larry was duration, the slow, steady movement of time. But even throughout that first, vast, lethargic year, the pasty gray things served on platters, the immutable presence of Father Larry, even then I knew that another force was journeying toward me, some sort of balance, an opposition, something to save me. I knew now that worlds could shatter completely, civilizations could be obliterated. At night I would wake and sense the rush of Jimmy moving constantly toward me, traveling through the night.

△

In the middle of New Mexico, the land of enchantment, a man in a Gremlin, one of the ugliest cars ever to traverse the endless highways of America, bounced to a stop along the dusty shoulder. I got in.

"Where you headed?" he asked.

"Doesn't matter," I said. "California, I guess."

He took me as far as some little town in the middle of Nevada, the land of casinos and missile-testing ranges, where he had bought some land and was planning to open a gas station of his own. Maybe because I was thin and dirty, ragged and smelly, he felt I needed some assurance of better things to come.

"There's no such thing as hell," he told me. "If anyone tells you different they're a shamefaced liar and don't believe a word of it. Tell them Raymond J. McTaggart told you the truth of the matter and I should know. I died once, you see."

He was a red-haired, green-eyed man, very friendly, very kind, he bought me a couple of Hostess pies, one of those three-for-ninety-nine-cents specials, although most people don't realize that you can buy one for thirty-three cents when they do that, so they buy all three, when they only want one or two. He was wise to that scheme, he only bought two, gave me both of them, and told me about his near-death experience. He was in a car accident. When you die, he said, your first few days are

spent in a warm, moist, jungle haze of orange flowers and tropical birds, an ecstatic state of communion with the mysteries of
the universe in which the singing birds and a clear, bathwater-
warm pool filled with blue and luminous fish instill you with
all the answers to all the questions. He'd known the answers
then, but had since forgotten them.

"But I do remember," he said, "that there ain't no hell. Who
needs it? Things are bad enough down here, aren't they?"

"Yes," I agreed, "they certainly are."

It all sounded very serene, not bloody at all, but I had my
doubts. There was a kid at the orphanage who was dead, one of
the walking dead, and he never mentioned anything about exotic
birds or tropical fish. He mumbled about insects and poisonous
concoctions and stared out of black eyes that didn't see you. He
had white, cadaverous skin and black hair. His name was Edward
and he floated through the halls, a wisp of strangulated smoke.
It was rumored that his parents were still alive, his mother at
least, reputed to be in league with the devil, a prostitute or rock-
and-roll singer or librarian somewhere up north, that she had
given up Edward because he wasn't human, was fathered by a
lizard demon or a mortician's convention. He may not have been
human, but he did have blood. I know.

His bed was two away from mine, at the far end of the room,
against the wall. He sat there on the bed, there were just the
three of us, me and Edward and Jimmy, bored as usual. Edward
took a tack out of the wall, studied it vacantly for a moment,
then quickly, as if suddenly possessed, jabbed it into his thumb.
He stared at it there, for a few endless seconds, then pulled it
out, violently, and watched the blood flow. A deep, rich red
next to his creamy skin, far redder than the blood of my parents.

We sat and watched it flow also, Jimmy and me, it was an
aesthetic experience of considerable impact; the red blood, white
skin, midnight-black hair and the rich evergreen of his pocket
T-shirt, all vivid and contrasting each other to produce an
exquisite feeling of apathy and nausea.

Nobody said anything, not for minutes, we just sat and
watched the blood flow. It was a hot, sticky day, fans were hum-

ming, and the muted sounds of voices drifted through the open window. Finally, Edward twisted his neck up slowly, gazed at the two of us. It was the first time I had even felt him aware of my presence. He stared quizzically, as if waiting for further instructions.

"Do it again," said Jimmy. "In the other thumb."

He flashed a quirky, toothless grin and plunged the tack into the opposite thumb. He pulled it out quickly this time, then stood up, held his bleeding thumbs out to the sides, snapping his head back and forth to look at one, then the other, as the red liquid trickled down his arms. He just stood there, smiling and smiling, offering his bleeding thumbs to the world, a sacrifice to alleviate the boredom of an endless afternoon in that stale-aired orphanage that reeked of oatmeal and disinfectant. Jimmy yawned, the blood slowed down. Edward bit into the wounds to keep it coming. The fans hummed. It was hot.

"I'm bored," said Jimmy. "Let's go."

I followed obediently. Jimmy was my only friend and I was terribly infatuated with him. We went outside and burned ant-hills on the sidewalk with a magnifying glass. Their little black ant bodies curled up, then crisped.

Δ

"Goin' to California with an achin' . . . in my heart . . . la, la, la, la . . ."

The longhair sang off key, but I couldn't hear him too well anyway, the windows were all rolled down, the flat Nebraska wind whistled through my ears. When he couldn't remember the rest of the lyrics he started telling me about his ex-girl-friend, a woman straight from hell. She was magic, a sorceress of sorts, had turned him into an iguana and kept him trapped in an aquarium in her apartment for weeks.

"But fuck that," he said, "and fuck her. California, that's the place for me, I've had it with this midwest bullshit. Sunshine, girls in tight shorts all year long, the best green bud this side of

Maui, and jobs, you know, real jobs, that's where all the money is these days. I'm off to the promised land, son, California."

The dark strip on top of the windshield kept convincing me that the sky was navy blue and it disconcerted me a bit. He let me off in a small Nebraska town with a laundromat, a 7-Eleven and no name, no name and no people, except for the chubby woman behind the counter in the 7-Eleven there was not a soul to be seen. The sun was high overhead. I scratched my scalp and tried to get some sense of direction, trudged back up to the interstate and stuck out my thumb.

"Going home," said the wide-eyed man in the Mustang convertible as I settled into the stained seat, burrowed in among Styrofoam containers and empty cans of Mello Yello. "Although I don't really imagine that I have a home, anywhere you hang your hat, you know . . ."

He laughed nervously and tapped his fingers on the wheel, trying to keep time to the frenetic music that was playing in his head. It got so loud once or twice I could almost make it out, I think it was something by X.

"Back to Indiana, I made my money, now I'm getting the hell out of . . . there." He waved his hand back behind him in the general direction of California. "I know Indiana sucks, I don't have any illusions that I'll be happy there. There's nobody there anymore, really, no friends to go back to, they've all left, I guess, or maybe I never had any. There's my parents, but I really can't stand them. Sure, I'll be alone. But, Jesus, I can't ever be as alone as I was on those endless, convertible-filled freeways, the blaring heat, the mirrored sunglasses reflecting all those painful shafts of light . . ."

He clenched the steering wheel, tightened his face, closed his eyes as spasms of existential despair racked his body. I thought we might crash, but there was no need to worry. We were in Nebraska.

He mumbled some final warning, something about skin cancer and Mickey Mouse, then dropped me off next to the sign that said, "No Name, Nebraska, pop. 216." There was a laundromat, a 7-Eleven and no people.

It was the same town. I hadn't moved.

I hurried back up to the interstate. The afternoon got smeared into a mass of faces and automobiles, they were all going to California, hordes of them, with hope and dreams in their eyes, or they were leaving California, fleeing, back home, with loneliness and the fear of death in their eyes, and I only traveled in circles. I didn't know they had circles in Nebraska, but whichever direction I went it led me straight back to that ugly little town.

"Hi!" said the golden young man in the AMC Pacer. "What's your name?"

I had to think for a minute.

"Matt," I said. "I'm Matt."

"Oh," he said. "I'm Frank. Going as far as Peoria. Home to visit the folks. On vacation, I live in California now . . ."

He loved it. It was beautiful. No rain. And he was only ten minutes away from Disneyland. Once his parents were dead he didn't think he'd ever go back to Illinois. Except for their funerals, of course.

"Although, sure, I miss home sometimes," he said. "But, no jobs, you know, just no goddam jobs. You know what I mean."

"Yes," I confessed. "The toothpaste factory laid me off a week ago."

"Well," he said, screeching to a stop along the shoulder, "good luck to you! Nice talking with you! Have a nice day!"

I was back. The woman in the 7-Eleven waved and flashed me a conspiratorial grin. I dashed into the laundromat for refuge, all the dryers were filled with clothes, spinning, circling, whirling madly, every single dryer, yet nobody was there, where were all the people? I opened one and stole a UCLA sweatjacket, ran as fast as I could, away, up to the highway. Everything blurred, faces, more faces, going west, going east, Los Angeles, Laguna, Long Beach, Danville, Detroit, Dubuque, people with shiny cars and no hope, suntanned and frightened, everybody, the whole nation was packing up and going to California, or narrowly escaping with the tattered remains of their souls. Whish, zing, zang, the cars sped by, I zoomed up and down that stretch of highway, straight and narrow, back and forth, around and around, doors opened, doors shut, it smelled like weeds and fertilizer outside. The earth was flat and endless, the highway was flat and endless, the sky was blue and flat and endless and thin veils of cloud hurried past, maybe they were heading to California, too, or maybe they were hurrying back, I couldn't tell, my sense of direction was slightly confused. I thought I might be delirious, but the nice woman at the 7-Eleven, Pat was her name, she bought me a cup of coffee and a donut, that cleared my head and I stumbled back up to the highway.

Eventually I passed out in a wheatfield, exhausted from speeding back and forth, listening to all those tales of rootlessness and palm trees. I don't remember how I finally escaped that town, sometimes I think I never did, but I look around, see buildings or mountains or people walking by or people looking at the sky or people playing hackey-sack, and I know I'm not there anymore.

Δ

The first night after Jimmy arrived at the orphanage, almost a year after I had, I was lying in bed awake, scenes of ruptured intestines dancing merrily through my head. There was a brief flash, a flicker of movement. Jimmy had floated from his bed to the window, a movement so quick and flowing that I doubted whether it had happened at all, whether he hadn't been standing there silently by the window all night. He lifted the screen and began to ooze into the night as stealthily as he had moved from the bed. I sprang up and ran to the window.

"Hey," I said. "Where are you going?"

"To get something to drink," he said. "You want to come along?"

"I can't do that," I said, taken aback by the implications of such a venture.

"Oh," he said, and vanished.

Immediately I wished I'd gone with him, out, somewhere,

anywhere away from that miserable orphan hell. Dreaming orphans filled the room, a virtual barracks, Edward and the others, the ghosts of their parents visible in their nervous, hungry sleep. I lay down, couldn't rest, worried about Jimmy. He was a beautiful child, an angel-faced mulatto, small and thin like me, he looked like an expensive piece of candy, his skin the color of Kahlúa and cream. Jimmy was something like pure wish. He didn't talk much, the other orphans didn't take to him. There was always a boredom on his face. But that face: it whispered of human sacrifice by the light of a raging Haitian bonfire, witch doctors and voodoo, the impenetrable beauty and fear and loneliness of the endless night. He told me he came from France.

I lay there sweating and staring at the ceiling, wondering what Father Larry would do to that face if he caught him. Sometimes discipline was lax. Other times it was harsh, red, bulgy-eyed rage hurled at us with belts and fingernails and Ping-Pong paddles. There was no telling if you'd be slapped on the wrist for tossing Molotov cocktails out your bedroom window at the smaller orphans playing in the yard, or if you'd be chained to a bookcase without food and water for three days for not eating your vegetables. I was relieved when Jimmy came crawling back through the window, several hours later, carrying the remaining half of a six-pack, his tiny wrist woven through the plastic loops.

"Have a beer," he said, seeing I was still awake, and he tossed me a can. It was Hamms, the can still slightly cool. I opened it and beer bubbled over onto my bedsheet. I took a sip. It was foul-tasting, bitter and warm. I took another drink.

"Where'd you get this?" I asked.

"Wasn't easy," said Jimmy. "I killed a man. Coming out of the Quik Trip."

"Really?" I said.

"Yeah," said Jimmy. "But don't tell. They might watch me more close if they knew I did that."

I drank my beer, listened to the other children breathing rhythmically. A feeling grew inside me, if not happy, at least different.

"You know," I said finally, "if Father Larry catches us drinking, we'll be in big trouble."

Jimmy looked at me.

"Oh," he said.

Father Larry didn't catch us, not that night at least, not for many nights. If Larry was duration and low-intensity warfare, Jimmy was the quality of the instant, a state of emergency, a nuclear blast. Jimmy was a sort of sixth sense that had nothing to do with telepathy, but that I felt inside my body, cohabiting with the churning of my organs, tissue, muscle, blood. We leaked together into the night, ran, shivered, swam in the river, moved. Begged wine off of Stevie, the idiot who lived under the bridge and read Shakespeare, or stole beer from the Quik Trip when old Leonard was looking the other way. Drank and drank and even laughed and pissed and puked up our government peanut butter in the backyards of respectable East Liberty families. The nights slipped out of focus, mornings ached, events disappeared sometimes, I don't remember throwing up on that woman's shoes, the one who smelled like pizza, muttered about the black age we were living in, when young, vicious hoodlums would accost you in your own front yard, while you were minding your own business, innocently watering the geraniums, and vomit on your shoes. She dragged me by the ears into her blurry, rumbly car of spilled dogfood and fuzzy dice, took me to the orphanage and angrily presented me to Father Larry. Jimmy had finagled his way back into bed, was already sleeping, cozy, warm, dreaming.

"Turning in their graves," announced Father Larry, after the hideous woman had been placated with promises of swift and violent retribution. "I can hear your parents now, turning in their graves."

"Really?" I asked, honestly intrigued by the thought, not understanding the motivation for this turning, just stunned by this sudden movement of the dead, not to mention Father Larry's incredible hearing. "Are you sure it's my parents? In Des Moines?"

He slapped my face with a sharp *thwack*, mistaking my

innocence for insubordination. His backhand hung in the air, uncertain, an untamed animal with a will of its own. His body relaxed, he rubbed his eyes and looked at me with exaggerated sorrow, droopy-eyed pain, as if it was him I'd hurt, as if it was his shoes I'd thrown up on.

"It's late," he said. "I'll deal with you in the morning."

He escorted me to bed and I slept, black, throbbing and short. That next morning was like the mornings now when I wake up by the highway in tall, dewy weeds, with diesel trucks thundering by only inches from my brain, insect bites covering my body and the former contents of the empty bottle of Ernest and Julio Gallo Rhine Wine I am clutching oozing out my ears, not sure just exactly which state I'm in. Except that morning was worse because there were no tall, green-smelling grasses to pee in, only Father Larry to face, and runny oatmeal.

After breakfast Father Randy played the soundtrack to *Saturday Night Fever*, Edward began rubbing leftover oatmeal on his chest and Jimmy vanished into a timewarp and hovered invisibly in an alternative, Larryless universe. Father Larry took my hand and led me upstairs. The orphanage air was heavy with disco and despair. Larry rubbed his eyes again, gazed at me, then stroked his chin in sad contemplation.

"Well?" he asked. "What have you got to say for yourself?"

I had absolutely nothing to say for myself. The night before was a dim haze. I wasn't sure exactly what I'd done.

"I'm sorry," I said. "I'll never do it again."

"Oh," said Father Larry, "you'll never do it again. You'll never do *it* again. Tell me, Matthew, what exactly is it that you'll never do again? Sneak out of the orphanage? Go out carousing, boozing, doing drugs? Terrorizing our neighbors? Accosting innocent women? Throwing up on them? Utterly humiliating yourself and all the rest of us who have worked so hard all these years to keep up the good reputation of the East Liberty Home for Boys? Those who have fed you, clothed you, cared for you?"

He paused. I glanced at his plump, soft fingers. My head was about to explode. The two bites of oatmeal I'd had for breakfast came back up, but I bravely held it in and swallowed it again. Father Larry didn't notice. He was on a roll, seething with the injustice I'd done him, he paced deliriously, spewing forth words like *heathen, ingratitude, delinquency, schizophrenia* and *hydroelectricity.* I began to drift, lost myself in the maze of his rambling lunacy, spun out on his ravings about the virtues of stamp collecting. But then he pounced on me, snarling, writhing, a jabbering carnivore, he spit the words into my eyes, his red face only inches from my own.

"Who was with you?" he demanded. "I know there was someone with you, you little shit, who was it?"

I froze. I swallowed. Ingrained deep in my being was the one truth that every schoolboy knows to be most sacred. To narc is the gravest sin imaginable.

"Nobody was with me," I said. "I was alone."

"Liar," he snapped. "Liar, liar, pants on fire! It was Jimmy, wasn't it? Wasn't it?"

I said nothing, stared in stunned silence. Then, in an instant, his wild, trembling rage was transformed into sobbing, shivery woe. His body shook with grief, he fell to his knees, pleaded to the paneled ceiling, wailed of his great efforts, his love, he did his best to lead us right, but he was so weak, so very, very weak. His face ached with the suffering of humanity, I must confess I had the impulse to pat him gently on the back. It only lasted a moment, he regained his usual composure, and he calmly dismissed me with a warning to never let it happen again.

But it did happen again. Often.

Δ

"Got any dope?"

No, I didn't have any dope. The truck driver was obviously disappointed.

"That's why I picked you up!" he yelled, so as to be heard above the roaring diesel engine. "Thought you might have some dope!"

The noise made conversation difficult. Three small bullet holes dotted the passenger's side of the windshield. He told me he had some *Playboys* I could look at. I thumbed through them. Then he brought out the good stuff.

"These are pictures I took!" he yelled. They were neatly arranged in book form. "These first ones, that's my ex-wife! My girlfriend thinks I threw them away, but I kept them, for sure! Then these, these here are of my girlfriend."

There they were, all right, in the flesh, not bad-looking women for such a homely idiot. His girlfriend was sucking an unidentified penis in one shot. I assumed it was his. I didn't ask.

"Nice-looking women," I said.

"Sure are." He grinned, stupidly. "Look them over for a while."

Not wanting to offend the man, I looked them over for a time span long enough to prove my admiration. Then I gave them back. We drove in silence. I could think of nothing to say.

A warning of a DOT car ahead crackled over the CB. He told me he'd have to let me out, if he got caught with a hitch-hiker it'd be his ass. So he let me out at a rest stop, somewhere between Tulsa and Oklahoma City, and rumbled along his way.

I sat there most of the night, in that rest stop. Drank the coffee out of the bottoms of a couple of Styrofoam cups left lying around and picked crumbs off the tables. Spent fifty cents on a pack of Donettes from the vending machine, so it was a pretty good night all told, except for the noise from the pinball machines. Turnpike rest stops are really very comfortable and I'm grateful for them. I'm not tired yet, but I suppose it'll hit me later this morning.

I'm walking along the tracks now, just off the road. The present seems somehow unhinged: this is the summer of my twenty-second year and I'm still here, in the middle of it all. Who'd have guessed? I'm all buzzing and full of caffeine, walking on the tracks, I like to walk on the tracks. Always walking on railroad tracks, at dawn or at dusk, nightfall or late afternoon, it gives me a sense of freedom and direction, lines stretching on forever, withered planks, balancing on a thin beam. I like to walk.

Sometimes, like right now for example, I step back and I look at myself and I ask myself just what exactly I'm doing, bouncing around this glorious American landscape like a schizophrenic superball. What's the point? But then I remember. I remember exactly what the point is. I'm looking for Andalusia. I haven't forgotten her, not ever. I always felt that we'd meet again. Someday. A glorious reunion, three frenzied days and nights of lovemaking as the sun stands still, of exchanging stories, all the trials and tribulations we've endured during our endless separation. Now that I really think about it, three days isn't nearly long enough. Maybe forty days, forty days of rain, as we sit by the fire, absorbing each other, merging our souls. I guess we'd have to drink a lot of coffee to go that long without sleep, or else do a lot of cocaine.

She is out there. Somewhere. My brain is getting cramps and I can hear the rush of traffic increasing on the turnpike. The sun's coming up. Not a cloud in the sky, it's going to be another hot one.

Off I go.

TWO

Δ

1

There is the road, greedily sucked under by the tires. There is
the numbing panorama of the passing Kansas landscape, ver-
dant and waxy. There are fathers in the fields, in the trees and
on rectangular billboards, fathers both dead and alive, too many
dead. There is the voice of the man, Martin, rattling in my ears.
There is no past and no future. There is the gun.

Sometimes, guns go off.

"It's scary out there. People on the freeway, shooting each
other! I had to buy this."

He waves the gun in my face. I watch billboards instead:
the *Mona Lisa* smiles at me, urges me to buy a particular brand
of motor oil. I wonder if she was really a da Vinci self-portrait
as they say.

"Only nice thing about California, all those women in bikinis,
let me tell you. Everywhere, I couldn't take it, I was horny all
the time. I met a few nice women, had some really good sex,
you know, but most of those California women are cold as ice.
You know? Think they're movie stars or something."

The little man is wearing a red T-shirt that says *Take the
Pepsi Challenge* and matching red sweatpants. He gives me a
sly smile.

"Meet a lot of interesting women on the road, huh?"

"Oh," I say, "yeah, I suppose there's been a few."

"You know it," he says in his squeaky, frenzied little voice.
"I remember I hitched down to East Texas once, you know, to

see some relatives. But I sure didn't see much of my relatives. This woman picked me up, just the most beautiful thing you can imagine, long blond hair, tits the size of grapefruit and the biggest sex maniac in the world! Things like that don't happen all the time, well, you probably know that, but boy, did I get my share."

I pick up a videocassette from the seat beside me. *Paradise Lost*. There is a naked woman on the cover licking an apple.

"That woman just loved to go down on me," he says. "There was nothing she wanted to do more than suck my dick. I stayed with her for a week, you know, just constant sex, sex all the time."

I find it difficult to imagine this mousy man cavorting with a voluptuous nymphomaniac in East Texas. We're zipping through Kansas in his Plymouth Swinger. An old man with a speech impediment and a truckload of pecans took me from the Oklahoma rest stop to Coffeyville, just past the border. And then he picked me up. Martin. He fidgets as he drives, his eyes dart back and forth between me and the road, he bounces the gun lightly against his thigh. The car smells of pink bubble gum, Aqua Velva and secreting glands. The ashtray is stuffed full of cigarette butts, but nobody's smoking. I look out the window at trees and houses.

"I'll bet that's happened to you quite a bit, huh?" he asks. "That you've been picked up by women? That, you know, wanted to have sex with you?"

"By women?" I say. I have to think for a minute. "No, not really very often at all."

"How often? Twenty times? Thirty?"

I can think of only three, and two of them had just been released from the reformatory, were thick and pale, with an abundance of tattoos.

"I don't know," I say. "I can't count them. Not that many, though."

He chatters away, jiggles in his seat. I move my hand up to my mouth, lick the palm, feel the salty taste on my tongue. Close my eyes for a moment, try to imagine a life: lush, mahogany, not so linear, filled with human beings and a vague sense of understanding something.

"When you're out like this," he says, "you know, traveling around, here and there, you must go for long periods of time without any."

"Oh," I say.

"Without any women," he says. "Without any sexual contact. Don't you just lose it sometimes, aren't you horny all the time? I mean, what do you do to relieve the tension?"

"The tension?" I say.

"Do you ever, well, you know, masturbate?"

I don't answer just yet. Not so long ago I saw a newborn baby. Not as large as Martin, but otherwise comparable: excitability, attention span, wardrobe.

"Oh," I say. "Masturbate."

"That's all right if you don't want to talk about it, I know it's not a, you know, a subject that people generally talk about, that they feel comfortable with, if you're offended . . ."

He taps the gun against the steering wheel.

"It's OK," I say. "It's not that big of a deal, I guess everybody's done it."

"Yes, yes!" he says. "Everybody, you think? Yes, you know, but you're right, people act like there's something wrong with it, like you're not, you know, normal. They tell you it's a sin and you'll go blind or your dick will fall off, and you know they do it all the time themselves. So you've . . . you yourself have masturbated?"

"Yeah," I say, "I guess so."

"And you still do it? Whenever you, get the urge? Do you do it often?"

"Oh, no," I say. "Not really. I wouldn't say that."

"Say only every other day then? Once a week? How often?"

He rubs his nose on his shirt sleeve.

"I don't know," I say. "Not that often."

"Really? Monthly, maybe? Bimonthly?"

He touches the gun to his chin, thoughtfully.

"Wow," he says. "You must not have a very strong sex drive. Statistically speaking, I'm in the majority."

Martin has a truly enormous libido. Sometimes, he tells me, he masturbates three times a day. Sometimes three times within a fifteen-minute period. Sometimes, at his job, he'll get so agitated that he just can't take it, he'll be ogling his female coworkers and have to get up from his desk and hurry into the bathroom. He wonders about how I do it. My technique. He wonders if I ever worry about size, if I worry that I don't have a normal-looking penis. He wonders if I worry that I might not have a normal sex life, if I wonder about other people's sex lives and how I compare. He wonders how often I do various things, in which parts of the country, in what positions. He wonders with whom and what I personally find most enjoyable. He is a curious man.

"I read polls," he says, "to make sure I'm normal. I often worry, you see, because doctors told me I have fourteen times as much adrenaline as a regular human being. I'd take lithium, but it makes you fat and impotent. But I'm working on improving myself, you know, on normalizing other aspects of my life. I read *USA Today*. I heard that in the future they'll get rid of those who aren't normal. I used to drink Coke, but I drink Pepsi now. I took the taste test."

I glance at his shirt.

"What an abundance of choices," I say.

Yes, not so long ago I saw a newborn baby, Jessica Moon's. I watched it through a window, so perfect in its lack of statistics. More and more information, less and less meaning. It's election year again.

"That video," he says, *"Paradise Lost,* it's great, you know, the hero, he loses his virginity in the produce section of a supermarket. The women, they all have tits the size of mangos, tits the size of muskmelons, tits the size of cantaloupe."

"Well," I say.

"It's great just to talk about sex like this, you know, not everybody would be so easy to talk to, so comfortable. You can't always talk to people about what you really want to, about the really important things. They might be offended. You're not offended, are you?"

"Not very often," I say.

"This is really great. That you're so open-minded. Like, for example, I'm really horny right now. Normally, I might pull over at a rest stop and masturbate, or if I was in kind of a hurry, which I am, you know, I might even just sit here and do it as I drove."

He pauses.

"Would you be, well, offended, if I did that? Right now? Just pulled it out and did it?"

I look over at the eager little man. I'm tired. Suddenly I'm tired and I want to go to sleep for a good long time.

"No," I say. "Feel free."

"Really? Do you mean that?"

"Sure," I say. "Why not?"

I hope he won't. I lean my head against the window. The door lock jabs into my shoulder. The sun shines hot on the glass. Albino cows stare at me. A car drives by with no driver. A column of smoke curls up in the distance, off behind some trees. Something is burning.

"This is great," he says. I can see him out of the corner of my eye. "Are you ever curious to, you know, watch how other people do it?"

"Not really," I say. I change the subject. "How long have you lived here? In Kansas?"

"Most all my life," he says, and is silent for a moment. "I know there's better places to be. Here," he says, and thrusts the gun into my hands, "hold this for a minute."

I hold the gun. It's heavier than it looks.

"Feels good in your hand, doesn't it? Smooth? Cool? Kind of scary, huh?"

I shift it into my right hand and back again.

"Go ahead," he says. "Fondle it a little."

I run my fingers along the barrel.

"Yes," I say, "you're right. Kind of scary."

I hold it out to him. Both his hands are occupied. I set it down on the seat between us. He goes on.

"Jesse Jackson is too black, don't you think?" he says. "Never be president, he's too damn black. Bill Cosby could be president, he's just a regular guy, he isn't a nigger. He looks good on TV, his wife has great legs, you ever see legs like that on a white woman? Sill though, president? Vice-president maybe, anyone can do that. Johnny Carson and Bill Cosby, there's your dream ticket. Who does Jesse think he's fooling? He's a black man straight through, always, forever, only that one thing, a black man."

He picks up the gun. He strokes himself with his left hand, twirls the gun with his right. He drives with his knees. He runs his fingers up and down the stubby barrel. He cocks it.

"I fired it once, you know," he whispers. "By accident."

He points it at a passing road sign that says NO SHOULDER. He points it at a tree. He points it at a nickel on the floor beside my foot.

We hit a dip in the road. The car is jolted, I fall forward. Martin moans and ejaculates. The gun flies into the air, clatters onto the dashboard, then slips off and down onto the floor. I look at Martin, gasping, eyes closed, knees on the wheel. The smell of his semen rises in the air. I look at the cocked gun on the floor, at the road. I close my eyes.

Martin slams on the brakes. I open my eyes. A station wagon speeds past us to the left.

"Shit," he says, "I missed my exit! I have to turn around!"

I open the door and dive out onto the road. He waves, distractedly, makes a U-turn across the grass and speeds away.

I stand here by the highway. The sun is hot on my scalp. A fiery dry wind rolls down the plains. Cars whiz by. I don't stick out my thumb just yet. I only stand here.

I stand here for a half hour or so. There is a billboard way off down the road, I can barely make out the figure of a man in his underwear. Something about this billboard disturbs me. I walk backwards, away from it, thumb extended. I wonder why exactly I'm in Kansas heading north, when my plan was to go south through Arkansas and Louisiana to New Orleans. Then a pickup truck stops, it's a girl, blond and pretty, she motions for me to get in back, then cracks her window.

"I'm going to Iowa," she says. "West Des Moines."

"Oh," I say. "OK."

I climb in back. Her doors are locked. I guess she's afraid I might bludgeon her to death with her own tire jack, rape her, and then cut her into tiny little pieces and feed her to my dog. I don't even have a dog, but I don't blame her. You never know what sort of people you might meet on the highway.

Here I sit. It's nice, I don't have to talk to anybody. I can just feel the sun on my face. The wind. Watch haystacks go by, and barns. Restaurants called simply RESTAURANT, as if to further discriminate would be pretentious and absurd. It's kind of bumpy here. I could stay here forever. I don't really want to be in Iowa. Everyone in Iowa is gone.

Δ

Once, when I was small, I was lost and alone and drowning in the river. I can see it all so clearly, the falling off the bank, and then the water all around. My eyes were wide open and everything was slow. Time was different, everything foaming and undulating. Whorls of brown water, slimy green river plants. I went straight to the bottom, I couldn't swim a lick. I remember holding my breath and just sitting, knowing that at the age of six I was going to die. I wasn't scared. Everything was quiet. Everything was huge, an atom or a universe, surrounded by water. Andalusia had told me I was born under the sign of a small child falling asleep in the snow. That the moon was in its milky infancy and one day I'd make choices. But first, I was drowning. I held my breath. I looked up. I thought I could see the sun up there, on the other side of all that water, a huge brown ball. It rippled. All that water and light and time and death.

She was there, huge, moving through the water toward me, her hands out, my lungs ready to explode, splashing, swimming, and we were out. I breathed and breathed, Andalusia dragged me to the side, she was crying and hysterical, but I was calm. On the shore she pressed my chest, trying to squeeze the water out, but it tickled, and I laughed. She glared at me for a minute like she was mad or confused, but then she laughed too.

She said she was so scared, if she'd have lost me she didn't know what she'd have done. She was laughing and crying at the same time. It wasn't a conscious knowledge that happened, it was a slight movement, in my glands or muscles, biological knowing; we would never be apart. We belonged together. It was in her, too, I know it was. I know that she remembers, just like me.

Sunday nights I sat with Mom and Dad on our dying sofa. It was worn down to the cardboard stuff on the arms, but we always had plenty of blankets. We watched movies, or *Colombo* or specials about wildlife on public TV. I always scanned the *TV Guide*, hoping *Vanishing Point* would come back on. Dad yawned and scratched his belly, Mom fixed us sandwiches and grapes, but then she usually fell asleep, which was good for me. It meant I could stay up past my bedtime.

"Shhhh," Dad would say when the movie ended, a yellowed finger to his lips. He'd cover her with a blanket, leave her there on the couch, swing me into his arms and carry me up to bed. He told me stories and played with my toes. I was special, I only had nine. One foot was lumpy and deformed and minus a toe, the one next to the big toe. I was happy that way. When we went walking, on beaches or in mud or on other planets where the ground was made of Jell-O, my footprints were unique. Dad told me that monsters had attacked once, he'd fought them off heroically, but not before they'd made off with my toe.

"No sir," I said, "Mom told me it happened in the hospital, that a doctor cut it off."

He gave me a look filled with danger and hidden knowl-

"Your mother," he said, "doesn't know everything. It's best that way. There are things it's best we didn't tell her. She'd only worry."

He told me stories that Mom never would, scary stories, populated with cloaked riders on horseback moving through misty woods. He'd tickle me until it hurt, then tell me to go to sleep. Afterward I dreamed, the dreams scared me sometimes, but I was old enough then. I knew I could always wake up.

On honey-colored autumn days, Dad sat with me, fuzzy sunshine filtering through the burnt-orange leaves. We collected walnuts on the damp ground. The moist shells stained our hands, brown and black and green, our fingers smelled rich, like something that throbs beneath the crust of the earth. Dad told silly jokes and I refused to laugh. He laughed to himself and gazed up toward the impossible blueness of a September sky. He talked about the spirit of History, genetic mutations, the choices that every molecule must make. He talked about dinosaurs and leaps of faith, stock-car races and the view from the Himalayas, baseball and sorcery, space exploration and the pretty girls in Spain and Bora Bora. He rarely talked about working down at the mass-mailing factory where he pumped out envelopes that said, "Dear Mr. / Mrs. / Miss_____, you may already be the winner of a sum of money so huge that the zeroes wouldn't all fit on this page!" but when he did it was always a warning.

"Go to college," he said. "Out here it's a constant struggle not to become a machine. They try to steal the substance of our beings and transform it into replicable simulations of death."

He took me out for banana splits and peanut butter parfaits and asked me what I wanted to be when I grew up.

"I don't know," I said. "I don't really think I want to grow up."

He smiled and told me I was wise beyond my years.

When he came home from work he smelled like sawdust and glue. Mom listened to a music box while he was away, there was a girl on top sniffing flowers and it played "Edelweiss." She'd just listen, over and over, staring out the window or float-

ing around the room like I wasn't even there. *Bloom and grow,
bloom and grow, love our homeland forever* . . . I'd watch her
amazed, too young to connect such a nostalgic, patriotic song
with Nazis, concentration camps, the end of civilization. *Bloom
and grow, bloom and grow* . . . All this time I was growing, right
under their feet. I couldn't stop.

I made up countries. I drew maps of them, oceans, islands,
mountains and deep, scary forests. There were places where
everybody's name started with an L, places where all the buildings were igloos, countries of elves, of gnomes, of women on
horseback. I made up languages for them. House = blablabla,
dog = qorphk, cat = umm. That I was the only one who understood did not seem a disadvantage, ensured my sense of who I
was, alone, a creator of cultures. I inhabited my worlds with
curious pilgrims, shadowy felons, venomous lizards, hippos and
steam. I gave them a national anthem, the song we always sang
in music class at school. *This land is your land, this land is my
land . . . from the redwood forests, to the New York Island . . .
from the Des Moines River to the shores of Donutland . . . this
land was made for you and me.*
   I was kind to animals and old people, sickened by the abuse
of frogs which was so rampant in our neighborhood: the firecrackers down the throat, the popsicle-stick crucifixions. I was
comforted by the knowledge of the spot reserved for me in
heaven, with Jesus and Andalusia, the Beach Boys and Clint
Eastwood. Despite the fact that we were constantly hopping
from church to church, the songs remained the same. Whatever
the adults sang, for us kids it was always "What a Friend We
Have in Jesus." I knew that it was true.
   When I was older I spent the better part of a year hitting a
tennis ball onto our roof. This project wasn't born of any desire
to improve my tennis game, only of the strange marriage of
boredom and a love of unpredictable rhythms; would the ball
bounce once, twice, three times on the roof? Would I overshoot
the roof entirely and have to go running around to the other side
of the duplex, into the alley, or the Tyndalls' backyard? The

possibilities were endless. But winter came and the balls wouldn't bounce in the snow. I turned to minor vandalisms with the neighbor kids, ringing doorbells and running away, throwing snowballs at cars, spelling out obscenities in antifreeze, so that when spring came we could read the dead grass in neighbors' lawns. We weren't angry; we just had time.

But that spring I got my paper route. Mornings, when I came back, I'd find Dad sometimes, in the kitchen, surrounded by a chaos of coffee cups, ashtrays and hard, gluey books, wild-eyed and writing furiously. He'd have been up all night, scribbling and muttering and smoking Lark cigarettes. I'd mumble something about donuts or birds and go up to bed for a couple more hours of sleep before school. He'd still be there when I got up again, cranky and covered with the cracking green seaweed of sleep. Mom would scold him and tell him he'd best not be late for work again. It was always an odd feeling to find him there like that, in a strange sort of fugue state. It was disturbing, but it was also a comfort: in the middle of the night, somebody was there.

Collecting was the only thing I hated. There was a woman with a snarling Doberman; she always stood in the crack of her door, between me and the dog, and her husband was always yelling in the background. The Littles never remembered who I was. The Dwyers' house was always dark, the family huddled around the television.

"A dollar forty," I said.

"Shhh," said Mrs. Dwyer. "I want to catch this."

"Symptom," the voice on the television said, "loss of equilibrium or balance."

I just stood there.

"Possible condition," said the voice, "middle or ear infection. Polyp or tumor in middle ear. Trauma to ear or head. Brain infection. Feline infectious peritonitis. See also listings under tilting head in one direction, falling over, inability to stand steadily."

There were old people who always listened to the radio or the ticking clock, alone. There were young couples who always

argued about riding lawn mowers, women who constantly fried
fish and potatoes. Everybody's house smelled different. Musty
or like cat litter or garlic or like Mrs. Guntherson's that always
smelled like violets and confusion.

"Every day," she whispered, as I stood in her kitchen,
clutching my change purse and receipt book, "I wake up to find
myself in unknown territory. I never know what to expect next."

She paid me my money and I left.

Teakettles ringing. Raindrops spattered on the windowpane, goldfish suspended in each. I wasn't sure where I was; I
was a child, like any other, on a gray-smeared rainy day, longing
for otherworldly beings and laughter. The moment stretched
on, I watched out the duplex window and I knew: I would
remember this moment always, though I didn't know why. Perhaps it was only because I asked myself these questions: Does
time have an edge? Where does the future hide before it arrives?
So much had been forgotten; my infancy, my birth. What was
there before the beginning, and back before that? Thoughts were
always changing, though I knew I'd been there forever. The
rain drummed on the glass, the future stretched out, crystal-
lized. There would be journeys by ship, foghorns, oceans and
lips. There would be running and strange passages of time. My
father was at work, I could hear it in the distance, ching ching,
hummmmm, the grinding machinery, factory sweat, the gravel
parking lot at dusk. Mother napped upstairs, dreamt. The quiet
was alarming. The future hung, suspended, nudity and a house
full of animals. Parrots, turtles, cairn terriers and at least one
chimpanzee.

Clouds dipped low, rain subsided, there were puddles and
slippery grass. The street was empty, wet and waiting. A younger
child came running, laughing, galoshes in puddles and shorts
to his knees, but then falling; falling and scraping and screaming, just outside my window.

I went to him.

I was running, I was there, I took the younger child's hand,
I carried him inside. "Shhh," I said. "Shhhh." I was calming

and calm. I fixed him chocolate milk and a Band-Aid, I kissed his knee. He sniffled. I was good, so good, because no one would ever know. I smiled and sent the child on his way.

I held that virtue in, a secret, all my own. It warmed me. Jesus was watching, I knew. *Let the children come to me.*

It started again, the rain, washing prisms away. The future would be filled with new tennis shoes, springy, to help a boy leap over puddles and rivers. The future would be filled with dripping leaves and moss on trees, the color of limes. There would be bells and horses and minibikes. There would be wandering brick streets under full moons. There would be death and heaven, ghosts and alleys, levitation and laughter.

Teakettles ringing, distant. Windowpanes gleamed: the world was out there, waiting.

2

There was a light drizzle, not falling, just hanging in the air. There were ice witches flying past the moon, piercing the night with jarring shrieks. There were whines of jackals in the distance. There were the two of us, me and Jimmy, sitting by the black river, clenching cold beers with bare fingers.

It was October.

The grass was wet, it seeped through my pants to my skin. I longed for warmth and bed, but we wouldn't go back yet to the orphanage. Something held us in the raw darkness. West, across the river, was blackness hiding something insubstantial, once known but not remembered. Jimmy stared out, through everything and into something that I can only describe as the night. He had incredible eyes, Jimmy, powerful brown sorcerer's eyes filled with black magic and intensity. I wished I had those eyes. The world would be mine with those eyes. The dark forces of Pluto would be at my command. I could decimate my enemies with a glance if I had those eyes. But I didn't have them. Jimmy did. Unless I plucked them out with a spoon, like Jimmy did with a cat he caught one night, he would keep those

eyes. I didn't have a spoon with me. Besides, Jimmy was my
only friend.

"Come on," said Jimmy. "Let's go."

I followed, along the river, over crunchy weeds and hardened mud. We came into town, climbed the steep embankment
into backyards. We moved past creaking swingsets, weather-
beaten lawn chairs and a nude, armless Barbie doll, cold and
forgotten, legs protruding from a sandbox. All the houses were
closed up, barricaded against the cold and the night, but we
could stand out there, with our hands in our pockets and look
inside. Real people ate pork chops and thumbed through magazines, screwed in light bulbs or sat on recliners, silent,
entranced, the blue glow of the television illuminating their
empty faces. We could watch them or we could watch our own
breath as we exhaled. They were warm and well fed, bored and
silent and unaware of the dangerous mammals that lurked outside, watching them, waiting. Sometimes I felt sorry for them
or envied them. Mostly, I just hated them. Quietly and methodically we destroyed their shrubberies and scratched obscenities
in the paint of their garages. Then we moved along.

"Doesn't look like anybody's home here," said Jimmy.

No lights in the kitchen, no woman loading the dishwasher,
no movie of the week throbbing in the living room, no tales of
horror or suspense. No car in the driveway, no car in the garage.
Jimmy had a rock in his hand, materialized from nowhere. He
began chipping away at a basement window, one audible crash
and a tinkle, tinkle as the fragments floated down to the basement floor. We were silent, listening. No sound. He cleaned up
the edges, slid through the window, onto the washing machine
and down. I followed.

It was pitch-black and dank. Cool air rushed through the
window, strange shapes rubbed against me, silky and decadent.
Blindly, I followed the sound of Jimmy's faint breathing up the
warped stairs. Streetlight yellow glow shone through upstairs
curtain cracks, enough to make out furniture and appliance
shapes. We examined vases and wall hangings and the insides

of kitchen drawers. I found a few crumpled bills and a butter dish full of quarters, dimes and nickels. Jimmy found the pennies in a can that had once held cashews.

"Come on," he whispered. "The really good stuff'll be upstairs."

Up the carpeted stairs we tiptoed. Shadows danced in the hall, my shadow, Jimmy's shadow, a murderer's shadow. Killer on the loose, carving knife gleaming, sharp glimmers of light bouncing across the ceiling. A soft nightlight glowed from the crack beneath the door at the end of the hall. I closed my eyes, heard slashing in my head, a blade through air and flesh. I wanted to scream, took a deep breath, it was only robbing, only robbing, no murder. A tingle of fear, excitement and death, adrenaline rush, fight or flight. *Flight,* said my bowels, but I moved along the wall, stayed calm, my fingers gliding over ruptures in the paint. An open door, an empty bed, Jimmy rustled through drawers, quickly, quietly began filling a pillowcase with polished objects.

"Why don't you check out the other bedroom?" he whispered.

The other bedroom. The thin line of light at the bottom of the door. I reached out, held the knob, felt the bloody smoothness against my palm. I turned it. Zombie shrieks filled my head.

"Nobody in here but us chickens!"

The henhouse was empty, no farmers, just a Donald Duck nightlight and me, the snarling, bloody-fanged wolf. Jaws and hair and teeth, teeth clenching teeth, bones grinding, glands salivating, all teeth and jaws. Into the drawers, the letters and photographs of sweaty Disneyland relations, the pantyhose—all the better to strangle you with, my dear—and the perfumes, face powders. There was an embroidered plaque on the wall with the Twenty-third Psalm in red capital letters, YEA, THOUGH I WALK THROUGH THE VALLEY OF THE SHADOW OF DEATH, I WILL FEAR NO EVIL; FOR THOU ART WITH ME; THY ROD AND THY STAFF THEY COMFORT ME. There was my shadow, tall and ominous on the wall before me. I found two Eisenhower silver dollars and an Indian-head penny, shoved them in my pocket. I examined the double bed, an odd excitement as I looked for mysterious stains.

"Matt, come here. Check this out."

I moved through the doorway down the hall and into the other bedroom. Jimmy was kneeling by the dresser. The second drawer from the bottom was open. I could barely make out the object in the darkness. It was a gun. He pointed it at me.

"This is great," he said. "You can use these for a lot of things."

"Is it loaded?"

"Two bullets," he said.

He pointed it at the mirror. He pointed it at the empty bed. He pointed it at a little porcelain music box on the dresser, bone-white figures, a deathly-pale girl and her smooth, white dog. He pointed it at a painting of a shipwreck that hung on the wall. The closet door was cracked open, a flannel sleeve protruded. He pointed it back at the girl and her dog. Her neck was twisted, her mouth open, as if hearing a call in the distance, but her cold eyes stared steadily at me.

Lights shone through the window. They shone in my eyes for a moment, then circled about the room, illuminating everything in turn: mirror, shipwreck, gun, Jimmy, the girl. Then the lights were gone and there was only the sound of a car idling in the driveway. The engine shut off. Door slammed. I looked at Jimmy. He went to the window.

Footsteps echoed up the walk. I couldn't move. The girl stared. The front door opened. Voices entered, loud, clear voices. As if they had nothing to hide and nothing to fear.

"I thought I told you to get Dial soap," said a heavy male voice. "I know I told you that. Is that so hard to remember? Dial soap?"

"This soap was on sale," answered a woman's voice. "Maybe if we win the Publisher's Clearinghouse Sweepstakes you can have your Dial soap. It's not such a hardship to wash with this for a while."

"You can't even rightly call that stuff soap," said the man.

"It doesn't make me feel clean. We're not saving any money if I have to use twice as much soap, are we?"

There was stomping directly below us. A brief silence. Jimmy pushed up on the window. It didn't budge. I listened to my heartbeat. I felt the dark air move against my body as words were spoken below.

"Now I won't be able to sleep all night. The thought of it, waking up in the morning and having to use that . . . stuff."

Jimmy moved to the other window. I followed with my eyes.

"It leaves such a disgusting film. I hate it, you know, that film. Why couldn't you have just bought Dial soap?"

"Why don't you just drop it? If you want your Dial soap so bad run down to the Kum and Go and buy yourself a bar."

Jimmy shoved up the window. It made a sharp, squealing noise. We froze.

"Oh, right, Miss Economics here, and now she wants me to use up my gas, to go out in the cold for one bar of soap."

"Well then, don't complain!"

"Don't complain? Sure, sure, always it's don't complain, when you're out wasting my money, buying soap that I'm going to have to use twice as much of!"

Their voices were getting louder, more violent. I felt my feet against the smooth wood floor. My nine toes in their tennis shoes. They felt somehow separate.

"You don't have to use twice as much! This is perfectly good soap, for Christ's sake! Here, look at the label! S-O-A-P, soap! Made out of the exact same gunk as your precious Dial soap, I bet. Here, read the label. Sodium tallowate, sodium cocoate, coconut acid, water, fragrance, titanium dioxide, chromium hydroxide green . . ."

"Shut up! Just shut up! It's crap, that's all it is, cheap, crappy bar of shit!"

"Read the ingredients! Read it! Read it! Take it! Take it!"

Something banged against a wall, something shattered. A shriek, more stomping. Jimmy turned to me.

"Storm windows," he said. His arm moved, bringing the gun

from his side up by his shoulder. For one long second every-thing was silent.

"Are you finished? Are you quite finished with your little tantrum?"

"Why don't you just . . ."

"Oh, Jesus, look what you've done! Just look! You big . . . big . . ."

"Big what? What, Jackie? Go ahead, say it. Big Cyclops? Big what?"

"Shit for brains, that's what. That's what it is. Why don't you think? Why don't you just once think before you fly off the han-dle? Just look . . ."

"You watch it, Jackie. Don't push me, Jackie."

"Give me a break. I can't . . . I just can't deal with it any-more. Look at this. I'm going down in the basement to throw in the wash."

Jimmy looked at me.

"The basement," he whispered. "The window."

A door slammed. Then silence. Huge feet clomped down the hall downstairs. The upstairs light flicked on. Muffled steps and breathing ascended, closer, a large presence was moving toward us, I could hear blood rushing through thick veins, the churning of internal organs, the slow, steady exchange of car-bon dioxide for oxygen.

"Get under the bed," whispered Jimmy. "I can shoot him if I have to."

I crawled under the bed. Heavy breathing moved closer. Jimmy slid the open drawer shut and slipped into the closet. The man entered. Legs and feet were all I could see from my position on the floor. He turned a light on. He moved toward the bed. His feet were immense.

"Bitch."

The word was almost inaudible, yet heavy, low to the ground, it sank down into the thick layer of gray dust around me. The dust crawled up my nose. His boots were shiny. He paced.

An old shoe lay next to my head, worn, dusty. It wasn't his. It was much too small. Just about right for my feet. Or Jimmy's.

A long-legged spider scurried up, out of the shoe, across my hand and out into the open. The boot came down firm, silent but for the soft squish as spider guts oozed in different directions. The floor was hard and cruel against my pelvic bones. I felt my breathing was too loud.

He sat on the bed. The mattress wheezed and sank. My head was smashed flat into the floor. I had to turn it to the side to avoid having my chin crushed up into my skull. There on the floor beside me was a bone. Not a pile of bones. Just one bone. I swallowed. The sound reverberated through the room. He shifted his weight. Springs groaned. I studied the bone. It was long and narrow, not quite long enough for a human adult. It was dusty and decaying. It wasn't smooth. It wasn't white. But it was a bone.

I rolled my eyes up in my head so I could see his feet. He shifted his weight again. The mattress sank further, my back pressed toward the floor. My lungs. I couldn't breathe.

I closed my eyes. Something crawled across my leg. He stood up, I gasped for breath. The floor quaked with his weight. Dust swirled up into my nose, my throat, coated my lungs. He walked to the dresser. He knelt. He pulled out the drawer, the second drawer from the bottom, and let out a short cry.

"That bitch," he said.

He knelt there for a moment. He stood. His feet moved toward the doorway, he turned off the light and vanished into the hall. I strained my ears to hear. Voices whispered everywhere, below me, above me. Soft laughter, the beating of hearts. The darkness was filled with the movement of shapes and noises. I heard fabric sliding against wallpaper and flesh, fingers thoughtfully rubbing chins, cold air moving through the broken basement window far below.

Jimmy moved. I felt it along my spine as he slid out of the closet and disappeared into the hall. I was alone.

A violent silence pulsed through the house. Through the air. I felt the electric currents in the floor. I stretched out my head and neck. Listened. Branches clawed at the roof in the wind. Mice scurried in the ceiling, the walls. The man returned.

He stood, facing me. He was huge. He seemed to be looking right at me. It was hard to tell. He had just one eyeball,
large, black and unblinking, sitting in the middle of his forehead like a satellite dish in the middle of the desert, collecting
messages from outer space. He stepped toward me. I closed my
eyes. I could feel the porcelain girl watching my throat. I could
sense the shipwreck, reflected in the mirror. Something moved
against my foot, hot breath and fur. He stepped again. I opened
my eyes. His boot was red-brown leather, so close to my face I
could lick it. I did. It tasted just like I had always known a boot
would taste.

He turned, moved to the closet. Opened the door. Removed a solid-looking metal rod and vanished again, into the
hall.

Creakings, footsteps, weird laughter. A low moan. Wind,
rodents, the flitting of bats. Silence.

Then, there he was. In the doorway. His slight figure forming spontaneously from the air, the dust, maybe the bone.

"Come on," said Jimmy. "Follow me."

I just stared. Jimmy glanced at the porcelain girl. She shattered noiselessly into shards which scattered across the floor.
He walked over to the bed. He kicked me in the face.

Something in my nose made a crackling sound. Then it bled.
I moved. Down the darkened hallway, slowly, listening. The
house shook from the wind, somebody was humming a funeral
dirge downstairs. The soft music filled the house. I followed
Jimmy down the steps toward the eerie yellow electric light
below.

She had her back to us, kneeling in the far corner of the
living room. She was small and black-haired, carefully folding
towels and washcloths and enormous Fruit of the Looms. She
was humming. He had his back to us also, but he was standing,
several paces behind her, watching her and tapping the metal
rod lightly against his palm. YEA, THOUGH I WALK THROUGH
THE VALLEY OF THE SHADOW OF DEATH. He stepped toward
her. He was graceful for a man with such a hairy neck. He raised
the pipe. Jimmy made a dash for the back door and I followed.

He swung it open wide and the cool breeze of freedom rushed over us. I listened for a scream or the sound of metal against flesh but there was nothing and we ran.

We ran. The door slammed behind us and we ran. Through backyards, past barbecue grills and empty children's swimming pools, Big Wheels and baseball gloves. We ran. An old man cursed us as we trampled his young forsythia bushes. We ran. And ran. I didn't stop my feet, didn't pause to breathe, he was there, maybe, behind us, thump, thump, thump, running, flailing, yelling, had to run, couldn't stop, couldn't breathe, distance, somewhere, anywhere, away, run . . . Finally I collapsed, down by the river on a hard patch of soil and stones, collapsed and sucked in handfuls of icy air, wheezed and gasped, cold oxygen shocked my insides, but I had to, had to breathe. I lay there forever, breathing hard, while Jimmy played with the gun, aimed it towards the river, stared at outer space.

"Wow," I finally gasped. "You saved my life."

Jimmy pointed the gun at a beer can imbedded in the bank. He pulled the trigger. The explosion shattered the night, bounced off stars and trees. The beer can was gone.

He stood, listened to the echoes. The night was scarred now. Huge and thirsty. He turned and walked, right on the edge of the bank. I followed, struggling to maintain the balance that seemed to come so naturally to Jimmy. Before long, we arrived at the orphanage.

"What are you going to do with the gun?" I asked.

He thought for a minute.

"Hide it," he said. "Somewhere where none of the kids will find it. I can keep it under my mattress for tonight."

He paused.

"You never know when you're going to need a gun."

We climbed up the rainspout and in through our bedroom window. Nobody was awake. Nobody seemed to be breathing. We crawled into bed.

I lay there in bed. I listened to my breathing. In and out, in and out. I listened to my heart. Everything was so quiet. I didn't sleep. I couldn't stop listening. I couldn't make it stop.

The gun was a Smith & Wesson. The next day Jimmy buried it in a well-insulated shoebox, out on the edge of the property, by a cluster of maple trees.

Four nights later we crept into the orphanage early in the morning, after a long night, pissing on people's doorsteps and putting dogshit and dead birds in their mailboxes. When we got back, everybody was already up. Somewhere in that nebulous zone between drunk and hungover, clink, clink went the breakfast dishes, the blaring morning sun beat hot on red and tired eyes. Larry glaring, disgusted nostrils and lips. Runny, slimy oatmeal globules, like papier-mâché vomit. Topped with government butter, it slid down our throats and then sat there, germinating, throbbing, then growing until everything inside me was oatmeal, my brain, my spinal cord, everything.

"You take care of Matthew," said Father Larry to Father Randy after breakfast. "I'll deal with this one."

He led Jimmy out of the room. He would deal with that one. Randy dealt with me.

Winter was coming and with it an end, for a while, to the blurred nights under starry skies, the moving with no thinking, the beautiful dark motion that helped me to forget. Those nights had been all that kept me going, kept me from slitting my wrists in the bathtub with a razor blade, like Jimmy told me his mother had done.

"Wow," I said. "Was her name Alice? Did she get sucked down the drain?"

"No," said Jimmy. "The drain got clogged up with bloody chunks of hair. We had to get a plumber."

But I knew Jimmy's mother was somehow linked to Alice and Andalusia, could sense that this bathtub connection went deeper in my life than I could figure. There was something funny going on.

If unloved, we were not forgotten. Every Halloween they came, busloads of sorority girls from the university, to help us carve smiling or snarling faces in pumpkins. The local television station was close behind, dutifully recording this heart-warming scene of philanthropy for all to see. Edward, the white-skinned orphan with such deeply red blood, jabbed the pumpkins with such disinterested violence that the sorority girls were soon huddling in the corners, pretending to be happy and whispering to themselves. The orphanage was not civilization as they knew it. With all of our parents dead our childhood notions of civilization had been laid bare as the flimsy toothpick structures they always had been, built on violence, property laws and the desire to purchase a riding lawn mower. Despite Father Larry's obvious desire to simulate a Catholic priesthood there was no pretense of Christian values among the orphans, no belief in any higher authority beyond Larry. Still, women's church groups flocked in on Thanksgiving, heavily laden with boneless turkey, instant dressing and cranberry Jell-O. Then we would all stand in a circle, clasping hands, and hear of these women's personal relationships with Jesus Christ. Tears would form in the corner of their clear blue eyes and we would sing, always we would sing and always the same song, "Kumbaya." *Some-one's singing, Lord, Kumbaya.* I've never been able to escape these women, they follow me everywhere. From the orphanage to the Salvation Army in Santa Fe, from the Walla Walla Jail to Oliver's Gospel Mission in downtown Columbia. Always hold-ing hands and always singing "Kumbaya." *Someone's praying, Lord, Kumbaya.* Wherever I go, the exact same women, some-times with southern accents, sometimes without, teary blue eyes, quivery voices urging everyone to eat more biscuits. Always plenty of biscuits. *Someone's crying, Lord, Kumbaya.* Then, when they were gone, it was always the same, with bums or convicts or lunatics, just like it was at the East Liberty Home for Boys. We would sit late into the night and laugh at them and talk about their breasts.

It comes in fragments, mostly, I can't seem to tie anything together. The winter didn't end, the head aching cold, the gray, the bare feet on cold tile floors. For two weeks I woke up and it was the same leaden sky, the same smell of death, the same

date on the calendar, January 12. The winter refused to budge.
Fathers snapped at us irritably, ears became brittle and snapped
off the heads of young children, hearts froze and ice covered
limbs were found in the empty fields. The sky was only a blanket of gray. We were cut off from the stars and from each other.
Our vocal cords froze. We could not speak.

On Wednesday nights Father Larry gave us the opportunity
to express ourselves nonverbally. He held orphan fights using
the same basic philosophy as cockfights. He would sit there with
his cronies, townsfolk mostly: TV repairmen, bankers, plumbers
and those who dealt with the skins of dead animals. They'd
scream and jeer, spew cheers and insults, make wagers and
threats. Hurling fists and bloody noses, crunching jawbones,
grinding teeth, screaming, screaming, a loud, vicious din filled
the air and hair and teeth and blood. It was mandatory at first,
but they soon tired of watching those of us who were not highly
motivated and too small to do any real damage, so Jimmy and I
were relegated to the sidelines. There was no shortage of more
virile orphans who enjoyed nothing more than pummeling and
being pummeled.

Father Larry was fond of quoting John Steinbeck.

"A boy becomes a man when a man is needed," he would
say. "Well, boys, tonight a man is needed."

Carlos Beckman was their needed man. He was big and ugly,
his head looked like he'd been hit with a bat when its shape
was still solidifying. He only lost once. He had been sick all
week, puked up green liquid after dinner, coughed up red spot-
ted hunks of mucus. A solid, gelatinlike substance had formed
on either side of his bed, clear yellow, but splotched with red,
and on Lyle Grundy, who slept in the bunk below his, until
Lyle couldn't budge, was shellacked to his bed with hardened
phlegm, and Father Larry had to use a chisel to set him free.

Carlos was beaten that night by Willie Buford. Carlos wasn't
pleased, became quite outspoken in his promises of retribution
the following week and fulfilled them with a smile. We all
watched as he turned Willie into a twisted mass of bones and

blood. He was taken out in an ambulance. Four days later they brought back a skinny red-haired boy and told us it was Willie.

"That's not Willie," I said to Jimmy. "Willie had brown, kinky hair. Don't you see? That's not Willie. They're lying."

"Who cares?" asked Jimmy. "What's the difference?"

He was right. Still, it kind of disturbed me.

Government funding had been cut, Father Larry announced one night at dinner, and they would have to let some of us go. It was time for us to make sacrifices, but the process would be entirely fair. Four names were chosen by lottery and the unfortunate children were given a cheese sandwich, wished all the luck in the world and escorted to the door. Little Timmy Pinecone glanced up at the plaque above the door, in honor of Desmond Boekki, an orphan and former resident of the East Liberty Home for Boys who had clawed his way to the ownership of a large multinational corporation. Timmy sniffled. He was only six years old. He was gently prodded out the door and we never heard from him again.

They watched each other suspiciously, the orphans, if they watched each other at all. Usually they watched television. One evening after our usual feast of potato stew, Father Larry led us excitedly into the rec room where a new, huge, blaring color television was waiting with remote control, sixty-seven channels and stunning SPEKTRAVISION color. The old black-and-white had been trashed, the Ping-Pong table had been removed and we now had a genuine TV lounge.

"A gift for all of you from me," said Father Larry, "to fill your otherwise bleak and empty lives."

"Clean your oven—while you sleep!" said the lovely, manicured housewife. Handel's *Messiah* played during commercials for plastic guns and hand grenades. A famous actor, who would be elected to the U.S. Congress a few years later, declared that he'd maim and kill before he'd switch his brand of aftershave. A constant wave of entertainment and information was emitted from the screen and lodged directly into the waiting

brains of staring orphans. The colors were so bright, vivid elec-
trifying colors that would seize the nerve endings in your eyeballs and embed the feel of cold steel burning hot in your
forehead. It was hyperreal. I snuck off with Jimmy and drank or
hid in dark closets or read some of the books I found in a crate
in the basement, Edgar Allan Poe and *Huck Finn* and *The
Stranger,* or I masturbated, once, twice, three times a day, anything to use up a few minutes, to distract myself from the
oppressive gray. Sometimes Jimmy would get tired of me and
go away. Usually, though, he came to get me, stood by my bed,
bored and quiet while I stuck a book or drawing of faceless
people under the mattress. His face was always smooth, it didn't
show things. I was the only one who saw how angry he was. I
watched him do things, mean things to people's property or pets.
He'd come back over and not say anything, just give me a look
that said, "You see?" I did. It felt good to be angry instead of
just sick. I damaged houses with him sometimes, or cars or lawns
or riding lawn mowers. Mostly, though, I was just the audience.
The others watched television, I watched Jimmy. The amount
of violent imagery we received was comparable. What I missed
out on in murders and car chases I made up for in tortured cats
and elaborate concoctions of urine, antifreeze, spit, grass, mud,
Fresca, blood, spoiled milk, oil, cat litter, dogshit, plastic army
men, dead bugs and the ashes of *Remembrance of Things Past*
heated to a boil and dumped on top of police cars.

Everything seemed in a fog that winter, disconnected and
stupid. Only the pain seemed real, connected me in a meaningful way to Father Randy. Larry always dealt with Jimmy in private, Randy dealt with me. It wasn't as bad with Randy, he didn't
really care, I could see his boredom as he beat me, inflicting
pain was only a job. He never gave long, convoluted speeches
about the fall of man and why Jimmy Carter would live to regret
giving away our canal. I didn't know what went on with Larry
and Jimmy. Jimmy never said.

Just after Groundhog Day the winter began moving in
reverse. February shifted and groaned back into January, the

dying Christmas tree was put back up and the anticipation grew of more presents, donated socks and underwear and silky disco shirts. For the first Christmas most of us had received only used clothing: stained jackets, stretched and abused sweaters with most of the sparkly things fallen off, underwear with holes. But Jimmy got a brand-new cobalt scarf from Father Larry. It was striking on him, I must say, made him more exotic-looking. He didn't belong with the rest of us, it was clear. He was dangerous and wise and beautiful. We were just orphans. Carlos Beckman resented that scarf, he picked Jimmy's little body up with one hand one day, as we were slipping backwards in time toward another festive holiday season, he held Jimmy against the wall and asked him if he thought he was better than the rest of us orphans, if he and Larry were buddies, how nice and warm he looked in his cute little fucking scarf. Then he let on that he was tempted to wrap that little scarf around Jimmy's little neck, nice and warm, nice and tight, until Jimmy's little eyes would bulge out of his head, his little lungs would gasp for air and his little Adam's apple would explode in pain.

"Carlos," said Jimmy quietly. He didn't say anything more. He stared at Carlos. What could Carlos do confronted by those eyes? They were Jimmy's eyes, no one would ever dare pluck them out with a spoon, nobody else would know how to use them. For a second I thought I saw actual fear in Carlos' face. He put Jimmy down and wandered off to the television lounge, shaken and dazed.

Jimmy walked to the window and looked out, toward the cluster of maple trees on the edge of the yard.

In late December, time shifted again, began moving in its more traditional direction. Christmas came only once and January returned, haughty and dark. In East Liberty the townspeople drank, shot their pets, committed adultery. At the orphanage nothing changed.

One night I woke. The furnace had just shut off, there was only lonely silence and cold. I'd been dreaming, I'd woken with a scream in my mouth, fleeing the House of Usher, over the river, anywhere. But the House of Usher was everywhere and scary uniformed men with shiny buttons and flashlights saying, "Right this way, sir, there's oatmeal waiting for you over here, sir, and television." I lay there and caught my breath, stared at the ceiling, then sat up in bed. Jimmy was sleeping, all still and peaceful. I felt the most incredible longing. His flawless, serene face. There was a sharp crack, his head split open and his thoughts came out. It was all silky blackness, so smooth, undisturbed, restful. It closed back up and I was left only with the image of perfection. I got out of bed, felt the cold draft on my neck and my toes, stood above Jimmy, watched and listened. I listened to him breathe. So slow. Regular. I wanted to feel his breath next to me. I wanted to share in his dreamlessness. In, out. In, out. His eyes opened once, for just a second, he was looking straight at me, yet he was looking at everything and mostly at nothing. They closed again. I walked to the window. No moon, no stars, only winter black. I shivered. I lay down on the floor, reached out my hand, slid my palm across the cold tile. My heart lurched, as if skipping a beat. I closed my eyes. I understood then what I longed for, what I loved and needed. I went back to bed, crawled beneath the flimsy covers. I slept.

Spring came.

"You know what I do with orphans?" asked the brown-toothed man on the park bench with a bagful of dead squirrels. "Cut them into little pieces."

He grinned.

We stole a bottle of wine and drank it down. We smoked cigarettes. We caught a ride back to East Liberty with a wild-eyed middle-aged woman who was looking for her husband on a corner in town.

"He must come," she said. "For it's been eleven years and this is the very corner on which I was raped." She said the word *raped* as if she was ripping it out of the air with her teeth.

Her husband was not on the corner, only a black cat. It nearly killed the poor woman, the discovery that her husband had been turned into a cat, and then he vanished behind some bushes.

She sobbed, her body shook, her breasts pressed into the steering wheel. Then she sat up straight, drove us to the orphanage and gave us a stern warning.

"Be cautious," she hissed. "It's the full moon. It makes men's blood boil. Society is a hole."

She drove away. It was late. Father Larry was waiting up for us. Father Randy wasn't.

"Go on up to bed, Matthew," said Larry. "I'll deal with you in the morning."

I climbed the stairs. The hallway loomed before me, dark and full of enormous closed doors. I felt dizzy. Larry was coming up the stairs behind me. I ducked into the bathroom. Larry and Jimmy went by, into Larry's room. I peeked out. The door was open a crack. I stood outside and listened.

I heard them sit down on the bed, heard the rustling of Larry removing clothes and his soothing voice as he reprimanded Jimmy. The words were so soft, they slid out of his lips, slithered into Jimmy's left ear, gloshed through the mucous membranes of his cerebellum without leaving the slightest impression, then out the other ear and eased around the crack of the door where they reached me. The words were varied, they flowed in a bizarre stream, "punished . . . hurts me more . . . beautiful child . . . garden . . . night of man . . . omelettes . . ." I heard caressing, the sound of Larry's fat jiggling, as if an electric current were passing through his body.

"Wear this," Larry said, "and this. Yes, that's it. Look at you. Here, read this passage."

Jimmy read.

" 'His was an inpenetrable darkness. I looked at him as you peer down at a man who is lying at the bottom of a precipice where the sun never shines. But I had not much to give him, because I was helping the engine-driver to take to pieces the leaky cylinders, to straighten a bent connecting-rod, and in other such matters.' "

"Beautiful," said Larry. "Please, go on."

I couldn't help myself, moved my eye to the crack, watched the bodies glowing palpably in the moonlight. Jimmy was

dressed in a loincloth with leopard spots and wearing a feather
necklace, reading *Heart of Darkness*. I felt beer and illness
churning in my stomach. I turned away. He kept reading. I'd
never heard Jimmy read before, he pronounced everything right.

" 'One evening coming in with a candle I was startled to
hear him say a little tremulously, "I am lying here in the dark
waiting for death." The light was within a foot of his eyes. I
forced myself to murmur, "Oh, nonsense!" and stood over him
as if transfixed. Anything approaching the change that came over
his features I have never seen before, and hope never to see
again. Oh, I wasn't touched. I was fascinated. It was as though
a veil had been rent. I saw on that ivory face the expression of
somber pride, of ruthless power, of craven terror—of an intense
and hopeless despair. Did he live his life again in every detail
of desire, temptation, and surrender during that supreme moment
of complete knowledge? He cried in a whisper at some image,
at some vision—he cried out twice, a cry that was no more than
a breath: The horror! The horror!' "

Larry moved his hands over Jimmy's naked chest.

"You are my heart of darkness," he said. "My own dark con-
tinent. I want to help you to grow up into a civilized young man,
to marry and own a boat. But I have no control sometimes."

I ran. Back down the hall, down the stairs into the dark. I
could hear the television, still gurgling quietly, always on,
twenty-four hours a day. I stepped into the lounge. A minister
was being interviewed on a talk show. His name was Daniel,
he was with the Church of Christ with the Elijah Message. He'd
put his dead mother in a refrigerator and was planning to bring
her back to life. God told him what to do. He'd brought in experts
from Australia, people who'd done this sort of thing before,
brought the dead to life. I switched the channel. Larry's face
was on the screen, moaning, and dancing cannibals, muscle and
meat on their breath, sticking between their teeth.

"Matthew," said Larry's image, "it's past your bedtime. You
shouldn't be watching this."

My eyes were glued to the vibrant colors, they moved in
and out, a kaleidoscope of images. Rats and vultures, feasting

and fornicating, searching for a human sacrifice. A woman with big hair praising Jesus or selling charcoal lighter fluid. Words flashed on the screen. "The two U.S. presidents who never officially fathered a child." It was *Final Jeopardy*. Advertisements for financial magazines. Waterbeds and diet pills. Spilling brains. Larry and Jimmy, the scene I'd just witnessed.

"Go away," I whispered. "Leave me alone."

I wanted to scream, but I'd forgotten how. I heard Jimmy upstairs, climbing into bed. I thought about food, thought about vomiting. I ran from the room and up the stairs, into my room, past Jimmy, already sound asleep it seemed, and into bed. The first hint of pale light was creeping through the window. It was the ugliest light I'd ever seen.

We were standing by the highway, waiting to throw large rocks at passing cars. It was a bright, blue spring day, unseasonably warm, verging on hot.

"It's time for us to leave," said Jimmy.

I was startled.

"Where will we go?" I asked.

"Anywhere," he said. "We can be outlaws. Rob banks."

"Or 7-Elevens," I suggested.

"Whatever it takes," he said.

A car drove by, we threw our rocks. There was a loud thunk and we scurried into the cornfield, toward the orphanage. Old people cursed loudly.

"We have to travel light," said Jimmy. "Only grab what you really need. Meet me out by the maple trees."

I got my toothbrush, a flashlight, a change of underwear, a tattered copy of *Of Mice and Men*. Shoved some Life Savers in my pocket and stole a rhubarb pie from the kitchen. Out on the edge of the yard Jimmy had the gun.

"Start walking," he said. "Toward the road. I'll meet you in a minute."

I stood, slightly dazed with the sense of departure. I was fourteen years old. Jimmy tucked the gun in his pants and walked toward the orphanage. I saw him disappear into the door. I turned and began to walk. The ground was moist. The sun was hot on my hair. I squinted at the sky. There were no clouds. I listened for a shot. My feet made a gentle slurping noise on the earth, sticks cracked beneath my weight. The sun was high, I felt dizzy. A tense, giddy feeling inside. Where was it? My ears could catch nothing from the brightness and heat that engulfed me. What if Jimmy never came? I stopped walking. I held my breath. There was something, there, in the distance, the quiet sound of the afternoon splitting in two. I felt the weight of my body on the earth. The road was just up ahead. Birds flew, noiselessly. I felt Jimmy's presence behind me, turned, and he was beside me.

"Come on," he said. "We've got to move."

He moved. I followed.

THREE

Δ

1

The pretty girl in the pickup truck sits up front while the wind blows my hair against the BUSH QUAYLE sticker on the window that separates us. She has *Calculus* and sweaters, a boyfriend and a voter registration card. Once, I had such things. A father with a motorcycle, a mother with tapioca pudding. I think that was me. Everybody needs a past or they're likely to turn into a lunatic or a messiah. All I'm sure of anymore is that a long time ago I lived in the bathtub with a woman named Andalusia. Lives pass before me like billboards and rest stops and through me and over me. Illegal aliens with bad tires, skateboard sadists with bad teeth, suicidal teenagers desperate for affection. Dancing earth children frolicking under exuberant Colorado skies, smearing their well-tanned bodies with the juicy pulp of ripened fruit. Unemployed men everywhere who hate Jews or fags. Methodist preachers, ex-convicts, men with large purple birthmarks on their necks. I latch onto their lives for an hour or ten minutes or the entire distance between Baton Rouge and Desolation. I dip into them like a tongue in sugar, grow dizzy with the sheer volume. Their lives become mine, for I have no life of my own, just a series of observations.

"The past is no different from the present," Jessica Moon once told me. "We make it up as we go along."

Jessica Moon fed me stir-fried veggies and cheese fondue. She was a goddess of food. Hazelnuts, blackberries and wild mushrooms would throw themselves at her feet as she passed by, sacrificing themselves for her nourishment. Cauliflower, rutabaga and asparagus would hurl themselves from passing produce trucks to be near her, papayas and mangoes adored her, would make treacherous journeys from Acapulco, thousands of miles on the hats of vulgar American women, to immolate themselves before her. We would wake in the night to find white radishes and broccoli quarreling noisily, elbowing each other for the position closest to the mouth of the tent. Every morning a mound of fresh edibles was stacked there, waiting. She fed me, she fed Antonio and Wendy, she fed the child growing in her womb. She made sandwiches she sold for a dollar or whatever people could afford to pay. She spent the money on jade beads, Arkansas quartz crystals, luminous amethyst, hematite and onyx, transformed these little gems into dazzling necklaces containing secret histories of the universe, stories of lunacy and rebellion and the spaces between words. These she sold on the streets and spent the profits on gas for the van or tiny moccasins for the life that was forming inside.

"My father was one of those people," she told me, "who loved to plant things. Tomatoes, Russian olive trees, anything. He would plant them and that was it. He'd forget. I like to feed things, to watch them grow. Here, have another tofu-avocado sandwich."

I remember voices and hair, a look in the eyes or the color of shoes. Mostly I remember the food. An All You Can Eat cafeteria at Ormond-by-the-sea, a similar establishment in Las Vegas, plenty of mashed potatoes. Hot dogs for a dime at a grocery store in Denver. Hotcakes for a dime from an angel of mercy at the Market Street Diner in Wheeling. I remember lasagna, clam chowder and chicken parmesan. A man in Alabama gave me a bag full of kiwi fruit. A man in Idaho gave me macadamia-nut cookies. Mom used to mix milk, sugar and vanilla and freeze it on a stick. The food I dream about at night! Barbecued ribs, mushroom pizzas, octopus prepared in its own ink. I never dream of Hostess pies, of peanut butter cheese crackers or of Snickers bars. These I steal from 7-Elevens, Kum and Gos, Snag and Dash, Gas and Pass, or from all-night grocery stores. Sav-U-Plenty,

Cheep-O-Foods, Hinky Dinky and Piggly Wiggly; America is a neon glow. The food is kept in warm, well-lit places.

Once it is gone, you can never really remember the texture of hunger. I tell myself this now. I know it is true, yet I can't really believe it.

Unlike Jessica Moon and the man with the kiwi fruit, the pretty girl in the pickup truck doesn't feed me. She barely even speaks to me. I sit in back with the wind and the sun, watch the passing billboards and apathetic livestock, she sits up front with her calculus book and a mound of sweaters, listens to a tape recording of her boyfriend. He tells her that he loves her, he loves her pickup truck, he loves her mathematical mind, he loves her political commitment, he loves the way her breasts heave beneath whichever one of her sweaters she chooses to wear.

"You are with me always," I hear the tape recorder say through the thin glass that separates us. "In my mind, so real that I can touch you. Oh, that feels good. Your belly. Your wool sweater, the red one with the little deer on it. Your breasts."

"Come on, Davey," says the girl, "I'm trying to drive. You don't want to cause an accident, do you?"

There's a snicker from the tape recorder.

We don't crash. She lets me off, way out in West Des Moines. I walk several miles. Straight down University Avenue, past cream-colored condominium villages, past the movie theater, the college, the taverns and the shacks. Down Keo Way and into downtown. It's been ten years. I have come home.

Des Moines. I think of girls in red hats sledding down hills. I think of golf courses, loneliness, the statistical mean. A place where people own too much insurance. A place that instills deep in one's body the sense that we've already failed.

It's night now. High school kids from Des Moines, Indianola and Polk City drive Novas and Camaros in circles around me. They honk horns and shout out of open windows, crouching down to drink beer in the backseats while the drivers keep saying, "Keep it down! There's a cop up ahead." The night is balmy, the beer flows and the young people all blur together into one thing; the weather is perfect for a mystical and alcoholic ecstasy of this sort, breezy and filled with scents of ethnic food, exhaust fumes and rubber on the pavement. These are the best nights for sleeping when you do not own a blanket. But there's that flirtatious warmth floating in the air, it forces me to stay awake.

I walk. Teenagers standing in gangs on the corner smoke cigarettes and watch me go by. Girls in black T-shirts whisper and laugh when I have passed. Why am I downtown? I could pay my respects at my parents' cemetery, or visit the old neighborhood, the duplex. I could look for ghosts. Maybe Mrs. Tyndall and Marcie are still living next door. Or Olivia Barnhouse, the evil woman across the street who summoned demons. Somebody might recognize me. I pause, look at my reflection in a store window and know how ridiculous this is. What happened to the twelve-year-old boy with the paper route and the curious awe? I search for a resemblance. Maybe something in the eyes. This is all that connects us, a thin strand, ethereal, like a cobweb, a continuation of blood and bone cells, molecules and membranes. Even the chewing gum I swallowed then has passed out of my system.

Δ

Dad's was a magic presence that shielded me as a child from the harsh realities of life. Whenever Olivia Barnhouse, the evil woman across the street who summoned demons, would frown at me from behind her thick black curtains, releasing the wicked, snarling guinea pigs from the depths of hell beneath my bed, Dad would simply sprinkle oregano around my mattress and I'd be safe for the night. When drooling lunatics came to our door selling magazine subscriptions, Dad explained that there was nothing to fear; insanity was simply one of the many different ways that the universe had for communicating its intent to us.

"It's a known fact that there are five times as many women as men in the world," the salesman said, "and I have the ear of a woman."

Dad was always able to see the pattern in seemingly random communications. My Bible-story coloring books, Mom's scribbled grocery lists, the notes the milkman left, maps of ancient trade routes, words spelled out with dead grass in neighbor's lawns. Biorhythm charts in the newspaper, foreign words that Olivia Barnhouse shrieked at new moon or on Wednesdays, excerpts from editorials, scientific reports, legal treatises or folk tales, Clint Eastwood westerns and bullet holes in walls, the color scheme of the jars of moldy leftovers in our refrigerator.

"Don't specialize," he told me. "That's the key. Don't ignore anything the world wants to tell you."

In retrospect, I'm amazed how well he functioned, what a useful member of society he was, pumping out mass mailings or filling cars with gas. Until things fell apart.

I found out that Dad couldn't always be there, even before he was murdered in his sleep. I was eight or nine, sitting in old Mrs. Danish's backyard, I'd followed a monarch butterfly there, captured it and stuck it in a jar. Hidden from the old woman's view by the towering anise and mint and tomato plants, I sat and pulled thin little carrots from her garden, munched them, dirt and all. It tasted like eating the planet itself. The drowsy scents of licorice and spearmint filled the air, the drone of bees buzzing about the white-flowered heads of mint tea. Everything was strange and near, the world colorful and raw, the tulips, zinnias, tomatoes ripe and filled near to bursting with juice, hanging from the vines. The world itself was ripe and alarmingly recent. Mushrooming bushes and spores, jutting, exuberant flora, the menace of red petals, slumbering clouds. Life was abundant, swarming and decaying, and the odor rich, so sweet as to nearly turn my stomach, if it wasn't for the gentle breeze and the hum and the crunching of carrots in my teeth.

Ricky Sedlacek lived on the next block, could spit a looey fifty feet with deadly accuracy and was possessed by the devil. He came up behind me with a couple of thugs from his block, Joey Sassatelli and his little sister, Petunia. They stood and stared at me until Ricky announced that I was an ugly little dickface and probably a tattletale and that they were going to give me a pink belly. Before I could move they had me down on the ground, Ricky had my arms, Petunia held my legs, Ricky lifted my shirt and began thumping away at my belly with his hand, like a drum. Thump, thump, thump. He spit on my eyelid and drummed away, his palm rapping against the rawed flesh of my belly. Joey stood and watched, grinning evilly, while rhythmic vibrations of pain shot through my body. Thump, thump, thump. I tried to kick, tried to squirm, couldn't budge, could feel my skin turning pink, then red. I wanted to bawl, but I couldn't let them see me cry. Boys don't cry, but I'd never known human beings could endure such pain. I thought of tales of torture I'd heard from the Tyndall kids, men tied out in the desert with their eyelids removed, bodies dipped in marmalade and left to the ants. Thump, thump, thump. It lasted forever out there with the sun beating down and the nauseous odors of mint and zinnias and licorice. I screamed, finally, screamed for all I was worth. Ricky shoved Petunia's sock in my mouth to make me shut up. I couldn't breathe, my nose was filled with tears and snot, I was choking on a smelly pink sock. Thump, thump, thump. I was sure it was the end. The earth rumbled, trumpet music blared, the sky was filled with doves, and I saw her, there in the sky, the clouds parting before her, it was Andalusia, smiling down at me, her arms outstretched and a pink box of Mr. Bubble in her hands. I felt myself beginning to float up toward her and then Ricky stopped.

They sat for a minute and admired the rosy color of my belly. Ricky called me a little crybaby fucker. Petunia took back her sock and they hurled tomatoes at Mrs. Danish's house. The juice splattered like blood against the white wood siding, dripped down in streaks. They ran off toward their own block.

Mrs. Danish never came out. I sat and cried. It felt good.

"What happened?" Mom asked when I walked into the kitchen. She could still see the tearstains on my pliable little cheeks.

"Nothing," I said. "I've just been sneezing. Maybe I'm allergic."

She didn't ask questions, but gave me grape Kool-Aid and Double Chocolate Coconut Cookies. They were warm and gooey and brown and the memory of pain subsided as I filled my stomach and smeared melting chocolate on my lips and face and shirt.

Like the stranger, I didn't cry at their funeral. I just watched. The sky that day was pale bright, like a desert. I could see a striped hot-air balloon, hanging in the distant sky.

The summer before he was dead, Dad had a mustache and a gut. He experimented with facial hair—Fu Manchus, Peter Fonda sideburns, goatees—and ate ice cream all the time. We went to the beach that summer, all of us, the man-made lake north of town, Saylorville. His belly hung out over his swim trunks, covered with black hairs, it looked like a fuzzy sort of Cyclops head, the belly button staring out. He was pale, reading a book. Mom flipped through a magazine and drank lemonade. I came out of the water, ran wet and shivering toward them, the sand sticking in globs to my feet, my ankles. I sat in the sand, wrapped myself in a towel, shivering. An image popped into my head, a white dome on top of a cliff. Dad was watching me, reading my mind.

"This telepathy is a bad sign," he said. "The neofascists on the rise again. Only five years after Nixon, all this psychic phenomena."

This was one of Dad's big projects that summer, mapping out the coincidence of psychic phenomena and the rise of the right wing. I lay out on my towel. Two browned teenage men were stretched out behind us on Coors towels, displaying their hairless muscles. I knew they were thinking about sex.

"Matt," said Dad, "did I ever tell you about the Dome of Silence?"

I shook my head no. The sun was bouncing off the water, white glare, I had a headache. People were throwing Frisbees to dogs, laughing, drinking beer. I wanted to be one of those people, I thought, running down the beach, not a kid with his parents.

"It's in Greece," he said, "on the top of a sheer cliff in the middle of the sea. You have to climb hundreds of feet up a rope ladder to get to the monastery. Nobody speaks there, even the birds are silent. Even the rain that falls there falls without a sound, on shrouded men walking garden paths, lips closed tight. The ocean is mute as well, the wind tiptoes past, there isn't a sound that's allowed to intrude. I spent several months there. I vowed I would make a sound, just a small noise, a whisper . . . but I couldn't make it come out. The silence was too overpowering."

"Neat," I said. "Can I have money for a Sno-Kone?"

"Wait," he said. "Listen. It nearly drove me crazy at first. Total silence. But then there was this humming, welling up from inside my own head. It was a song, vibrating in my temple, voices and melodies and animal noises. It was the strangest thing."

Behind him, Mom was looking up from her *Gospel Herald*, listening.

"Eventually, I came out of that place, of course. I came back here to go to school. I had this incredible urge to fill the world with noise. And then I met your mother."

He was staring at me without seeing. Mom stood up, she looked sick. She was walking down the beach then, and crying. I didn't understand it; Dad chasing after her, talking the way he did, joking, trying to make her stop. She kept crying, all the way home in the Volkswagen, carefully, calmly crying.

We stopped at the Dairy Sweet and Dad bought us ice cream. Girls' softball teams piled out of station wagons, couples on motorcycles ate banana splits. Mom apologized for ruining our fun. Dad was cracking jokes, splurging. It felt good then, like that was how it was supposed to be, a family, eating ice cream, together. We were fat and sticky. Our skin glowed from the sun.

In September Dad got laid off, on my parents' twelfth wedding anniversary, five months before my twelfth birthday, seven months before the two of them were killed, just four days after I'd committed my life to Jesus. I'd been going to the Zion Lutheran Church youth group on Friday nights, they called it Arnold'z and we could play all the pool and pinball we wanted for only fifty cents. Some of the kids smoked dope in the parking lot beforehand, but I wasn't that advanced yet. Then one night they took us to see a film about the end of the world. Graphic images of famine, nuclear blasts, blood pouring from the moon, plagues of locusts and boils, all the torments reserved for the non-Christians who Jesus left behind. After the film a man suggested that anyone who wanted to be saved step forward. I was sitting with my friend Teddy, a fat boy who looked sort of like a blown-up Arthur Rimbaud with zits. We looked at each other, nervously. We stood, stepped down with various other young people who were shyly moving to the front of the room, were led into the back. A man explained everything to us back there and asked us to commit our lives to Jesus, to say it out loud, to ask Jesus to forgive us. We did. He gave us tiny, lime-colored Bibles and we rode our bikes home. On the day Dad lost his job I was playing hooky, contemplating the tempting sinfulness of my classmates, my newfound path. I rode my green Schwinn one-speed up to the park at the top of the hill, found Dad there, sitting, looking out over the city. It was that time of the year, with the fading light, the first colored leaves, when the whole day seemed like dusk. He should have been at work.

The economy was getting slow, he said. His boss didn't like him anyway, because he was always late and he had a bad attitude, too human. He'd never officially been hired full-time permanent, so they didn't have to give him Unemployment.

"Don't tell your mother," he said. "I don't want to ruin this day for her. I'll tell her tomorrow."

He looked so tired. Twelve years they had been married. Four months before I was born.

"I'm still going to get my ten-speed, aren't I?" I asked. "For my birthday? I've got to, Dad. I've just got to."

He didn't seem to hear me.

"Alaska," he said. "I was scheduled to leave on a fishing boat for Alaska."

Then he smiled.

"Get back to school, you little hoodlum," he said. "I didn't give up my college education so you could turn out to be an illiterate."

I sat in class that afternoon playing with my pencil and staring out the window. It was a Trusty pencil, rubbery, it would bend like crazy without breaking. I thought about Dad. I knew then, for the first time, that he was missing out on something, that he had given something up. Because of Mom, because of me. I watched the hands on the clock. Miss Tierney gave us a spelling test. *Dividend, rhythm, planetarium, doubtful.* Spelling was my best subject, I usually got perfect papers. This time, I intentionally misspelled, as if that would help me.

That night the kitchen was filled with burning torches and roses, an invisible string quartet played delicate music of love and sorrow, voices from the air asked my mother if she had a request. She wanted to hear "Edelweiss." *Bloom and grow, bloom and grow, love our homeland forever.* Meanwhile, Dad presented us with the most glorious feast I'd even seen. Octopus in its own ink, dragon tongue in pineapple sauce, seventeen varieties of mushrooms, sautéed in butter, flaming chocolate unicorns in brandy.

"My Lord!" exclaimed Mom. "It's a miracle on the order of the loaves and fishes."

"It's a mite beyond that," said Dad. "Him, he had everything handed to him on a platter. He never had a family to feed. He didn't have to put food on the table for twelve years."

Mom took his hand and smiled. He smiled back. He poured red wine in crystal goblets. I didn't know it then, that this would be our last supper before everything began falling apart. I shoveled octopus into my mouth.

After dinner I rode my bike through the early darkness. Leaves were falling, yellow, and blowing. The breeze chilled me. I played a video game at the gas station, Space Invaders, spent three dollars in quarters. I rode home then, left the bike in the front yard and went in.

The kitchen was empty. I started up the stairs, could hear Mom humming in her bedroom, knew she was brushing her hair. I stood. There was something. I looked down over the kitchen. Dad's papers were spread on the table, he'd been writing again. A soft noise, like a balloon letting its air out, a quiet collapsing. I descended. Large slash marks covered the pages, papers were crumpled in balls on the floor. A brisk wind blew through the back screen door, carried something with it, a new sound.

I moved toward the door. He was out there, sitting on the back step, his head buried in his hands. I knew then what it was, that sound. His body shook and the leaves with him, in the wind. Father was crying.

2

By the time we reached the highway I was tired of carrying the rhubarb pie I'd taken from the kitchen, ate a piece, gave a piece to Jimmy and threw the rest in a ditch by the side of the road. Jimmy was carrying nothing but the empty gun, shoved into his trousers. Our futures stretched out before us in either direction, we couldn't go back to the orphanage now. East or west, my whole life had come down to this decision. Maybe because we didn't realize that west is the traditional direction for outlaws to flee, that west is where the future lies and the secrets of the night, the American dream, hope and possibility, mystery and visions, or maybe because neither of us even knew which direction was which, we headed east, toward the old world, the past.

Our first ride took us across the Mississippi to East Moline.

"There she is," the sawdust salesman who was driving said. "The mighty Mississippi. Kind of makes your heart get all woozy and furry-feeling, don't it?"

He was wearing sunglasses tinted orange, a suit jacket and a tie.

"Maybe we could get a raft," I whispered to Jimmy, "and float all the way down."

"Don't be stupid," he said.

The man mumbled something about riding lawn mowers and let us out. The sun had set behind us, the crackling afternoon had slipped to the west. The night was crisp, moon-soaked, everything sparkled, edges more defined. Objects jumped out at us and demanded our attention, telephone poles, the geometric configurations of wood and wires, vivid brick walks, lawns speckled cream and green, flattened by months of snow and boots. In the cloudless spring night all the earth's warmth had been sucked up into the blackness. The wind passed right through my flimsy jacket.

"Wait here," said Jimmy, and he strolled off into the town's darkness. I shivered and paced. I tried to imagine heat. It was useless. I realized that Jimmy might never come back, that he had struck out on his own. What did he ever need me for? I was doomed. Jimmy was my savior, my protector, my view of the world. Jimmy was beyond language, a beautiful silent film. Jimmy was Jesus, my father and Charlie Chaplin all rolled into one. Jimmy did more than reveal secrets, Jimmy was the secrets. If he didn't come back I'd be empty again, with nothing to watch. Moving was more than I could do, all by myself. Alone, I would die.

He returned with a blanket. We crawled behind the shrubbery of a small church building, out of the wind, and wrapped ourselves in the big gray blanket that smelled of dog. A long night passed on the hard ground, I slept for five-minute periods then woke with a start, a shudder, the sense that something was coming after me, was creeping up on me while I lay there, defenseless in the blanket. In the morning I woke with a noise in my throat, the sun shone yellow in my eyes. We walked wordlessly back toward the highway, covered with dew. My teeth chattered. Traffic was slow and the rides did not come easy.

Jimmy would spot highway patrol cars in the distance and we would dive into ditches, lie flat on our bellies and hold our breath. We were picked up, let out, slept outside in bushes that made me itch. It rained sometimes. We spent a week in the Indianapolis airport, after getting a ride from a man in a turban who didn't speak English. It was a warm place to sleep, an easy place for Jimmy to steal things from. Posters of sunny islands beamed down at us, frazzled, well-dressed people ran around with luggage, we rode the escalators and ate onion rings and cherry pie and roasted almonds that we stole or picked off other people's plates. We slept on blue padded benches, through countless announcements of imminent departures and calls for Mr. Somebody to come to the white courtesy phone. We never bathed, except for our faces and hands in the bathrooms, and I knew that we smelled. It was something we had in common and I started to like it, my smell, Jimmy's smell, the two smells mixed together. Somewhere in Kentucky we found a warm barn, slept in the cab of an enormous tractor. Back in Indiana we slept in a cemetery. We traveled slowly and not in a straight line. Jimmy had decided we were going to New York. Living was easy there, he said, he'd been there before. He knew the ways of the natives and the streets. And, he said, it was an easy place to vanish. That was all I wanted to do.

"Hop in, boys, make yourself at home, where you headed?"

"New York," I said.

The man smiled. The car was luxurious, crushed blue velvet, cigar smoke and the frozen liquid smell of automotive air conditioning. He was middle-aged and mustached, wore a nice suit and gave us brandy-scented words of encouragement.

"I think what you boys are doing is great, goddammit. You guys are just like Kerouac and Cassady. Not many kids have the guts to wander the highways anymore. When I was your age, I'll tell you, everybody was doing it, I was out there, zipping back and forth from New York to San Fran, seeing it all, doing things. Kids today are too damn content. Have much luck getting rides?"

Jimmy was silent on my other side, staring out the window.

"Yeah," I said, "it's been pretty good so far. Sometimes it's kind of slow, we had to wait three hours this morning. Then some guy with a big purple birthmark on his neck picked us up."

"Sure," said the man, "you meet all kinds on the road. Purple birthmarks, red birthmarks, harelips, it's all the same. Back in my day you never had to wait, not more than fifteen minutes. Anybody'd pick you up, people trusted each other, loved each other. By the way, my name's Earl, it's a pleasure."

He extended a hand. His grip was large and confident, his palm not sweaty at all. I liked Earl. I felt safe with him.

"Back then everybody was out. Experiencing, protesting. On the road, drinking in the greatness of the American night, feeling the hot breath of life roaring in our faces, overwhelming our hallucinogenically enhanced sense perceptions with the sweet, sad rush of romance and freedom, filling our lungs with the Kerouacian dream, rolling down endless, mystical highways, coming face to face with the chilling and awesome mysteries of love and death and destiny, out naked and free under the void, the inscrutable face of the godhead . . ."

"Wow," I said. Jimmy rolled his eyes. Earl went on.

"I see it on TV now and they make us look silly. Sure, I know we were just kids, all those radical politics were sort of ridiculous, I suppose. I think Carter's a good man, it's just he's a bit incompetent, you know? You have to grow up, everybody seems to say so. You have to vote Republican sooner or later. I don't think Reagan's all that scary, I don't think he'll blow up the world or anything. It's just that we've got to get back to something. Maybe he'll make America more like it used to be. It's not that I believe him, you understand. But I admire the way he can get other people to believe in him when there's really nothing there. I admire his knack for manipulating public opinion. A president should be able to do that, I think, manipulate the public. Sure, I'm married now. I sell dental equipment, dental equipment never hurt anybody. I've got a decent sort of life, a nice house, a car, a couple of daughters."

"You're a father," I said.

He nodded.

"Two of the sweetest, most beautiful girls you ever saw. Damn, I love those girls. Let me show you a picture."

He reached across our laps, dug through the glove compartment, through matchbooks, legal documents, yo-yos and breath mints, pulled out a photo. They stood in a plastic wading pool, blond and smiling, the smaller one wrapped in a green alligator inner tube, the older one with her arm around the other's shoulder, protective.

"Four and six," said Earl. "Although I guess Elizabeth would have been only three when this picture was taken. If it wasn't for those two little angels, damn, you know, I miss the old days sometimes, there was something there that's missing now. Something to be said for security, sure, but listen, I was out and wild, I didn't go to Nam, I was twenty-three and my uncle paid to put me in college. He'd been to Korea, he knew. War is hell, he told me, not that that's really profound, but he saved my life in a way. I didn't spend much time in classes, though, I was out, on the road, sticking my fingers in. Walked across the state of Alabama just for kicks, got threatened, slept with older women a lot. Me and my buddies, once in Minnesota we were tripping our brains out and Steven, he steps on glass, this was at this lake, you see, we're just swimming in the lake, this wild clear lake, really blue, you know, you can't always find lakes like that. But he cut his foot all up, bleeding like crazy, and we head for the town, to go to the hospital, but we have to stop for ice cream on the way. So then all these fascist cops and townspeople are getting bent out of shape because we took some geezer's towel to wrap up his foot. I don't know. Crazy times."

He paused and put his cigar out in the ashtray.

"What were we looking for? They said if you were looking you'd already found it. They said a lot of silly things like that."

Earl wore glasses and didn't have to pay much attention in order to drive. A billboard for Scotch told us that we were the kind of people who only settled for the best.

"It was good," Earl said, "because everybody you met, even if it wasn't a person, if it was a rock or an ice cream cone or a lake or an idea, it's in that meeting somewhere that something happens, these lines take off and move in different directions, everybody's full of lines and then they go off, I know I'm not explaining it right, but just think about a rodeo."

Ohio was filled with signs. Some promised Columbus and Zanesville were just up ahead. Others advertised fast food and motor oil. I pictured horses and lassos and squirming bulls in the dust. Jimmy was fidgeting next to me, his leg up tight against my own.

"I used to box," said Earl. "Back with my uncle, back when I was a kid. I was pretty good, we boxed a lot. Once I started tripping I never wanted to box anyone again, but still, I loved my uncle. You know what I'm saying? When I was just a kid he took me to the Ohio State Fair. There were these tiny little black people, the littlest people in the world, shaking maracas. I never forgot that. My uncle was missing a finger, he only had nine. Those were days, all right."

"I only have nine toes," I said. I hoped he might want to take a look.

"Sure," he said. "Everybody's missing out on something."

I studied his face. He had bags under his eyes, lines in his forehead.

"You know," he said, almost to himself, "I really think the sky was a more appealing shade of blue back then. Those damned nuclear tests the government runs, you never know how they've fucked up the atmosphere."

It was true, I knew. Back in the neighborhood with Andalusia the sky had been royal blue or cornflower or periwinkle. Now it was just the color of mentholated cough drops. What with the altered sky, the death of God and the fracturing of time, the old days definitely advertised an appeal.

"I was in love once, you know," Earl said. "Oh, I was in love with my wife, too, of course. I still am, in a way. I was in love with her at the same time I was in love with Rebeca. I was capable then of being in love with more than one person at the same time. Rebeca had bucks. Never pass a rich girl by, if you can help it, that's my advice, a rich girl's just as easy to love as a poor one. I met her at the American University in Mexico

City. So beautiful! White-skinned, long black hair, her accent a combination of Wales and North Carolina. You should have heard her speak Spanish, exquisite. Oh my. We went to Oaxaca, to the ruins at Monte Albán. We were communing with the mushroom gods, *hongos* they call them in Mexico, best *hongos* in the world come from Oaxaca. The sky was red, strange shafts of light bouncing out of secret keyholes, illuminating lunatic hieroglyphs, an eclipse of the sun. Rebeca had a knife, slaughtered some sort of two-headed beast and drank the blood, right there, on the summit of the temple, the glow of the sky bathing her in pale, silent light and then *Are you coming? Are you coming?* she asked, Jesus H., was I coming? I could have come five times a day with that woman. She was my lost half, my other self, I could have merged with her for eternity and vanished in bliss! *Yes,* I said. *Then take my hand,* she said, *and don't look back."*

Earl paused and lit up another cigar.

"What more could I have wanted? What was I afraid of? But I froze. I froze! My wife, well, she wasn't my wife then, but she was in San Fran, pregnant, it was a miscarriage in the end, but I didn't know that then. Hell, it might not even have been mine, but that must be what stopped me. That must be it. What else could it be? Fear, I suppose. I don't know. *Take my hand,* she said, and the wind was swirling her black hair around her body, her hair was dancing a tale of sex and love and eternity, I reached out, my sweaty little fingers, there was a flash of lightning, but no. Something held me back. Her face was up, toward the void, and she saw it, whatever it was, and I knew I'd never have a second chance, the sky ripped open and she vanished in a blaze of brilliant orange light."

Once again, the sun was setting behind us, reflecting its light in our rearview mirrors. The road was filling with cars as we moved closer to Columbus. Make those pesky roaches disappear! declared a billboard. On the other side of the road a long woman in black smoked a long cigarette.

"But I don't regret my decision," he said finally. "Hell, no. No regrets, that's what I always say. Vanishing into some sort of timewarp, or whatever the hell it was, you know, that idea doesn't really appeal to me. Who knows what it's like on the other side? Hot and crowded, probably, with live chickens in canvas bags, like a Mexican bus. Hell, my wife's nice enough, two of the most beautiful daughters you ever saw. Sure, they're responsibilities. Sometimes you have to face responsibilities. In a way, you know, vanishing into thin air is just taking the easy way out."

"Yes," I echoed, "the easy way out."

The car thumped over a dead animal in the road. We drove in silence.

"Look at me," he said. "I talk like I have a history, like it's just a straight line. From boxing with my uncle to groovy hippie love to Mexico to marriage to conservative values, selling dental equipment and owning life insurance. That isn't it. I used to be hell with a yo-yo, you know it? But, look, it was different then, people would give you rides and food and love. People these days don't pick up hitchhikers. Fear, that's what it is, people are afraid. And, well, sometimes you have to be, you have to keep in mind that you have two little girls who depend on you, who'd have an awfully hard time trying to make it through life without their daddy. I don't pick up everyone I see by the side of the road anymore. I figured you boys looked harmless enough."

Jimmy was staring at the empty landscape, a bulge on his thigh where the gun was strapped on. I looked back at Earl. He was staring again, puffing his cigar.

"But, wow!" he said, suddenly returning. "You guys are going to have a blast! Experience, New York City! Just always try to make sure you have a warm place to take a shit. Whoa, here's my exit, sorry I can't take you all the way there, sorry I can't go along. Some of the best times are actually those by the side of the road. I had to wait two days for a ride one time and it was pure magic, I met parts of myself that had spent their entire lives hiding in an apple orchard."

He pulled over, we climbed out.

"Enjoy yourselves, boys," he called after us. "Live it up while you're young! Remember, these are the best years of your life!"

He waved. We were on the outskirts of Columbus and it would soon be dark. Green, Gatsbyesque lights shone from the city's center. We moved as if in liquid, as if rowing, as if backward, ceaselessly toward them.

There was something apocalyptic hovering in the donutshop air, something coming, rapture or death. It's always at three o'clock in a bone-weary morning that you run into your destiny, slurping a coffee or eating a long john. We'd gone in to escape the chill of the Columbus night, Jimmy and me. He bought me a cinnamon roll, while he ate a croissant. Maybe he really was French.

She was sitting next to him, smoking a cigarette, her copper bangs hanging down over her eyes as she searched the bottom of her coffee cup for something, a motive or a reason to live. She mumbled to herself. She had a can of sardines in front of her.

"Excuse me," said Jimmy, "but I couldn't help noticing that you have a can of sardines and nothing to open it with."

She lifted her head and looked him over.

"What of it?" she asked.

"I have a sardine-can opener you can use if you'd like."

He pulled it out of his pocket and showed it to her. She just stared. She was not unattractive. Her shoulders were broad and the symmetry of her metallic-colored hair was slightly askew. She looked to be about eighteen. She was.

"My name's Melissa," she said, and she ordered a cremefilled donut.

"Jimmy," said Jimmy.

"My dreams come in pairs," she said, "and one of them is always true. I think I may have dreamed about you."

A blond man with glasses and a small child were seated on the other side of me. As he read the newspaper, his golden, doughy little boy inserted a huge donut, bigger than his own head, into his mouth. Just shoved it straight down his throat and beamed up at his father.

"Daddy," said the cherub. "Daddy. Daddy. Daddy! Daddy!"

"Hmmm," muttered his father. "What, Jason?"

"Daddy, what happens to people when they die?"

The waitress wiped crumbs off the Formica in front of me. I chewed.

"Where are you from?" Melissa asked Jimmy on my other side.

"France," said Jimmy.

"Speak some French for me."

"No," said Jimmy. "It brings back too many painful memories."

That was a lie. He was a liar. When he was bored, Jimmy doused cats with gasoline, set them on fire and watched them try to flee from their own burning selves.

"How old are you?" she asked.

"Eighteen," said Jimmy.

She laughed.

"Daddy? Daddy? Daddy?"

"What, Jason?" asked the blond man.

"Billy Bodigger says when his little sister got smushed in the back of that garbage truck she went up to heaven and Steve Johnson says she's just laying there in the ground getting ate up by bugs. He said that's what happens to dead people, they get ate up by bugs, and Mary Marble saw a ghost at her grandma's house. Daddy, what happens to people when they die?"

"Well, Jason," said the man, leaning back and touching various parts of his head with his fingers, "that's a very sticky issue . . ."

I picked a raisin out of my cinnamon roll.

"It's OK, Jimmy," said Melissa, "I like younger men. Although you aren't really my type. Most of the men I've been with have been tall and blond with glasses and slightly schizophrenic."

The blond man paused and turned his head. He took off his glasses, wiped them on his shirt and looked up, suddenly, at the neon DONUTWORLD light, as if hearing voices. He turned back to his son.

"Some people say that everything just sort of goes together

when you die, like it's all the same thing and it's sort of an intense white light or something. Like how everybody thinks love ought to be. I read a book about that once."

"Actually, that's how I met my best friend, Jennie," said Melissa. "We were always with the same men. I'd be with some guy and I'd see him with her the next week, or she'd be with some guy and I'd end up with him a night later. So I introduced myself and discovered we have a lot in common besides our natural affinity for tall, blond lunatics. For instance we both come from bad family environments. Our parents are shit. But it's OK that you're short and dark-haired and have no need for corrective lenses. It's better that way. You have the most intensely beautiful brown eyes I've ever seen on a human being. Kind of like my dog, Beauty. I know, it's a stupid-assed name for a dog, but my parents named him. He died last month. Beauty is dead. The symbolism is kind of overwhelming, don't you think?"

"Of course, these days, most people think when you go you just don't exist anymore. When you're dead, you're dead. I can imagine a lot of things worse than simply not being around."

I stared at the endless rows of donuts in the bin, each donut unique, yet all smashed together, no room to breathe. All smashed together, yet each donut would face his destiny, would be chewed and digested, alone.

Melissa was caressing Jimmy's thigh and seductively removing the filling from her donut with her tongue.

"Where you headed?" she asked.

"New York," said Jimmy. "Eventually."

"Well," said Melissa, "you can stay at my house for now."

"OK," said Jimmy. "Let's go."

They stood up and headed for the door. Wait. What was happening? The donuts just sat. Others were eaten. Finally one with those who ate them. Nourishment and true communion. I felt everything moving around me, felt trapped in the center and alone.

"You know," said the man, "I think the worst thing would be to exist in some strange sort of limbo. Maybe you exist, but nobody knows it, nobody can see you or hear you, you just float.

You can't make anyone feel you there. That's what they say happens with ghosts. Buried wrong or bad karma. That would be the worst thing. That's the biggest fear."

His little boy wasn't listening to him anymore. He was watching a tiny black bug move across the Formica. He squished it with his thumb.

Jimmy and Melissa were out the door into the parking lot. Something inside me, a fear, a hole, finally willed my body to rise and hurry after them. I saw my reflection among the sticky fingerprints on the donut-shop door and everything vanished behind me. I was climbing into a vaguely family-oriented car with a copper-haired girl and my beautiful friend with his maple-frosted skin.

"Who are you?" said Melissa.

"Matt," I said. "I'm Jimmy's friend, Matt."

She looked at Jimmy. He nodded. We drove.

We didn't even make it to her suburban home before the inside of the sleek cushioned car erupted in a frenzy of lust. Just past a record store called Magnolia Thunderpussy the car had to be pulled over, clothes were ripping, pale pink flesh and creamy brown intermingling in the front seat, lips and hair, grunting and slurping, probing fingers. I didn't know what to do. It seemed inappropriate for me to be sitting there in the backseat. I knew I should step outside, walk around the block, at least look the other way. I didn't. I wanted to watch Melissa. I wanted to watch Jimmy.

I'd never seen sex before. Melissa's acrobatic flexibility amazed me, their heads were down under the steering wheel, legs in the air, joined at the hips, Jimmy thrusting into her. I was intrigued by the glimpses of her pubic hair, the dimples on her knees and on Jimmy's butt. Jimmy looked at me once, watching him. Almost imperceptibly, he smiled. I'd never seen him naked before. I'd hardly seen anyone naked before, though I imagined it often. I had distant, frightening memories of dressing rooms at the beach, musty, warped boards, a thick odor and fat, hairy men. One glimpse of Marcie Tyndall in our bathtub, bubbles falling off. This was the curse of being an only child, of being raised in an orphanage run by prudish perverts, of living in towns where pornography wasn't sold on street corners.

When it was over Melissa caressed Jimmy's body like a pet. I could feel her expelled passion in the air around me and smell her words, hanging in the fragrant, grassy night. Her words reeked of algebra tests and fingernail polish, adolescent longing and funeral flowers. She smoked a cigarette, took a swig from a bottle of schnapps in the glove compartment.

"You'll stay with me, little boy," she said, her fingers skimming over his hair and tiny neck. "In my room. My parents are stupid, they won't know. Fuck them anyway. Maybe I'll even tell them. What could they do? You're so beautiful, just like my dog. My dead dog. He was so silent and strong. He was the only beautiful thing I ever had in my life. I hate my parents. Do you hate your parents? Of course you do. Everybody does. They're all such dolts. They're so old. They don't understand anything. I have my own television in my room with Cinemax, so don't worry, it'll be cool."

She sighed.

"It's weird," she said. "Sometimes things can still surprise you. Even when you're eighteen. Sometimes things don't suck that bad."

Her father was an orthodontic-supply salesman, her mother was a nuclear engineer. Or maybe they were both chiropractors, I'm not quite sure. The house was sumptuously furnished and hushed. Metal objects would fall to the floor, the noise absorbed into lush carpeting. There were plump cushions, fragile bowls of thin mint candies and Scotch in the walnut liquor cabinet. The house was sterilized, vermin-free, ordered in the midst of the world's chaos. With the exception of Melissa's room. She had posters of Kafka and Jim Morrison and seminude young men with muscles and smirks, photographs of things surreal and electric. There were clothes and books, tapes and albums and ashtrays strewn carelessly about.

"You sure your parents won't look in here?" I asked.

"Wouldn't dare," said Melissa. "They'd be afraid of what they might find."

She lay back on her bed and lit a cigarette.

"You can sleep in the bed with me," she said to Jimmy. "You can sleep on the floor," she said to me. "You can shove that pile of stuff over by the closet and make some room over here."

I covered myself with her soiled laundry. It was mostly black, smelled of smoke and perfume and sweat. The lights went out.

We stayed. Her parents came and went, made little noise, asked no questions. They were faceless, odorless. We stayed in her room and watched game shows and soap operas while Melissa went to school sometimes. Graduation was ahead, her future stretched before her.

"Suicide would be a viable option," she said, "But it's so trendy these days. Jennifer Grady o.d.'d on Valium over Christmas, people would just say I wanted to be like her. Fuck me dead! She wore the ugliest Gore-Tex bodysuits you ever saw."

She fed us Chee-tos and diet Coke. We watched MTV, smoked cigarettes, she played the Dead Kennedys or the Circle Jerks or Dan Fogelberg, read Jim Morrison's poetry, stuff about voyeurism and film, modern life compared to a trip by automobile.

"He's still alive, you know," she whispered, as if someone might overhear. "He isn't really dead. I heard he was living as a vagrant, on the streets of St. Louis."

She gazed at the book reverently.

" 'We all live in the city,' " she read, and paused for effect.

She was in love with Jimmy. She asked him questions. The replies tended toward monosyllables and were usually lies. Me she ignored, except to ask me to pass the bottle of Scotch.

"Four-thirty," she would say every day, "time for Scooby Doo on Channel 94. It's the greatest show. Scooby and Shaggy are always so stoned and Fred and Daphne are always going off to fuck in the van."

She was insatiable. I could feel the yearning grow, and jeal-

ousy, hers and mine. I lay there every night among their discarded undergarments, listening to their pants and moans.
Sometimes they did it in the middle of the day, right there in
front of me. A gummy rose light spread through the gauzy red
curtains and highlighted her broad, pink rubber nipples, Melissa
all flesh and freckles, the yellow sheets stained with a violet
liquid in the shape of a newborn baby, Jimmy's skin perfect,
the color like the penuche fudge that Andalusia used to make
me, polished and blemish-free, his miniature arms and legs, his
sculpted features. Kafka glowered at them, Jim Morrison
approved. Sometimes Jimmy would vanish inside her, sometimes they'd both explode into fragments. That was love, and I
wanted it. I lived in a perpetual state of arousal, not quite sure
which of them I wanted more. Melissa was smarter, but Jimmy
was more mysterious, more beautiful and filled with a quiet,
empty rage. Quietly, I masturbated, and dreamed of them both.

She took us to a party in some huge suburban home filled
with swanky teenagers and a band called Bad Food playing in
the basement. The parents were in Monaco or Morocco. An
almost mystical combination of boredom and violence pulsed
through the house, hovered over crowded stairways, scurried
back and forth between the throbbing back patio and a living
room in decline. We wandered through a vague malaise without referent, a fashion of dissatisfaction, shark's-tooth earrings,
skateboards, black leather and an occasional Gore-Tex bodysuit. In the basement we were all jammed together, one quivering mass of raging, giddy, excitable young people, a medium
for the music to work its way through.

"I love Bad Food," Melissa said. "Their music's so listenable,
almost pop, you know. What's the word I'm looking for? Bland,
that's what it is. But on the other hand it's really nihilistic. So
there's sort of an irony there, you know?"

The lead singer was mumbling something about heroin
addiction and whips. Girls in cheerleading uniforms were
swaying back and forth up front. Elsewhere, basketball and petty
vandalism were discussed. As me and Jimmy rummaged through

the refrigerator upstairs, the disillusioned youth took turns vomiting on the parents' belongings, fucking on the parents' waterbed and shattering the stained-glass windows to let in the refreshing winds of chaos that swirled about the cul-de-sac. It was like a tribal dance, a hundred tribes of one, thrashing, gyrating, bouncing up and down on the grand piano, a flow of desire, an erotic bloodletting, an almost incestuous ritual of mass destruction. Glass and china and Oriental rugs. The waterbed burst, a tall, thin girl in a sailor suit and a young man with a chain dangling from his nose came fleeing from the tidal wave, screaming nonsense syllables. The girl who lived there rolled around on the floor with a tube up her nose, giggling and exclaiming, "Aren't they going to freak? Aren't my parents just going to freak?"

Melissa was getting drunk. I lost track of Jimmy from time to time. A tiny girl with white hair whispered to me.

"Did you hear about Mary Wachendorf? She tried to kill herself this morning, but she mistook her mother's calcium supplement for Valium."

"Stupid bitch," said a girl in a Gore-Tex bodysuit. "She just wanted to be like Jennifer Grady."

Two young people were painting elaborate phalluses on the walls. A girl sat in the corner reciting avant-garde poetry.

"What an idiot," said a large boy with horn-rimmed glasses. "She thinks she's a rebel. You can't be a rebel when everything is permitted. Nothing is true. Nietzsche said that, and then the Jim Carroll Band."

By the time we stumbled out to Melissa's car the drapes were on fire and the dog was in the driveway, either passed out or dead.

"Wow," said Melissa. "Just like Beauty."

We'd only gone five or six blocks when Jimmy asked to be let out of the car.

"I'll meet you back at the house," he said. "I have something to do."

"Something to do?" said Melissa. "At two in the morning you have something to do?"

Jimmy stared at her and yawned. She stopped the car. He got out and vanished into a dark backyard.

Melissa said nothing the rest of the way home. I followed her into the house, relaxed on the leather davenport and stared at a swordfish hanging on the wall. Dumb fisheyes and a pale blue sheen. I wanted to be like that giant dead fish, thinking nothing at all. I let my mind drift into a numb haze.

"Come on," she said suddenly. "You're coming with me."

I followed her out to the car and got in. We drove in silence, parked next to a small park with swingsets, a jungle gym and several trees. She pulled a bottle from under the seat and took a big swallow.

"I'm sort of drunk," I said.

She looked away from me and tapped her fingers on the bottle.

"Don't think I like you," she said. "I just didn't want to drink alone."

"Oh," I said. "OK."

She started eating a Twinkie from her purse.

"I'm so fucking hungry," she said. "All I've had to eat today was a liter bottle of 7-Up."

I opened the window. The night was warm and empty. Summer was near with all its possibilities.

"Jimmy's going to leave me," she said, "isn't he?"

I was startled.

"No," I said, "I don't think so."

"Liar," she said. "I know he will. Nobody ever stays. I love him, you know. I really do."

"I'm sure he loves you, too."

"You are so full of shit," she said. "Here I am spilling my guts to you and you just sit there and lie to me."

Spilling her guts. I thought of my parents. I listened to insects, chirping in the distance, watched the flat red clouds pasted overhead. I took the bottle from her and drank, plain vodka. It tasted horrible and burned.

"Where are you from, anyway?" she asked. It was the first time she had ever asked me a question about myself.

"Des Moines," I said. "Des Moines, Iowa."

She laughed. "Des Moines, Iowa? Where the fuck is Des Moines, Iowa?"

I turned toward her.

"Where the fuck is Columbus, Ohio?"

"Yeah, well, I guess every place sucks in its own way, doesn't it? But at least I don't live on a farm and slop the hogs and shit."

She lit a cigarette.

"You probably had a real nice, cozy little life there, didn't you? Pigs and horses? Christmas trees and family dinners? Bowling alleys and pickup trucks? Yee haw! Did you ever have a dog? Did you ever have a dog that got run over? While it was sleeping in your own driveway?"

"No," I said, "I never had a dog."

"Well, I did," she said. "The most beautiful dog in the world. Fuck."

She was silent for a moment. She took a drink.

"He loved me so much. He was the only one that ever did. He used to sleep at the foot of my bed. Oh, fuck. Why? Why him? Why me? You don't know, you can't know. You can't even imagine how it felt."

"My parents died," I said. "Two years ago. Murdered in their sleep."

"That's not the same thing," snapped Melissa. "Your parents only love you for income-tax purposes."

I stared out the window.

"Why is he going to leave me? I just want him to love me. He's so beautiful. His eyes, you know. I just want something beautiful. Is that so much to ask?"

Where was Jimmy? He wouldn't leave for good, not without me. What did he ever need me for? I took a drink.

"You love him, too," she said, "don't you? Little faggot."

"What?" I said, startled. "Me? He's my best friend, that's all. He's my only friend. My parents are dead."

"I don't want to hear about your dead fucking parents! Oh, Jesus fucking Christ. Don't you ever think about anything but death?"

I stared at my hands. I was trembling. If people could tell just by looking at me that I wanted to hold my naked body against Jimmy's they would hate me and kill me and lock me in jail.

"Oh, fuck," she said. "I just wish I was dead."

She looked like she might cry, really, or maybe she was just faking it. Her despair seemed like something out of a made-for-TV movie, overdone, a luxury. Then she turned toward me and I could see it, something, back behind, something real.

"What am I going to do with my life?" she asked. "Really, what? Go to college and drink every night, have a few abortions? Go to bars and funerals and kill myself in middle age? Have a bad marriage or two, sleep with married men? I don't want to do any of that. I don't want to do anything at all. I want to have sex on a beach somewhere, with palm trees and shit, waves rolling over me. I want love. I want my dog back."

She looked at me, as if she was expecting some kind of response.

"I don't think about the future too much," I told her. "Mostly I just worry about eating and sleeping. Things used to be better, but they aren't so bad now. I like to move."

She considered this.

"I think I'd like that, too. To move. I think I'm scared. Believe that? Me, scared." She lowered her voice. "Tell me. What's the very worst thing you ever did?"

I thought for a minute. I knew what it was, but I couldn't tell her that. Most of the other things I could think of were just me watching Jimmy.

"I sniffed the neighbor's underwear," I said. "When I was little. That seems worse than stealing, I think, and torturing animals."

She laughed. "That's really funny," she said. "I wish my worst thing was funny. It isn't. I was really drunk. I ran over my own dog in the driveway. Nobody knows it was me. Everybody blamed Janet Winters and I let them, but it wasn't such a big deal. A dead dog isn't something you're supposed to get all choked up about. I'm cynical, you know. Jaded."

She sat, smoking.

"It hurts, doesn't it?" she asked. "Really, you know exactly what I mean, I can tell it. It just hurts."

"Yeah," I said, "a lot of the time."

"Which hurts more?" she asked. "The cold and hungry part or the lonely part?"

The windshield was clear and the red clouds moved past, opened up, the sky deep beyond with stars and things. Where was Jimmy? I couldn't answer.

"That's what I was afraid of," she said. "And you even have him with you."

"It isn't always so bad," I said. "Being out feels good. The orphanage wasn't, but out, I don't know. There's these times, you know, when you're in somebody else's house, or even outside, looking in, and there's wind all around you. It's exciting. Sometimes you get this feeling like someday, somewhere, things will be good."

"Funny," she said, "that's not a feeling I get."

"You know," she said, "I really don't dislike you. You're kind of OK. I guess I'm just jealous. Because of Jimmy and all. I know he'll leave, and you'll go with him. And I'll be alone again. Even if you are a faggot, I don't care, people have sex with just about anything anymore, don't they? Robots, electricity, inanimate objects. Everybody's looking for love."

I looked at her, quiet.

"I don't know. We might stay."

"You know," she said, "I always knew, I guess, that love and death are basically the same thing. Everybody says that. That one is just a preparation for the other. I just never thought . . . I mean, with Jimmy . . . I just never thought it would be so obvious."

Her face was so real and close. The freckles, the copper bangs. So close I could have lifted my arm and touched it, with almost no movement at all. I could have.

"You've got really cool eyes, too," she said. "I never noticed. I mean, Jimmy has those deep, spooky eyes, like pools you could get lost in and never find your way out. You have spacey blue eyes. Jesus Christ eyes."

"Jesus was a pervert," I said. "Always putting little kids on his lap and washing men's feet."

She laughed. She squeezed my knee, it tickled.

"You're funny," she said. "I never knew you were funny. You should talk more often, people might like you."

"That's not true," I said. "The less you say the more people like you."

She considered this.

"Me," she said, "I talk too much, especially to crazy blond men with glasses."

The insects were louder now, the swings in the park jiggled from a small, listless breeze. The slide reflected a silver streak and I looked for the moon in the sky. It wasn't anywhere I could see. Melissa rested her head against the window and closed her eyes. I looked for one of the dippers in the sky, couldn't find them either. I traced trapezoids with my finger and connect-the-dot foreign countries, faces and chandeliers. The trees churned, an invisible rumbling, the sound of their growth.

"Come on," she said finally, "we should head home. Jimmy might be back by now."

She started the car. It moved gently, the whole night felt peaceful around us. Houses were dark, streets empty. She was so calm.

It didn't last. Jimmy was waiting in the front yard.

"Where did you go?" demanded Melissa.

Jimmy shrugged.

"Don't give me that, you little shit," she said. "I have a right to know. I'm the one that shelters you, I'm the one that feeds you, if it wasn't for me you'd be out on the streets somewhere, I'm the one that takes care of you! Don't give me that look, what do you think I am, some stupid bimbo who wears pink sweaters and puts bows in her hair like Tammy Mahoney? I got a thirty-one on my ACT, you little prick, do you really think I believe that you're from France? Where have you been? Fucking some other girl you met at the party? Susie Cobbs? Fuck me dead. Say something, goddammit."

Jimmy said nothing. Melissa screamed, stomped, cursed and stormed into the house.

"It's time for us to move along," said Jimmy. "Watch."

I watched him move toward the house, scratch a word into the paint with a sharp stone.

"I got some good stuff tonight," he said. "Jewelry. Money, too. Let's go."

I walked up to the house. The word was BITCH. I heard her inside, running down the stairs. Jimmy moved, quickly, like spilled gasoline across the neighbor's lawn. I ran after him. She was out now, calling after us, tears in her voice, apologizing, she didn't mean it, he could do anything, she'd just had a little too much to drink, please come back . . .

I looked over my shoulder, saw her there, standing in the doorway, bathed in the blue light of the streetlamp, sobbing, but it was no use, for he was gone, farther every second. I turned and so was I.

The car slowed and stopped. Me and Jimmy hurried to meet it and climbed in. A spring storm had formed in no time, the temperature had plummeted and it was starting to rain. The highway glittered black.

"Well, look what we have here," said the blond, flat-topped youth to his close-cropped companions. "A nigger and a long-hair. Is this one a boy or a girl? Or something in between?"

They laughed. They were easily amused. They had skate-boards and bad teeth.

"Beer?" asked the grinning teenager.

"No, thank you," I replied.

They insisted. It was very cold. They poured it in our laps. They hit us with their fists and with a small board. They took all the money and jewelry that Jimmy had stolen. They took the gun. They took our clothes, they took the copy of *Of Mice and Men* I had stuck in my back pocket, they jerked us around by the hair, they made rude comments about our mothers. They drove us out into the country and threw us, bloody and naked, into the pouring rain.

We crawled through the dark, through the mud. I had thought I'd known cold. It was hard to move, there were no lights, nothing to give us a direction, a point of reference. We were off the road.

Finally we came to a bridge. We huddled underneath, in the wet grass, out of the rain. I shivered so hard and I felt the shivers begin to change into sobs. I moved next to Jimmy for warmth, saw only his eyes, shining and cold in the dark. I reached out my hand to touch his face, the water running down it, it felt like glass, it felt like nothing on earth. I didn't cry.

FOUR

△

1

Once I was there, naked and cold beneath the bridge, with Jimmy in the pouring rain. Now I am not. What the future holds I cannot say, although I have reason to believe it won't be much better. The present holds this: midgets and bridesmaids whirling through the streets of Des Moines and me, Matt, furtively eating a stolen Almond Joy in a Quik Trip bathroom.

Quik Trip bathrooms are strange, back behind the storage room of Styrofoam cups and pornographic magazines, they give me this fugitive feeling. I chew noiselessly, carefully fold the wrapper and place it in the trash, turn the water on full blast, so they will not hear me, eating stolen merchandise in their very own unisex rest room.

Paranoia flourishes in such a place.

I don't want to be one of those people who steals candy bars from convenience stores and eats them in the bathroom. I want to be a different kind of person altogether. I want to be one of those people who walks proudly up to the counter and says to the smiling cashier, "Sir, I'm afraid I haven't a cent to my name, but I am hungry and I want to work. I will gladly wash your windows and trim your shrubbery, scrub your floors and your toilets, for the privilege, kind sir, of eating one of your candy bars."

I want to be one of those people, but I'm not. I'm too shy, I think. So I steal.

An alternative: To be one of those people who would be found not guilty, by reason of insanity, *because they are unable to distinguish between right and wrong.*

On the wall, there's a Jim Morrison quote. Jim Morrison is everywhere, Traveler I should say, he cannot be escaped. Below this quote, in a less steady script: "There is a fissure in my vision and madness always rushes through." The graffiti is the same in rest rooms from Cumberland to Truth or Consequences. In Los Angeles it's slightly darker, in New York it's more surreal. In El Paso it's mostly in Spanish and I wonder if it says the same things. Defecation is certainly a lonely business. Even here messages are transmitted. Eat, excrete. Whatever we consume must be transformed and eliminated or we will die. Somebody must be listening.

I stand, flush, wash my hands and face, let the automatic hand dryer blow warm over me. I move out into the crowded store, filled with snarling young people, policemen, other shoplifters and dazzling white light. I hesitate at the candy counter as if I might actually buy something, then tighten and move, like I've just remembered that I'm in a terrible rush and there can be no time for Milk Duds or Hot Tamales.

Outside, it's Iowa, the night is uncanny. A wedding party glides through the streets flowing lavender and lace. Teenagers mingle on the corner, threatening. There is a convention of dwarves at the Marriott Hotel and they spill out onto the street, drunk and rowdy and short. This Quik Trip is subterranean, huddled beneath a towering office building. My perspective feels skewed. Ten years. There are video rental stores, new Burger Kings, a skywalk system, a giant umbrella sculpture. Life progresses more quickly than I can adapt.

I move up, toward the freeway. The midgets, the flower girls, the brooding teenagers with dangling cigarettes and muscle shirts, these fall back behind me. Once I am above it the downtown seems to shimmer, holding something vital within it. Lights in windows rise and sparkle. Ahead, down the freeway, the dome of the state capitol glows gold in the night. I walk east, toward it. Off to my left, down Sixth Avenue, if I passed invisibly through buildings and trees then curved, up along the river, I would be home.

I stop. Stand. A slow car shimmies past. I remain still.

I long for closure. Surely, this would be the place. Everything returns to its source in the end, so I've been told. Yet whatever I would find will not be here. Andalusia will not be here, avoids the place, banishes it to a dark corner of her mind. She has another home now, with stone walls and a fireplace, the smell of pine. She spirals outward, exploring the many faces of love and solitude, always returning, a little bit wearier, a little bit wiser, a little bit more content. Home.

In my head there is a duplex, an alley, a backyard. They exist in a universe not even parallel to what lies waiting, just beyond the horizon of my vision. The impulse is to move toward that place, but I fight it. Strangers sleep there now, their snores drifting out of open windows. This is not what I need. I need to go on.

Δ

One of Dad's coworkers came to see him after he lost his job, brought him a card of condolences and thirteen dollars from the staff at the mass-mailing factory. She was a bony woman with a flabby waist and gray-brown hair tied back in a ponytail. Her mouth was all pinched up, like she was holding a needle in it, ready to sew.

"We're all real sorry," she said, sitting in our living room, smoking a cigarette. Mom seemed nervous, kept offering beverages and chips. Dad sat, looking at his knuckles. "But we're all scared, too. Who knows which of us will be next? I'd love to take some time off for a while, but the way they've finagled it so we don't get Unemployment, shit, I couldn't afford it. I got payments up the butt."

She leaned back in the couch, coughed twice.

"They're making big changes," she said. "There's a new guy in charge, name of Ron. I swear, half the people I meet are

Rons. My ex-husband, he was a Ron. My boyfriend's a Ron, my oldest boy's a Ron. Last night I was down at the Last Chance Saloon, this guy starts hitting on me, sure enough, he's a Ron, too. It's OK, I don't mind getting mixed up with Rons. Rons are partyers, that's for sure."

Dad stared out the window. Dad wasn't a Ron. I wasn't a Ron either, none of us was. I felt glad of this.

"My ex, he'd drink anyone under the table. My boyfriend, he's a drinker, too, and a fighter. The boy doesn't drink yet, not that I know, but he's a scrapper. Fighters and drinkers, that's what Rons are about."

She paused, puffed on her cigarette.

"This isn't a bad little place you got here," she said. "I used to live in a duplex, back with Ron. We rent a house now, though, it's nice having a little privacy. Had any luck finding a job?"

Dad didn't say anything, didn't hear.

"No," Mom said, "but there's some good prospects. We're expecting some calls. Would you care for a donut?"

"Sure," the woman said, "I'd always eat a donut. Something else about Rons, they don't mind a little extra something to hold on to."

She laughed. Mom went out to the kitchen. Dad stood up, walked outside. He walked down the street, around the corner and out of sight. I knew where he was going. He was going to the bar.

Mom came out with chocolate donuts, still in the box. She stared at the indentation in the chair where Dad had been sitting. She looked frightened.

"Donut?" she asked. She sat on the arm of the couch, perched dangerously, like a doomed goldfish bowl. The woman took a donut. I took a donut. We sat there, chewing and swallowing. The sound of something metal scraping against the sidewalk came from outside. Nobody got up to see what it was.

Mom and Dad started to fight, usually after a silent dinner. Mom banged carefully around the kitchen, refused to look at Dad, sealed leftovers in Tupperware, quietly slammed draw-

ers, wiped the table with a vengeance, wiping just around his
elbows. He just sat and doodled, spirals and curlicues and lips,
or stared out the window. That was how it worked. She fumed,
he refused to acknowledge her fuming, she moved around, he
remained still, neither of them spoke, the energy of hostile
silence filled the kitchen, the tension grew so thick my vision
blurred, until everything snapped, one question, one word, an
"Excuse me" or "Are you finished with that fork yet?" and the
kitchen exploded into a frenzy of vicious whispering.

"I'd like to wash that fork now. You're always holding on to
your silverware, just playing with it until I'm done washing the
dishes, and then you don't just wash it, you never can wash it
yourself."

"Look at the kitchen," Dad would say, lazily, loudly. "There
are things growing in the sink, for Christ's sake. One fork is
going to make such a difference?"

At first I liked to watch them fight, it was something new. If
they ever fought before, it was private or polite. There was
something inherently rewarding about seeing my parents at each
other's throat, when they'd always seemed a united front against
me, against climbing trees during thunderstorms or setting lizards loose in the yard. Still, it was scary, once they were into it,
the fury was a little too much. I sat out on the back porch, where
I could listen without feeling threatened.

One night Mrs. Pennel, the new lady who'd moved into the
other half of the duplex, came out and sat with me. I knew she
fought with her husband, too, because I could hear it through
the walls. They were a couple living a parallel life to my parents over there, but with one exception; they didn't have me.
Mrs. Pennel dyed her hair different shades of red instead and
kept an ugly little dog, a Lhasa apso named Sir Quentin
McDonald.

"Sucks, don't it?" she said.

I nodded.

"My folks used to fight a lot, too. Sometimes I think the only
reason I got married was to get away from all that. Huh. Same

old thing here, but now I get to hear your folks fighting anytime I've got any peace and quiet over here."

"I'm sorry," I said. "I can ask them to be quiet if you want." She laughed.

"Nah," she said. "Better for them to get it out in the air. But I'll tell you what. Ben's working late tonight and we got us a couple of tickets to see the Oaks play. You wanna go?"

The Oaks were the Chicago White Sox triple-A farm team. My Dad used to take me all the time when I was little, we sat and ate peanuts. He drank beer and let me sip off it, he smoked cigars some, too. I liked the way that baseball made time last forever. Baseball was so stable and patriarchal, so civilized. The billboards in the backfield advertised herbicides, pesticides, restaurants owned by the mob. Sometimes, when I was older, I rode my bike through downtown, dodging the traffic, all the jacked-up muscle cars and pickup trucks early in the night, blasting out Led Zeppelin tunes. Then over the tracks, across the rickety bridge and off through the parking lot, behind the stadium. There was a hole back there, in the Hiland potato chips sign; the baseball players could win a car from the potato chip company if they hit the ball through it. It was a decent-sized hole, but it hadn't ever happened, not as long as I'd been around. I'd climb up the sign and stand out there in the cool night, watching the players, so little, like toys or wishes on the field, the distant crowd just a blur of colors and noise. Once every couple of innings the ball would be hit in my direction and a thrill would spin through my fingers, hanging on to the edge of the hole. The center fielder would come so close I could yell out to him, and sometimes I did, after he'd fielded the ball with his animal grace I'd say, "Nice catch," or "Atta boy," and if I knew who it was, if it was Lamar Johnson or one of the better hitters, I'd call out his name.

"OK then," Mrs. Pennel said, "let's get going."

I stood up, glanced back into the kitchen. Mom and Dad were still at it.

"Better ask your folks," she said.

"Naw," I said. "They won't care."

She nodded and we left. On the way she talked about mint juleps and lawn mowers and high school athletics and fudge. I just listened. We crossed the river and I thought about other places, about some sort of escape. Mrs. Pennel parked, lit a cigarette, asked if I liked the color of her hair.

"Yes," I said. "Very much."

It was the color of tomato soup. I hated tomato soup, but it also matched the plastic bags they delivered the weekly advertising newspapers in. Me and the other kids in the neighborhood would steal those bags off people's porches, turn them into water balloons and throw them at cars. Mrs. Pennel's hair reminded me of the thrill of running away.

The stadium was packed, it was September, real cold, but it was free-T-shirt night. I put mine on right away, happy and proud. The stands were filled with busty women, children in hats, men from halfway houses selling peanuts or Coke. We sat back in the bleachers behind home plate, and ate popcorn and Sno-Kones. Mrs. Pennel drank beer, a beer every inning. She went down to the concession stand in between, and usually missed the whole visitors' batting. During the seventh-inning stretch she started telling me about her family.

"My dad's a mobster," she said. "Me, I don't want nothing to do with it. Ben, sure, he's just a mechanic, but there's some future in that, at least he's honest, you know? I got a weird family, kid. Did I ask for this? Did I ask for my father? No, I might've asked for Charles Bronson for a father if I'd of had a choice."

"I didn't ask for mine, either," I said, "I would've asked for Evel Knievel, maybe, and Farrah Fawcett Majors."

She laughed, spilling popcorn everywhere. The organ started playing, people stamped their feet along with it, I could hardly hear anymore. I didn't know why she was telling me these things, I was only eleven. That was just the beginning, though, my whole life it's gone on, people confiding in me, confessing, telling me their troubles. I never minded listening, I knew that people had to talk, and I learned things. Still, something always felt wrong, like I was eavesdropping, like they were telling the wrong person. Like I was somebody different from who they thought I might be.

People were stamping like mad, we jumped to our feet, yelled *Charge!* It was exciting, even though we were losing by six runs, you could tell there was still a chance. You could tell it wasn't too late to turn things around.

It was. We lost, but I didn't care, I got to ride home with Mrs. Pennel. She laughed and honked her horn, shouted at other motorists, swerved all over the road. Red taillights and foggy rear windows stretched on across the tracks, drivers congested the downtown streets, jerked and maneuvered, cutting each other off, cursing. The night seemed filled with raucous possibility, anything might happen. I'd never ridden with a drunk before.

She took me down the freeway, the wrong direction, away from home, and my heart leapt. I didn't want to go back, I wanted to keep on moving. The freeway was enchanted, filled with strange cars and danger. People exited and merged. She glided around a circular off ramp, much too fast, tires squealed, and then we were moving down a suburban street, a West Des Moines neighborhood I vaguely recognized, associated with some dim childhood memory of large packages or a cafeteria-style restaurant. I searched for a landmark, but nothing was where it should have been.

"That's it," said Mrs. Pennel. She was pointing to a car dealership, new cars lined up in gleaming rows, red and blue and white. "That's the garage where Ben works. His car's still there."

She pulled into the lot.

"You wait here," she said. "I'll only be a minute."

A streetlight was making a loud buzzing noise. I tried to look through the big picture window to see what was happening inside. I was sure it was something secret, something daring and risqué. She was in there a long time. I could see shapes moving around. I wondered if they were screwing , or maybe even fucking. Johnny Tyndall had explained the difference to me, and when she came back out to the car I was dying to ask which it was. Her face was flushed. She laughed.

"Men," she said. "I'll never understand them. What is it about car engines that's so damn appealing?"

She laughed again, she seemed happy. She started the car and we moved silently back toward the freeway.

"I'm thirsty," she said. "I'm thirsty and hot."

Her neck was damp with sweat. My heart was beating fast. She was going to take off her clothes, I thought, she was going to tell me things. Things that nobody else in the world knew. She lit a cigarette.

"Don't ever smoke, kid," she said. "Don't ever start, believe me, it'll kill you."

She was quiet. The freeway was open before us, we moved. I wanted to keep on moving, follow the traffic's orange blur. Why didn't people with cars just keep on forever, why would they stop? When we got to our neighborhood she yelled things out the window at people she knew, sitting on their porches. At home, she stumbled out of the car into the duplex lawn, I stumbled too, a sympathetic response. She lay down in the grass, she started laughing. It was cold out.

"Good night, Mrs. Pennel," I said. "Thanks for everything."

She didn't answer. I went inside. Mom was in the kitchen, making a list. The heading was WHAT DO I WANT. There was a book on the table with clouds on the cover, one of her books about how to use prayer to be happy and make the world a better place. I grinned, waiting for her to notice my new T-shirt, waiting for her to ask where I'd been. It was way past my bedtime.

"Hi, Matt," she said. She was twisting her hair, so far away she was bordering on invisible. I left her there, went up to my room, took off my shirt. I stuffed it in a drawer on top of my lime Bible. Out in the yard I could hear Mrs. Pennel laughing.

Expected calls didn't come. Good prospects faded and the air grew heavy in our half of the duplex. When I went collecting for my paper route, entered the muggy homes of strangers, I'd hear them whispering about me in their back rooms. They gave me extra tips and offered me food, nasty leftover casseroles with tuna and green peppers or ham-and-bean soup. They talked about how cold and rainy it was outside. The Hooeys were always on the phone, the Vander Meydens were always reading magazines. The Coffins were always standing around or hanging from their ceiling. Those people were busy, living their lives. Back home it was different, it grew quiet and there wasn't even a smell.

Dad went into a serious decline. It was a classic case, by the book. He stopped writing, only occasionally scribbled something on paper and then crumpled it into a ball. He didn't talk much either, words seemed bottled up inside. He started drinking Pepto-Bismol by the bottle, morning and night, so much Pepto-Bismol that his skin turned pink. I knew he used to drink it when he was a little boy. His father, my grandfather, who died before I was born, owned a drugstore, and he would pilfer it off the shelves for a cheap high. Now he was reliving his childhood. Still, that wasn't an excuse.

Dad's teeth were yellow, he didn't brush. He'd never practiced proper dental hygiene, that particular vice wasn't a result of his unemployment. But the combination of his pink skin and his yellow teeth made him appear fluorescent when the light hit him a certain way. It was eerie. There was always a look of profound constipation engraved on his face.

Nights sometimes, when I got up to do my paper route, I'd find him passed out on the kitchen floor. One night he was wearing a toga and a laurel wreath, his fingers were bloody around the nails. Another night he was surrounded by turtles. Dad had always had a way with reptiles, he kept pet lizards in the bathroom. But lately, he'd been vegetating on the sofa, watching *Family Feud* or *Wheel of Fortune* or stumbling on down to the Bob and ? bar, around the corner and down a few blocks, already dizzy from the Pepto-Bismol.

Saul the chameleon was the first to go. I lifted him by the tail, plunked his motionless, dry brown body on the speckled kitchen counter, where Mom leaned, staring out the window at the fallen leaves.

"He's dead," I said, scrunching up my face as if I was about to cry. "He wasn't fed in days."

Mom ran upstairs to her bedroom, sobbing. A week later Hector the gecko died and finally Sparky the green lizard. I dug graves for them in the backyard, put stones on the earth with their names written in permanent black marker. I talked about the funerals at dinner while Dad played with his vegetables and Mom stared vacantly at smudges on the wallpaper. I asked for more juice.

At school, girls were starting to develop breasts and I was realizing how stupid my teachers were. October sank in, it grew dark early, all my daylight hours were spent memorizing facts, learning fractions, taking part in small rebellions against the teachers; at a certain time everyone dropped their pencils or belched. When Mr. Parsons' back was turned we bombarded him with chewed bubble gum. We communicated in codes, allowed notes to be found implying things about his sex life. We were at that tricky age when they still made us walk in lines from class to class, didn't let us chew gum, sat us alphabetically. Still, we were old enough to recognize injustice, senility and pattern baldness.

Meanwhile, Dad went out every night, Mom read books on the power of positive thinking or else sat and cried. Sunday mornings she took me to church. Dad never said anything about it anymore.

"I hate this," I said on the way. "Church is stupid. Those people are all stupid."

American Top 40 played on the radio.

"I hate this song," I said.

She clenched the wheel, stared straight ahead, silent.

"When is Dad going to get a job?" I asked.

She didn't answer. The streets were dead and filled with brown winds. Dogs choked on their own chains, molding pumpkin guts rained from above. Soon, children would dress as mummies, nurses or ex-presidents and go door to door, begging for sweets. I felt Mom was responsible.

"Everything will work out," she said finally. "It's not for you to worry about. Just let it be."

Everything would not work out, I knew. Snow would cover us soon, then grow black and refuse to melt. Things were twisting inside and they lied to me, patronized me, refused me the things I needed. I needed a new bike. I needed Levi's jeans and brand-name shirts, not generic jeans from JC Penney and striped crewnecks from discount stores.

I sat in church on Sunday mornings, whichever church it was, Catholic or Lutheran or Jehovah's Witness, while people around me sang or prayed or mumbled their sins. I stared at the back of their heads and zapped them. I imagined that I was blowing them up or making them vanish into air. There were a few that I spared, people I liked the looks of. A young woman with a baby and an unrepentant swath of long, black hair. A man with a beard who snored softly, a small child with a sinful nature, and one old woman in the front pew whose hair was the most intriguing, icy shade of blue I'd ever seen. I imagined them as my friends, as belonging to a club. Others I stared at, clenched my fists and then blinked. Once, it actually worked. A man in a suit, two pews ahead, balding in back, he just plain vanished, nothing but a wisp of pale smoke left behind. Nobody noticed, or else they didn't want to make a fuss about something like that in the middle of the sermon. The preacher was talking about a TV miniseries he'd just seen, *East of Eden*, starring Jane Seymour as the bad woman. I just sat, absolutely still. I couldn't believe what I'd done.

That night in the duplex Mom got down on her knees and prayed. She prayed for strength and guidance in this our hour of need. She asked God to speak to her, to tell her what to do. She didn't know I was there, but I watched, from the hallway. She'd just about given up, stood on her feet, all exasperated and pained, when a voice started speaking. I thought it was the clock radio at first, but that was unplugged, saving us money. The voice was speaking to her from our three-way lamp. It spoke in a foreign language, I couldn't make out a thing. Mom listened for a minute, then turned the knob. The light got brighter, the voice a little louder, but it was still in a foreign language. Eventually, it stopped.

"Yiddish," Mom said. "I'll bet that was Yiddish."

She wandered into the kitchen. Dad was out, at the bar. I fiddled with the lamp off and on for the next couple of weeks, but it wouldn't do it again. It wouldn't talk to me at all.

Δ

In the beginning was the Word, and the Word was Rain. Rain, rain, nothing but rain. There had never been anything else and there was no end in sight. Memory of warmth had been obliterated, the meaning of dryness was lost to us. Nothing could be grasped then, under the bridge. Our bodies were slick, glistening blue and brown in the drizzly cold light of morning. Eventually something had to happen; it was the cold waiting that couldn't be borne. The night had been endless, a stretched-out, soggy worm. Back, lost in it somewhere, had been mean teenagers, budding law enforcement officers, who should have had orthodontic work in their younger days, before it was too late. What did their teeth have to do with my life? Their teeth were all I could think about, their crooked fangs and gaps.

I closed my eyes, lay back in the mud, sinking. I let go. Warm liquid flowed across my thigh in a stream. The heat of the urine created a brief physical sensation bordering on ecstasy. The earth swallowed me.

Down, toward a center of molten lava, everything swirling liquid fire, erupting volcanic geysers, pink orange light. I let myself go. Down, toward the center where Andalusia lived, waiting. Down, past layers of granite and clay, hematite ore, down past my parents' rotting bones, all the decaying bones of history, all fusing together, dancing, pulsing. My name was forgotten. The earth was breathing, decaying, dying, dead, and I was sucked inside, part of it, moving down. Every language ever spoken, every word engulfed me, the fossilized remains of dinosaurs, the crumbled ruins of ghost-filled cities, everything bleeding toward the center, and mud, mud, everywhere mud and lava and skeletal ancestors and mud. The past was moving, living, changing, dying and being born again, it filled my lungs like solid matter. Osmosis, liquefication, fluidity and flux. The past, the present, the future moments blended, my own life unrecognizable through the mud. Food and faces, bathrooms and car doors, I wondered where I'd fit in. I couldn't breathe. My own name was spelled out in illegible symbols, carved in broken bone and vapor, but it couldn't be read, it couldn't be differentiated from any other name or stream or mineral vein. I felt it covering me, like a placid breath of honeysuckle, this knowledge that I was gone for good. I felt myself smiling. I would never move again. I couldn't feel any part of me or remember a thing. Mud. Nothing but mud. Nothing at all.

"Get up. Get up, now."

I felt a hand pulling me up. I wanted to stay, I was moving back through it, quickly, a pain in my chest. I held my breath, tried to blow myself up like a balloon and splinter into fragments, to latch onto words, manic oceanic, hypnotic bubble stream, but it was too late. I remembered my name.

"Matt," said the voice, "stand up. Now."

I was standing, my naked feet still sunken in the mud. I opened my eyes. It was Jimmy, pulling me up. I blinked. Even the gray light of morning was dazzling. I was here. Here and there. There, under the bridge. It hurt.

I just stood for a moment, taking it all in. Grasses were wet and things seemed brighter in the mist, dancing. Colors, brown and walnut and mahogany, greens and pink and bronze.

We climbed out from under the bridge and into the drizzle, ascended the slope of the ditch. We looked at the bridge which had sheltered us, the gravel road which lumbered in two directions. One way and the other. We stepped onto it and crossed.

We did not speak, but trudged, pale, naked zombies on the land. The rain was light now, a falling mist. The stones were sharp on our feet, our bones brittle, muscles screaming. But we walked, ascended slowly, then reached it, the crest of a slow hill. We looked out over the land, the fields mottled deep, wet greens, and yellows, and mud. A house squatted in the distance, white and beckoning. The land rolled toward it, gave me a feeling of return, of solitude, of age. The image of a man appeared in my head, a man walking, alone on his land, the sky stretching around him, blue and larger than even the expanse of highways. But this sky wasn't large, only gray and leaking, and the man wasn't there.

We stood, absorbing the view. We were bruised and naked, splotched with congealed blood and muck. We descended.

The house vanished from our sight as we moved lower and lower, then reappeared dramatically, larger and warmer, as we found the peak of another hill. A vision, it took on shape and meaning. A pickup truck and a blue four-door beater car in front, trees and chickens, patches of red flowers and back, just behind it, a small brown barn. It disappeared one last time and then we rose, again, and there it was, directly below. We moved off the gravel drive, cut across the wet field, sticking close to trees and cows. The cows glanced at us, wary yet bored, in that stupid, nervous, content way that only a cow can look at you. We moved nearer, dropped onto all fours, slid under the electric wire that separated field from yard. We moved like beasts toward the house, on all fours and grunting. Halfway across the yard we could smell everything we'd dreamed.

"Breakfast," whispered Jimmy. "Bacon and eggs. Coffee and fried potatoes."

"Milk, too," I said. "Straight from the cow's udder."

I was startled by the sound of my own voice, the first time I'd spoken since the beating, edged now with a dangerous silliness. I took a deep breath, to calm.

"We'll sneak in the back door, hide in the cellar," said Jimmy. "Steal clothes and food when they go out to do their chores."

Chores. Jimmy amazed me, continually. Where had he acquired this rustic lingo? We moved farther, toward the house, over gravel. Chickens scattered, squawking. We peeked in the window. A plump woman and a young boy sat at the kitchen table, speaking. A box of Froot Loops stood there, another box

of cereal with the face of a bear, smiling in a stocking cap. The
floor was speckled linoleum, the plates and bowls seemed Dutch,
blue-and-white china. It was the essence of warm kitchen, the
definition of home.

And then, the inevitable farm dog found us, pointy-eared
and barking, yellow lips and teeth, barking, retreating, barking,
advancing, dancing in circles around us. Its bark was not judg-
mental, merely declarative. We stood by the window, not moving. Flight was not an option. Our future was here.

"Quiet, Jonah, hush now."

The voice came from around the corner of the house, past
the long porch, and was followed by the boy himself. He looked
to be close to our own age and unsurprised. He stood, his hands
in his pockets, bare feet against the gravel. His toes looked like
rounded beige stones, his hair the color of straw, his eyes clear
and blue as cornflower. He just stood and looked us over, two
naked strangers in his front yard. His lips quivered and slowly,
the process long and careful, as if sculpting his own features,
his face turned broad and grinning.

"God be praised," he said. "I was starting to think you might
never get here. I have been waiting a terrible long time."

2

His name was Cain. He took us inside, two naked strangers just
wandered in from the wilderness, to meet his mother, Leola. I
held my hands self-consciously in front of my genitals.

"Oh my," she said. "Don't tell me that filthy Zeb Cosmos
and his nudist Christian church are back in the area."

She was round and squat, like a pumpkin, cheeks white and
full, black hair pulled back tight in a bun. Her fleshy fingers
didn't stop moving, drying dishes, kneading dough.

"No, Mother," said Cain, "this is the answer to our prayers.
Angels of the Lord have been sent to us. Finally."

She looked us over. She was skeptical.

"Not to deny," she said, "that He, in His great wisdom, may
have directed these young men to our doorstep. Lord knows,

He works in abstract and incomprehensible ways. But angels? This one's got a bit too much pigmentation for an angel, wouldn't you say?"

She motioned at Jimmy with her thumb. Cain looked us up and down, up and down. He didn't seem to be dissuaded.

"What's your story, boys?" asked Leola, wiping her hands on her flowered apron.

"He's right," said Jimmy. "We're angels. Angels of the Lord."

"In disguise," I added, "to seek out the righteous and reveal the sinful hearts of the wicked."

Jimmy glanced at me, a look of slight surprise, as of a teacher discovering a particularly gifted pupil who had heretofore shown only mild interest and ability. My years of varied religious instruction would prove useful after all. Dumb amazement was being left behind. Fear of possibility had been beaten out by teenagers with clenched fists and small boards, washed away by cold May rain. A game, a game, fitting yourself into the rules of others. I was learning to cope.

"I see," said Leola. "Then I imagine you'll be wanting to borrow some clothes, hm? Naked isn't a very inconspicuous way to travel, here in the material world."

We were clothed in flannel and corduroy, dirty old tennis shoes. They fed us eggs and potatoes fried in bacon grease, hotcakes smothered in butter and maple syrup, milk as white and pure as the albino kitten that chased chickens in the yard. Leola leaned against the counter, threading a needle. There were large holes in the knee of Cain's jeans, which she was just preparing to mend. Cain sat pensively in his shorts. They had matching calluses on their knees, mother and son.

"So," said Cain, "what are you fixing to do about the problem?"

He was looking at me.

"The problem?" I said.

"You know," said Cain. "My brother. Seth."

I leaned back in my chair, thinking.

"There's no controlling Seth," said Leola. "He wets his bed and evil language comes from his mouth. He dabbles in sin.

There is little hope unless you are, in fact, the miracle we've been praying for. Seth is just plain bad, clear through to the gizzard."

My head hummed. Things were calm and far too real. The overhead bulb seemed to be vibrating, washing everything in a sharp, molecular light. The kitchen was decorated with pictures of nature becalmed, Jesus on the water and Bible quotes on wooden plaques. *In the beginning was the Word and the Word was with God and the Word was God,* and a longer one, *Behold thou hast driven me out this day from the face of the earth; and from thy face shall I be hid; and I shall be a fugitive and a vagabond in the earth; and it shall come to pass that everyone that findeth me shall slay me.*

"Genesis was always my father's favorite book," said Cain. "Back before he was dead. He used it to name us, but through some work of the devil the names came out pitch-wrong."

Leola turned toward us.

"Seth is the one who has fallen," she said. "It is Cain who brings me joy, whose offerings I approve."

"It's true," admitted Cain, "that our names are chock full of irony."

Their bad luck all started with Cain's twin, she told us, Abel. He was trampled by a raging bovine when he was just a few months old. Ever since then something seemed to be missing from Cain, he was always looking for something that wasn't there. Then along came Seth, supposedly a replacement, but he was just clean bad from the very start. He hung kittens from the drapes to get his mother's attention, he put toothpaste in Cain's hair while he slept. Then their father died.

"He was a great man," said Cain. "Almost a saint."

The overhead light grew suddenly brighter.

"Did that light just brighten?" asked Leola. "Or am I developing a brain tumor?"

"Sign from above," said Cain. "Clear as the dickens."

There was a clanging upstairs, violent screeching bells and sirens. My heart seized up and I looked at Jimmy, felt the panic rising in my throat.

"Oh, dear," said Leola. "The alarm again. Seth has gone and wet the bed."

She hurried upstairs to tend.

Cain carried our breakfast dishes to the sink.

"Whatever Mother may think," said Cain, "I know that you are angels. She's a good woman, my mother, but sometimes she has difficulty accepting the miraculous in her daily life. It isn't an earthly thing, naked strangers wandering into your farmyard on a Saturday morning. Even I can see that."

He turned on a tiny television that sat on the breakfast counter. A commercial blared, for cereal so sweet it would make your gums bleed. They were using this fact to their advantage in the advertising campaign, implying that bloody gums made you a member of some elite group. Small children were lip-synching a popular song and dancing in their psychedelic club-house.

"She's just wary," said Cain. "The last time I thought we had an angel on our hands she just turned out to be crazy. She was the most beautiful woman I ever saw, with long black hair and the most peculiar accent. Her name was Rebeca and I asked her if she'd go fishing with me. But she kept mumbling about slaughtering beasts in Mexico and vanishing. Then she went along her way. But that's not the same. She might have been beautiful, but she was fully clothed."

I turned his story over in my head. It sounded familiar, but I couldn't place it.

"Everything happens for a reason," said Cain. "Even the things that seem the worst, floods and murders and the like. I'm sure, as angels of the Lord, you would be in agreement with me there. Even the fall of man had its up side. It provided the opportunity for us to know God's grace."

This boy was beginning to irritate me. My ears were still full of liquid. Less than an hour ago I'd been nearly dead; life had taken on a quality of transparency, a window looking out on waves of texture and color, and I wanted to feel it move through me in silence. Jimmy seemed to vibrate, his body dark against the kitchen's white light, a muscular intensity. He was reading the back of a cereal box.

"Someday soon, everything will be fine. Everything is merely preparing us for this end. Nuclear holocaust is coming any day. Armageddon, you know. That's why I wish I was old enough to vote. America has a privileged and holy role to play in this drama. But I'll miss it all anyway, I suppose, all the good Christians will vanish in the sky. But do you see what I'm saying? Even death is OK in the end, even nuclear war is a grand opportunity to save lost souls."

Jimmy was figuring out if he was getting his Recommended Daily Allowance of vitamins. I coughed. Invisible particles were flying about the room, colliding randomly.

"We've hooked up an alarm system that goes off as soon as Seth's sheets get wet. There's a possibility of mild shock, but we feel it's a necessity. Satan is involved, it's clear. Electric shocks are often used as a cure for different manifestations of Satan, such as sexual perversion or Catholicism. Seth's bed-wetting is a symptom of a greater sickness, a sickness entrenched pitch-deep in our society. But things are starting to move. The forces of God have risen from their slumber. Things are fixing to change."

I needed to pee. My thoughts weren't moving in a line.

"But in the meantime," said Cain, "I guess it's simply imperative that we love our neighbor. Not our neighbor's sin, mind you, but our neighbor, nonetheless. Although lunatics like Zeb Cosmos and his nudist Christian church are exempt from this statute, I feel, due to the serious nature of their blasphemy."

I picked at a scab on my ear. I was sore all over.

"Hmm," I said. "Yes."

Leola entered the kitchen with a nearly hairless boy. He was greeneyed and wiry, smaller than Cain, and he spat on the floor.

"My brother," said Cain. "Seth."

He looked us over.

"Who are these dorks?"

"Flee from your wicked ways, brother," said Cain. "The Lord God has sent angels of mercy to fight for your wretched soul."

Seth laughed.

"Like hell. Those aren't angels of the Lord any more than my asshole is."

I liked this boy immediately.

"Never mind him," said Cain. "He speaks with the tongue of Satan. The fact of his antagonism is only further proof of your divinity."

I studied Seth's face. At a glance it was canine and red like a barn, but the more I looked the more the lines of it moved, somehow wrong, as if his features had been lifted off of someone else.

"They wandered in naked from the wilderness," said Cain, gesturing toward me and Jimmy.

"No wonder they look a little rough around the edges," said Seth. "If they're angels, how come they look like somebody beat them up with fists and small boards, made rude comments about their mothers and left them out to freeze in the rain?"

I thought fast, groping.

"We just came through purgatory," I said. "We've been fighting to save the damned."

"Purgatory?" asked Seth. "What's that?"

Wrong religion, I realized. I searched my past life for the appropriate vocabulary of guilt and salvation. Were they Mormons, Presbyterians, or simply Unaffiliated Lunatic Fringe?

"The lake of fire," I said. "Hellfire and eternal damnation."

"Oh, that," said Seth. "I'm not scared. I can suck the butane out of cigarette lighters and breathe fire. I light my farts, too. It makes a green explosion. I'm already damned, you know. I might as well make the best of it."

"I've tried to tell him," said Cain, "that Jesus can save anyone, even the very worst. Jesus could have saved Hitler, had he only opened his heart. Jesus could have saved Charles Manson or the Beatles."

I looked at Jimmy. He was staring at the refrigerator. There were little magnets shaped like fruit holding up notecards with Scripture quotes for the day.

"I'm no Catholic," said Cain. "I know that the pope is an idol. But I do believe in confession. I do believe it is the only way to save ourselves. God's ears are wide open, just waiting to hear."

Seth was clipping his toenails onto the linoleum floor.

"You angels wanna get drunk?" he asked. "I got a fifth of Southern Comfort hid out in the barn. We could get pitch-drunk."

Jimmy turned, looked at Seth.

"Pay him no mind," said Cain. "He'd try to tempt the Lord Jesus himself if he could."

"Damn straight," said Seth. "Somebody ought to have made a man out of that one. I don't think he'd of been such a pansy if he was all drunk on wine and buzzing from chew."

Cain sighed.

"See?" he asked. "See what I mean?"

Seth turned to me, winked. I smiled.

"You know," said Leola, standing at the counter, "I sometimes get the queerest sensation, it is just most certainly bizarre. Like our entire lives are just some huge allegory, what with the kids' names and all. But I've yet to figure out what it means, what God is trying to say through our lives."

She sighed, seemed to shrink.

"Don't worry, Mother," said Cain. "It will all be made clear on the Judgment Day. In the meantime there are some things it is best not to know. Knowledge can be a dangerous and misleading thing. Earthly knowledge is most certainly not all it's cracked up to be."

"Amen," said Leola. "Amen to that."

Morning moved to noon and the rain stopped altogether. The air grew hot and sticky in a humid haze. We sat in the kitchen and ate orange slices of jelly coated with crunchy sugar. I could squeeze my limbs and wring out water into puddles on the kitchen floor. Leola busied herself preparing food, Seth played with a toy bus, shoved little plastic people or Bible picture cards into it. The very fact of sitting in a warm kitchen was difficult to grasp, but so easy to take part in.

At lunch there was more food, sandwiches with thick slabs of ham and mayonnaise, potato salad, tangy and sprinkled with something red. The texture of the potatoes in my mouth seemed so alive as to be almost dangerous. I felt flushed, feverish. I sat in the bathroom forever afterward. The air deodorizer smelled like pine trees and I could hear birds singing outside in the heat.

In the kitchen, Jimmy was flipping through a copy of *Reader's Digest*. Seth was watching the television. Cain and Leola were moving, busy. Something about Leola made me like her, her sturdiness, her quality of being a mother. I've always had a fondness for those who fed me, even the crazy ones.

"This afternoon," she said, "my women's Bible study group is coming over to pray for Ronald Reagan in the upcoming primary elections. Afterward we'll stand in a circle and sing 'Kumbaya.' I'll want you to join us."

"Oh, you can never forget it!" exclaimed Seth.

He stood up and walked out the door. Through the window I watched him move across the yard to the barn. On the television there was a commercial for a cola beverage, with young men and women frolicking on the beach, wearing very little.

"So much ignorance in the world," sighed Leola. "So much misinterpretation of Scripture. Why, one young man once tried to tell me that Jesus himself was a communist."

She wandered into the next room, carrying wildflowers in a vase.

"Lord have mercy," said Cain. "Next thing you know they'll be saying the Holy Spirit was a lesbian."

He followed his mother and we were alone in the kitchen.

We stepped outside onto the long porch. The afternoon was vague, uninterested. The fields glistened and dried.

"What do you want to do?" I asked Jimmy.

"Drink Southern Comfort in the barn," said Jimmy. "Take all the money in the house and get the fuck out."

I sat on the porch swing and oscillated. There were toads in the grass by the porch's edge.

"Maybe we could take Seth with us," I suggested. "We could form a gang."

Jimmy looked out over the yard, the chickens, the flowers, the albino kitten. Her name was Pitch. She wasn't just white, Cain had explained. She was pitch-white.

"He can't help us," said Jimmy. "We don't need him, he'll only hold us back. These people are weird."

I wanted Seth along, I knew it. On the porch I was realizing it, what I wanted to do. I didn't like Cain at all. I wanted to take his brother away, to make him my own.

"We lost the gun," I said.

"We can get another one," said Jimmy. "Once we get to New York."

Jimmy had saved my life, earlier that very day. It seemed like years ago. Something was wrong. I felt mean and oddly independent. I wanted to kick something, to slash tires, spit blood.

"We need transportation," I said. "To get back to the highway."

"When did you start thinking so much?" asked Jimmy. He stared across the yard, towards the fields, the cattle. The farm dog Jonah emerged from nowhere, Pitch held still and curious, watched him bounding. Something black fell from a tree overhead. The dog devoured it.

"Maybe Seth has a gun," I suggested.

"Maybe," said Jimmy, "maybe not. Maybe guns will rain down on us from the sky. Who the fuck knows? Maybe tonight we'll die again."

He turned, went back into the house. I knew what I wanted didn't fit into our needs. I knew this, but couldn't stop. I let the swing take me, forward and back, forward and back, my bare feet gliding against the smoothed, painted wood of the porch.

The women came, their faces indistinguishable from those who had preceded them and those who would come after. *Kum-*

baya, my Lord, Kumbaya. We stood in a circle, holding hands, women spoke and tears rolled down their cheeks. Seth was notable in his absence.

"Come upstairs with me," said Cain afterward, as the women were putting on their coats and moving toward the door. "I want to show you my room."

His room smelled like wax and sweet, acrid flowers. Candles were everywhere and marigolds and black roses. Orange and black, the room was like a weird Halloween church. On the wall an enormous photograph of a man, bearded and brooding. He wore eyeglasses and a brown suit. The picture looked old, realer than death. Cain's room was a shrine to his dead father. He slept here.

"He was a truly great man," he said. "His memory is everything to me. It guides me through my every day, helps me do what I know to be right. He sold plaques door to door with the Twenty-third Psalm on them or the story of creation. The old farmer who shot him was hard of hearing. He thought my father said *I've come for your youngest daughter.* His actual words are lost to us now, forever. But the farmer was acquitted and we hold no blame against him. Anyone can be used as a tool of Satan, particularly the blind or the deaf."

He struck a match and relit one of the candles that had gone out.

"So, you see," he said, "this is the root of the troubles in our home. We have but one parent."

"Oh well," I said, "one is better than none, isn't it?"

I closed my eyes, felt trapped in the midst of something unspeakably living and warped. I opened my eyes. He was still there, Cain. I felt it then, beginning.

"Maybe you've met my father. In heaven."

"No," I said, "I don't believe so."

"Are you sure? He was a great man. Almost a saint."

I felt saliva on my clenched teeth, realized that I hated this boy. I hated everything he had and I did not. This knowledge made me queasy and warm. He was so stupid, just like I used to be. He still believed in things.

"Maybe I did see him," I said. "Maybe I saw him in hell."

Cain took a step back. The window was open and a soft breeze hustled through the room, the flames of candles flickering just slightly.

"You're lying," he said. "This is part of it, isn't it? The punishment."

I said nothing.

"Oh, I know," he said, "I know that Seth is not the only reason God sent you. I'm the one who first opened the door of this household to Satan. I'm the one who must be cleansed first. Oh, I've hidden it, I know. From my mother, myself, even God. God is just like the rest of us, you know. Cheated, lied to and misunderstood."

"God is just like the rest of us," I corrected him, "dead. He died some two years ago, stabbed right through the heart."

A look of alarm spread over Cain's face. He stepped back again, narrowed his eyes. His face seemed to be moving about, not sure which shape to take, which emotion. My heart beat fast, I could feel a slight stiffening in my crotch.

"You are just waiting, I imagine, for my confession. You will continue to torment me until I have confessed myself clean. If I must speak the words aloud to rinse my soul then that is what I'll do."

He took a deep breath. The air seemed ready to burst.

"I have touched myself," he said, "in a lewd and lascivious manner. Three hundred and twenty-seven times in the past two years alone. And that does not include the two times that I came to know Elaine Sodmutton, or . . ."

He stopped.

"Or what?" I asked. "Say it all."

Jimmy stood back behind me, silent, breathing.

"Or that one sick and evil evening of bestiality in the fields."

He was trembling now. I didn't flinch.

"I know that that is not love," he said, "for love is clean and pure. A woman leaves her father, cleaves to her husband. The body and the head. It is all so simple."

I smirked.

"Is that it?" I asked. "Everything?"

"Yes," he said. "Everything. All of it."

"Do you feel clean?" I asked.

"What more must I do?"

I could feel Jimmy behind me, warm, his pulse. I was tingling, static electricity rising from my hair. I felt like I was alive, alive, but in the wrong way.

"I have matches," said Cain. "There's gasoline in the garage. Whatever it takes. The kingdom of heaven must be mine."

The room was hot, the humidity hanging and the waxy smell of candles burning. I began to sweat. I'd crossed over into something else altogether. I said nothing, thinking too fast, the thoughts all gathering there in the back of my head, rushing out over me and escaping, intoxicated by my own power, the power of my very own words. Parts of myself just stood back behind the rest of me and watched. There was nothing I could do to stop it, I was so glad of that fact, it was coming too fast, I let the torrent take me.

"You have a knife?" I asked.

Noiselessly he moved to the desk, beneath the enormous portrait, the eyes of his father, and opened the top drawer. The blade was sharp, cruel, used for whittling maybe, or cutting open dead animals. The blade shone silver.

"A cross," I said. "Deep in the palm of each hand, so it scars."

He stared at me, trembling. The candles threw shadows on the ceiling, glowing orange. The marigolds stank.

"Do not blow this one chance of redemption," I said. "For the Judgment Day may be close at hand."

He held the knife out, his eyes calm now. He twisted the blade quickly, he cut. Into the palm. Blood in bright lines, and he screamed. It was hot then. I could feel my teeth swimming.

His father's eyes moved over us. Candle flames flickered and outside light moved across the room, the sun out for a second or two from behind the clouds. The flowers and blood shone bright and the sun was gone again.

Cain was on his knees, the puddle widening on the floor. It

crept into the denim of his jeans, a black spot growing, moving up his leg.

"Jesus Christ," I heard my own voice saying. "We're not angels, you dumb shit. We're orphans."

His mouth was open wide, uvula hanging, the straw of his hair pushed back by his eyes, opened wide like portals. He sobbed then. The blood was everywhere. I moved, grabbed the white sheet off the bed, knelt and wrapped it tight around his hand.

The sheet grew pink quickly, then red. Cain was bent over, eyes screaming, on the floor.

"I don't understand," he said, and the pain was running through his face in streaks. I looked back and Jimmy was looking at me.

"God has sent you," said Cain, "whoever you are. You are my punishment and I will bear it. I am clean now."

"I'm sorry," I said. "Nothing can make you clean, or us. We've gone too far."

What a kick, I thought, to be bad past the point of redemption. I stood, turned. My face was hot and red. I moved past Jimmy, toward the door.

"But you can't beat me," he said, angry; I could hear the grinding of his teeth. "You can't beat us at all. I will fight you. And I will win."

I stepped out the door. Jimmy followed. I turned, looked into his eyes. I looked for myself in the reflection.

"That was stupid," he said.

He walked on past me, down the steps. Inside, my heart fluttered, cold with disgust. I felt my warm forehead and shivered. I needed a mirror, I needed to see what I looked like then. I swallowed, my throat raw, and followed Jimmy downstairs.

Leola was trimming bushes out around the edge of the house.

"Was that screaming I heard upstairs?" she asked.

"We were praying," I said. "Perhaps we got carried away."

"I figured as much," she said. "You seem like good boys.

You sang 'Kumbaya' quite beautifully earlier. The women were all quite moved."

Jimmy crossed the gravel toward the barn. I followed. We could hear Leola behind us, humming to herself.

Inside the barn a darkness and an odor staled, damp hay and dead rodents. Seth was seated in a spot where the light shone down through a window, creating a halo about him. The bottle in his hand glowed a rich liquid brown. He took a swig, looked up at us and offered the bottle. Jimmy took it and drank. He passed it to me and I felt the liquor run hot down my throat.

"We're going to have to leave now," I said. "Soon."

"Oh yeah?" he said. "Which place are you going? Heaven or hell?"

"New York," said Jimmy.

Seth took the bottle.

"Your brother is bleeding," I said. "Cain."

He looked up toward the rafters, took another sip of Southern Comfort.

"Let me come along with you," he said. "To New York."

Dust motes danced in the ray of sunlight that covered him. I felt light, buzzing.

"It isn't an easy life," I said.

"I'm not a stupid kid," said Seth. "I fondle a twelve-year-old deaf girl who lives across the way sometimes. Elaine Sodmutton. I'm past the point of being saved. I shoplift in town and smoke cigarettes and chew. I've smoked pot, too."

He drank deep, showing off.

"Sometimes," said Jimmy quietly, "we have to kill people."

The dust from the hay coated my throat. My body was floating, my feet firm on the ground. I put my hand on my belly. My hand was cool, my belly was hot.

"I'm up for anything," said Seth. "I've got to get out of here, I've got to be free. This place stifles me. My mom and Cain are so pitch-stupid it's making me crazy. It's time I cut out on my own."

"How old are you?" I asked.

I was whispering and I didn't know why.

"Eleven," said Seth, "but almost twelve."

"Shit," I said, "you're just a kid."

"Age doesn't matter," he said. "I'm worse than most kids twice my age. I steal things from stores all the time. I smelled my mom's underwear once."

"We have no mothers," said Jimmy, and the whole barn seemed to quiver with the words. "Or fathers, either. They are all dead."

Seth watched Jimmy's lips, obviously impressed now. He raised his hand absently to his chin, ran a finger over his own lips.

"Did you kill them?" he asked. "Your own parents?"

Jimmy said nothing. He took the bottle from Seth and drank, slow and smooth, a natural act.

"Matt," he said, "we should be going."

"Wait," said Seth. "You've got to let me come, too. You wouldn't be sorry. I know I have a bladder-control problem, but I'll get over that any day now. Once I'm away from my mom. Dad always loved me best. Love isn't equal or fair. Cain always says that, but he's the one who's got it now."

I could read the longing in his strange features. He seemed so innocent. I wanted him along. I wanted to leave Cain with nothing, split in two. Even after what happened inside, I couldn't stop it from growing inside me, that rage.

"They don't want me at all anyway," Seth said. "They want to turn me into my brother who got trampled by a cow before I was even born. They think if they can empty me of myself, Abel's soul will come rushing in to fill me up. I won't have it. I won't be anybody else, it would just be too weird, I think, to be somebody you aren't. Especially to be somebody who's only a dead baby."

Birds fluttered across the barn, in the rafters. I ran my fingers over a bale of hay, prickly.

"You're lucky," Seth said, "having dead parents. That's every kid's dream."

"It's an incredible freedom," I said, "You can do anything you want. You answer to nobody. I wonder if you can handle it."

His eyes were begging. I looked at the rafters, rubbing my chin.

"Sure," I said, "you can come along."

I looked at Jimmy. He showed no expression. I looked back at Seth.

"We can take a blood oath," I said, "and swear each of us to stick to the band and never tell any of the secrets. We'll have a special mark to hack into our victims. And nobody who doesn't belong to the band could use the mark and if he did he must be sued. And if he did it again he'd be killed. And if anybody that belonged to the band told any of the secrets he'd have his throat cut, and then have his carcass burnt up and the ashes scattered all around and his name blotted off the list with blood and never mentioned again by the gang, but have a curse put on it and be forgotten forever."

"What's the line of business of the band?" asked Seth.

"Only robbery and murder," I said. "We'll stop stages and carriages on the road and kill the people and take their watches and money."

"Stages and carriages?" asked Seth.

I nodded.

"Must we always kill the people?"

"It's best," said Jimmy.

"Some authorities think different," I said, "but mostly it's considered best to kill them. Except for the ones that we ransom. But first off you'll have to steal your mom's car for us."

"I'll do better than that, I'll get the truck. I drive it all the time in the fields, and I've even taken it in all the way to Columbus."

"Ever meet a girl named Melissa?" I asked. "Hanging out in a donut shop?"

"No," he said, "I don't think so."

"Either did we," said Jimmy.

I had to stop and consider this. Was my memory to be trusted?

If Jimmy denied her existence, how could I prove that I hadn't just imagined her?

Leola called us in for dinner. Cain was sitting on the porch, his hand hidden under a jacket. The evening was growing still and green around us, like something immense and open, a cavern under sky.

"We can go right after dinner," whispered Seth. "Might as well get fed first."

On the table were chicken thighs, mashed potatoes, thick, lumpy gravy, hunks of doughy substances and apple butter. Cain sat directly across from me, his maimed hand remaining under the table. The food passed in circles, bowls spinning, dizzying. I ate greedily.

"Are you feeling all right, Cain?" asked his mother. "You look a little peaked."

"I am fine," he said. "In fact, never better. I've been washed in the blood of the Lamb. I feel as if I've released a heavy burden. A bit light-headed perhaps. Are you sure *you're* OK, Mother? You look a bit pale to me, as if you may be coming down with an illness."

"I do?" said Leola. "Well, I don't know. Now that you mention it I am a bit tired. All the excitement of the day, I guess."

I chewed. Bird feathers dripped past the window outside. Blind beetles hurled themselves toward the kitchen light.

"What are your plans?" Leola asked. She was addressing me.

"Well, ma'am," I said, "I reckon we'll be leaving soon. We have a great deal of work to do. And we wouldn't want to overstay our welcome here."

"Nonsense," said Cain. "Angels of the Lord could never overstay their welcome in this house."

He held his dull butter knife in the air.

"There's so much work left right here, isn't there?" he asked. "Surely you could keep busy right here. I know what they say about idle hands and the devil's work, but certainly . . . certainly you could keep your hands busy right here."

I shoveled mashed potatoes into my mouth. Seth spilled his milk, grinning. We watched it spread across the plastic table-cloth, evenly, lethargically, then just stand as if a solid thing. Animals bleated low, the sounds of dusk. Nobody moved then, for a long, long time.

We sat on the porch, waited for Seth with the keys. The sky was sinking. Evening would last forever, it seemed, the sun would never leave us. I was anxious to be gone from there. Seth hurried out.

"Come on," he said.

We climbed into the seat of the pickup truck. He started the engine and we were off, down the gravel drive, kicking stones and dust behind us. Fields rose on either side, crops shimmy-ing in the breeze, muted greens and golds in the hazy early-evening light. The length of the day seemed contained in our very breathing, subdued. Night loomed large on either side.

"New York," said Seth. "All right. Fucking all right."

"Do you guys know how to get there?" he asked. "This road'll take us straight-on to the interstate, but after that I'm lost."

"We'll get there," said Jimmy. "One way or another."

The creek lay before us, the gully, the bridge. The night before seemed so distant, a fable. I was dry in the truck, mov-ing. The bridge rattled and we were past it.

"Yee haw!" said Seth.

Jimmy sneered.

"Yee haw?" he said. "Jesus."

The road stretched on, alternating between patches of dirt and gravel, ceaselessly straight. The sky lived with new colors, cold dark blues, moved closer to black. We crossed bridge after bridge, gullies below, but no intersections. Only those two directions, forward and back.

"When do we hit the crossroad?" asked Jimmy. "Where's the fucking highway?"

"We must have missed the turnoff in the dark," said Seth.

"There hasn't been anything," said Jimmy. "It's nothing but straight, nothing but gravel and bridges."

We crossed another bridge. Clusters of lights trembled in the darkness on either side of the road, every mile or so. We drove in silence. No crossroads, nothing but clusters of lights and bridges, the country sky filled with stars: white dwarves and supernovas, the whole works of the universe. Every so often we rattled over a bridge, the dashboard shook, the stars blurred.

"I have to piss like a Russian racehorse on roller skates," said Seth. He brought the truck to a fast stop, just on top of a bridge.

"Shit," said Jimmy, "I thought you were an outlaw."

"I am," he said. "Even Jesse James had to pee now and then."

He jumped out of the truck. I sensed cows in the distance, a whole mob of them, black and chewing, but I couldn't make anything out in the fields. Seth's pee made a tinkling sound in the creek down below. He climbed back into the cab.

"Anybody else have to use the facilities while we're stopped?" asked Jimmy.

Seth yawned.

"You guys got any food?" he asked.

Jimmy turned.

"Food? Where would we have got food from? First tell me, where the fuck are we? Where does this road go? You want food, is that what you want? Say, is that the McDonald's arches up ahead?"

I felt my face fill with blood. Jimmy didn't usually get mad, not out loud. I felt feverish, tom-toms and exploding eggs, a war in my head.

"All right," said Jimmy, "I'll go find us some food."

He hopped out of the truck.

"Why don't you let me come along?" I asked.

He walked off toward a cluster of lights in the distance. They wavered and dimmed. The night was turning cold. I couldn't see him anymore.

"He wouldn't need to be like that," Seth said. "Holy shit, it's my truck, ain't it? I'm the one that's doing you guys a favor."

"Don't worry about it," I said. "We've just had a rough day, you know. We'll be OK. I'll watch out for you."

"Shit. You think I need somebody to watch out for me?"

"I'm just saying," I said. "You know. I mean we'll look out for each other."

We sat, quiet.

"A lot of people without families," I said, "those guys got nobody, they're just useless. But we're different, see, we watch out for each other. We could get our own place sometime, with goats and rabbits and chimpanzees, live way out away from anybody, on our own."

"Not me," said Seth. "I don't want to clean up no rabbit shit. I thought we were going to New York."

"We could have animals there," I said. "Live off the fat of the land. But all I mean is the main thing, that we all got each other and that's why we aren't useless like lots of other orphans."

I sank down into the seat. Seth played with the shift lever.

"I am hungry," he said, finally.

"It's hard sometimes," I said. "We'll have to scrounge a lot."

"That Jimmy's a mean fucker," he said. "I don't know. Hey, what's that moving out in the fields?"

I didn't see anything.

"Probably just cows and such," said Seth. "I'm not scared. Not at all. Did you ever fuck a girl?"

I laughed.

"Of course," I said. "All the time."

"I wish I had one right now," he said. "It's cold, you know? I just wish I had one to keep me warm. Elaine Sodmutton or such."

He rubbed his cheek with his fingers.

"Say," he said, "you know what we could do? I mean, it's not the real thing and all, but. No, that would be stupid."

"What?" I asked.

"Nothing," he said. "I was just thinking since it's so cold and all, I could pretend you were a girl and you could pretend I was. You know, close our eyes and all."

I didn't say anything.

"I don't mean being fags or anything like that," he said. "I mean shit. Don't get the wrong ideas about me."

"OK," I said.

"Just to keep warm," he said. "I don't mean kissing or any of that shit, I mean I'm just cold. I'd just sit next to you and close my eyes and pretend you were Elaine."

"OK," I said.

"OK?"

"OK. Just to keep warm."

"Sure," he said. "It's just if we started the truck we'd maybe run out of gas."

He moved up close and put his arm around me. He was little and really pretty ugly. We just sat there like that for a long time. Dark splotches moved along the horizon, the stars made eerie whining noises.

"Want to see my dick?" he asked. "It's getting some hairs on it now."

I laughed.

"OK," I said.

He unzipped his pants. His penis was small as a toothbrush and hard and pink and hairless.

"See?" he said. "Here and here and here. Pubic hairs." He zipped back up. My own was hard now, too, pressing up into baggy corduroy. I wondered about Jimmy, about all those bridges, about time. We were stuck on some road that might never end, only two directions forever, out here in the middle of the wilderness, Ohio. The moon rose, halfway full. It looked like a hunchback, somehow evil. Seth squeezed me tighter.

"You're OK, for an angel," he said. "I sort of like you."

"I sort of like you too, I guess," I said.

He squeezed over closer. His teeth were chattering. There was something out there, in this night.

"What if he doesn't come back?" he asked. "What if he gets killed?"

He was scared. Maybe he was right to be. Maybe this time Jimmy wouldn't come back. Maybe I'd pushed him too far, with Seth.

"Who would kill him?" I asked.

He didn't say anything. The cluster of lights in the distance went out, vanished. I heard conspiratorial moos from out on the land. I wondered if cows ever killed people, rabid cows or vampire cows. I heard footsteps, gravel, breathing.

"Maybe you should lock your door," I said. He'd done it before I even had the words out and then there was a face at the window and I screamed. And Seth screamed and there was blood on the face and it was Jimmy, he was holding something in his hands and there was blood on his shirt and his hands and dripping down.

"Open up," he said.

Seth didn't move. I didn't move either. My insides were shrieking, a chasm opened up, blood and tissue and organs belly-flopping into it. There was blood smeared on his face. Was that Jimmy? Anything could happen out here in Ohio, anybody knocking on windows, dripping with blood.

"Open up," he said. "I got us some food."

It was some kind of dead animal in his hands. I unlocked the door and he climbed in. Blood ran all over the seats.

"Jesus H.," said Seth. "You're fucking crazy."

"You want to starve?" asked Jimmy. "Go on, start the truck. I checked a map. The interstate should be a few miles ahead."

Seth just sat there. It was a feathered mound, dead and wet with guts.

"It's only a chicken," said Jimmy. "We'll cook it over a fire."

Seth closed his eyes. Behind us a rumbling. A cloud of dust rose, its reflection brown in the moonlight and treacherous in the rearview mirror. I could see my own eyes watching it.

"Let's go," said Jimmy.

It came closer, a car.

"Shit," said Seth. "It's him."

"Cain," I whispered. "Of course."

The bridge was shaking. I knew it was going to collapse underneath us, there was really nothing there.

"Fucker," said Seth. "I'll kick his fucking teeth in if he tries to stop me."

He was almost upon us.

"There's no turning back now," I said.

I looked at Jimmy for affirmation.

"There never has been," he said quietly.

The car stopped, thundering, behind us. Seth stuck his head out the window, shouting.

"What do you want? You can't stop me. I'm gone."

Cain stepped out onto the gravel. He looked distressed.

"Seth," he said, "you have to come quick. It's Mom, something's happened, you have to come, I called the doctor already, but I don't know what to do, you have to help me . . ."

I clenched my fists, listening.

"What?" asked Seth. "What?"

"She's sick bad," said Cain. "I don't know, it came down on her all of a sudden, like a knife . . ."

"He's lying," I whispered. I swallowed.

"She's back there all white and muttering, I can't make sense of it, I think she might be dying, Seth."

Seth stared at Cain. He turned forward, gazed into his own wrists.

"Damn him," he said. "God damn him."

I could feel him slipping away. My face was burning, my throat raw. He was mine. To watch out for, to take care of.

"He's lying," I said. "You know that."

"I don't know anything," he said. "Fuck, you know. Cain or Jimmy, they're both pitch-crazy as a headless chicken. Neither direction's any good."

"Seth," said Cain. His hand was wrapped in gauze.

"I'll go then," he said. "Back up the car so I can turn around."

Cain stepped back into the car. Seth started the truck and threw it into reverse.

"Wait," said Jimmy.

He opened his door and slid out. I followed.

"What?" asked Seth. "What?"

"We're going," said Jimmy.

"Oh," said Seth. "Oh, I see." He looked straight ahead. "The highway's miles, you know."

Jimmy shrugged.

"We've walked before," I said.

"It's just, you know, what if she died on me?"

He sat, waiting. Cain moved back, the car, out of our side-ways vision. I stared into Seth. I slammed my open hand into the side of the truck.

"Get the fuck out," I said and I felt sick. Things were churn-ing inside, building, I felt it like fluid in the back of my throat. He backed away and I stumbled forward, fell to my knees at the side of the bridge. I leaned over to puke, saw the gully, moving below, dizzy, heard the truck rumble away, farther, gone. My face was so hot and I felt Jimmy waiting behind me, with his dead animal. My mouth hung open, I gagged. A thin line of spittle webbed down from my chin. I knelt there like that. Nothing came.

Δ

Pause now. Zoom backward, upward. See the boy from above, crouched over, trying to puke or to weep. Between Earth and the planets small dark clouds creep past. In outer space Pioneer Venus orbits the next planet over, snapping photos of a barren world, like Earth drained of its seas. On Earth, a volcano erupts in Washington State, creating a moonscape of ash. Race riots rage in Miami, a former actor is running for president. And how many billions of miles to the edge of the solar system? How many googols of light-years to the nearest star, the next star, the brightest star, the edge of the Milky Way? Does the concept of infinity make atrocity more palatable?

I stand here now, by the freeway, eight years later. It's in the spaces between rides; these minutes or hours at the side of the road, the passing cars, the dirty looks. It is here that slowly, over time, you begin to collect an idea of yourself. There's no other body to absorb you, no other life to step into or step back from; you can look back over your actions and discover which ones were really yours.

Manipulating a young boy to cut himself, deep in his own palm, that one wasn't mine. I will not take the credit. I'm a decent sort of person, I give money to beggars if I have it, help blind men cross the street. No, that particular action could only have come from Jimmy, somehow, from the darkness of his soul. At the age of twelve I put my own on automatic pilot.

But I loved him. There are many things I will confess, here by the side of the road, all alone. I have loved only twice, Andalusia and Jimmy. Oh, there were others, of course: a girl named Frita Bob who threw up her food, Jessica Moon and Antonio and Wendy and Dwight, various men in hotel rooms or bushes. They are all behind me now, with Jimmy and the others. I've done what I had to. Andalusia is waiting, just down this road.

I know that I am worthless until I find her. I know I haven't used all the things that I've learned. I know that I lie, even now, to myself. And there are other things. Things I could never say out loud.

But how many stars populate the sky, how many ghosts populate the history of the universe? We're really such tiny things. Still, everything is expanding away from everything else, isn't it, a cosmos without edges, so every place is in fact the center of the universe. On the bridge I wiped my mouth with the back of my hand, though there wasn't any vomit there, and turned up toward Jimmy.

"Don't ever leave me," I said. "We've got to stick together."

He knelt down beside me, put his hand on my shoulder. He loved me. I was shaking.

"Just don't be stupid, that's all," he said. "We've got to get by, you just can't be stupid. That's all."

He tossed his dead chicken into the ditch. We walked on together toward the highway.

FIVE

Δ

1

My head bobs and I wake with a start. A voice is saying something, but it's as if I cannot hear. My head is surrounded by an ethereal layer of gauze, everything is overly filtered.

"Corals, hydroids, jellyfish, sea anemones. These are members of the phylum Coelenterata."

The woman driving says nothing. The silence between us is filled only by the radio and the gurgling of my stomach.

"So," I say, finally, after miles like this, "what's your name?"

She pinches her mouth together, a look of disgust at this intrusion.

"Linda," she says.

She looks sideways, away from me, as she drives. She seems to have something on her mind. She seems angry and confused.

"I'm Matt," I say.

I play with my seat belt. Space passes us, locations. Time constrains us, so rigidly unidirectional, but space lends us freedom. A multitude of directions, despite the despotic, linear nature of the interstate. Driving encourages rational thought, a faith in progress and Western civilization. Still, these towns slide by without the slightest pretense of distributing knowledge. Newton, and beyond. Grinnell, What Cheer, East Liberty. My path and my goal do not coincide. I want to go to New Orleans, to curl up in a seedy motel room. Sleep for a good long time.

I lean back, close my eyes. The radio goes on.

"Porcupine fish, black iguana, painted turtles and dusky shrews. These are vertebrates; that is, animals with a spine."

"Phylum, genus, species," says the voice. "Classifications, arbitrary divisions. The things we'll do to make everything fit together as some sort of organic whole. To make the numbers come out right. A work of art, a system of thought, a life."

I sense billboards that I've missed with my eyes closed and lost forever. Even on this rational highway dark figures loom in designer briefs. This may just be imagination; many things are, they say, and objective reality was dismissed years ago. Still, such bleeding and starving goes on. Hair spray is bought or a new satellite dish, to tap into someone else's dreams: advertising executives, politicians, perpetual states of desire. It's election year again. Why such billboards, such underwear?

Davenport is just up ahead, blue lights stretching on toward the Mississippi. It is hazy and dark still, the sky pregnant with rain. There were blue lights like these, long ago, in Des Moines, at the airport. We used to drive down at night to look at them, linear Christmas lights showing us the way, me and Mom and Dad. Planes came mumbling down over us, the car radio played soft music. Simon and Garfunkel or *Jesus Christ Superstar*. Mom and Dad seemed happy. They were giving me things that money couldn't buy.

In other cars children watched the sky, couples necked and groped. Somebody was shot once, a drunken argument, but it wasn't fatal. Many things aren't; we recover and do something else.

"Where you headed?" I ask.

The woman winces, as if I've made a motion to smack her. She glares at me, eyes like hot pokers. She turns back toward the road, intense on the dotted line.

"But the aberrant," says the voice on the radio, "duck-billed platypus, dodo bird, jackalope. The albinos, the melanomatic."

I watch for Andalusia, in the cars that pass us by. These people, their hair is all frizzy and electric from the humid heat. They're all watching the sky, hoping for rain.

Before the Lost Nation exit the woman pulls over. She sits, without a word. She turns to me.

"Go on," she says, "Get out. You can't know. You wouldn't understand."

I don't move. I just watch her angry face.

"You have it," she says. "Exactly what I need. The courage to drift. I don't have the courage, but I'm drifting nonetheless. Not of my own free will, mind you. I've lost everything I had to tie me down."

She shoves a newspaper at me.

"Look at this, it's news. My baby died. My baby up and died, never even belonged yet. Never even made it."

I sit, searching for something to say. I can't tell which story in the paper is the relevant one. The biggest headline is the heat, the lack of rain. Sweat dampens Linda's forehead, veins skip in her neck. I can smell her garlicky, human breath. I want to help her, but I don't know how.

"Nobody cares," she says. "It's only the news."

"Where you going?" I ask.

"Just get out," she says. "I'm going somewhere else. Please, just get out and leave me alone."

I step out of the car, shut the door. It makes a loud, hollow sound. Gnats swarm about my head, my stomach falls half a foot then catches itself: the courage to drift. That isn't me, that isn't me at all.

The clouds have vanished, only heat remains. It's that damn greenhouse effect, everyone tells me so. At my feet a tiny brown toad begins its treacherous journey across the highway. The woman drives away.

Δ

We caught toads and huge, juicy frogs down by the river, me and Andalusia. We fed them fireflies so they would glow, pale, through their translucent skin. It only took one fly to make them glow, but we fed them dozens. We'd walk through the neighborhood like phantom knights, holding out our luminous toads as night lights. We could save anyone. Long-haired women trapped in tall stone towers, circled by flocks of evil crows. Wizards who crawled through the ruins of their burned and gutted sanctuaries, their magic powers lost. I bumped into her as we walked, wanting to be close. When she looked down at me, my glowing toad held out in my cupped palms, she would giggle, and then laugh. When she laughed it was like an earthquake.

I was a small child, I know. My hands were covered with frog slime. We walked through a vacant field where kids rode minibikes and caught monarch butterflies and tiger swallows and the weeds were tall enough that you could hide yourself and never be found. To our left the wizard drooled and raved, on his hands and knees. To our right the stone tower, red hair hanging from the window in the pale moonlight. We could save them.

"We can do anything, can't we?" I said to Andalusia. "You won't ever leave me."

She set her shiny frog down in the weeds and it hopped away, like all our dreams, not looking back, preoccupied, searching for critters to eat.

She told me that everybody left everybody, sooner or later. People come and people go. But probably, if she ever left, we would meet somewhere again. She broke off a stalk of milkweed, sucked it between her teeth. Down the path older boys were riding their minibikes up a ramp, jumping over each other. Everybody wanted to be Evel Knievel, all of us kids then, we wanted to break every bone in our body, just like him.

Later, Andalusia was gone, and the field, too. It burnt down when the Trumleys and Johnny Rice were playing with matches they stole from the Kwik Shop. The Trumleys, Mary and Lee, they started it, but couldn't stamp it out; they were barefoot.

Johnny had shoes, but Johnny ran. The day became strange, all sirens and shouting, and I stood in my living room, had a nightmare that a tidal wave of creamy acid was rushing down the street, the tops of telephone poles exploding. I was wide awake.

Nothing was left of the field but a black, charred stubble. The woman who owned it sold it then; they built apartments there. That was good, for the year of the building, a vast construction site to play in, we had dirt-clod fights and prowled through the basements and boards and sawdust. When they were done it was only squishy apartment floors and five hundred new neighbors, mean single people mostly, and a few divorcées with bratty kids, kids who told on us when we threw things over the fence at cars in the apartment parking lot.

When I was older I stopped throwing things over that fence, but then I started again, while Dad was in his period of jobless despair, drinking Pepto-Bismol and lounging on the sofa. I needed things to do. One Saturday afternoon I went to a movie at the mall with some boys I knew from school. It was just before Christmas, traffic and slush everywhere, red taillights blinking at people who looked tired or sick. The movie was something violent, gunshots and explosions, teenage girls getting hacked apart by psychopaths with butcher knives and syringes. Only one girl escaped, the virginal baby-sitter, the one who didn't smoke cigarettes. We sat in the back of the theater and blew pop at each other through straws. A mother picked us up afterward, we drove out of the mall parking lot, slow through all the congestion and prickly green ribbons hanging from light posts. Someone suggested McDonald's.

"I'm expected home for dinner, I think," I mumbled, but the mother, whoever's mother it was, said she'd treat and pulled into the McDonald's lot.

My mom had been working there for a couple of weeks. She was cheerful about it, said it was fun, she was learning things about french fries she'd never imagined and the people she worked with were really great, high school kids and college students home for break. I held back behind the crowd of hungry shoppers and movie watchers, hoping she wouldn't see me, my own mother, there at the cash register, in bright yellow stripes, her hair all tucked under a paper hat, smiling at strangers and asking, "Can I take your order, please?" I was hoping that none of the kids would recognize her. I was nervous, tingling with shame.

The other mother emerged from the crowd with enormous white bags filled with hamburgers in gold Styrofoam, french fries and Cokes. I hurried after her, heard the voice of my mom calling after me, "Matt!" I kept right on walking.

At home, Dad was gone, too. I sat there in the empty kitchen for the longest time, listened to the dripping faucet, ripping apart my Dad's Lark cigarettes to study the tiny balls of charcoal in the filters. The sun went down outside somewhere, and eventually I realized that I was sitting in the dark. I stood up and turned on a light, but it was all wrong. I turned it off again. A car pulled up out front, somebody letting my mom out, a cheerful goodbye, thanks for the ride, do you work tomorrow? I'll see you tomorrow then, bye now.

I hurried up to my room, shut the door, lay on the bed. I listened to the Pennels in the other half of the duplex. Usually I could hear everything they said, and if not, all I had to do was put a glass to the wall. That night they were talking loud.

"Did you hear what that man on the TV said?" Mrs. Pennel asked. Her voice sounded breathless, like a kid playing hide and seek. "He said that eighty-five percent of the American people claim to have had a supernatural experience. That seems awfully high, doesn't it? Did you ever have a supernatural experience?"

It was quiet. I couldn't tell if the man was saying something or not.

"That reminds me," she said. "I was thinking about Christmas dinner. Do you want I should get a regular turkey, one with bones? I was thinking of trying the boneless kind. Are you partial to bones in your turkey?"

The knob on my door turned, the door opened. I froze, shut my eyes. I could feel my mom move into the room, could feel her looking down at me. I made my breathing slow. I wished she would go away. She stayed for a minute, then went out, quiet, so she wouldn't wake me. My wish came true. She left me to myself.

The photograph: Mom caught with her eyes closed, seated, hands in her lap, smiling, almost ecstatic in a long white dress. I was scrunched up next to her, enjoying my play of boredom with the posing. Dad stood behind me in a dreadful black suit, his hand on my shoulder. His face looked stunned, by mystery or insight, almost fearful. Mom's hair was piled on her head, tilting in his direction, a unifying effect: there we were, the happy nuclear family, a holy trinity of sorts. Father, Son and Holy Ghost. Joy, boredom and dread. Either way, a unit, an equilateral triangle with Mom as hypotenuse. There was your proof, there was reality. Beyond that photograph things were no longer solid. We were phantoms, wavelengths of hostility and grief, acting without effect. A family called the Louds had let a television crew into their home, to film them in their natural environment. Maybe if we had someone filming us we would have been happy, we would have been real. In the meantime, I sat halfway down the steps, staring at the framed Sears portrait on the wall, listening to Mom and Dad in the kitchen. Less and less did eavesdropping seem wrong or even dangerous. It was a right, a legitimate means of acquiring knowledge. Nobody told me the things I needed to know.

"Tomorrow they're going to train me in drive-thru," Mom said. "You know, I think I'll really like that, talking through that intercom. Jeannie, she's that girl I told you about on the North basketball team, she kills me. She's always talking in funny accents over the intercom, pretending she's somebody else."

I pictured my mother there, trapped in the drive-thru, her hair hanging out the tiny rectangular window. Cars lined up for miles, honking and screeching, demanding their food.

"All that red meat," Dad said. "All those dead cows, that chunky black lard sold to cosmetics companies. All that grease and uniformity and Styrofoam. What have I done to you?"

"I knew I never should have told you what they do with that lard," Mom said.

I could hear running water in the sink. More than likely she was washing the dishes.

"I sure won't wear that makeup anymore," she said.

"There's no getting away from it, is there?" Dad asked. "We pay taxes and Latin Americans are tortured. We work and they convert our souls into plastic and death. We don't work and our children go hungry, our lizards die, our wives work for slave wages at greasy hamburger joints."

They were quiet. When Mom spoke her voice was softer but nearer, next to Dad at the table.

"We'll get through this. Just for a little while, huh? I like doing this for a little while, it's a change. You always took care of me, ever since the start, you were always the strong one. Maybe this is an OK thing, everybody has to have their chance to take care of the other one. I never gave you much before. You just rest now."

I peeked through the railing of the steps, into the kitchen. They were there at the table, but Dad leaning over, his head in Mom's lap, she running her fingers through his hair. Their clothes and bodies ran together, I couldn't tell where one started and the other stopped. I pulled my head back in.

Δ

We stood by the highway in the middle of the night, me and Jimmy. I was shaking with chills. A man, Tom, picked us up in an oblong green car.

"New York?" he said. "Why that's exactly where I'm headed. To lose myself in the blur. Become myself through the exhilarating drug of anonymity. I'll take you all the way there. You'll wake up in the morning right in the heart of Manhattan."

"Are you from New York?" I asked.

"Don't burden me with your expectations of who I am," he

said. "I am not. I'm not who anybody thinks I am, not even myself. Don't be surprised by anything I do. Don't be surprised by anything that you do, or anybody else. Nobody is really themself."

He was a curly-haired man, with a head white and square, like a marshmallow. He would not take pictures well, they would always come out looking like someone else. His face reminded me of Seth's, only in the way that it didn't seem to be his own. His glasses were thick, his age about halfway to death.

"Oh," I said. "Then who are they?"

"Smartass," said Tom. He shifted gears. He started talking and didn't shut up. He'd been to California to find himself, to peel away the layers and learn what it really was that made him, what he wanted and needed and loved. From the day he was born, was given fuzzy blue jumpsuits with little green bunnies, had plastic barnyard animals hanging musically above his crib, taught to say Mama and Dada and uh-oh, he'd been nothing but an extension of others. His father was a Freudian, his mother a reincarnation therapist. Masculine and feminine essences, phallus and lack, forever trapped in their ongoing dialectic. He paid therapists and masseurs, watched whales off the Big Sur coast. He freed himself from the blather and plunged into the void. Finally he had found himself and discovered there was really nothing there.

I pressed closer to Jimmy, away from the man. I chewed on my finger. We were surrounded by mountains.

"All form," he said. "No content. It seemed very liberating at first. But now I'm finding a profound need to distract myself from this knowledge. I crochet, I drink. Mostly I just drive and consume. People are always speaking so disfavorably about distraction, I really can't understand it."

The white line glowed and snaked. Animals waited on either side, in the dark. Trees rose around us, we burrowed further into the depths. The radio played songs about unfulfilled lives, about running away and finding something better.

"I'm not interested in the details of your lives," said Tom. "Why don't you get some sleep?"

"We're orphans," I said.

"You think that makes you any different?" asked Tom. "Dead parents are just as inescapable. I can see plainly that you never adequately resolved your Oedipal complex and probably never will. You seem to have a strong oral fixation."

I quickly removed my finger from my mouth. Short poles with glowing white reflectors scurried along the road, orange stripes, a sign post in the dark, CONSTRUCTION NEXT 438 MILES. At night there were no workers, only projects abandoned, bulldozers and sweaty flannel shirts.

"One of you may as well stretch out in the backseat," said Tom. "It's more comfortable back there."

I climbed over the seat, stretched out on the vinyl, had to bend my legs. I was growing, still, in the midst of everything. We drove through tunnels, pale, lunar, vibrating. Money or tickets changed hands, we entered the turnpike. The mountains grew dark around us. I could see only patches of the nightsky, passing slowly through the opposite window, the occasional orange rooftop of a Howard Johnson's. The night flowed easily, the pleasant hum of the engine, that feeling of being in somebody else's hands, a driver, capable and decisive. Back somewhere behind me, Cain's hand was scarred for good. If I could only ride in other people's cars, watch Jimmy doing this or that, I wouldn't have to think. Listening to the engine was just like being drunk.

"Morning," said Tom. "We're here."

I sat up. It wasn't quite what I expected. Where was the enormity, the hustle, the pulse of the vortex? I looked around. The buildings were tall, sure, I could feel a current of energy. I wanted to leap and sing and run, but I was disappointed, too. There didn't seem to be much more here than in Columbus or Indianapolis.

"So this is New York," I said.

"This isn't New York," said Jimmy. "This is St. Louis."

Tom stopped for a red light.

"Smart kid," he said. "Didn't I tell you not to be surprised?"

My heart sank. Jimmy stretched.

"I'm not surprised at all," he said. "Why don't you stop somewhere and buy us some breakfast?"

Tom pulled over by a coffee shop.

"We humans," he said, "always intending destinations, always disappointed if we don't get there. But alas, unpredictability becomes in itself an expectation and we are trapped again. No escape, it seems, from the falseness that forms us."

He bought us eggs, bacon, toast and coffee. He read the morning newspaper, said goodbye and left us there, in downtown St. Louis.

A misty city at night. An arch rising high overhead, shining and twisting like a steel reptile, glittering and black. An arch. Was this whole city just a giant McDonald's playground? We walked. A twenty-four-hour restaurant downtown, mirrored walls, so many reflections of bums and cranky waitresses and potential killers in checkered pants. One cup of coffee, refills weren't free. Everything twisting and bending and scattered. We moved.

Lobbies of ritzy hotels were bright, silver, warm. All those rich people just waiting to have their things taken. It was exciting to be with Jimmy, to know that he might do anything, that we might do anything. In the gift shop he slipped a pack of Camel Filters into his pocket. In the lobby he tapped the pack down. We sat in chairs freckled with flowers and I watched the sensuous curve of his lips wrap themselves around a cigarette.

"What was it like?" I asked. "With Melissa? All that fucking, I mean."

He shrugged.

"I've never done it, but I'd like to," I said. "Sometimes I just wish somebody would touch me there. Anybody. I'd do most anything."

He handed me the cigarette. I took a drag, squinting.

Security guards and bellboys, gold strings hanging from their jackets. Cars pulling up in front, black windows. Heels and glass and electric laughter. Inside the hotel nobody was scared. They didn't realize that a fur coat was a violent act, a limousine, a steak dinner, just as much as anything me and Jimmy might do.

I gave him back the cigarette.

"I'll steal a purse," he said. "Watch."

He smiled at me. It felt like a hand on the back of my neck or a tongue. His face was so smooth, his lips. He moved toward the front desk where women with pearls and enormous red hair were feigning exhaustion, leaning on older, casually distinguished men. The floor was littered with their smaller bags, cosmetics cases and purses. The desk clerk smiled at me, thinking I belonged. Jimmy was invisible, *whish* and he had it and was moving toward the door and I moved that way too, separate so no one would know we were together. We ran out and far away, across the highway and out of breath, in the big park under the arch. Jimmy rummaged through the purse.

"Tampons," he said. "And silver toothpicks and lipstick and tiny bones and a plastic mouse and eyeshadow. And letters and more lip stuff and a picture of a woman sticking her tongue in another woman's ear and a handkerchief. And a dead snake and a glass eye and pills. And money."

It was warm. We slept close together on the grass in the park. Jimmy used the purse as a pillow, I had a fancy handkerchief. Insects bit me, but I imagined that our dreams were the same, me and Jimmy: blizzards of cotton balls covering everything, women in towers, broken-down wizards, a place of our own, tending the rabbits. My hands on Jimmy, moving down his chest, his thighs, staring into his eyes.

The next day Jimmy went off, promised to meet me back in the park. I'd never stolen on my own before, it was always just watching or helping. That day I did, from a Walgreen's drugstore downtown. Unlike Jean Genet, this was not an existential decision, rejecting a world that had rejected me. It was just that I'd been terrorized by dental hygienists in elementary school with their pills that turned our teeth pink, their slides of gummy, toothless mouths. My own father's mouth had repulsed me as well, yellow and splotchy brown stains, teeth that looked like

escapees from institutions for the dentally deranged. I wanted
to brush. My teeth were all gunky and heavy, I could feel the
decay. What a vertiginous drugstore it was, round mirrors overhead and swiveling cameras pushing me down toward the black-
and-white checkered floor. I moved myself strategically, a bishop
roaming diagonally, a knight, forward, forward, side, slinking
along counters filled with stacks of peanut brittle, bubble bath
and lotions, panty hose in eggs. Nonchalant, whistling, a pawn,
a rook, an iguana: move in, a flick of the tongue and the toothbrush would be mine. I imagined a room in back where evil
scientists monitored the video screens, waiting for shoplifters
to abduct and use as guinea pigs. So much surveillance, everyone on film. I stood in front of the rows of white and red tooth-
brushes, not daring to touch them, examining dental floss instead,
comparing prices on mouthwash. The aisle was long and empty,
the camera swiveling the other way. I held my hand in the air.
A woman swung around the corner, walking straight toward me,
her pale blue smock like the sky across the river where Lennie
could see the future unfolding, tending rabbits, the fat of the
land, but then a mercy killing, George's gun at Lennie's neck,
the smock moving closer. I stared into the cinnamon red of the
mouthwash. Would Jimmy do that for me if this woman seized
me, tried to lock me away and torture me, would he put a gun
to my neck and kill me, let me slip out altogether in the middle
of love? We weren't like other guys, we had each other. The
woman moved past me, loped around the next corner. I grabbed
a toothbrush and shoved it in my pocket. The camera froze, staring right at me. Paste was too much to ask for, I couldn't push
my luck, walked toward the door, stared straight ahead, waiting
for shouts and rough hands and the noose of a rope. I pushed
open the door and was out on the street. The concrete was hot,
the street full of sun. I dodged people in suits and ran toward
the park.

    I spit on the brush to moisten it and luxuriated in the clean-
ing, a full ten minutes I scrubbed my teeth and my gums, the
brush turning pink with blood. I was laughing and hungry, the
sun on my face. I'd done it, all by myself. That night I got a tube

of Ultra-Brite from the bus-station gift shop and another brush,
for Jimmy. He brought me things, too, blueberry bagels and
candy bars and ice cream. This was the place, St. Louis. Life
would be good.

In the daytime park employees found us on the grass and
told us we couldn't sleep there; it was the law. We rested in a
smaller park with a fountain over by the big hotels and the baseball stadium, where business people sat and ate their lunches
on sunny days. A man offered Jimmy ten dollars to touch him,
but Jimmy grabbed the money and ran. I ran, too. We turned
into night creatures, playing video games in the bus station,
drinking coffee in the twenty-four-hour restaurant with mirrored walls, watching the reflections of the bums, waitresses
and potential killers in checkered pants. Outside, young people
stood on corners in twos or threes. The waitress asked us, wasn't
it past our bedtime? A potential killer in checkered pants patted
Jimmy on the head and said something about how much he liked
the feel of mosquito repellent on his skin. We left, walked around,
a few lonely cars cruising the downtown, pale hallucinations,
breathing corpses, cops, all of us moving in circles until the sun
would come up. Women were dried-up and painted, children
had glass embedded in their bare little feet. It was easier to find
places to sleep during the day. Rainy days were the worst,
sleeping in the hard bus-station chairs made my head ache and
the public library was blocks from downtown. We tried to sleep
in the huge chairs in the lobbies of hotels, but you couldn't
sleep in hotel lobbies in St. Louis; it was the law.

I learned how to walk without looking scared, how to be
invisible, to look impoverished and insane. How to talk to myself,
gesticulating wildly, muttering *motherfucker* or *CIA* every few
yards so people wouldn't bug me. How to slide down the streets,
steal candy bars, bananas and bran muffins for that extra fiber
we needed so bad. We washed up in fountains on hot days,
collected the wet change from lovers' wishes. Sometimes we
split up. I liked to hang out with tourists by the arch or in bookstores in malls. I'd follow families around, pretend they were

mine, wait for them to leave their table at McDonald's or Wendy's and eat the food they left behind. A few blackened french fries, ketchup, the corner of a bun. Nights we found each other again, me and Jimmy, like fruit-shaped magnets and refrigerators, in the park, under bridges, usual places; we brought each other gifts: stolen tangerines, macaroni salads, shirts or jackets we'd found discarded on the street. I learned to eat and run, find dry corners out of the afternoon rain, search for quarters on laundromat floors. I asked strangers for money. Most just ignored me or said "Afraid not!" in a tone implying that they were good citizens and I was hardly human at all. Others threw me change so I'd have to chase nickels or dimes, careening across the sidewalk. Some suggested various paths to salvation, some offered money if I'd do certain things, but I wouldn't, I only loved Jimmy. Some threatened me, some called me by names usually reserved for vermin, some said they'd call the cops, if I didn't watch out. United States senators from southern states, in town for a tobacco convention, chased me with a stick, demanding I cease to exist. Life became that running away, that begging, that scrounging and walking, pressing from the inside of a bubble. Circling the city and screaming from there, hurtling through forgotten spaces where only spirits wandered, I conversed with pigeons, ran down alleys and through top-heavy rainstorms, listened, moved, glandular, following the city's cycles of mood, smelling coffee beans and sauerkraut, sticking fingers in the crevices, spewing nonsense syllables and peeing off tall buildings.

Sometimes I was angry. Cold, insect-filled nights, chased away by security guards, body chemistry skewed by bad coffee, there was nothing to do. Frozen nights, bright, sweaty days, back and forth and zombified. Sticky and dirty and eyes filled with crust, I walked and wanted to spit, finding that people were cruel and alien and that words said nothing and I wasn't myself, I wasn't anything but some hostile will getting away from itself; I was a stranger and the others as well; unknowable and hungry, I was the walking, no different from the walking and eating and visions of city, concrete, men and women walking clothed, genitals out of sight and the people were this: this walking, obeying, falling into patterns, these clothes and sunglasses, to cover penises, vaginas and eyes, this endless devouring, and I was sick in the heat, always sweating and wanting to spit.

There were odd sensations sometimes, in St. Louis; when I would step over some bum into the bus station bathroom, see blood dried on the tiles; I would feel like maybe it was my own. When I would see a mime hurl himself in front of a bus, hear the crunch of his body under the tires; I would feel a strange excitement as the crowd gathered around, the ambulance. But there were other times when I would stumble onto some terrible beauty, saxophone blues in the park, fire dancers, or a rich smell of baking pastries on a deserted corner. It was like I'd found a girl sunbathing topless in a huge cemetery, in Georgia or New Mexico, her pale breasts exposed, basking in the dull heat of the sun, surrounded by tombstones and the spirits of the dead.

Only Jimmy was really with me, was really alive. Together we were so hungry and smelly and filled with hate for the world, shattering glass on the streets, chasing rats, stealing food, scrawling our screams in black chalk under bridges, on stairways, in parking garages. So many idiots and droolers and hustlers out on the street, so much debris. We smoked cigarettes, felt our lungs turn black, coughed out gobs of bloody phlegm on the sidewalk. We moved with the synapses, electrically jumping into traffic lights, red light, yellow light, green light, existing. Cardinals fans jostled through the streets on Sunday afternoons, schizophrenic men fed us chicken and beer in the park and kissed me on the neck, we met a dwarf named Phen in a donut shop who let us stay in his tiny apartment for a night while he sat up watching reruns of *Dallas*. Other nights were too short, the sun like a bludgeon at dawn, a pasty film in your mouth, scabs on your scalp, scattered pieces of dream: a welcome apocalypse, a steak on a grill. Cops beating up children, sidewalks and traffic. Young boys slicing crosses into their hands.

Mostly, I walked. Ankles aching, feet tired and brain feeling like it was expanding, contracting, bubbling sometimes, if I'd just stick with it a little bit longer I knew I would get there,

finally, after all, someplace, a corner of my brain, a doorway on
the street, an animal's lair, someplace I could call home.

I found him in front of the bus station, sitting cross-legged
on the sidewalk. Jimmy was elsewhere: flirting with danger,
sacrificing animals, lips and concentration and eyes, tearing
about. I didn't know what all. Me, I was aimless that day,
watching old blind men play chess, roller-skating mohawks and
lunatic zombies preaching to students with dark glasses. His
eyes caught me, throughout the afternoon, pulled me toward
him, but I resisted, crossed the highway and circled the arch,
walked back, looked at him and then quickly away. He was old
and bearded, drooling, but his eyes shone a peculiar light.

"You," he said finally, quietly, firmly, as I walked past his
spot, and I turned and stared. He smiled. I walked toward him.
He smiled some more.

"What?" I asked. "What do you want?"

"Sit," he said. I don't know why; I did. His eyes were amber,
his beard tangled, he smelled of bourbon and sweat and aged
skin. I felt calmed, my feet resting.

"You have strayed," he said, "from your true self. You are
moving in circles, but you don't know why. If you move long
enough, however, that movement can in itself become your true
self, can fill you up like a quality. Do you understand what I'm
saying?"

I thought for a minute.

"No," I said. "Haven't got a clue."

"Good," he said. "You have money. Buy me a bottle of
whiskey or a jug of wine. It will all be explained in due time."

Pigeons waddled by, a woman with a baby fed them bread.
The baby was chewing on his mother's newspaper, a picture of
Cuban refugees swarming to Florida. I wondered how hard it
would be to cook a pigeon.

"You want me to spend my money so you can get drunk," I
said.

"No," he said, "so I can stay drunk. Listen. I'm not just anybody, like some people are. My name is Traveler. Go, now, hurry. I will wait."

I didn't move. He shooed me on with his hand, then closed his eyes and raised his head toward the heavens. I wasn't going to spend my money on this bozo.

I wandered off toward the deli where Jimmy liked to eat blueberry bagels. He wasn't there, either. Elsewhere, only that. I felt heavy. I stopped. A liquor store sparkled beside me, newspapers, cigarettes, a sleazy-looking man behind the counter with slicked-back hair. I bought a liter jug, slid my money across the counter and left, the man watching for the cops. I headed back toward the bus station, feeling a wild buzz in the back of my brain. He was there, and nodded to me.

I was so tired. I sat down beside him.

"You can call me Traveler," he said, "although others would call me the Lizard King. Tell me, boy. How old do you think I am?"

I studied his lines, his wild hair, hanging jowls. He looked close to a hundred, but I thought it would be better to underestimate, so as not to insult his pride.

"Seventy-two," I said.

"Not quite," he said. "Thirty-six. Don't worry, I'm not offended. It's just that I've lived a lot in that time. I've experimented with twenty-seven-hour days. I've passed through four seasons in a single summer. It has worn on me, this living business. Someday, years from now, I'll be all used up."

I looked up at the sky. White trails, barely cloud at all. There was something peculiar about this man. He was wearing an orange scarf. He had a quality of uncertainty about him, not in his demeanor, in his actual existence. His outermost coat was blue plaid. I wanted to stay with him.

"Is that your real name?" I asked. "Traveler?"

"Of course it's my real name," he said. "I gave it to myself. The way I figure it, there are two options. You can name yourself, or you can let others name you. Wait, make that three options. You can name yourself, let others name you, or remain nameless, an empty vessel without qualities, even unto your self. Hold on. Name yourself, let others name you, remain nameless, or continually change your name, at every opportunity, for whatever purpose suits you. Although that might just be a subtopic under the first option of self-naming. Anyway, you get my basic drift. What's your name?"

I thought hard. If I gave him the name others had given me I might be lessening myself in some way. If I made up a name I might be stuck with something stupid forever. I didn't trust my own judgment. If I remained nameless I'd be an empty vessel. What did he want me to say?

"I don't care," I said. "Call me whatever you want."

"Good," he said. "I'll call you Matt. It seems to suit you."

Was I really myself, so obviously? That woman from my dad's factory said all Rons were fighters and drinkers. Cain's and Seth's names had been chock full of irony. Who did the naming, what did it mean? In the Bible it was Adam. Later, God changed people's names whenever he got restless. Jacob into Israel, Abram to Abraham, Saul into Paul. In a spy thriller I stole from a bookstore in the mall Nazis changed their names and moved to South America where they plotted to make a comeback with Adolf Hitler's clones.

"It's good to have you listen," he told me. "I need that grounding in some sort of dialogue, you know. I remember one winter I was living in a cardboard box in a park in San Francisco. The cold wouldn't have been so bad, but that rain, holy shit! I'd be drenched and shivering and I lost my voice. I felt somewhat nonexistent there for a while. Where do you sleep, Matt? Do you have a box of your own? I tell you, cardboard's not a bad way to live, if you've got a couple of blankets, too, it beats the hell out of the bus-station floors. I don't sleep indoors anymore, not even in the cold, it cuts me off too much from the whole of Being."

"Mostly in the park," I said. "But more inside lately, in the bus station and such. There's plenty of covered doorways and that, and if you know the right places there's almost no competition. I've got blankets, I lose them sometimes, but I always get more."

He was picking at his ear, he didn't seem to be listening.

"I once made love to an elm tree, and we became one. It was beautiful. Later I fucked the leaves as well, all piled on the ground, I buried myself in them, it was like a beautiful tomb. It felt good to be dead."

"I used to rake leaves with Andalusia," I told him. "She'd bury me in them, I'd breathe in their dusty smell. They were all crunchy and recently alive."

He offered me a slice of Wonder bread with cheese on it. As he talked, his lips smacked, and he didn't have many teeth, four or five at most. The teeth he had were yellow with spots of brown around the gums. His teeth reminded me of my father's. Traveler reminded me of my father, if my father had been old and smelly and probably insane.

To our left, a stray dog urinated. He watched it.

"City dogs," said Traveler, "are all the same, have you noticed? The strays, I mean. Over time, certain traits will dominate, the traits they need to survive in such an atmosphere. Quickness, bodies not too large, the tails that stick up, short, so they can't be grabbed. City mongrels, a fine example of Darwin's theory."

The day was moving toward dusk. The bleating, frantic sounds of rush hour. A cacophony of screeching brakes, honking horns, the color peach. Other people moved around us.

"I once formed a rock-and-roll band in Los Angeles," Traveler said. "I managed to produce several pop hits and a few quite disturbing and poetic tunes, if I do say so myself. I was looked on as a messiah by screaming teenage girls, became a prophet of sex and death. Cosmic transformation seemed just within reach. College kids took drugs and stared at lava lamps to the throbbing, tyrannical strains of my melodic deliriums. Everybody needs to lose themself in something larger now and again."

The other people were everywhere now, hurrying. Those

people had homes, lived up above, rode in taxis, wore clothes that fit them. I was still wearing Cain's rancid clothes, corduroy and flannel, they hung off me like hope for salvation and a home-cooked meal. The other people would go home, eat pasta, change into other clothes that fit them, and then dash into the night, moving through it in dizzy patterns, as if it was nothing more than a television commercial for imported beer. Those people weren't us.

"It was a fast life and I had to give it up, the sex, the drugs, you know the story. I disappeared, returned to anonymity, drifted. Most people seem to think that I died in Paris or some such thing. It doesn't matter. I'm happy, now, conversing with alley-cats and street urchins. Although it has been over a week since I last purified myself with cat urine, I feel I've reached a state of peace. Relatively speaking, of course. I'm not dead yet."

"You're Jim Morrison," I said. "I knew a girl in Columbus who read me your poetry."

He smiled.

"I'm Traveler now," he said. "Sometimes, you'll find it's best not to remember your past. Everybody makes such a big deal of forgetting, like it's the worst thing in the world. In the long run, it's the only thing. They say everybody was born, don't they? Well, I don't recall it. Must have been one of my black-outs."

He rambled on, talked about Blake, the poet, and his phi-losophy of excess. He talked about the Apollonian-Dionysian struggle for control of the life force and occasionally exposed himself to passersby on the street. He was warm, he had blan-kets and jackets and food sometimes, I started coming to see him every day. I brought him wine, I'd snuggle up next to him and listen, I got used to the smell pretty quick, I felt safe there.

But at night, on the hard ground, I still had scary dreams. I dreamed that a man was following me, a man with the face of a lizard and an orange mustache. I woke with a start, looking for Jimmy. Jimmy was sleeping next to me, behind some bushes in the park. It was hot, his back was bare, he was facing away from me. We had pillows Jimmy had stolen from a hotel and a sheet we found in the trash. It had some bloodstains here and there, but other than that it was a perfectly good sheet. I was shaking and sticky with sweat. I itched. Mosquitoes were always attacking my ear, one at a time, as soon as I killed one, another would take its place, right there next to my very same ear. I always felt as if someone was following me, chasing me down. I wanted to reach out, I wanted to touch Jimmy's face. He was so beautiful when he slept, I wanted to run my fingers down his face and his neck and his back, a blank piece of paper, I could have written my dreams on it, my life story. Wizards in ruins, women in towers.

2

The sky blossoming in the late afternoon. I sat on a bench in a park by the water, watching children play on the swings. Jimmy was down by the river, scrounging for money or food. A middle-aged woman brought two children, smartly dressed, a little boy and a little girl. The girl dragged a chubby, ugly doll along with her. The boy pressed buttons on a computer game. It made loud bipping noises.

The woman sat beside me, as the children ran off to play. She was a little bit plump, with long, auburn hair. Her features were bland, she looked like she might sell furniture polish on TV. She flipped through a *Cosmopolitan* magazine. She looked sad.

"These articles," she said, "they're so depressing. It's all about what shit men are, while encouraging us to do anything within our means, step on people or kidnap babies, to get enough money for a nose job. Ten Reasons to Stay with Mr. Wrong. Are You Getting Your Share of Orgasms? Take Our Quiz and Find Out. All these quizzes about sex and dating and nutrition. I always fail, I never stack up."

I wasn't sure if she wanted me to respond.

"Don't worry about it," I said. "It doesn't seem like anybody does. Nobody I've met."

She reached out and brushed my hair away from my eyes, as if forgetting that she wasn't my mother.

"What a good boy," she said.

She looked out, at the children pushing each other off the jungle gym.

"Are those your kids?" I asked.

"Oh, no," she said. "They're very sweet. Smart, too. Dinnie got into the very best preschool, she speaks three languages already. Ethan is more of an artist. He paints, he sculpts, he plays the violin. He's only five. But I'm just their nanny. I can't have children of my own."

"Oh," I said. "Do you want to?"

"There's nothing I'd rather do," she said. "But I can't. I just can't."

I liked her, her face was kind and maternal.

"I'm sorry," I said.

"Oh, it isn't your fault," she said. "It's just because I'm a monster."

I studied her carefully. Her eyes were brown. Her skin looked like bubble gum, the kind you got with baseball cards, pink and soft, speckled with powdered sugar.

"You don't look like a monster," I said.

"You're such a nice boy," she said. "But listen. I'll tell you. Did you ever remember reading about those psychology experiments they did years ago? Where they took a bunch of people and they told them to administer electric shocks to other people?"

"Sorry," I said, "I don't read much psychology."

"Well, I'll tell you how it worked. The people delivering the shocks could see that the people they were giving them to were in pain. The shocking machine was clearly marked DANGEROUS at a certain level, where it could even cause death. None of this was real, of course, the shocks weren't really being delivered, it was just actors. But the people giving the shocks didn't know that. These psychologists sat there and told the people to keep on giving shocks. To just keep on raising the level and raising it. It was supposed to be an experiment on how pain affected learning. Well, the disturbing thing was that many of the people just kept on giving these shocks, to what they thought were innocent people, just because they were told to do it."

She paused.

"The doctors were very intimidating, sure. With their white smocks and their briefcases and glasses. Still, that's hardly an excuse."

She leaned her head back, stretching, ran her fingers along her clavicle.

"I was one of those people," she said. "I shocked them."

The babble of children's voices filtered through the air. A cool wind blew in from the water. I didn't know what to say.

"How could I have children after I did a thing like that? How could I pass my genes along? I know what I really am, I know what I'm capable of. I could snap at any minute, I guess, go around with a cattle prod, shocking people on the street. They gave me therapy afterwards, you know, free of charge. They told me I was a twisted mass of guilt and anger inside. OK, I said. So what do I do? You know what they said?"

"No. What did they say?"

"They said I should ignore that fact, as much as was possible. They said I should do nice things for people, go on with my life. They said if I pretended to be something I wasn't, that is, a good, decent person, eventually I might turn into one. I might lose myself in the role. They suggested I work hard, make money, buy things. They suggested jogging or a new hairstyle."

I heard teasing voices from the playground. The victim threw rocks at the other kids and ran away bawling.

"But how can I forget?" asked the woman. "Whenever I see Holocaust movies on TV, now, I'm the Nazi. How can I identify with the Jews anymore, after what I did? I'm the Nazi. I used to like to watch atrocity as much as anybody. Bodies being bulldozed into ditches, you know, that sort of thing. I used to love that luscious sense of outrage, that self-righteous anger. I could sit there and say *how could they do that?* How could *they* do that. But now I can only sit there and say *how could we do that.* I hate those smug people who say *how could they do that.* I used to be one of them, I know. I miss the old days."

I reached over, squeezed her hand.

"It's OK," I said. "Shockers are people, too. Everybody's a person, if you think about it."

She ran her fingers through my hair.

"Such a good boy. I can see, clearly, that you are not the kind of person who would deliver powerful electric shocks to innocent people. I can see that you are full of joy and goodness. What lucky parents you must have, to have a nice little boy like you."

I smiled at her. I didn't want to make her feel bad, but on the other hand, I craved her sympathy.

"I'm an orphan," I said. "I live on the streets."

"Oh dear," she said. "That's dreadful. We can't have that. That won't do at all."

"Oh, it's OK," I said. "The streets aren't so bad. It gets cold at night sometimes, but it's better than the orphanage."

"No, no, no," she said. "Why, look at how skinny you are. You haven't eaten in days, have you?"

"Sure," I said. "I eat sometimes. I was skinny even before my parents were dead. I had a paper route then and we lived in a duplex. That was in Iowa."

"Iowa. You don't say. Oh, you poor boy. You listen to me. You wait right here. Don't you move."

She hurried off across the park. I sat, smelling the water, watching barges. There was so much happening, so much going on in the world. She came back with a gyro.

"Here," she said. "Eat this."

I ate. An idea popped into my head, perfect in its symmetry, its possibilities.

"What's your name?" I asked.

"I'm Amanda," she said. "Who are you?"

"Matt," I said. "I'm Matt. I was just thinking. Maybe I could be your kid. Maybe you could adopt me."

I bent my face into an expression of anxious longing, without being too obvious about it. She sighed and looked away from me.

"Oh, Matt," she said, "I'd love to do that, really I would. Like I told you, I can't, I just can't. I'm a seething mass of anger and potential violence. I don't want you to turn into one of those things, too. Not a sweet boy like you."

I held her hand again. She put her arm around my shoulder.

"I'm not much trouble," I said. "I don't eat much. I could mow your lawn for you. I'm a good mower, I keep my lines real straight."

"Oh, Matt," she said. "It's just that I've got. I don't. Oh, I don't know."

We sat there together, watching kids slide and chase each other around. I didn't ever want to leave. But the two little children came running up, her charges.

"Miss Lacey," said the girl, "Miss Lacey! Ethan got mud on his L. L. Bean's."

"Shut up," said Ethan. "Come on, Miss Lacey, or Dinnie will be late for her ballet."

Dinnie said something harsh, in a foreign language.

"OK," said the woman. "I've got to go. But here, take this." She pressed a ten-dollar bill into my hand. "Maybe I'll see you around here again. You take care, you hear?"

She kissed me on the cheek. I smiled at her and sniffled, like I was holding back tears. I folded the bill carefully, put it in my pocket.

"Oh dear," she said. "Yes, just for one night, OK. Come on, let's go."

I fell down and embraced her ankles. I stood up, smiling.

"Oh yeah," I said. "There's one more thing."

"What?" she said.

"I've got a friend."

She took the children to their lessons, came back for us just after dark. She seemed different from before, nervous. We walked with her through the downtown streets without talking.

This is where things got predictable. We were saved from our lives of petty crime, of stolen paperback books and ice cream for dinner, taken in and reformed. Educated and employed, we

grew into tall, robust young men, dated, joined fraternal orga-
nizations, did TV testimonials for the Boy's Club or the YMCA.
Amanda adopted us, married a widower with two children of
his own, a twelve-year-old Korean girl genius, already gradu-
ated from college, and an eight-year-old blind Hispanic juggler.
A television sit-com was inspired by our lives, filled with good-
natured racial ribbing and drug problems solved in two-hour
specials.

Or rather: we raped her and killed her, lived in her apartment for months without detection. We watched cable TV, drank
brandy, ran up outrageous bills on her credit cards for pizza and
silk pajamas.

But no. Just when things seemed set, when I was walking
down the street waiting for compassion to finally win the day,
or for the power of darkness to obliterate everything, a light
shut off in a window overhead. A woman's laughter fell to the
street and stuck to the sidewalk like a spoonful of mashed potatoes. Was she laughing at *us?* People moved furtively in doorways and bushes, all these secret purposes. A disruption, an
estrangement, an eruption of nightingales. Amanda jangled her
keys, we entered her building. Bright lights, a security guard at
the desk, a buzzer on the door. Between the street and Amanda's twentieth-floor apartment everything bent. The halls were
narrow, bright and silent, the carpet an extravaganza of spiraling reds and purples and little gold sprinkles. A fat woman
walked toward us with a black thing on a leash. Her hair was
twisted and teased, mascara running down her cheeks. Amanda
was breathless, fumbling with her keys, sliding the door open,
and there we were, in.

There was one room and a kitchen. On the other side of her
picture window were the arch, the river, the highway and bridge,
cars streaming back and forth, between Illinois and Missouri.
There was a small balcony with a potted plant and a yellow
director's chair. Amanda leaned against the refrigerator.

"Can I get you something to drink?" she asked.

"Whiskey for me," said Jimmy.

She laughed, a nervous, high-pitched giggle, then shut up

and twisted strands of her hair around her finger. Jimmy sat on the floor. The only chair was a beanbag. Amanda poured milk into wineglasses.

"How alone I am," she whispered.

The phone rang. She dropped a glass, it shattered. Milk seeped into cracks between the tiles. The phone rang. Amanda put her hand on her chest, gulped in air. Jimmy held his body tight, a cheetah. Cheetahs are the fastest animals, and strong. The phone rang. I didn't move.

"Don't answer it," said Amanda. "They'll want to come in. We can't let them in."

"Who?" I asked.

"Two is enough," she said. "Two is too many already."

The phone rang, slightly louder, understanding Amanda's fear. Jimmy moved to the sliding glass doors. He always knew what to do. Cheetahs are graceful and muscular and always get their prey. He slid the door open, stepped onto the balcony.

Amanda stepped carefully past the broken glass onto the carpet. She leaned against the wall, closed her eyes, put her head in her hands. I stepped out onto the balcony with Jimmy. The view was striped with cool colors. There were fountains way down below and enormous flowers, a circle of red, surrounded by a circle of orange, a target. I leaned out, the wind all through me in the open. The sound of traffic below made the city seem peaceful and alive.

"Look how far everything goes," I said. "There's so much."

"It sure looks that way, doesn't it?" said Jimmy.

He threw pennies out toward the street.

"By the time they hit," he said, "they're going fast enough to drill holes right through people's skulls. It happens all the time down there. People are walking along and they get killed by a penny."

I imagined the sidewalk below littered with dead bodies, pennies embedded in strangers' skulls. I just stood, silent, feeling large. Looking out over all those lights, the blueblack clouds over the dark spot that was the river, seeing how big and beautiful everything was I felt that there was no end to the possibilities, the places one could go. New York, Paris, Reykjavik. Minneapolis, Milwaukee.

We moved inside.

The air inside was quivering with heat. The walls were beaded with sweat and vibrating, something pounding on every side. I wiped my forehead with my sleeve. The phone was ringing again and her television was on, flashing scene after scene of street people, earthquake victims, terrorists, casualties, the old and infirm. Drug addicts, veterans, nuclear proliferation. Cripples and refugees and single-parent families, crumbling school systems, children eating paint, oil spills and right-wing death squads. A phantasmagoria of dark suffering eyes, idiot munchkins, bigots and torture, trampled gazelles.

"Shut the curtains," she said. "Hurry."

I could see a swarm of something flying straight toward our window, like a flock of giant black birds. I pulled the cord, then listened as beaks or fingernails beat against the glass. Jimmy was cool, smoking a cigarette. Amanda shut off the lights.

"At the current rate of expansion," said a voice from the television, "nothing will remain true. Ecosystems will collapse, populations will explode and facts will simply cease to exist."

"Please," said Amanda, "you've got to leave me alone."

She collapsed onto the beanbag chair, incapacitated. I opened a closet door, scrutinized the contents: sweaters, leotards, a typewriter, a tennis racket, a cattle prod, photographs, empty shoe boxes, Gregorian chants, domes, a river of ice. Acceptable levels of death, contaminated groundwater, dead rhododendrons, a trip to Jamaica.

The pounding continued, the nervous phone.

"I've let two of you in," Amanda said, "and now the whole rest of the world is trying to follow. Listen, I can't handle starving Ethiopians on my doorstep. I'd love to help you, but really, you've got to go."

She curled up into a fetal ball. Jimmy opened the refrigerator door, the glow streaming out into the dark room like the sunbeams that carry Jesus. He picked out a couple of beers, a hunk of raw meat, an apple.

"Let's go," he said.

We walked to the door. It was rattling, being pounded on, but when we opened it no one was there.

"Bye," I said. She wouldn't lift her eyes to look at me. We moved on down the hall, rode the buzzing elevator to the lobby. On the street it was cool again, it felt all right. We'd take care of ourselves.

The summer passed, moved into fall. My skin felt like it might crinkle up and fall off my body, dried-up and oily, my hair heavy with filth. At least my teeth stayed clean, I was always conscientious about stealing a new brush when the bristles got soft, although I never did floss. We kept a watch out for truant officers, anyone who looked like they went to a school. We took ice cream and potato chips from supermarkets, ate at restaurants sometimes and ran out without paying. I was bored with parks and hotel lobbies and streets and the arch. I played video games when I had quarters and almost every day I sat with Traveler, let myself be carried along by the mellow rhapsodies of his voice. He told me about how he used to prowl suburban neighborhoods in Denver, swoop down on unsuspecting barbecues and swipe the meat they were roasting over charcoal. Since then, though, he'd given up both stealing and meat.

An old bag lady came to sit with us. She was all flapping lips and sagging, splotchy flesh, the smell of decay. She chewed tobacco and spit.

"To find and know yourself," said Traveler, "is the only path. To perfect your own soul."

The woman coughed.

"Hogshit, honey," she said. "Don't let this bozo feed you all this eagle-in-the-sky existential bullshit. Man is a social animal, with responsibilities and obligations. Born into discourse, living and swimming in discourse, nothing if not a discursive element. All this talk about the soul to distract us from our real need for organized collective action."

She was wearing purple wool socks, layers of plaid skirts, a sweater, thick and matted wool with green stripes.

"Certainly," said Traveler, "the relation to the Other. But in the long run, to attain enlightenment is an individual project, in the sense that it is a matter between you and the One Absolute Being."

The woman pulled a cigar from her pocket.

"Come on, baby," she said, "light my fire."

Traveler seemed absent for a moment, wistful. He dug some matches from a pocket, held the fire toward her in his cupped palm.

"Listen," said the woman, "I can't quite bear this spiritual enlightenment crap. I haven't always been the sorry creature you see now before you. I studied linguistics at Vassar. I was married to the Secretary of Housing and Urban Development, the bastard. The story of my descent is a complicated one, involving a diagnosis of schizophrenia, a corrupt legal system and a daring escape from the asylum tower with a rope made from cooked spaghetti and hardened pudding."

I liked this woman. She reminded me of my mother, if my mother had been eighty years old, into theories of discourse and living on the streets of St. Louis, collecting scraps in a shopping cart.

"So here I am," she said, "living in poverty, on the streets of the city. I have little use for spiritual values, I'm looking for a revolution."

She blew a smoke ring, up, toward the October sky.

"You know," she said, "I must admit, I was somewhat surprised by the texture of poverty. I always imagined it as something sort of warm and slimy that I could just sink into. It isn't like that at all. It's grainy and coarse. It's hard work."

"You need to learn detachment," said Traveler. "All revolutions fail in the end, progress is only an illusion. Time moves in cycles."

The woman spit a glob of black chew onto the cement.

"Blah, blah, blah," she said. "Cyclical time, cynicism, feelings of impotence. Any excuse not to battle the dominant ideologies. You can't just remove yourself from history, you old fool."

A man in a suit walked by, fished some change out of his pocket and threw it to us. He looked wealthy, plump, a lush glow on his skin.

"Sir," said the woman, "may I ask your opinion? Do you feel history displays an evolutionary quality, ever-ascending spirals of advancement, as the oppressed masses throw off their chains and dance on the graves of their capitalist masters? Do you feel capitalism is a doomed system which is eating up our planet, as the wealthy squander unrenewable resources and litter the landscape with their gaudy plastic trash? Or would you be inclined toward the more Eastern view, history as a series of repetitions, yin and yang, cycles of wealth and poverty, progress and decline? Do you feel the universe will eventually implode, at which point a new universe will be born from its ashes and all that has happened will simply repeat itself, with a few minor variations? What Nietzsche referred to as the eternal recurrence of the silly? Or do you think that the universe will simply hit a dull, lifeless state of entropy which will last for all eternity? Or perhaps you would take the view that while the universe is decaying it is simultaneously evolving, life forms growing more and more complex, and in this process there is hope that some new stage of life will emerge, something so amazing that we could no more imagine it now than a caterpillar could conceive of its eventual butterflyhood?"

"Uh," said the man, "I don't know. Is this some sort of contest? Is there money to be won?"

"No money," said the woman.

He hurried away. Perhaps he wanted to find somebody, or maybe somebody wanted to find him. Perhaps he used a phone, did not rely on chance encounters. I couldn't know such things. In the park drums played, there was dancing. In the meantime, people in the crowd were getting ripped off, losing their concentration, imagining a better world, eating chili dogs.

"I know you, Traveler," the woman said. "I've talked to you before and I know who you are. I was at that concert in Miami where you exposed yourself. How inspiring to see the Lizard King waving a Colt 45 in one hand and his dick in the other at a bunch of screaming teenagers. That was your greatest moment, you know. You've mellowed. You seem to think you can escape from your past. You seem to think you can move through the world, recording observations, as neutral as a camera."

"It's true," conceded Traveler, "that I was fond of the image of the voyeur in my poetry. An image for America in the electronic age. But without detachment there can only be pain. To alleviate suffering one must learn to remove oneself from it."

"To learn not to feel," said the woman. "Obviously you are a member of the booboisie, that class made up of the gullible and the stupid."

She scratched at her crotch, started chewing on a donut. On the other side of the street Amanda walked by, hunched into her coat. I didn't call out to her.

"Would you like a donut?" the woman asked me. "A young girl gave me a whole bag last night at closing time, I didn't even have to dig them out of the trash. Now she is a saint, truly."

I took a donut. It was frosted with dried, crumbling chocolate, pale and falling off. The donut was stale and delicious. Traveler drank his wine.

"But you must understand," said Traveler, "that joy and sorrow are the same thing. The two are inexorably intertwined."

"Is a donut the same as a rumbling stomach?" asked the woman. "Is a warm bed the same as a rainy street? Not to me, honey. Not to me. Give me a swig of wine, I need to wash this donut down."

"I have everything I need," said Traveler. "I am happy."

The woman took a drink, handed back the bottle.

"You are duped," she said. "The romanticization of poverty. The wise and happy bum. I don't believe you even exist, you are just some sick hallucination created by the bourgeoisie to convince me and the rest of the street people that we should be content with our lot in life. They've drugged the water, everybody knows that."

She stood up and wandered off, mumbling.

Traveler was gazing into the distance, where the drums were, and other sounds, indistinguishable. I felt I was beginning to understand the connections; donuts and desire, love and freedom, confusion and life. It started to drizzle, wet and hard, but it couldn't reach us there, under the deli awning, and we were warm together, even if Traveler was a sick hallucination, he kept me happy and warm, covered with clothes that other people had thrown on the streets.

"Something has to be done," I told Jimmy at the gateway to the park. "Because we've got awfully bad karma."

"Shut up," said Jimmy. "I don't need that crap. I stole you a nice wool sweater, made in Peru. What did you get me?"

I brought him a bag of melon chunks and a book I'd stolen on the Zen way of bike riding. We ate the melon together, slurping the juice, staining our lips green. We ate pistachio nuts and crunched the red shells under our feet. He threw the book in the trash.

"I don't ride a bike," said Jimmy. "I never have. Why don't you find me a book on the Zen way of breaking into houses and stealing stuff from rich people. That I might have a use for."

I vowed to search for such a book. I needed to give him something that he wanted. I always felt on shaky ground with Jimmy, like if I didn't give him things he might just leave me. I knew, still, despite everything I'd learned, about stealing and running, without him I'd probably die.

I picked the other book out of the trash. Back when I was little, I used to have a bike.

Later that week Jimmy got sick and at first I was thrilled. I brought him soup, medicine, hot orange juice and toilet paper from the library bathrooms, sat with him while he slept and mumbled. We were not the sort of street people who would just get sick and die, be found like that and buried without a name. We were not the kind of street people that nobody cared about, who lived and died all alone. I'd often imagined Jimmy hurting himself, hit by a car, or fallen from a rooftop, bleeding on the sidewalk. I would run to him, hold his head in my lap, kiss his lips and lick the wounds. He would need me, wouldn't be able to live without me. But now he only got worse, mumbling about fires and wheelchairs and costumes with feathers. He shook with chills, his face gray, his lips all dried out. The night was mean with frost, he needed to be indoors. The cops at the bus station knew us by then, might arrest us, stick us in boxes and ship us straight back to East Liberty. Jimmy was burning up, I got scared. I went to Amanda's, stood outside the glass door, ringing her buzzer. "I'm not home right now," Amanda's voice said, "I've gone away on a much-needed vacation. But please, leave your name and message at the sound of the tone and I'll call you next week." The tone sounded. How could I talk to nobody? How could I tell a machine that Jimmy was dying? That I was, we all were, what could I say? I went back to Jimmy. Something had to be done.

"Maybe I should call the authorities," I said. Jimmy was barely conscious, couldn't give me instructions. I didn't know which authorities to call in situations like this. The Center for Dying Homeless Orphans? "Stay here," I told Jimmy, as if he might leave.

I called the hospital from a pay phone.

"Suppose I had a friend who was dying on the streets, but was running from the law," I said. This was a hypothetical situation. They asked if my friend had insurance. He didn't.

"I'm afraid we'll have to refer you to the free med clinic," they said. The address was right downtown, a few blocks away. I pounded on the door, felt my forehead as I waited. Was I getting sick, too? Maybe we *were* the kind of street people who'd be found dead on the streets after all. An elderly man opened the door. He gave me aspirin and Band-Aids, said funding was cut. "It's all that we've got," he said and sent me away.

The night lasted forever, the sun cracked my skull. I asked strangers for money, a man in a bowtie slapped me so hard I fell to the ground and then gave me three quarters. I took Jimmy into Wendy's, where we sat in a corner booth, drank hot tea with sugar. We stayed there all day, the employees gave us dirty looks, but Jimmy got better, drinking liquids and snoring. I realized Jimmy couldn't be killed. He was the one who would never lose his powers.

After Jimmy recovered I experimented with giving, to bums and cripples on the streets. It seemed a kind of insurance, bartering with destiny. I didn't tell Jimmy, figured he might be mad. Some days I had money, some days not, it depended on if I'd been begging myself, or if Jimmy'd stolen some wallets. I only gave when I didn't have much, when giving meant I'd have to scrounge harder or go a little bit hungry. Otherwise it didn't feel like giving at all. It made me feel decent, like a real human being. I think I always wanted to feel like a good person, just a good person gone bad.

"Dairy products build up phlegm," Traveler warned me, "and you have to go into the fear. Through the fear and out the other side. It's the only way."

"I'll keep that in mind," I said.

"No, really," he said. He looked sad in a way, like I'd never seen him. The day was hazy and cold. "Sometimes you fuck up, you know. We're lucky now, when we fuck up it doesn't much matter, to anybody but ourselves. I remember when I was a rock star. I remember Los Angeles. What an ugly city. Too many motels, murders, money, madness. Too many m-words there . . ."

I sat, waiting for him to come to some conclusion. He never did, just drank some soup I'd brought him, paid for with real money. We sat like that, quiet, as the cold dusk filtered down around us. Traveler fell asleep, snoring gently. I tucked my blanket around his shoulders, left him there like that, went off to look for Jimmy.

I'd discovered I could steal books from chain bookstores in the malls and then sell them to used bookstores for money. Most of those stores didn't have any sort of electronic detection system, you could tell by standing around the entrance, picking up a book on display near the front, and then just stepping back a little bit as you read it. Buzzers didn't go off and you knew. At the used bookstores I could get cash or credit for other, better books. Everyone came out ahead. I found the book for Jimmy and bought it with credit. *The Zen Way of Breaking into People's Houses and Stealing Their Worldly Possessions.*

We sat reading on the steps of a huge office building, just down the street from Amanda's building, all metal and reflecting glass. "As you liberate your fellow sentient beings from the bondage of their material things," it said, "concentrate on those which are small, valuable, easy to pawn: money, jewelry or the smaller kitchen appliances."

It was cold. Sleeping in the park was impossible and we were so tired. I knew it couldn't go on. We were into November, everything dead.

"We've got to go," said Jimmy. "New York, someplace warm."

I went to the bus station the next day and Traveler wasn't there. I walked around and came back and he was still gone. I felt empty and a strange terror inside. My stomach was all bunched up, I had food, but I couldn't eat it. I kept walking, the wind was wild, and cold. Gusts blew down the street between buildings, like in a tunnel. It made my eyes water, I bent into it, people were blown around the sidewalks and paper bags and trash. A man fell to the sidewalk, suddenly, as if struck from above. I leaned over him, saw a penny embedded in his skull. I ran.

I ducked into a phone booth, stood, staring at the numbers, the wind rocking the booth, whistling. The glass was creaking. A woman sat back against a building, watching me. She looked like a rodent. She looked like she hated me and wanted to kill me. I looked away, pressed my fingers against the glass. It was cold and smooth as outer space. I stared at the phone, then picked it up and listened. The crackling dial tone was like no sound I knew. I thought of Andalusia, of Melissa and Seth and Traveler. I even thought of the orphanage.

I had dimes. That was not the problem.

I hunched over, my forehead in my hands, and found that I was crying. I had never been like this. I tried to tell myself that joy and sorrow were the same thing. I stopped then. But it hit me again, harder this time, like something thrown from a roof-top. I cried hard and I couldn't stop.

3

Others are dead. I, on the other hand, watch colored light streak the horizon between the sky and the Earth. I move. I feel larger than just myself and this time seems to contain more than just what is.

These are the facts:

Δ

The man Kenny is beside me, driving this car. He's a Viet-nam vet and he's magic. He has a beard and a plaid shirt, cream and navy, burnt sienna and plum. He sells drugs sometimes, though he's been lying low by request of the Feds. He has money, but prefers to travel without using it, collecting emer-gency travel funds at police stations or town halls along the way. He's going home to Virginia, deep into the hills and valleys, to get some things together, repair his scepter and contemplate the loss of his woman. He can make things appear. Food. Gas. Women. Matter is just slowed-down energy after all. Mind is pure energy and one must only know how to harness the source. He has other theories as well.

"Now just look on a dollar bill," he said to me last night. "Whose picture do you see? George Washington. And you know who the founder of the Masons was? Go on, take a guess."

"George Washington?" I ventured.

He nodded. "And then there's the pyramid. What the hell is a pyramid doing on an American dollar bill? It all ties in. The eyeball, window to the mind. Pure energy. The only two pres-idents who weren't Masons were Lincoln and Kennedy. And we all know what happened to them."

The Masons are the Antichrist, he told me. It wasn't too difficult to figure out. You just have to use your Mind. He said other things as well. Prestidigitation and Agent Orange, jungle heat and heroin, swamps and sorcery, black voodoo depths and Coca-Cola. I closed my eyes and let his words fill the darkness, his words and the heat. He smells like wintergreen, which makes me think of sledding down hills in Des Moines in the snow, despite the fact that it is hot, hot, hot, even at dawn there's this burning on the land. He is quiet now and I'm thinking about the sewage dump in Des Moines, back behind trees and railroad tracks, it glowed and looked like the surface of the moon. I think about the feel of Andalusia's fingers on my penis, in the bathtub, and the taste of skin, Jimmy's once in Florida, or Frita Bob or a man in Wyoming who tasted like menthol cigarettes, and I remember huddling for warmth in the coal car of a moving train, on a cold night, with a strange, black-haired vagabond named Berke. The coal chalked black on my shoes and hands and it smelled like a charcoal grill. I roasted marshmallows with Jessica Moon not long ago on a crisp mountain night with the stars singing like fireflies in the universe overhead.

Kenny says, "Sunrise always reminds me of slaughtered children."

Δ

Children sleep, open-mouthed heads on pillows, against windows, in cars that pass us, serene. The sun is just up, nobody needs to talk. At dawn I feel new, just born, as if I'm seeing the world for the first time, as if I have no history at all. We're through Kentucky and into West Virginia now. We stopped last night in Lexington, got food from the authorities and gas so we could keep on driving. They always have funds for that purpose, Kenny told me, because town authorities would prefer that people like himself and myself keep right on moving through. There's a bond here between us, an unspoken understanding. We are outsiders, we do what we must. They had a shelter there, but it was dark and hot and rodent droppings squished under our feet. He took a pillow and we moved outside of town, slept for a little while in the car. He's a veteran and a magician. He doesn't have to sleep in a place like that. I wouldn't have been so picky; it was cramped in the car and now the muscles of my legs ache something fierce.

Δ

Vietnam: a country on the east coast of the Indochinese Peninsula. Embodying the oldest continuous civilization in Southeast Asia, it is today best known as the principal arena of the Vietnam War (1957–1975), one of the bitterest and lengthiest conflicts of the twentieth century.

Population: 57,036,000. Area: 127,242 square miles. 57,605 Americans dead in the war, 303,700 wounded. 499,000 South Vietnamese dead, 220,357 wounded. Approximately 440,000 North Vietnamese dead. These figures do not include civilians. According to the encyclopedia in the Lexington library, chemical herbicides destroyed enough food to feed 600,000 people for a year and enough timber to meet the country's needs for thirty years.

I was just a child. This is what I know.

Δ

"I wake in a cold sweat, sometimes," Kenny says. "It's never left me, that fear. The war was a brutal experience for those of us whose mental faculties were already in questionable balance."

He laughs. I'm not quite sure if he's serious. I like Kenny, he's good-natured and gregarious, but it occurs to me that I'm waiting for him to explode. Although I've ridden with a dozen Vietnam vets and never seen one snap, I impose my prejudices every time, my own notions of instability and sudden violence. I imagine their minds stretched taut between two worlds, between this moment and some crucial event in the past, much like my own. I wait for the vibrations to get too intense, the mighty twang, an explosion of frenzy and fear.

"You follow baseball?" Kenny asks. "If the Cubs don't do it this year, I swear they never will."

△

They don't believe it's true anymore, that something can't arise from nothing. A universe from a vacuum, a scream from an empty room. This is not true either:

As a child I went down to the railroad tracks. When it rained the rails became slick with black grease which stuck to the soles of my feet. I spread raw bacon on the tracks, then ran as a train came thundering from the distance. The bacon derailed the trains, cars burst open, spilling grain in mounds. Animals emerged from the trees, deer and zebra and tribes of rabbit, to feed. We children, we buried ourselves in the grain, only our noses sticking out, listened for each other's murmurs, whispering, until strangers came, men in black with salt shakers. We pretended we were victims, dying.

We still are, but so much remains secret: the way our own lives walk beside us, arbitrarily remembering and forgetting.

Back home in Des Moines, when I delivered the paper and walked across lawns in the dark, sometimes the fear would begin. Black things, large and wriggling, the very stabbed and bloody heart of the night, following close behind me, footsteps in my ears, green eyes glowing from the emptiness on the other side of picture windows. I had to do something to distract myself from that dread. I whistled. I wasn't much of a whistler, but I whistled anyway, always the same song, it wasn't a real song, just one I made up in my head. But it gave me a rhythm, a movement, kept me aware that even in my fear I was safe, and at least for the moment, alive and moving on.

Later, in St. Louis or Minneapolis, I would find myself alone and late, in the midst of wet and deserted streets, eyes in the alleys, heartbeats on fire escapes, cigarettes glowing in darkened doorways. I wanted to whistle then, but Jimmy'd warned me not to. Whistling, he said, would be the same as slicing your own throat. Whistling was a dead giveaway. It showed everyone you were scared.

Δ

We left St. Louis, me and Jimmy, for New York, although we never got there. Cold gusts of wind, sleet. In Hannibal there were dozens of Mark Twain gift shops and Samuel Clemens restaurants. I stole a copy of *Huckleberry Finn,* while Jimmy got popcorn and sunglasses. Huck and Jim, George and Lennie, Jack and Neal, we weren't the first ones. But our history was muddled, filled with things I didn't know. Was Father Larry dead? Did Jimmy come from France? In East Liberty, the white-skinned orphan Edward had stuck tacks in his thumbs and watched them bleed. Our thumbs wiggled in the freezing wind. Barns and trees, falling leaves, kaleidoscopic landscapes, bristling brown fields. People saw our thumbs and stopped to pick us up.

We received rides from lean, leathery, solitary men in cars with doors that wouldn't open from the outside and a history of trouble with women. We received rides from those with something to get off their chests, from those who needed to release the pressure of misery and hopelessness building inside. We received rides from those who had lived lives of misery and hopelessness in the past, but were over that now; through the grace of Jesus, the revealed truth of karma, the fraternal brotherhood of Amway distributors or the simple discovery that the secret of happiness was to let go of all expectation and desire.

We received rides from men and women hungry for symbols. We received rides from those who might be described as marginal, although what exactly they were the margins of I cannot say. There was kindness, there was hope. There was confes-

sion and regret. White lies, drunken mistakes, love betrayed.
We provided a service, an ear, we forgave them their sins. They
took us farther on our way.

"My girlfriend left me," explained the man who'd lost his
eye in a wet-towel fight in a junior high locker room. "I declared
my love for her on the second anniversary of the day on which
we first consummated our desire, under a thick blanket on a
Greyhound bus. We were both going to Los Angeles then, to
find something better. But she mistook my genuine sentiments
of love for sarcasm. Just last week she ran off with a nineteen-
year-old drifter named Toby who gives full body massages to
aging, wealthy widows and drives an MGB."

We became receptacles for stories, anecdotes and interesting facts. Theoretically, hummingbirds cannot fly. There is only
one mammal, aside from humans, which is sexually active con-
tinuously, a kind of monkey, and they are, of course, insane.
There are psychopaths who wander into big-city hospitals, pretend they are doctors and treat the sick and dying. Government
files exist proving the existence of intelligent life beyond our
planet. A man from New Hampshire, with a license plate that
said LIVE FREE OR DIE, explained that the universe contains
eleven dimensions, but we experience only four. There is a
mentally retarded child in Alabama with an IQ approximating
that of shelled marine life, who, nonetheless, can tell you what
day of the week any day was, if you give him the date, going
back for the last six thousand years. Leap years and the transi-
tion from B.C. to A.D. do not faze him. There is an orphanage
somewhere in the midwest so luxurious that children are liter-
ally murdering their parents to get in.

Words, words, words, we collected them, tried to fit them
in somewhere, stored them, forgot them. For the most part these
men and women were not interested in our lives, they had their
own set of assumptions concerning us. We had no integrated
vision anyway, we merely agreed.

"The problem with America today is the lack of assimila-
tion," we were told. "Immigrants no longer feel the need to
adapt, to Americanize, goddammit. If they didn't want to be real

Americans, why didn't they stay in Cambodia, for Christ's sake?"

We nodded, vigorously.

The moon waxed. We watched the eyes of strangers to detect those individuals inclined toward human sacrifice. The moon waned. Eventually, we arrived in Minneapolis.

It wasn't New York and it certainly wasn't warm. Our maps were no good, our destinations never achieved. But we stayed. Christmas bells, Santa Claus on every corner. Jangled nerves, Eskimo bars for dinner, bad sleep. We huddled in the stairway of a parking garage at night, walked the downtown mall in the daytime. The public library was enormous and clean, but there weren't many comfortable chairs. We didn't have the right clothes, the snow wasn't innocent, our skin dried and blued. We asked for money inside downtown stores and skyways. People were generous for the holidays, patted our heads, wished us a festive season.

The crazed woman held a screaming baby.

"Spare some change?" she asked, panic in her voice, thumping the baby's back as its whining increased. "I got to feed my baby."

I gave her two dollars I had in my pocket.

"That was stupid," said Jimmy, as we walked away. "It's only a trick, it's acting. The baby's only a prop."

I told myself otherwise. Long days I had on my own, we separated, walked, explored, scrounged. We spent Thanksgiving at a mission, where women stood in a circle and sang "Kumbaya," fed us turkey and cranberry Jell-O. They sang and they sang and they sang.

One day while I was fishing quarters and dimes out of a blue fountain inside the mall, a couple offered Jimmy money to let them take pictures of him naked. They had no fingerprints, no hair on their bodies, no permanent address.

"It was easy," Jimmy told me. "She told me how to pose and he showed me all his cameras. He had one that killed people at the same time it took their picture, but he never used that one on me."

"Did they take a lot?" I asked.

Jimmy shrugged. The city would be filled with his image. I glimpsed them everywhere, passed under tables, delivered on dark corners, set down in briefcases and then snatched up by men in dark glasses. Glossy photos, secret flesh, hidden between pages of scholarly books, hurriedly shut whenever I approached. A splattering of warmth moved in surreptitious undercurrents through this, the coldest city in the world. They had posed him in their hotel room in brilliant white light, sweat streaming off the lunar baldness of their heads.

"Hold this teddy bear," she said.

"Touch yourself here."

"Tilt your head sideways."

Jimmy went back for more sessions. I was terrified they'd kill him or turn him into a slave. The photos circulated just outside my vision and Jimmy always came back, sometimes with scratches or bruises or welts on his arms.

I wandered through the seasonal hustle and bustle, armloads of packages, gift wrap and tinsel and bells in the streets. It was rumored that Jesus wandered the skyway system as well, but I only saw shoppers and traffic below on the streets. Mornings were deserted, frozen, out of context. Jimmy's heart beat irregular rhythms, we wandered through dreams of the west. Pine trees in parks, blue, almost electric. The sky lightening, electric as well, everybody waking and busying and neon-charged. This is what happened and this is what happened: Jimmy smoked, I shivered, everything blue and gray and broken. Old people with purplish skin walked zombified as naked bodies were tossed up from the river. I wanted to fuck somebody, I wanted to fuck Jimmy: I knew that would change everything, transform my life into something warm and distant.

I woke once, a cold morning, five A.M., walking, shivering, waiting for some place to open. So many mornings, the cold, the people who looked at me like they thought I was scum, the dull rage, the scrounging for change so I could drink a cup of something hot. In Minneapolis the streets were filled with us. The man was screaming at his girlfriend, at five in the morning,

"I'm tired! I'm tired of living on the streets!" She put her hands
on his shoulders. From across the street I could see him shaking. I walked on, curled up in the back stairway of the parking
garage, tried to get a little more rest.

Δ

When we crossed the border into West Virginia, the green
sign said, "Welcome to Wild, Wonderful West Virginia!" Kenny
is talking again now, something about the different kinds of
vegetation in Vietnam, but I'm barely listening, I keep catching
myself singing that John Denver song about country roads taking me home, to the place I belong, and I read the familiar
phrases on other cars' license plates. You have a friend in Pennsylvania. New Jersey, the Garden State. Indiana—Back Home
Again.

I've been here before, West Virginia. I recognize the sounds
of the screaming earth. Things seem skewed, horizontal, houses
built into the sides of things. On the land around us there are
trees and grass. In Vietnam there were different things, swamps
and granite hills. I imagine Kenny there, feet stuck in yellow
ooze, looking past the physical reality of jungle and dismem-
berment to a threshold of liquid light, some dazzling white beauty
on the horizon, just past annihilation. Snakes and parrots and
vultures. The varieties of life. The spice. Coriander, cumin,
cayenne pepper.

The road divides, the sign points us to Cumberland. Kenny
veers off in that direction, while I'd prefer to move toward
Wheeling. I was in Cumberland once before, I froze to death
there, the winter before last. Eleven degrees and nowhere to
go. The town was evil, the shelters closed, the damned walked
down by the railroad tracks. Finally, the police let me sleep in
their doorway. People stepped over my huddled body through
the night. At six they kicked me out, but the donut shop was
open then, I traded *The Complete Works of William Shake-*

speare for a cup of coffee and a long john. I'd stolen it from a
chain bookstore in Washington, D.C., and it was too heavy to
carry around anyway. I only read *King Lear*. Leaving that town,
I was spit at, but then a car pool of Taco Joe's employees listening to Aerosmith took me farther on my way.

There is no logical procession of geography; the shortest
distance between two points, for Kenny, is not a line. He is
magic. He might easily arrive in Virginia the day before yester-
day. The backseat is filled with tropical fruit and red balloons
that weren't there minutes ago. Cumberland didn't exist then
either, but now the sign says it is so.

Cumberland. A pickle is, in fact, nothing but a cucumber. A
cucumber which has been pickled. I never realized that, until
it dawned on me in a diner in Eugene, just two weeks ago, eating sandwiches with Jessica Moon. What did I think a pickle
was before then? I didn't think about it at all. But now, there is
a knife on the seat, between me and Kenny. I think about that.

"Murder isn't such a big deal," Kenny says, "once you realize that death is an illusion." He lights a cigarette. "Existence
is murder. People think just because they're reading a book or
watching a film they aren't murdering anybody. But it's everything. Reading, breathing, meditating. Murder, murder, murder. What's the fuss? But torture, now that's a different thing
altogether. Now that's a big deal."

I avoid the temptation to nod, whatever I may actually think.
He's watching the road anyway. In my silence, agreement is
implied.

He licks his lips. The AM radio plays the Doors, *Texas Radio
and the Big Beat*, Jim Morrison singing, or Traveler.

"It's all about power," Kenny says. "The unfortunate fact of
our times is that most of the power lies in the hands of the
bureaucracy of evil, actors and former heads of the CIA. Vietnam,
El Salvador, Guatemala, Chile, East Timor. As long as the
president doesn't personally visit our neighborhoods and rape
the girl next door, who gives a shit? As long as he doesn't take
her away, dunk her in filthy water, shove her head in bags of

lime and stick lit cigarettes into her nipples in our own lawns
and basements. As long as he doesn't sit in our own fucking
living rooms and shove his presidential dick up our own cunts
and assholes, doesn't pry our own skulls open with crowbars
and leave our bloodied, rotting corpses splattered with
presidential semen hanging from trees for the vultures. Our
government's just a giant sex killer, an enormous Son of Sam."

The way Kenny smokes. I can't get the word *combustion*
out of my head.

"Now take this war on drugs. Listen, the FBI, they are
entirely aware of the fact that I sell drugs, they've told me this.
They have the proof, they simply don't care. They are holding
it there, thinking they can use it to control me, anytime they
please. They don't give a shit about drugs, they're the ones who
make the most money off it. They want to control us, that's all
it is."

There's a billboard up ahead advertising a wax museum.
We pass it without comment.

"They are mistaken about me, however. I know the secrets
of power, it's all about Mind and words. It all comes down to
speaking the magic words."

He may be on to something here about Mind and words. I
can't deny that truth sometimes lingers in the unlikeliest vehicles.
Gremlins, Darts, El Torinos.

"I can make just about anything appear," he says. "I'm a
powerful man in my own way. Although with my scepter broken
I feel a little bit empty, a little bit dizzy. Like I need something
to hold on to, while my thoughts keep flying by too fast for me
to get a grip on. I'm always thinking, that's something you should
know about me. When I was a kid I tested a genius."

"A genius," I say. I know that's no guarantee of luck or even
safety. The seed that is our sanity falls on the rocky ground
regardless. Or the thorny ground or the sandy ground. I look
out over West Virginia and understand how scarce the fertile
soil truly is.

"I've got something stuck in my teeth," he says.

He picks at his gums with the blade of his knife. The sun is moving up, the heat increasing. Nothing else seems real. This is where I'm at.

Δ

3.5 billion years ago, the first living thing. By 700 million years ago warm seas hold worms and other creatures with specialized cells grouped in organs for feeding, locomotion, reproduction and so on. 4 million years ago we walk on two legs. 40,000 or 100,000 disappeared in Guatemala? 500,000 or 3 million homeless? 6 million or 8 million Jews killed by the Nazis? One theory says that the Holocaust was only possible because of the outrageous inflation that plagued Germany in the twenties. Carrying bags and buckets full of bills, paying millions for a loaf of bread, numbers had lost all meaning to the German population. Or maybe they had themselves convinced they really didn't know what was going on.

That smell of wintergreen, Kenny's smell, it makes me think about Christmas. I'm not sure if it's after-shave, chewing tobacco or Life Savers. On the radio the Allman Brothers sing about being born a ramblin' man, a gambling father who wound up on the wrong end of a gun, birth in the backseat of a Greyhound bus. The sunrise is blue and bright and we are driving into it. I think about Alaska, although I've never been there. I think about snow.

Δ

It snowed in Des Moines, even the winter that Dad had no job and Mom was working at McDonald's, right before Christmas. It gave me this sense of a fresh start, the smell of it floating down. On Christmas Eve I sat in my room, reading books about UFOs, stars and galaxies, Hal Lindsey's predictions of the coming Biblical apocalypse in *The Late Great Planet Earth* and the Book of Revelations from my tiny lime Bible. I was ready for the end of the world. I was bored, getting erections then letting them subside so I could enjoy the distraction of getting another one. I could hear Mom downstairs doing the dishes. Other Christmases it had seemed to take forever for her to wash those dishes, I would sweat and pace, imagine what waited in all those packages under the tree. That year I didn't want the waiting to end, didn't want to find out. I wanted to sleep, but I'd been sleeping twelve, fourteen hours a day every day of school vacation. There was a quiet downstairs, low voices, Mom and Dad. I heard her coming up the stairs.

"Matt? Matt, we're ready."

I lay there for a minute, not wanting to respond, wanting to disappear. I'd been listening to the neighbors in the other half of the duplex again.

"Matt?"

"I'm coming," I said, but I didn't move. Mrs. Pennel was screaming at her husband for ruining her Christmas somehow. She said she wanted her Christmas to be perfect, like in the commercials for Butterball turkeys on TV, with a lot of happy relatives smiling and sitting around the table.

"We don't have any happy relatives," her husband said. "It isn't my fault if your father's an asshole. He's your father, not mine. You're to blame if anybody is."

For a second there, like a flicker in my gums or my nasal cavity, I'm sure that I realized my future: this would all be over soon, I'd be alone and lost forever. It was the time between the bed and the crisis that I didn't want to endure. But there was a dim hope that something magic was about to happen, that my gifts would be fabulous, that everything I'd ever wanted would be in boxes downstairs.

I went down, past the Sears portrait on the wall. The living room was dark and blinking, Christmas lights masking-taped across the walls. Mom had cut a few branches off the bluish pine bushes in front of the duplex, since we didn't have a

Christmas tree that year. They were tacked onto walls and perched on the end table, next to Mom and Dad on the sofa. Candles burned on the windowsills, melting Christmas trees and tall red and white sticks. They smelled like bayberry, coconut and wax. There was a blank look on Dad's face, a dull pain, and such a bright smile on Mom's that I had this urge to set her hair on fire, throw all the gifts out the window and electrocute myself with the Christmas lights.

I sat quietly beside them.

"OK," said Mom, "before we open the presents, I'll read the Christmas story."

She opened her Bible. She did this every year. Before it was always a justified ritual, to prolong the suspense, an exquisite sort of pain. Now it was just stupid.

"And it came to pass in those days, that there went out a decree from Caesar Augustus," she began, "that all the world should be taxed. And this taxing was first made when Cyrenius was governor of Syria."

Dad's eyes glassed over. His stomach rumbled. The Christmas lights flashed off and on, on the wall, our faces glowing red or orange or blue. Out the window the street was empty, white mists of snow snaking across it. Nothing was happening anywhere. I tried to imagine I was someplace else. I couldn't think of anyplace else to be.

"... and she brought forth her firstborn son, and wrapped him in swaddling clothes, and laid him in a manger; because there was no room for them in the inn ..."

I wondered what the presents were. They weren't a bike, I knew that sure enough. How easy it would have been for the candles to tip over, for the house to burn down. What would we save, where would we go?

"And, lo, the angel of the Lord came upon them, and the glory of the Lord shone round about them: and they were sore afraid."

She finished, shut the book.

"Turn thou us unto thee, O Lord," said Dad, "and we shall be turned; renew our days as of old. But thou hast utterly rejected us; thou art very wroth against us. Lamentations, Chapter Five, verses twenty-one and twenty-two."

He folded his hands in his lap. Mom's face was confused. She coughed.

"OK," she said, and she knelt on the floor, picked out one present for me and one for Dad.

"Thank you," said Dad and we started to tear off the paper.

"Don't rip it," Mom said. "We can reuse that paper next year, if you're just a little bit careful."

We unwrapped them slowly, picking off the cellophane tape, folding the crinkled wrapping paper. Dad got a really nice pen. I got an enormous bag of M&Ms.

"There's more for you, Matt," said Mom. There were two other boxes under the tree and they were both for me. We hadn't got Mom anything. I opened each one carefully, drawing out the agony. The first was a J.R.R. Tolkien calendar with pictures of hobbits and dragons and elves. The other one was a pair of shoes. I felt sick. Shoes for Christmas.

"Mom," I said, "these aren't Nikes. I told you I needed a pair of Nikes."

"Oh, Matt," she said, "these are just as good as Nikes. See? They've even got the stripe on the side, they look almost just the same."

Mom sat between us and put her arms around us. I felt all squished around inside. I couldn't wear those shoes to school. They were dorky and ugly. Fake Nikes were worse than the shoes I had. It would look like I was trying to fool someone.

I squeezed out from beside her, hurried up to my room. I lay on my bed and I hated her. I hated everything. I remember it then, thinking that I'd be better off without parents at all, I may have even wished it then, the first time: that I didn't have her. That she was dead. I listened. Next door someone was crying, a door slammed, the sound of shattering lights.

4

It was kind of pointless collecting for my paper route, nobody had any money after Christmas, they mostly told me to come back later. It was dark early, but fresh snow on the ground made everything seem brighter. Mom didn't hear me come in, she was crouched on the floor of the kitchen, clutching the phone.

"Yes," I heard her say, "thank God I finally got a human being. I've been trying Dial-It services all afternoon and all I get are these stupid recordings. They haven't been any help at all."

I could tell that she'd been crying. I moved soft into the living room and listened.

"I tried Dial-a-Prayer, Dial-an-Inspiration, Dial-a-Thought-for-the-Day. I just wanted somebody to talk to, I guess. I tried Dial-an-Attempt-to-Make-Sense-of-the-Modern-World and Dial-a-Stab-at-Order-in-the-Midst-of-Chaos. I even called Dial-a-Meat-Free-Recipe and Dial-a-Horoscope. My horoscope told me this would be a difficult month. It said I'd be faced with sickness, blindness, ignorance and deceit. It said I'd have to confront the endless assault of boredom and the mundane. It said this would be a good month just to stay in bed, or else to go shopping to perk up my spirits. I'll tell you, I'd love to stay in bed, but somebody has to feed us. I'd love to go shopping, but that's just the problem. We're all out of money."

On the way home I had stopped at the bowling alley, spent two dollars of quarters on video games. The sounds were still in my head, the ching ching ching of the video games, the crashing of bowling pins, the crescendo of smoky voices and laughter.

"It's just, I don't know what to do. I feel all empty and useless inside, like everything is falling apart. Whatever I do, it doesn't seem to be worth anything at all."

Coming from the bowling alley I'd passed Dad at the bar he went to. I'd opened the heavy door and stepped inside. It

was warm and smoky, the red bar lights glowing fuzzy. I stood
there, snow melting off my tennis shoes. Dad was sitting at the
bar. Even in the darkness he looked pink.

"I feel like I've been forgotten, like nobody will listen to
me. I feel ugly and small."

Dad had been staring at the TV, some news show, wars in
the Third World, starving African babies, disaster everywhere,
in bright colors. The newscasters were calm and sexy in an inor-
ganic sort of way. "Dad," I said, but he didn't hear me, he didn't
look. Nobody looked at me, they were all laughing or watching the TV. There was a commercial for beer, with rugged
men on mountaintops, shooting the rapids, laughing with
gusto.

At home, the TV wouldn't come in right, the picture was
garbled. Nobody fixed it. Nobody fixed anything, we were all
too tired.

Mom kept talking and talking into the phone, everything,
her job, Dad, the bills and dead lizards. Other things, things I
never would have known. She talked about her parents, farmers
who'd died in a boating accident when I was a baby. She talked
about the way she would feel when she was just a little girl,
waking up in the night and crying, for no reason at all. She talked
about being pregnant, how she wasn't married, and I realized
that I was the baby in question, I was the only one she'd had.
She said she was always afraid that Dad had only married her
because of that, and that really, he never loved her at all.

I wasn't sure how I should feel about these things. It seemed
like a different world, like things a kid shouldn't know. She said
she felt so exhausted all the time, like she just wanted to curl
up somewhere and sleep for fifty years. I sat there listening until
she hung up. She said thank you before she did, and her voice
sounded better. She went into the backyard, walked in the falling snow.

I went over to the phone. Next to it was a list, WHAT DO I
WANT. I'd seen Mom making this list months ago, when I went
to the baseball game with Mrs. Pennel.

WHAT DO I WANT:

To do something well and know that I am accomplishing something without having to have the "feeling" that comes from recognition and praise from other people. What particular thing would I like to do well?

House: Get done each week: Laundry, ironing (a few sessions), Mending (each week's plus grad. reduce accumulation), menu planning and groc. shopping, clean out frig., vac. and dust all rooms plus one xtra cleaning task.

Reading, writing letters, eve. free for Jeremy, Matt, visiting, etc.

Matt: More patience.

Teach to assume responsibility.

Jeremy: Learn to really listen and understand him.

From marriage: A feeling of warmth, of being loved, listened to. I want our marriage to be imp. enough so that he'll take the time to think and talk about us—how we can grow in our understanding of each other. How we can complement each other and learn from our differences. I want him to face honestly his fears, needs. I want to be able to share my deepest longings, dreams, moments of inspiration, beauty, learning. I want to sit down together in our home and talk or read or listen to music and have some of our experiences of physical lovemaking grow out of moments of emotional and spiritual closeness.

I put the list down. Teach to assume responsibility? Physical lovemaking? I looked out the window for her, couldn't see her at all. I felt like I had acid running down my throat, like I understood nothing at all. Dial-a-Listening-Ear. I called it.

"This is Joe," said the voice, "at Dial-a-Listening-Ear. Go on. Tell me your troubles. I want to hear them. That's why I'm here. I care about you."

I waited. "Yes," I said, finally. "This is my problem. I was kidnapped by space aliens and taken to the distant planet Raygatron, where they inserted fuzzy disks into my brain. They put tubes in my belly button, they told me they were doing experiments so that they could rescue the human race."

"I see," said the voice. "Go on."

I didn't say anything.

"I understand," he said. "Mmm hmm, yes."

I sat and listened. Periodically the voice would affirm his agreement and understanding. I hung up the phone.

Lizard ghosts haunted me at night, I didn't get the clothes I wanted, or the bike. Dad continued being pink and silent. He'd put an ad in the paper to sell his motorcycle, but nobody called. It was winter. People drove in cars, or took the bus.

My parents fought in their quiet, often silent way. I was talented when it came to provoking tensions.

"Is something wrong with the phone?" I asked at dinner one night. "I tried to call Bobby McGrane earlier but the phone was dead or something."

I knew full well that it had been disconnected, had been waiting all week for men in white suits with enormous wire cutters to pound on our door, stomp muddy through our kitchen, rip out cords and wires indiscriminately. I drank my water, looked up at Dad.

"The phone's been disconnected, honey," said Mom quietly. "You'll have to make arrangements with your friends at school, or else borrow the Tyndall's phone for a while."

She cut into her meat. Dad stared at her.

"The phone's been disconnected," he said.

She didn't look up, continued slicing through flesh and gristle.

"Bastards," he said.

"Jeremy," said Mom, "please. I told you the bill was due today. I guess we can make do without a phone, just until you get back to work."

"Sure," said Dad, "That's fucking great. Under 'phone number' on job applications I'll simply write *nonexistent. Unable to communicate with the outside world. Lacking the necessary tools for discourse in the postmodern age.*"

Mom didn't look up.

"Seems to me," she said, "you don't have to worry about that until you actually fill out some applications."

Dad put down his fork. He got up from the table, grabbed his jacket, slammed the screen door on his way out.

There was a thaw in late January, just before my twelfth birthday. I took my bike out, my old one-speed, and rode it, up Skyview Drive, huffing and puffing up the steep incline and then resting at the top, looking out over Des Moines, the melting snow, sand on the streets, potholes and rusting cars. The view from up there was enormous. I could see the capitol building, wooded areas and golf courses, the end of town and the places beyond it. I felt omniscient. I felt angry. I needed a new bike, a ten-speed. I felt like I wanted to risk something, to destroy something, to fly.

I started down the long hill, felt the gathering speed rushing into my face and held my hands back, in the air. I flew down, no-handed, straight, cold air rushing up into me and through my hair. I was smiling and blood was rushing, the bottom of the hill was coming up so fast and I knew there was sand there but I was flying and it wasn't even the sand that did it, I felt the front tire begin to wobble, just a little bit, I felt the fear, reached for the handlebars but knew it was too late, I was flying and the bottom of the hill was there before me, the bike slid sideways and I was scraping along beneath it, then beside it, and rolling and the cement and sky all around.

It was only along my hand that I was bleeding, my knuckles bleeding, dry in the cold, and one deep gash in the side of my hand that wouldn't stop. I sat in the middle of the street and there was nobody around. I stood. The front fender and tire of my bike were all twisted, the seat sideways, the handlebars scraped. I smiled. They would have to get me a new bike now, they would have to.

I walked the bike slowly through the streets to my house, blood dripping from my hand, and my head was singing, tiny explosions. I felt all white and drained. I left the bike in the yard and walked into the house. It was quiet. I went upstairs. Mom was stretched out on her bed, sleeping, even smiling, she looked like an angel there in her white nightgown, white all around her, sheets and clothes and pillow, breathing gently. Her stiff, yellow uniform was crumpled in the corner. She smelled like french fries. I held my breath, leaned over the bed and let my blood drip onto the sheets, then walked out, leaving red dribbles on her bedroom floor, down the stairs and in the kitchen.

I washed my hand, put a Band-Aid on. I walked outside and down the street, not knowing where I was going, not going any- where, imagined her horror when she woke up and found the blood. I knew then that I was a terrible kid. I felt through the Band-Aid the deepness of my cut. I knew this one would always be with me, I was proud. I knew that it would scar.

When I returned home Mom was waiting for me, sitting in the kitchen.

"Matt," she said, "I want to talk to you."

She twisted her fingers with her hand and looked at the ceiling. *She won't get me a bike,* I thought. *She'll put me in an insane asylum for bleeding on her bed.* I got ready to hate her guts.

"I have a book for you. I brought it home from the Lutheran Church. I think you should look at it."

She set it on the table in front of her, like she couldn't bear to hand it to me directly.

"You're getting older," she said.

I picked it up, read the cover. *Growing to Manhood in Christ.* I knew what this was about.

"I know this is a difficult time for you," Mom said. "But this book might help. This book will explain everything you need to know."

She didn't look at me, she looked out the window. There were a boy and a girl on the cover of the book, smiling, holding hands. Mom felt she had to do these things, I knew, because Dad was falling apart. I took the book to my room, sat alone in the quiet, reading, angry and filled with shame.

"You may find yourself dreaming about a pretty girl in your

class," the text read, "dreaming about hugging her and maybe even kissing her. You may wake up and find a sticky wet spot on your sheets. This is called a nocturnal emission and it is OK. It is nothing to feel guilty about."

I peeled off my Band-Aid to look at my cut. She didn't even notice. I hid the book in the bottom of a drawer, under socks and underwear and my Iowa Oaks T-shirt. The book didn't help anything. The book had nothing at all to do with my life.

Δ

We walked down the Minneapolis street in a thin drizzle. Neon lights glowed over us, coloring the murky night. The man watched us, circled and followed.

"Just follow me on this," said Jimmy. "This is an opportunity. You can see what he wants, clear."

I put my hands in my pockets, watched. I liked rain in the city when I had an umbrella that hadn't collapsed, retreated into itself like a crustacean. I didn't have one. Lights flashed red, inside and out.

"Stop," said Jimmy. "Wait for him."

We stood. I felt the city growing, closing in. The man vanished and then was there, beside us and behind.

"Good evening," he said. "Do you boys like money?"

Jimmy's head turned slightly.

"You know all about money, I'll bet," he said. "About all the wonderful things it can do."

"Oh," said Jimmy. "Sure."

The man laughed, cold feathered particles from his throat.

"I know boys like you. Life has nothing to offer but sordid sex and mind-destroying drugs, you've found."

"We want money," said Jimmy.

"Heroin? Cocaine? What is it you use?"

"Are you hell-bent on corrupting us?" asked Jimmy. "Or do you just want to take our picture?"

The man pulled his coat collar around him, slick black plastic, reflecting smeared lights. He smiled.

"Yes, I have money. A hundred dollars for the both of you. You like money, hm?"

"Yes," said Jimmy, "we like money. A hundred apiece."

"Ho, ho, ho," said the man. It was getting closer to Christmas. "You think you're the only cute little boys on the streets tonight?"

He walked away. An insane man asked me not to give him a cigarette, no matter what. The rain stopped, then started again. The people on the streets drew no meaning from this, merely opened and closed umbrellas as the occasion warranted.

"He'll be back," said Jimmy.

"Everything falls apart!" exclaimed a man with rubbery legs as long as myself and ran into the rain laughing. Vampires distributed pamphlets. Taxis started and stopped, thick incense burned under awnings, jewelry and roses were sold. I tilted my head back, closed my eyes, felt the water on my face.

The man was back.

"One hundred and fifty total," he said. "My final offer. Half now, half later."

"Fine," said Jimmy.

"Follow me."

We slid around the corner. The man bought us Cokes and urged us to drink them down. He motioned for a taxi.

"I've never done this," I whispered to Jimmy. "What do we do?"

"We'll hit him with a brick," said Jimmy. "Take all his money."

We climbed into the cab. I sat back and watched the city moving around us, greasy light and tumult. The man stared out the window. I wondered. Where did Jimmy think we'd get a brick?

The apartment glowed electric, lit by the blue light of a television, soundless. Scenes flashed, blue jeans and domestic situations, a reminder that there was another world out there, of instant potatoes and world affairs, a world as alien to me now as freshly washed underwear. I had money in my pocket. The man was sprawled out on his bed, naked. His body looked ghostly, his face looked normal, like anyone you might see on the street. I listened for the rain, falling outside, but the walls were thick and there weren't any windows.

He crawled across the floor toward us. He knelt in front of Jimmy, undid Jimmy's zipper.

"You're so beautiful," he said to Jimmy. "Go on, take off your shirt. You too," he said to me.

I took it off, shy. I'd never been naked with Jimmy before, except for that time under the bridge. That was different. We were beat-up and tired and nearly dead in the rain.

The man put black army caps on our heads and armbands with swastikas on our arms. The man started sucking Jimmy's toes. I looked down at my own foot, my lumpy, four-toed foot. I stood a space away.

"Tell me what to do," the man said. "Make me your slave. Make me do things against my will. Anything. I have no will of my own."

I couldn't take my eyes off Jimmy. I was tingling all over, erect. The man moved his head up Jimmy's legs, put his mouth over his dick. Jimmy wouldn't meet my eyes. I didn't know what to do. I didn't want to be there with that man.

Then he was crawling over toward me.

"Spit on me," he whispered. "Kick me. Make me do things, anything. Be authoritative, take control."

I could feel the blood all in my head, I was blushing. I mumbled that he should suck my dick. He undid my zipper.

He moved his mouth down over me, it felt weird, melty and warm. I was in a different universe, no longer attached. Sensory data filtered in: marshy and humid. So, I thought, *this is sex.* Before it had always been something that other people had, I doubted it would ever happen to me at all. In grade school couples had skipped off together at recess, kissed behind the church across the street. Jane Coffin, Lisa Kothenbeutel, Todd McIntosh.

I was shocked and envious. I never knew how it happened. I guessed that one of them had to ask the other. Nobody ever asked me. I always figured it was my red Toughskins jeans.

I felt myself spurting in his mouth. I shivered. He drew away from me, wheezing. I pulled my pants up.

"Have a Coke," he said, and he gave us each a bottle. He'd been giving us beverages ever since he picked us up. I had to pee. He moved back onto the bed.

"Stand over me," he said, then, "One on each side."

I looked at Jimmy.

"Come on now, boys," he said. "It isn't hard. You want the rest of your money, don't you?"

Jimmy stepped up onto the bed, it sank with his weight. I moved up onto the other side. The man began masturbating, slowly. There was a camera next to his head. He looked sad.

"You," he said to me. "Take it out."

My bladder was fit to burst. His forehead was below me, beaded with sweat. Silent laughter, false mirth emanated from the television.

"Take it out," he said. "And pee on me. On my neck. My chest. You do have to go, don't you?"

He stared at me. I unzipped my pants.

"Slowly at first," he said. "Hold it back, don't let it all out yet. You've got to save some."

I released it as slow as I could, a thick stream, then tightened to stop. It hurt to hold it in. Our urination was choreographed, me, then Jimmy, me, then Jimmy. It splashed across his belly, his face. He smelled like lime shaving cream, his hands were warm and thick on my ankles. This wasn't like I'd imagined it would be at all, sex. As my pee dribbled over him I felt unclean. But it felt good in a way, too, like I was really *there*, like somebody knew it. I trembled. There was nothing beyond that room, nothing at all.

"Now, then," he said. "Both of you together, let it all out."

I let it go, a full stream, and it mixed together with Jimmy's, our pee merged and rained down over the body, as wet and salty as a true confession. The man took our picture, the flash blinded me. I could feel myself weird inside, I was bubbling over. Our love was finally being consummated, me and Jimmy, and the release of pressure was intense. I felt moisture in my eyes. The walls shook, fluid. I laughed. I laughed and laughed, I couldn't stop, the man leaning backward like he was swallowing himself whole, and I looked at Jimmy, laughing with me, laughing together, laughing, laughing, laughing.

Afterwards, he took us out for pie.

We sat in a diner with the man, late at night. Me, and Jimmy, and the man. In the plastic window we could see ourselves, and glare. The man played with his ketchup bottle. Me and Jimmy, we ate pie.

"It's all red," the man said. "Everything in here is red."

He wasn't lying. The tablecloth, the curtains, the tiled floor, the booths, even the skirts on the waitresses. All red.

"They do that at restaurants," he said. "It makes you hungrier. The color red. It makes you hungry."

He looked out the window at the street. I shoveled in pie. It might have been the red, or maybe just a poor diet, but I was starving.

"I want you to know," he said, "I'm not a bad guy, really. It's just I have to act mean at first, you know, tough. I couldn't be sure what you boys might try. You might have tried anything."

I held my fork still.

"What do you mean?" I asked.

"Oh, I don't know. I thought you might try to hit me with a brick or something and take all my money."

The pie was blackberry. I finished it fast and he ordered me another slice. The man told us about his life. He was born in northern Michigan. He did social work with battered women. Ever since he was a young boy himself he'd found that he enjoyed being the victim of degrading acts. He started crying.

"I'm sorry," he said. "For getting you into this. Really."

"You don't have to apologize," I said. "We did it. You paid us."

"But you're so young," he said. He blew his nose.

"We're at least eighteen," I said. "We're small for our ages."

"At least now I have pictures," he said. "I'll remember the moment. I'm so sorry."

He kept talking, we ate our pie. Silverware clinked, the waitresses' heels clicked against the tile floor. He wouldn't stop apologizing.

"Don't worry," I said, "you didn't hurt us. We're fine." I smiled big, to show him I was happy. "And I promise, we'll spend the money on something good. On really nutritious food with lots of vitamins. Chicken soup."

He was looking out the window.

"I don't want to be responsible," he said. "Like anybody else, I guess. I need to find somebody to tell me what to do. I'm tired of this life. I didn't ask for it. What if they found out about this down at the clinic? I'd lose my job."

"I'll bet you're real good with those battered women," I said. "You have a way about you."

"Sure I do," he said. "Everybody tells me that. That I have a way about me. I've rescued a hundred women from abuse, I've saved a dozen families from disintegration. So why do I need these fantasies to be fulfilled? To be dominated and abused? I still don't think I'm fulfilled. That's all I want. To be fulfilled. Is that so much to ask?"

"Of course not," I said. "Everybody should be fulfilled."

"I'd like to meet somebody," he whispered. "Somebody who'd take my life away from me and make it his own. Somebody in a uniform would be nice. Last week this woman came in and she had round cigarette burns all over her back. I sat down with her and we cried. We cried together and it felt good, we felt strong. But she went back to him. I met him once and I understand. I hate to say it, but I understand it. He could be a movie star or a politician. People would vote for him. He has that way about him, you know?"

Jimmy nudged me with his knee. He was ready to go. The man stared at his plate. When we got up to leave he patted our heads and gave us a present. The gift paper had little Christmas trees on it. I just wanted to be alone with Jimmy. I knew we wouldn't talk about it, the evening, the man, but still, it would be there between us, a kind of bond.

Later, on the street, we opened our present. It was a cheap plastic Instamatic camera, loaded with film. The sky was lightening. We huddled in our blankets in the parking-garage steps. I took Jimmy's picture while he slept, used the whole roll and stuck the pictures in my back pocket. The hazy fact of our love had now been proven. Our love had grown, like cities, out of commerce and war. The sense of our love was like curling down an off ramp with a South Dakotan in a pickup truck, fleeing some teenage girl's father. Our love was the quality of the instant. Our love was like I thought fucking might be on hot nights, tangled in sweaty sheets, lasting forever, wrestling in time, soaked together, desperate, intense, concentrated, hours and hours of it, arched backs, fingers intertwined, bitten lips, clenched teeth. Our love was proven but not released.

The next day we spent money. We bought Big Macs and a jug of wine. We sat in the park, it felt good for a while. Then it was too cold. I sold the camera to a woman in a purple suit for five dollars and we took a city bus to the highway.

It took us four days to get to Rehoboth Beach, on the Delaware coast. The town was deserted, the streets were empty. The locals watched TV in bars and hotel lobbies and watched us walk past. The wind blew. We sat on the cold sand and watched the waves rolling in, the gulls. We spent Christmas there, on the beach, together, wrapped in blankets. It was warm in the blankets and Jimmy talked to me.

He told me about the suicide note his mom left him when she slit her wrists in the bathtub. It was addressed to Jimmy's dad, who he never knew, blamed him for ruining her life, abandoning her with nothing but shit.

"She wrote that she was doing it because she couldn't stand to look at my face anymore," Jimmy said. "But I don't think I was that bad. We yelled at each other a lot, and sometimes if she tried to hit me I bit her."

"Where was that?" I asked. "In France?"

Jimmy's head was tilted back. He was so beautiful.

"Sure," he said. "France."

The clouds that day had a greenish tint. Fish jumped out of the ocean from time to time. I scanned the horizon, looking for UFOs or Jesus.

"They put me on a bus," he said, "to stay with my Dad in Iowa. But he wasn't there. I'm not sure if he was dead, or just moved away. They put me in the orphanage then, in East Liberty."

"Your mom," I said, "what was she like?"

He was quiet for a minute.

"Big," he said. "She was real big and dark. She sang sometimes."

I froze. It came rushing over me in waves. The things he was saying, it all made sense, it was all too incredible. Andalusia. Big and dark, the throaty voice. Andalusia was Jimmy's mother. It kept coming, wave after wave. Of course. My father was his father. In the duplex all those years, my father and Andalusia, carrying out their affair through the walls, their secret love that could never be revealed. He loved her, he had fathered her child, but then she had left. So this was it. Me and Jimmy, brothers all along. It was destined, we were complementary, doppelgangers, each other's lost halves.

A wave of pity flowed over me, my poor desperate father. I realized now that we'd had more in common than I'd thought. Andalusia. Then I remembered my poor, betrayed mother.

I looked at Jimmy. My brother.

"What was her name?" I whispered. "Your mother?"

"Tammy," he said. "Her name was Tammy. She didn't have any legs, but she used to corner me with her wheelchair and beat the shit out of me."

I felt tired. How could I know what was true? Still, he'd never talked to me like that before. I squeezed up close to him. He was staring out over the waves, and I wanted to hold on to him, to hold on tight. He was everybody I had. I put my arm

around his shoulder. He let me do it for a little bit and then he
turned to me and said, "Don't be a fag."

He got up then, walked on down the beach a ways, then
moved up close to the walls of tall empty hotels, and I couldn't
see him anymore. He came back later and we sat together again,
quiet.

That night, Christmas, we walked up to a dark house off the
beach, broke a window and went in. I remember standing there,
in the dark, feeling my heart scream and whistle, my feet against
the carpet, the enhanced quality of sounds in the darkness. I
took out my pictures of Jimmy. The images had all changed,
faded and blurred or turned into pictures of lightning, of cats. I
moved to the living room and watched out the picture window,
the ocean, the waves. We got close to fifty dollars and then we
were gone.

In Columbia, South Carolina, we sat in the public library
while it rained outside, but we couldn't sleep there; it was the
law. You had to pretend to read or the security would throw you
out. I watched a man in a lumberjack shirt reading *Model Airplane News*. He put it back on the shelf, perched comfortably
between the shining pink and white of *Modern Bride* and the
more rustic-looking copy of *Moccasin Review*. Shriveled bums
wandered in and out, pretended to read newspapers. An ancient
man whose face seemed slightly caved-in was reading with a
magnifying glass. Someone tapped on the window, someone with
holes in his shoes and a sense of eternal weariness.

That night we stayed at Oliver's Gospel Mission. They asked
for proof that we were eighteen, but they gave in easy enough
when we didn't have it. The men who worked there seemed
tired and hard, directed us to the showers. I was the only white
person there, but no one seemed to notice. Once you got to that
point, pigment wasn't an issue.

The mission: sweaty bodies, lumpy mattresses, this, that,
the other. Women came and brought us food, then clasped hands
and stood in a circle, sang "Kumbaya." The one in charge had a

luscious southern accent, and teary blue eyes. There was a Mexican teenager there who'd been sent up by his father to learn English in the states. I talked to him, I taught him a few words, words that Traveler had taught me; *susurrus, nimbus, lugubrious, convex*. He taught me Spanish words; the verbs *chiflar* and *pitar* both meant *to whistle*, but *chiflar* also meant *to lose one's head or become crazy*, while *pitar* also meant *to slip away or escape*. In both languages he said that the women had big breasts and I agreed. He had some money and the next morning we went to a donut shop, he bought me coffee and lemon-creme-filled donuts. All they had at the mission was runny oatmeal and burnt, dry toast, just like the orphanage. I sat with Eduardo and we laughed some, he told me about San Miguel de Allende, stone streets, stone buildings, all this stone that remembered and faceless women in black shawls who floated through town at midnight. I made up stories, told him I had a family, that I was on my way to Florida to be reunited with them at Disney World. I said there was a house there, with gardens and fountains and wide fields to play kick soccer in, zebras and tigers and gnus.

We walked back over toward the mission. A man stopped us, just outside.

"I'm looking for somebody," he said. "Two people, actually, two boys, and I'm wondering if you could help me. I have reason to believe they're near here."

He looked like a lizard, his face, with a disturbing orange mustache. I realized he'd been following me in my dreams. He took out a picture, held it out for us to see. At first I didn't even recognize myself. Jimmy, that's what clued me in. It was a grainy black-and-white photo of us at the orphanage, sitting around a table, waiting for cheese sandwiches.

"No, sir," I said. "Haven't seen them. I'm afraid they might be lost for good."

I could see Eduardo recognized us, too. He kept quiet.

"Oh, I'll find them," said the man. "They didn't just vanish, I know that much."

My knees were buckling, I needed a hand on something.

"What did they do?" asked Eduardo.

"I'm not at liberty to say," said the man. "Let's just say I need to find them and they need to be found. They might just be dangerous. Any assistance will be greatly appreciated. Financially, you hear what I'm saying?"

Eduardo nodded. The picture was less than a year before. My face had been altered, I wasn't sure how. How was I different if I'd been just as hungry?

"I believe there is an order to things," said the man. "I have faith in this fact. The guilty are punished, the runaways brought home. My father instilled this belief in me, a great man who didn't spare the rod. No doubt the universe is unfolding just as it ought to. I will find who I'm looking for."

Eduardo squinted at him, trying to understand.

"People have called me a sadist," the man said. "But those people don't know me as well as they should. I'm a complicated man, a man of many moods and bodies of knowledge. I won the Sports Car Derby when I was a Cub Scout, only eight years old. People don't take things like that into account."

There was a vague sense of doom and prolonged despair hovering about his head.

"You keep an eye out," he said. "You hear?"

He walked on, toward the mission. There were dozens of men there who might identify us. Eduardo turned to me.

"Don't tell me what you done," he said. "I don't know it, thank you. I know good person. Do not say it to me. I don't know it, I know nothing, thank you."

"Thanks," I said. "Good luck with your English. I guess this is goodbye."

He nodded, we shook hands. I turned, ran to the library to get Jimmy.

"There's a man," I said. "He's looking for us. I think he wants to kill us."

I was confused, but Jimmy moved fast. It took us fifteen minutes to get outside of town. A light drizzle was falling from a sunny sky. A car was waiting down below at a Juice 'n' Junk.

It sat running, a Ford Escort, while its driver ran in for a quart of milk or a bag of chips.

Jimmy looked at me. I nodded. The hill was slippery, the grass bright green and wet in the paradoxical sunshine. I slid, smeared the butt of my jeans brown and green.

"Will that be all for you today?" the smiling cashier asked inside. "Sanitary napkins or calcium supplement perhaps?" while me and Jimmy backed out of the lot in the customer's car. Jimmy drove.

We sped out two-lane highways into the Carolina countryside, dipping and rising, hills and valleys, moving on our own momentum. I felt a surge of joy, an exuberant tremor of fear, watching back behind us for flashing lights and sirens, laughing and spitting and mooning old women we passed as Jimmy drove on and on. We emerged from the rain, into light. We rolled down the windows and felt the cool air rush through the car, through us, and it was January, it was New Year's Day, but it felt like spring or September, a golden eternal autumn glow all around that would melt into spring right off, never pass through winter, all a haze of color and sun, blue sky and laughter, and we bounced through small towns with deserted pumps, signs that said GAS, past children on bicycles, wholesale carpeting outlets, used-car lots and Piggly Wiggly stores. Landscape colors swirled gold, old men walked raccoons on leashes, middle-aged women swung on porch swings in flannel robes, clutching a beer in one hand, a shotgun in the other. We sped past mistrust of strangers, southern hospitality, a will to stand firm against the onslaught of absurdity. Ghosts walked the streets, widows watched behind curtains. We sped on, between fields of peach trees and peanuts, Jimmy accelerated, increasing the distance between us and whatever lay behind us, whatever it was that we knew was chasing us and would never catch us now. I laughed and laughed and Jimmy laughed too, really laughed.

"This will make everything different now," said Jimmy. "We're in control now. We have our own car. We can go wherever we want. Having your own transportation makes all the difference in the world."

We crossed into Georgia, and south, on, toward Florida.

What opposed us was tangible now, and we were outrunning it.

Δ

"I watched them massacre the entire village," Kenny says. "Women and children and livestock. Every last one of them, and I just stood there and watched, as if I was numb. They were my superior officers, there was nothing I could do. Now I know better. I've learned the magic ways to power, harnessing the powers of the Mind."

There is the knife, sitting on the seat between us.

"But something like that never leaves you," Kenny says. "Watching in itself is a violent act."

I know that this is true and it disturbs me. Watching and listening, both. There are too many things in my head. I try not to think about it in the heat.

The observable universe, I think instead: roughly 10^{87} bits of light and matter scattered over 10^{69} orbic miles of space. The Andromeda galaxy is the most distant object in space visible to the naked eye, appearing as a fuzzy oval patch. About 2.2 million light-years away, it contains an estimated 300 billion stars, compared to only 200 billion in our own Milky Way.

They say there is simply no satisfactory way of picturing fundamental atomic processes in terms of space and time and causality. Theories are tossed about in which certain effects precede their causes. The result of an experiment on an individual atomic particle generally cannot be predicted. The statistical result of performing the same individual experiment an enormous number of times, however, may be predicted with virtual certainty.

Kenny still smells like wintergreen, he secretes this odor from his pores. It's getting hotter, the air moist and heavy. The restful period of dawn is over, the day seems headed for violence. My back is sticking to the seat and I turn my head, see myself standing by the side of the road. Our eyes meet for an instant, I don't wave, I never do, we recognize each other without so much as a nod, my two selves, and we move along.

This is not the first time. I see myself by the road often, my past self, my future self. I pass myself by hitchhiking, or there, standing by the road, I see myself driving by. For an instant, time freezes, colors reverse, like in a photographic negative. The past, present and future do not collide so much as briefly glimpse each other, just long enough to shudder and feel your kidney turn over.

Lately, however, I never see my future. There I am at fourteen, outside Indianapolis with Jimmy trying to get to New York. On the Florida coast I see us drive by in the stolen car. I see myself just last year, in the middle of the Nevada desert, or desperate, along the Coast Highway. But where is my future? I used to see myself a couple of years down the road, a little bit taller maybe, a little bit more or less hungry-looking, but now there is only a blackness up ahead. Of course, this gives me a feeling of dread. I can imagine only two possibilities, death or true love.

On the radio, R.E.M. sings about Driver 8 taking a break, the hope of reaching our destination, putting children to sleep.

I'm hungry again, my stomach cramping. Last year I finally made it to New York, like me and Jimmy never did. I remember only this: Stolen burritos were exploding inside me, I rushed from block to block, desperate for a bathroom. Uniformed men in hotels told me they were out of order or they didn't exist. In delis and corner groceries there were none to be found. At the police station they were unavailable, being fumigated or searched for clues. I stumbled out onto the street, cramps shooting through my bowels like blades, sharp, my head was bursting, nowhere, nowhere in that city a body could take a shit. People looked at me suspiciously, as if I wanted to take something from them. My teeth clenched, I squatted between buildings, let it out. It lay there like a dead animal, my feces steaming on the pavement. I used discarded newspaper to wipe. I stood and walked, calm then, empty.

We stop in Morgantown, the day's light entrenched now, walk into a grocery store to get breakfast, me and Kenny. We pick out Hostess pies and small cartons of milk and cigarettes. The girl at the checkout is flipping through *Soap Opera Digest*.

"Excuse us," says Kenny.

She looks up at us like we are something rancid that has just crawled out of an abandoned coal mine. She adds it all up.

"Two fifty-nine," she says.

Kenny gives her food stamps. She glares.

"You can't use these for cigarettes," she says.

Kenny is looking up at the ceiling as if distracted. He turns to her suddenly, jerking. He leans toward her, staring into her eyes. He whispers.

"You know, little girl," he says, but he stops then. I figure he'll take her neck between his fingers, snap it clean in two. I wait for this, unable to move. She backs away.

"Well," he says, looking away and speaking now in a conversational tone, "ring up the other stuff and give me the change, why don't you?"

She does it fast, not looking up.

"Oh," he says, "one more thing."

He picks up a nickel gumball, puts it on the counter with a fresh dollar food stamp. She rings it up. He pays for the cigarettes with the change.

"There," he says. "Now we're all happy as can be, aren't we?"

We walk out of the chilled store, across the warm asphalt of the parking lot, and climb into the car. I look back and catch her eyes, watching us as we drive away.

"Be best not to hitch in Virginia," Kenny says, down the road a ways. "The cops in Virginia won't stand for it, they'll throw you in jail, knock you around and not ask questions. Take my word for it."

"Well, then," I say, "I may as well just get out here. I'll hitch around it, back through Kentucky, or maybe I'll find a ride who'll take me all the way through."

To be honest, I've been looking for a reason to leave Kenny.

He may be magic, but there's always that knife on the floor, and I have this prejudice, I can't deny it, this fear that he might not be entirely stable.

"If that's what you want," he says, and he pulls over. He shakes my hand. He gives me some food stamps, a bag of raisins and a button, he says it's a special button, a lucky button. It says, *It's Only Rock and Roll, but I Like It.* I clutch it in my sweaty palm, stand here on the shoulder, the sun high and hot, and he drives away, leaving me here, thinking about directions, Wheeling, Cumberland, sweat in my hair, a light-headed feeling and the cars flying past.

Murder is not such a big deal, Kenny told me, once you realize that death is an illusion.

Something like that never leaves you, he told me. Watching in itself is a violent act.

The things I have seen, the things I have heard. The things that I know. Stars bright on desert nights like sparks etching their fire into your flesh. The building promise and wind of a tornado, luminous jadestones bluegreen on Big Sur beaches, rust-colored leaves on rainy days, the soft wetness of a human mouth. Bathwater bubbles, slippery fingers, the lonesome whine of a train that goes nowhere. The laughter of ducks, the textures of cheese, a shish kebab hot, strangers' reflections in donut-shop doors. Mandala designs cracking in tiled rest-room floors. Stones that bleed, a saxophone's moan, muscles of trees, faces like cats, others like lizards, a nimbus of light. The wink of an eye, vocal inflections, hidden meanings, a woman raped, a kitten on fire, the flesh of a mango, clouds blooming madness, traffic and emptiness, the ocean, the insects, sand crabs and piss, snow on wool coats, nectarine nightmares, a goldfish serene. A cross cut into a young boy's hand. The outside of windows. The cold absence in the bodies of the dead, the violent energy in those still alive.

And I have seen more than I told.

My legs feel suddenly weak and I drop to my knees. The ground is so close, stones on my palm, the sky all around, burning and blue. I am grasping for a reason, a destination, a direction even, someplace to go.

It must be close to noon, but I can't afford to be a cynic now.
I pray. To the cloudless sky, the asphalt, the gravel, whoever
will listen, I ask but one thing; forgive me earth, forgive me sky.
For the things I have seen.

I lied to the police when my parents were killed. I told them
I was out, delivering the news. But I was there, I saw it all. I
stepped out of my bed, I stood in the doorway and I saw him
stab them, I saw the knife, a shiver of light, cruel in the dark,
and I watched. I stood there in the doorway, I watched it all,
and then he turned around and I saw it, that face, the face of the
man who killed my parents.

SIX

Δ

1

At school we made applehead dolls for Iowa History Week. Applehead dolls, like the pioneer children used to make, back in the good old days, before everything got fucked up.

"Be careful not to make the eyes too big," Mr. Horner warned us. "Otherwise they'll come out looking like ghosts."

I gouged holes into the apple core, deep and wide and black. I thought it would be cool. Mr. Horner asked me to stay after school to talk.

"Are you having problems at home?" he asked. "Is something on your mind?"

He was an idiot and he bugged me. I loved my applehead man just the way he was. I thought he looked excellent.

"No," I said, and I wouldn't say more. Mr. Horner was convinced I was a deeply troubled child. He showed me black ink splotches and asked me to tell him what they were.

"Five penguins flying to the moon," I said, "dragging little plastic buttons. If you push the buttons it blows up the world. On the sides there's kumquats, lots of kumquats."

I didn't even know what a kumquat looked like. Mr. Horner looked frustrated and confused. He wasn't sure if I was playing games with him or if I was completely out of my mind. I took my applehead man and went home.

At night in my room it came to life. We built bonfires together in an ashtray I took from the bowling alley, danced wild around it, me and my applehead man. Wiggling digits, limbs akimbo,

we danced the nightsky, we danced our needs and hunger, we
danced shadows twisting and the stars falling down. We danced
blood sacrifice and we danced the first fire. Pyromaniacs, we
burnt paper and wooden spoons, sacrificed plastic pigs and G.I.
Joes and Mr. Potato Head, toys I dug out of the back corners of
my closet. We renounced everything, we danced some more:
the end of time and the beginning.

"Things have gotten bad," my applehead man told me. "Take
a look at me. I used to be red and juicy and tart."

In the morning at school, it was all I could do to keep my
eyes open. Chalk squeaked on blackboards, children moved
about in lines, girls who wore bras stared at my ridiculous shoes.
I only wanted to sleep.

Everything turned liquid and dark. When I got up to do my
paper route in the middle of the night, I'd find Dad rearranging
the furniture, putting up Christmas lights, splattering cooked
oatmeal against the walls and watching it drip down. In a way,
though, he seemed better, doing everything with a strange,
childish glee. I thought we were on the verge of something.
Something had to give.

The electricity got shut off and we lived without lights. No
candles even, no TV, no hot food. Dad would listen to the Pennels' television through the walls sometimes with a glass. He'd
crouch there, laughing at something moronic, *Hee Haw*, or *The
Addams Family*. I was awake all night. I couldn't sleep or I
wouldn't wake up for my route; without electricity I didn't have
an alarm. I heard things in the darkness, the whole world shutting down.

I played with myself, moved myself to other landscapes,
left my parents behind. Even then I was independent, my own
dark child. My head was filled with sex. Naked men, all sorts of
outrageous things. I wasn't sure how they'd got in there, I knew
this couldn't be my life. I got my hair cut at a real barber shop
with comic books of Aquaman and Dr. Doom, an old-fashioned
pop machine where you had to yank on the bottles. Clippings
of hair fell to the floor, men had their necks shaved and talked
about riding lawn mowers. How could I be a fag, getting hair-

cuts in a place like this? Fags were the kids like Bradley Van Meter who didn't care how many of his bones Evel Knievel had broken. Fags were arrested in a park north of town, but nobody saw the actual fags, only their names in black ink in the paper. Fags didn't exist in Des Moines, were shadows, invisible. It was only the air around their invisible spaces that moved, filled with all sorts of angry words, sermons, legislation, insults and threats. But I certainly didn't have the right thoughts for a twelve-year-old kid in this city, all those muscles and buttocks and smooth, sweaty chests. It had been a long time since I prayed. I took out my tiny lime Bible, read passages at random, waiting for a message from Jesus that made some sort of sense. I got down on my knees, I asked Jesus to get these things out of my head. I just wanted to be a normal kid, with Nikes and a ten-speed, playing Little League baseball. I wanted kids at school to like me. I wanted to be able to watch TV, to smell something cooking when I came home from school. But Jesus was sloughing off. Jesus was no help at all.

The world wasn't turning out to be the kind of place I'd been promised. I blamed my parents. It was their fault, everything. Everything was all wrong, I'll admit it, even before my parents died, everything was all wrong.

The day before they were killed, we fought.

There was a strange April ice storm and the whole world glittered crystal, blue and white, frozen. Three-foot icicles hung from our rainspout, cold diamond swords. I broke one off, carried it with me, delivered the news in a world of ice. I slid across it, everything sparkled, houses, cars, streets, all blue and translucent. The night was calm and crisp, and the stars.

When I got back home Dad was up, just smiling at the kitchen table. He looked different. Crazy, but in a saner way, his old self. He'd got a job.

"I start tomorrow," he said. "Six bucks an hour."

He looked like somebody off the cover of one of Mom's books about peace through prayer, smiling, with his hands in his lap. I tried to figure out how I felt. Empty and tired, only that. I went on up to bed.

The next day it warmed up, fifty degrees, and the world was melting. Kids flew kites, rode their bikes through the wet, sandy streets. Mom came home from McDonald's and we sat at the dinner table in the dark, eating peanut butter sandwiches.

Mom glowed. Then she started crying and they kissed, it was just like a bad movie.

"I knew it," she said. "I knew it was just a matter of time. I had faith, I did."

They kissed again. I wanted to puke.

"This means I can have a new bike," I said. "And some Nikes."

Mom looked at Dad.

"Don't count on it," he said.

I furrowed my brow, dramatically.

"What for? We'll have money now."

Dad picked at his rotten teeth.

"Why not?"

"We owe rent. Utilities. Your mother needs new shoes. The car needs work. Any extra money will have to be saved. If there was an emergency we'd have nothing. If one of us got sick. If something happened to me."

I flew to my feet. Why did she need new shoes when the shoes I had were worthless? Work on the car when I was still bikeless? They never thought about me, they didn't care. I yelled and waved my arms, I'd had more than I could take. I threw my sandwich on the floor. Dad grabbed my wrist. Physical contact, the hint of violence. *Just because you're bigger than me,* I said. I threw the tantrum of a lifetime. I was charged with the luscious fury of the self-righteous, that joy of hating when you know that you have been horribly, cruelly wronged. I stamped my feet around the kitchen, I called them names.

"Upstairs," said Dad. "Forget about dinner, you can go hungry. Selfish little shit, I want you to sit up there and think about things for a while, think about what you've said, and I don't want to see your face for a good, long time. Not until you've thought this over and you're ready to apologize."

I stormed up to my room hating, hating blind. Never, ever,

never never never would I say I was sorry, those fuckers, those selfish, cruel, never.

I lay on my bed. I thought it over for a good, long time.

Later, I went to the window. They were out there together, Mom and Dad, laughing on the lawn, in the moonlight, holding hands. After the way they'd treated me, they were out there having fun. They were talking to each other quiet, but I could hear the low murmur all the way up there. He pulled her to him, he kissed her. They stared at each other and he ran his fingers through her hair. Dad looked around the yard, then pulled off his shirt. His back was white in the moonlight, he had a little hunk of flab around his waist. Mom laughed and ran a few steps away, but he grabbed her, pulled her back, she was trying to get away, but then he kissed her again, and they were both laughing. Mom looked around and next thing they were on the soggy ground and Dad was pulling off her shirt. They rolled back over toward the alley, behind the trash cans, and I couldn't see them anymore, just their bare feet and ankles, twisting around in the grass.

I walked out into the hall, into their bedroom to check the battery-operated clock. It was midnight. It was four more hours before I had to get up for my route. I watched the orange numbers on their digital clock blending into each other every time a minute passed. I sat on their bed like that.

Δ

The stolen car broke down just outside of Destin, on the Florida panhandle. It didn't break down so much, I guess, as just stop running and we were gliding silent down the highway. We coasted as far as we could, another half mile or so, pulled off along the shoulder and started walking. I wonder now if maybe we just ran out of gas.

Then we were somewhere else altogether. Along the beach everything was a happy slow motion. We were a postcard pic-

ture, winter sun bright, sparkles on waves, a ship floating in the
air just above the horizon. Lumpy, erotic pillows of cloud moved
fast, like high-speed photography, but we barely moved at all.
Others on the beach were relaxed, not slothful. The seven deadly
sins didn't apply that far south. Here, people seemed content.
Old people strolled in pastel sweatsuits, children chased crabs.
Shells and salt water and daylight, all over the place.

Then I was running, barefoot, but slow in the sand, and
Jimmy too, running, a whirlwind of light. Jimmy's mouth was
open, his teeth white as the clouds. I remember then I was falling. The sky was filled with chrome globes, a man was pulling
in a line of flopping, silver fish. I hit the sand with a soft thud,
laughing, leaning back, toward sky, sky, ocean and sky. Jimmy
was there with me, laughing. He threw a Frisbee and I caught
it, ran, he tackled me and we rolled there on the sand.

I lay still, closed my eyes. I could feel his warmth against
me. I'd always wanted Jimmy, nothing more than that. There
was a bright orange spot, the sun, burning through my lids. I
opened my eyes. His mouth was smiling and I wanted to touch
it.

That night they lit up the beach, shacks sold Mai Tais and
beach towels, flamingo or beer or Donald Duck designs. We sat
on wooden slanting chairs. Nuclear families strolled past us,
radiant with sunburn. The old people had changed into shiny
white suits.

"He'll never find us here," I said. I was talking about the
man with the orange mustache. "He was wrong about people
always getting found. They never caught the man who killed
my parents."

Jimmy considered this.

"So he's still out there," he said.

He drank from a long bottle of beer. Beads of moisture glistened on the amber bottle, the label peeling off.

"Aren't you afraid that he's going to come back for you?" he
asked.

I'd never considered this possibility. I pictured the killer in
my head, his heavy eyebrows, his pale lips.

"Most murderers like to finish off any job they start," he said. "Killers are perfectionists. I heard that somewhere, I'm sure it's true."

Down the beach, somebody was juggling torches. I watched the fire moving, making zigzagging streaks in the air.

"You're lucky," said Jimmy, "that I'm here to watch out for you."

I was startled. The implication: that he'd take care of me. He always had, out of boredom it seemed, but the security was tenuous.

"I can take care of myself pretty well," I said.

"Right," said Jimmy.

From the corner of my eye I saw a flaming object fall from the roof of a hotel. It looked like a body maybe. But I turned to see and it hadn't happened at all.

Other things did, though. Happen. Jimmy left, the fog came. The man was there, looking for us. I found Dust.

Let me slow down.

"I'll go find us some pillows," Jimmy said, when we were tired and a little drunk. He stood out of his beach chair, but I had a surprise for him. I was thinking ahead.

"I already got some. They're over under the dock with the rest of our stuff."

I'd gone into the Ramada Inn earlier in the day, followed an old cleaning lady around. I tried to stay far enough back that she wouldn't notice me prowling about.

"Young man," she said. "Young man! I want to tell you something, young man. You come here, you listen to me. I have something to tell you."

I moved toward her to listen.

"Forty years," she said, "forty years I've been working as a cleaning lady, cleaning up people's ashes, their spills, their bodily fluids. Forty years. You listen to me. Don't you think that just because you're young you don't have to listen to me. For the last thirty-seven of those forty years I've been working third shift. Thirty-seven years. For thirty-seven years, I haven't had a decent night's sleep. You hear me? Thirty-seven years."

I waited for her to continue.

"That's all," she said. "That's all I wanted to say. I just wanted to tell you that."

I couldn't steal pillows from her rooms then, it didn't feel right. I moved up a floor, found an open door. A different maid was vacuuming with headphones on and singing along, a song called "Heart of Glass." I snuck in behind her, grabbed two pillows and ran.

Jimmy scratched his belly and yawned.

"You got pillows already," he said.

I just smiled.

"Seems you can take care of yourself pretty good, all right."

Everything I knew I'd learned from him. He wouldn't look me in the face, stared at the zigzagging torches. We walked over to the dock. I spread out a blanket and some shirts, fluffed up my pillow. Jimmy got up to leave.

"Where you going?" I asked.

"To find something silver," he said, and he walked away.

I didn't know if he was after jewelry or something more abstract. The beach night was sharp, a living thing. I watched tiny waves rushing through the darkness. Farther down a fire blazed, couples sat with beers, roasted meat. I could hear it crackling, smell the cooking flesh. There was a sliver of white moon like a fingernail clipping, hanging in the sky. I felt tribal, but there was only one of me.

He didn't come back.

Morning came, afternoon, dusk, night. I was surprised that the fear I felt wasn't more intense. He'd come back. He was only doing this to show how much I needed him. I walked barefoot across the stony highway to get Donettes and a coffee from the Stop 'n' Pop across the way. I was careful, watching for glass.

Another dusk and things were the same. The same and different, like strangers. A bank of fog hung out on the horizon and the sun sank into it, a black globe. Jimmy was really gone.

The fog rolled in. A strange dark light moved over everything, an eerie noise filled my head. I walked through it, objects distant or moving on the edges of my vision. The mist covered everything. Hotel lights rose up to my right, smeared red eyes, like an albino kitten. Like Pitch. People moved about with purpose, dark shapes, things happened, but I couldn't see them. I realized that I'd entered a dream I once had as a small child, a dream of a soupy, conscious fog, dancing phantoms, noise and silence, spirits and things, the living and dead all intertwining, licking each other's ears. Seaweed was the hair of it, shells whispered of missing persons. I was lost in this dream, moving down the beach. The fog so thick and moody, I knew if I just kept walking I could disappear, get so far into it that I'd never have to come back out.

Black-haired heads bobbed up out of the mist to my left, the heads just floating, the black hair hanging in air. It was a woman and another, white lace gowns that merged with the fog, their heads rolled groundless, dove and laughed, red lips on each other and floating black hair. One head vanished, the other twisted, rolled, back again, I could hear the surf murmuring over them. Both were down low and laughter, low lovesongs of laughter rose out of the fog, heads and waves moved black in the mist.

"Damned lezzies," came a man's voice to my right. "Nothing more repulsive than a couple of goddam lezzies fingering each other on a public beach."

I moved fast, away, into the fog. Shapes and voices, voices without bodies, words floating in the mist. I watched for Jimmy to appear, sudden, dark and beautiful, rolling in from the ocean.

There was something sexual about the fog, the way things remained hidden. I expected to see men in trench coats, the burning ends of cigarettes. Figments of my imagination were eating Fig Newtons and lamenting their fate. The mist poured out of rocks, a mirage. I walked and walked, voices all around.

"Do you like that yogurt? I do too. Do you like that frozen yogurt? I do too. It's better for you than ice cream, you know. Not as much fat."

"They aren't supposed to have weather like this. Why would they be having weather like this? No fog on the Gulf. Nobody's supposed to have weather like this, not here, not ever."

The fog had brought everyone out, trying to lose them-selves on the beach.

"I just am that way, that's all. I don't want to be that way, mean-spirited and all. I just am."

"Peter, I can't even see you. A foot in front of my face and I can't even see you. Peter? Peter, I just want to go home, this vacation isn't any fun anymore. Peter?"

"Jeremy, Jeremy, honey, would you pass me a papaya?"

I froze, dead still. It was my mother's voice.

"Mom," I rasped. "Mom! Dad?"

I could hear my mother sucking juice out of a papaya. I tried to move toward the voice, I ran faster, but it slipped into noth-ing. I realized then that things weren't real. I ran, farther into it, down the beach.

2

When the fog dissipated, I was lying shivery and damp on the cold grass of a private lawn. Behind me was an unrecognizable stretch of beach, the Gulf. In front of me was a house, large, glass and tile, clean Florida. A fountain towered in the yard, strange sparks of light floated inside. A hunched and whitened old man was seated in a lawn chair.

It was night, still.

"Hello, boy."

His voice was like powder, and his skin. His presence amazed me; the night's moisture should have wiped him clean, like chalk on a blackboard. Black, tiny eyes stared, an animal peering from its ruined cavern.

"Come here," he said. "Closer."

I crawled toward him, my palms through the dewy grass. He reached out his arm, ran a stained and wrinkled finger down my cheek. His finger smelled like cigarettes. His body stank of lotion.

My options weren't clear.

He withdrew his hand. From my crouching perspective the

house was enormous, a monument, pillars and stained glass. His breathing was forced and tired.

"I'm Dust," he said. "You know, as in *from dust we came, to dust we shall return.* But just call me Dust."

He was entombed in a white shawl. The lawn chair was yellow-and-green-striped. I tried to think of something to say.

"Do you need a home?"

I couldn't form words. I was hearing him differently, not through my ears. Through the tips of my fingers, just under the nails.

"Good," he said. "You can stay here with me. I'll feed you and clothe you. I'll give you everything you need. You can play on the beach, build sand castles, that sort of thing. Aren't you a lucky little boy?"

I stood up, sudden. I said, "My parents are dead."

"Mmm hmm," he said, looking away. "We'll soon share that characteristic, your parents and I. But why don't you come in? Join me for a steaming cup of café mocha. It's one of those International coffees. You know the commercials: for the moments of your life. But come, come . . ."

He rose, moved with amazing vigor. He was shrunken, smaller than me. I followed him into the house. It was filled with candles.

"Are you a mystic?" I asked.

He laughed.

"I'd hardly call it that," he said. "Even mysteries grow tiresome eventually. Florida is where people come to die. Welcome to the land of the dead, little boy. If you examine the landscape you'll see that this is, in fact, the underworld. But don't expect to find your own dead here, your father or mother. The sunlight hides them well, erases them. The nature here makes me nauseous, so loveless, so painfully bright. I prefer the artificial, the theatrical, things which disturb the senses in a less organic way."

"Andalusia," I said, "my old baby-sitter, she used to light candles sometimes."

He picked a tiny insect out of his shawl.

"I used to burn them from both ends," he said. "The candles. But I'm a bit old for that now, wouldn't you say? You, I imagine, are a little firecracker. So much life and energy you don't know how to contain it."

"I live like I have to, that's all," I said. "I'm an orphan."

He looked at me, his black eyes moving up and down.

"Yes, well, we're all orphans these days, one way or another," he said. "Don't be so impressed with yourself on account of that one fact. Round out your personality a bit, you're still young."

He was wobbling around the kitchen in the semidarkness, fixing the coffee. I stood in the dark living room, an enormous picture window gaping before me. I could see the expanse of water beyond.

"Everybody isn't an orphan," I said. "Not everybody."

"Oh, how charming you are," he exclaimed. "So innocent and dumb. I mean orphans in a spiritual sense, of course. Although on a literal level, I assure you, my own parents are quite dead themselves. They died on the same day, twenty-seven years ago, three thousand miles apart. My mother was in Seattle, my father in Birmingham. One was a car accident, the other a stroke. No connection, or so we are told. Are you familiar with Jung's studies on synchronicity? Anyway, these things are correlated more frequently than can be explained by chance. We can't say anything about cause and effect, you understand, we can only observe that they do happen. When I die, I hope my second wife wakes up screaming, with blood pouring from her ears. I'm not a vicious person, you understand, but I certainly do hate that witch."

Dust stepped through the doorway, his figure black for one moment and then blue in the candlelight. Steam rose from the coffee. Where was Jimmy? Where was he sleeping, who was he with? I was safe and dry. The fog had changed everything, things had been lost.

"Please, sit," he said. "You're a perfectly lovely little boy in an odd sort of way. Your skin isn't as smooth as I might have hoped. But you're so lean and young and bright-eyed. Simply adorable."

I could feel myself blushing in the dark.

"Please," he said, "don't be disturbed by the seemingly homoerotic nature of my affections. I assure you it isn't that at all. I've always been terribly fond of women. I'm a breast man myself. It's your youth I'm infatuated with. Your innocence. I've lived much of my life in an attempt to imitate great literature and I intend to die the same way. Chasing an image of lost youth, basking in the presence of a frolicking child. If you hadn't wandered into my yard I would have had to steal some toddler from the shopping mall, I suppose."

He sipped his coffee.

"I'm glad you came, it's better this way. Death in Destin, how absurd. They call this stretch of beach the Redneck Riviera. No canals here, no sense of sinking and plague, only the enormous Gulf as a continual reminder of what I'm approaching, the sheer expanse of it."

I sat, sipping café mocha. The chair was plush velvet. He was rich. Things were polished, the walls littered with beautiful works of art. A painting, the profile of a woman, long black hair blowing forward, surrounded by leaves. A black-and-white etching of an infant, perched on its dead mother's chest, among gray columns and trees.

"There are those who learn to accept the idea of their own death," said Dust. "Make their peace with the grim reaper, so to speak. I assure you, I'm not one of those. Not by a long shot."

I closed my eyes. I felt confused, almost as though I belonged there.

"Oh, forgive me," said Dust. "You must be tired. The sun will be up before long and I'd wager you haven't slept. Come, come, you'll have a bed of your own. We'll talk more in the morning."

I followed him down the hall, blind. The bed was huge and soft and clean. It wasn't a bench, it wasn't the ground, it wasn't a lumpy bundle of springs. It was a bed. The sheets smelled like flowery fabric softener. I burrowed in, sank. Immediately I slept and dreamed about a fat yellow cat shedding fur around my legs.

In the morning I could hear the hush of the Gulf. Different when it was outside and I was in. I lay there, blinking at the light, afraid to move. Somewhere, something was ticking.

I got up, feeling skinny in my underwear, walked around the bedroom. There were framed photographs on the walls of dwarves and mongoloids, tattooed women and nudists and twins. There was a bookcase filled with black and green and yellow books. I ran my finger along the covers. Rimbaud, Baudelaire, Lautréamont. I could stay in a place like this, I thought. I heard something coming, ran back to the bed, got under the covers.

"Good morning," he said. "Sleep well?"

"Fine," I said.

He opened the curtains. Sunlight streamed in through the bay windows, swept across the wood floor. The light was heavy, the cast of noon.

"What an appalling uniformity of landscape and skies," said Dust. "Another beautiful day. I'll be right back."

I felt myself floating in the bed, limp and exhausted in a way I hadn't been in months. Exhaustion had collected in my cells and molecules. The bed had only released it.

He returned with a plate full of cherry Pop-Tarts.

"I was going to fix you a Belgian waffle," he said. "Theoretically, a Belgian waffle would have been the ideal way for us to begin our first day together. In theory we will, in fact, be sharing just that Belgian waffle. In practice I'm afraid it's nothing but cherry Pop-Tarts."

I ate slowly, meticulously, savoring every bite. I was afraid Dust might be crazy, like everybody else.

"You're hungry, aren't you?" he said. "In more ways than one, I imagine. By all means, eat it up, there's plenty more."

He was so tiny and withered. He wore a silky yellow robe.

"Eating," he said, "always reminds me of death. That's the real connection, you know. The young are always trying to connect sex with death, romantic bullshit from the perpetually horny. Eating, that's the real tie-in, life continually consuming itself."

He sat on the edge of the bed, watching me. I felt like an invalid.

"Eat cautiously. Every bite you take is deciding for one thing and against another. Cherry Pop-Tarts instead of Belgian waffles. So much food, so many choices."

A breeze came through the window. I shivered.

"What do you want from me?" I asked. "What do you want me to do?"

He laughed.

"Why, youthful things, of course. Just be yourself. Act your age. Go frolic on the beach, play in the sand, laze the day away. Act bored, like there's more time than you could ever possibly fill. Have no responsibilities. Let others make your decisions. Say things that unintentionally display your naiveté."

He tousled my hair. His hand was rough on my scalp.

I didn't know where to begin. I sat up, out of the covers. In my underwear, against the clean white of the sheets, my body looked different. Harsh, like a blemish. I felt uncivilized.

"First, take a shower. Don't worry about your clothes, I've got clean things, new things for you to wear. Those things you had were misshapen and filthy. They looked like you found them in the trash on the street."

"I did," I said.

"You just love to play it up, don't you?" he said. "Bask in danger, commit crimes. Streetwise and world-weary. You're still a child! Look at those suffering eyes, that sensitive pout. People trust you implicitly, don't they? At your age I don't suppose you consider innocence a virtue. You flee from it. A frightened runaway, your greatest desire is to go running home to Mother, but your adolescent pride won't allow it. You are a good boy, filled with wonder. So many possibilities! You believe there is redemption through love. You suspect love is your destiny."

I felt I might throw up undigested cherry Pop-Tart goo all over the linen sheets.

"In the first place," I said, "my mother is dead. In the second place, I'm bad. I'm so bad you can't even know. I've done horrible things you wouldn't even believe."

"Please, spare me," said Dust. "I'm not interested in your story. By the time you've reached my age you will find you've pretty well lost interest in anything beyond the fragments of your own life. I can see what you are. A sweet little boy."

"Yes," I said, "always helping little old ladies across the street."

"Oh, I do love a smartass," he declared. "I know I've found cynicism the most effective tool in distancing myself from the ever-encroaching blot of organic decay. It's also a good tool for keeping other people's pain an arm's length away. Everyone is always trying to spill their pain all over you, have you noticed? Like a Bloody Mary or some syrupy liqueur."

I couldn't tell if this was supposed to be funny. I studied my own rib cage. There was nothing much to me, there in my underwear. Where was the substance? Dust kept staring at me. I didn't know what I was supposed to be.

"Ah, selves," he said. "Always groping for qualities, aren't we? Something to give us a sense of form in the presence of someone else's gaze."

He coughed, I thought his tiny body might collapse.

"Go on," he said, "take a shower. You can use the flamingo towel."

I walked into the bathroom. There were perfumed soaps that had never been used, decorative hand towels. This was civilization again. I showered. It was so long since I'd been clean. I felt the hot water spray over me forever, I shampooed. My hair felt weightless, smelled like strawberries. Jimmy wasn't here.

Back in the bedroom clothes were laid out on my bed. A pair of white shorts with little blue whales on them and an aquamarine T-shirt that said *Southern Alabama Shakespeare Festival*. Dust wasn't anywhere I could see. I dressed, walked out onto the beach. I looked up and down for something familiar. I knew this had to be an extrapolation of the other beach, the one I'd shared with Jimmy, but I recognized nothing. I was lost.

I played as well as I could, wading and splashing. I buried myself in sand, felt the weight of it on me, holding me down.

When I stood up the sand cracked, fell off in heavy clumps. I could feel Dust's eyes watching from a place I couldn't see.

People on the beach smeared coconut oil on their bodies, winced at the sun, as if in pain. It wasn't the sort of day on which anything would happen. Still, I watched for Jimmy. The day merely fulfilled its promise of emptiness. But there was shelter, there was food. I wouldn't leave it.

The days developed a strange continuity. We would eat cherry Pop-Tarts, sit out on the beach, playing backgammon and reading books. Dust talked and talked, told me endless stories about World War I, about Paris and newspaper reporting, about marriage and birds, but I could never fit all the pieces together. He showed me ancient brown pictures of himself in uniform, in North Africa, in houses and in water to his waist. He showed me photographs of his wives and newspaper stories he'd written. He told me he had a photographic memory, in the sense that his memories often lost their context. He taught me backgammon strategy. Once you got far enough behind, he said, it made more sense to leave yourself wide open, hoping to get more men sent back. Just when you were so far behind that the game seemed laughable it became clear that anything could happen. He'd tried to take that principle beyond into life, but it never worked quite so well.

I told him about Andalusia and fireflies and *Vanishing Point*. Sometimes, he pretended to listen. Some afternoons he disappeared, hiding in his room, while I wandered through the house, exploring. Carved jade Shivas, alabaster elephants, paintings of young girls watching the sky. Shrunken heads, wicker chairs and woven rugs that looked like they'd come from Morocco. Art and books, everywhere I turned. This was civilization, but nothing was alive. I flipped through the pages of *Death in Venice*, trying to figure out what Dust expected me to be. At night he lit candles, played raging symphonies on his immense, blinking stereo. Stampeding buffalo, bad rivers, birth and pain and anger, slaves rowing boats. Sprawling continents, islands and streams, genocide and coral reefs, the movement of time.

In the daytime the house was bright and time stopped altogether. I tanned, felt encrusted in a beautiful glass bubble. A
silent sort of happiness descended on us, a forgetfulness, like
the first moments of a late-afternoon nap. I lost memories and
guilt in the sunshine, ran through the sand, danced the limbo
with vacationing insurance salesmen, talked to elephant-tusk
vendors and the fishermen who found gold coins in the bellies
of bronze fish. Dust brightened and joked, canaries swarmed
about our heads as we sat playing backgammon. I understood
then, the affection of dogs, or more accurately cats, a love so
consciously rooted in self-gratification. It was the joy of having
my hair ruffled, of being fed and obedient. I knew then, if not
consciously, that love is whatever draws two together: a mutual
respect for Elvis, a shiny trinket, the cold night air, electro-
magnetism, the sound of a train in the night. Fear of crabs, sad-
ism, car crashes, childbirth, dying, the army or sociology texts.
The love I had for ocean breezes and the sun on my face was
not that different from the love Dust had for me. Our languages
were only slightly more compatible.

"I speak nine languages myself," Dust told me, "a fact which
has helped neither my career nor my sense of identity. I find
I'm a different person in whichever language I speak. I've
achieved no sense of consistency. There are those who consider
consistency a virtue. I'm not one of those. Although I do think
differently on the subject in German. I'm somewhat flexible in
regard to consistency."

The consistency of the day was lemon Jello-O with whipped
cream. Malleable, opaque. The consistency of my life, looking
backward, seemed the same.

I woke in the middle of the night once, from a dream about
planets. I could feel his presence in the silence, admiring me
as I slept. I didn't move or open my eyes. I could hear his rough
breathing, the air moving around me as he bent over toward me.
He almost touched me. The room grew large around us, emptying: the boy and the old man in a cavern, surrounded by the
echoes of our heartbeats. I could sense it then, his dying, and

farther behind it, my own. He stood watching for the longest time.

When I ate different things, I dreamed different things. When I ate citrus fruit I dreamed I was a kite, laughing. When I ate meat I dreamed of the man with the orange mustache, chasing me with a rope stretched taut between his hands. When I ate lemon Jell-O I dreamed about falling through an empty sky. When I ate cherry Pop-Tarts I dreamed about Jimmy. We ate a lot of cherry Pop-Tarts.

One day he was there. Not Jimmy. The man who was after us, the one who looked like a lizard, with an orange mustache, the sadist. He was outside, talking to Dust. He showed Dust a picture, Dust pointed down the beach. I clenched the windowsill. He looked up at the house, he looked right at me. He was wearing a suit. Even at the beach there was something dreadful about that man. I thought about thumbscrews, the razor pendulum, flaming bamboo under my nails.

He said something to Dust and walked away, down the beach. Dust came into the house.

"Tadzio!" he called.

"Matt," I said. "I told you my name was Matt."

He patted me on the head.

"So," he said, "you really are a criminal. You're being pursued. What fun! Not the innocent I'd imagined, alas. But tell me. Who's your friend, the other little boy in the photograph? Even in that grainy picture I could see his beauty. He's the one really, isn't he? Your own dark vision? I could see he'd be prone to such interpretation by those who want to love him."

"His name's Jimmy," I said. "He's gone. He isn't here anymore."

"Yes," said Dust, "I see that. But is he coming back?"

He coughed. He took a green bottle from his pocket, popped a couple of pills into his mouth."

"We don't know where each other are," I said.

"Don't be ridiculous," he said. "People can always find each other if they have a mind to. We emit radio waves from a corner of our brains. Call it telepathy if you must. Can't always be controlled, though, sometimes you get stuck in a nasty telepathic rut. My second wife, after the divorce I ran into her everywhere. Finally it was just too much, she had to move to Alabama."

"You see?" I said. "I really am bad."

"Yes," said Dust, "you're a rebel, a real James Dean. The young, how intrigued they are with death! When you get a little older you may find that you want nothing more than to distract yourself from your own mortality."

He paused and rattled. *Blah, blah, blah,* I thought. He went on.

"But yes," he said, "when I was your age I could hardly contain it, all that venom and rage. The atmosphere in my childhood home was so thick and sullen, rank cellars underneath. My parents busied themselves with their silly amusements. I wanted to blow something up, to hurl bricks through windows. You're just like I was. You want to hurl bricks through windows. By all means, shatter glass! *The seeds of filth contained in every soul begin to grow. The most austere of men are plagued by longings for foul amusements. Men of high esteem begin to see the world through criminal eyes.*"

In my head I could see it, all that beautiful tinkling glass on concrete.

"You," he said, "you're a real time bomb, just waiting to explode."

"I thought I was an innocent," I said.

"You change," he said. "You're whatever I want you to be."

I looked away, at the walls. Framed portraits, mirrors and masks.

"You feel that you've been cheated of something that's rightfully yours. You feel angry because you suspect that somebody else has it, this thing, that is rightfully yours. Sooner or later, I'm afraid, you'll discover that nothing is rightfully yours. We're all tenants in this life, with no more rights than these Cuban refugees we hear so much about, adrift in the Caribbean. Even the right to exist is suspect. I'm afraid we've abused it."

I watched out the window. Naked toddlers waddled down the beach, little human beings with entire lifetimes ahead of them. Eighty-seven years, I thought. I did math in my head. The year 2068.

"I'm dying, you know," said Dust. "Have I mentioned that fact?"

I could see him out there, his black eyes, swimming in the Gulf. The old man and the sea. I didn't know what to say. He was so ancient, used-up.

"How small it all seems now. How petty." His voice was shaking. "It's all so small, but so enormous at the same time, the things that fill my head. A girl in a white dress, a windy day in the park, the wind blowing the dress against her, outlining the shape of her breasts. Paris, a picnic, traveling by train at night. Trenches, gunfire, so many years ago. Niagara Falls. New York, the summer of '47, a dog, washed up on the beach. Fireworks. A poem, in Serbo-Croatian, that line about the wrecking ball, the meaningless light shining through. A flat tire in the California desert. The smell of varnish, my father's favorite hat."

He looked sad, far away. He ran his finger down my cheek.

"What?" I asked. "Just tell me. What do you want me to do?"

I knew he loved me. Not me really, but something beyond me, something that he thought was me, back behind him.

"I'll tell you what," he said, and his voice was cracking, "let's go out for dinner tonight, what do you say? We'll have Chinese food. Yes, that would be good. Go on, go to your room, get changed."

I walked past him fast, down the hall. Get changed, he said. Into what? I rummaged through the dresser drawers, scared of what came next.

There were red tablecloths, red booths, fans on the walls. Dust ordered something with shrimp and bamboo shoots.

"And what would you like?" asked the waitress. She was neither Oriental nor inscrutable. She looked restless and depressed.

"I don't care," I said. "Anything's fine. The same thing, I guess."

She squinted her eyes at me. She had long blond hair and muscular calves. She left us, limping, studying the words she'd written down on her pad.

"You don't care to choose, do you?" asked Dust. "Perhaps you don't believe it's possible."

Dust. He was always talking, always talking. He thought he knew so much. I played with my napkin, cut rows into it with my fork. I took packets of sugar from a blue bowl. They had pictures of wildlife on them and words on the back.

BAR-TAILED GODWIT (Limosa Iapponica). *The bar-tailed godwit is a Eurasian bird that must have established a beachhead in Alaska in relatively recent times. It flies home to its ancestral wintering grounds in the Old World for the rites of reproduction. Want to help save endangered animals and birds? Conserve and protect the natural environment. Clean air and water are needed by both wildlife and you. Tax-deductible contributions aid our vital conservation work.*

"My second wife," Dust told me, "believed that our lives can be stabilized and fastened down. That there's a generally acceptable way to do things and the closer one sticks to that ideal, the better off we all are."

"What about your first wife?" I asked.

He took a sip of tea.

"She's dead," he said. "She was into celebrating the dimensions of the vibration of Being. That wasn't a particularly happy marriage either."

I picked up a different sugar packet, a wolverine.

" 'The wolverine is our largest weasel,' " I read aloud. " 'He is found on all continents in the northern hemisphere in both arctic and subarctic regions. Though wolverines have often plundered trappers' catches, research has proven that they are not the savage beasts that legend has made them out to be. Want to help save endangered animals and birds? Conserve and pro-

tect the natural environment. Clean air and water are needed
by both wildlife and you. Tax-deductible contributions aid our
vital conservation work.' "

"I always thought the wolverine's reputation was unde-
served," said Dust. "I'm so pleased to have this verified, before
I myself become extinct."

The waitress brought our food, steaming bowls of rice and
mixed-up vegetables and seafood in a sticky sort of sauce. She
placed them carefully on the table, then stood there, watching
the rice, as if waiting for something different to happen.

"Yes?" said Dust.

"Excuse me," she said, "but I can't help telling you that I
sense something from the both of you. I feel that I'm with kindred
spirits. That I understand how you're feeling. I sense a loneliness, a confusion, a profound sense of disappointment with life,
combined with an intense urge to live, as fully as possible. As
humanely, as meaningfully."

She had a good face, the face of someone who would give
me change if I asked her on the street. She was not the type of
person who would insult me, suggest that I kill myself, chase
me with sticks. Dust cleared his throat.

"You are correct," he said, "insofar as we both feel victim-
ized by forces beyond our control: weather patterns, the state
of the economy, illness, genetic makeup. A predilection for the
dark and twisted. You sense perhaps that we both feel pursued
in some way, by danger or merely death. That we are inexorably drawn toward human beings, despite our tendency to live
in our own fantasies. That we consider ourselves outcasts or
runaways."

"I'm a runaway of sorts as well," said the waitress. "I was
working with prisoners back home in Maryland, legal services
for those already incarcerated. I wanted to help the low, the
desperate. Who is more low and desperate than a prisoner, I ask
you? I was going to go to law school next fall. But my days were
filled with murderers, rapists, the dishonest and the insane. This
killer, he drew cartoons, all these enormous people. In the real
world, he said, everybody's big. He said, you know why none

of my cartoons look me in the face? Because they know that I'd erase them. I couldn't take it anymore. I drank a considerable amount, I fought with my boyfriend. I was burnt-out, I had something my parents insist on calling a nervous breakdown. I bought a car on credit and drove down the coast, until I got here, where I stopped and went to work waiting tables."

I watched her face, intent on disclosure. She was not the type of person who would kick me or spit on me or tell me about Jesus. Dust started eating.

"This is the problem I must put to you, for it's the question I am continually asking myself. What does somebody do, somebody who wants to help people, somebody like me, when they get to the point that they can look at another person, a human being in pain, and feel absolutely nothing? Where does one go? Will a brief stay in Florida cure me? Or will I stay like this forever, cynical, burnt-out and sick?"

Dust put down his chopsticks.

"Oh, you'll recover," he said. "Everybody does, in the long run, I'm afraid, from that peculiar disgust with living. I can't imagine that you really feel nothing."

The waitress looked thoughtful.

"You know," she said, "on my way down here, at a truck stop in North Carolina, I ran into this woman, she had long black hair and the oddest accent. She was riding a motorcycle, she'd stopped at the truck stop to get a cup of coffee and a piece of coconut pie. She looked frantic and dazed. I felt so much for her, she looked so desperate, yet so hopeful, I didn't know what to do. I tried to strike up a conversation with her but she mumbled something about always being followed and hurried away. Something about that woman, I can't pin it down, it just stuck with me. Very disturbing."

"What an amazing coincidence," said Dust, "but I believe I've met exactly the woman you're talking about, in Utah. She was somewhat dazed, she'd lost several years of her life, she'd thrown herself into the source on top of some pyramid in Oaxaca, in Mexico, one afternoon during an eclipse, and then suddenly it was five years later. She said her body felt like she'd been

riding a Mexican bus all that time. How she got to Utah, she
didn't know. She woke up there, in a corner booth at Denny's,
in Salt Lake City, a cup of coffee and a piece of coconut pie
sitting before her. The waitress asked her what happened to the
gentleman who ordered the pie. Rebeca didn't know. She paid
for the pie, then ran, as fast as she could. She was a trifle disori-
ented when I met her, at an Amoco down the road."

I wondered if Dust had made this up. I never knew what to
believe. He went back to his food, eating it artfully, with fluent
movements of his chopsticks. The waitress sighed, mumbled
something, and walked off toward the kitchen. I used my fork.

We ate in silence. At the next table people were loudly dis-
cussing the best technique for removing blueberry stains from
flannel bedspreads. The food was making me tired. I studied
the designs on the fan above our booth, intricate mountain scenes
with monks and waterfalls. I read another sugar packet to myself.

LARGEMOUTH BASS (Micropterus salmoides) *This popular game fish is one of the most voracious of underwater
animals and is not averse to eating smaller individuals of
its own kind. It is the male which protects the young,
chasing off the female as soon as eggs are laid. Want to
help save endangered animals and birds? Conserve and
protect the natural environment. Clean air and water are
needed by both wildlife and you. Tax-deductible contributions aid our vital conservation work.*

"You know what Heidegger suggested," said Dust. "He
suggested that we can intuit Being in three moods. Joy, boredom and dread. Somehow, in these three moods we feel Being
moving through us, we become somehow more aware."

I was bored. He was always talking to me like I was someone else, someone who understood. I picked chunks of imitation crabmeat out of my rice.

"Lately," he said, "I'm afraid I've been intuiting this experience of Being quite a lot, but only through the mood of dread."

The tablecloth seemed so red. I was suddenly struck by how

real it was. I stared at Dust, his dry, puckered skin. I wondered what it would feel like to touch it.

"Of course Heidegger turned out to be somewhat of a Nazi," said Dust. "As was my second wife. She thought that by the age of thirty, one had made all the necessary choices in life. I was considered one of her necessary choices. I, on the other hand, understood that she was not the end I had in mind to the story of my life. She viewed love as fulfillment, whereas I've always seen it as more of a tool for imbuing one's life with a certain sense of drama and desperation. Real life, I think, is somewhat of a shabby imitation of art. But my wife. She flew into a rage, it was perfect. *I'm not some character in a cheap novel,* she screamed, *I'm your wife.* Now she lives in Alabama with a man who loves her so much that he once locked her in his own closet for two days."

I poured sugar into my water and slurped it out of a straw. I knew that this was the sort of thing Dust wanted me to do. He cracked his fortune cookie open.

" 'You have a potential urge,' " he read, " 'and the ability for accomplishment.' A potential urge! How wonderful. If only I can actualize this urge. What's yours?"

I cracked the hard cookie with my teeth. The fortune was typed in green capital letters.

" 'You are ultimately concerned. You love sports, horses and gambling, but not to excess.' "

Dust sipped tea out of a tiny circular cup. Outside, the sunset swirled into the Gulf, pink and crimson. Our waitress announced that a couple two booths away were celebrating their fiftieth wedding anniversary. They stood and everyone applauded. The old man started to say something, something about luck and devotion, but his wife tugged on his sleeve and said, "Nathan, you shut up right now, I'm not going to sit here and watch you make fools of both of us. You shut up right now."

He sat down and the waitress led the customers in a round of "For They're a Jolly Good Golden Anniversary Couple." Then we headed home.

"Remind me," said Dust, as we walked across the parking

lot in the cool evening air, "never to come to this restaurant again."

At home, I slept. When I ate Chinese food, I dreamed about Jimmy.

The man with the suit and the orange mustache walked down the beach. Three times a day he passed our house, always in the same direction. He showed my picture to strangers. People could tell he was weird, his thought processes malformed. I felt things moving toward a danger, a climax. Dust told me real life never worked that way, things never got resolved.

I woke one night, right in the middle, and he was there, at the window. I sat up with a start. He was looking right at me. I couldn't move. He was outside, I was in. He didn't even knock at the window, he just looked at me, like he was bored.

I climbed out of bed, walked across the floor. Time was moving slow, locked in glass. I opened the window. He stepped in, silent. He looked around: the bed, the dresser, the bookcase, the walls, with art on them.

"Nice," he said. "You've done well."

I was scared, like he was going to do something quick and violent, slap me or kill me or break things. It passed. I realized: this is only Jimmy, back now, with me.

"What's in the refrigerator?" he asked.

I sat on the bed.

"Are you hungry?"

"No," he said, "I just ate. I'm thinking about for later."

He sat down next to me. I didn't wonder how he'd found me. It was just that he had. I realized it then, who needed who. Jimmy needed me. Vice versa, of course, but somehow not as much. I had Dust. The air conditioning chilled me, I could hear it generate through the house.

"You could sleep here," I said, "until morning. Dust won't get up until nine."

He was looking at his feet. I felt guilty. I wanted to offer

him more. Taken in, I was smaller. But I was in. I had things
that Jimmy didn't. I was civilized now.

"Are you planning to stick around here?" he asked. "Until
the old man dies? Or should we just take everything we can get
and go?"

It was so easy then, with Jimmy. I knew who to be. I bounced
gently on the bed, felt the vibrating springs. I looked at the
ceiling.

"That man is looking for us," I said. "He's here, at the beach.
The one from Columbia."

He jiggled his feet, up and down. He looked like a little kid.

"I feel safe here. I don't want to leave yet."

"All right. Can I get in here? Will the old man deal with it?"

I lay back, rested my hands on my rounded belly.

"No," I said. "He's seen the pictures, he knows who you
are. He's nervous enough about me. It's best if you stay hidden.
You can sleep in here if you want and I'll get you food and
money and blankets. He's got great pillows, Jimmy, the most
incredible pillows you've ever seen, feel these pillows."

Dust wouldn't care, he was dying anyway. I wondered if
Jimmy knew. I felt like a shit. This was the worst thing I'd ever
done almost, lying to Jimmy.

Him, who was everything I had.

"Great," he said. "Real nice. Pillows."

He grabbed one, walked back to the window without a word.
He was gone again.

I left the window open, felt the breeze move through the
room, lay there in the bed sideways, stared at the ceiling. I ran
my fingers over my throat, my Adam's apple. It seemed the only
thing to do. My Adam's apple, bumpy and weird. I don't know
why. I closed my eyes, moved my fingers, back and forth, over
my own throat.

When Jimmy came back I gave him things, books and paintings and sculptures, all these silly artifacts scattered about Dust's
house. Jimmy sold them to tourists on the beach or pawned them

and bought Sno-Kones, Michelobs, postcards, swimsuits with giant fish and tiny Hemingway faces printed all over them, ceramic ashtrays, foam sandals, lick-on tattoos, cigarettes. He shared the cigarettes with me under the pier, let me lick the tattoos and press them onto his shoulder, changed into his Hemingway swim trunks right there in front of me while I studied his shoulders and stomach and back, stole glances at his briefly naked butt. Meanwhile, Dust spent more time in bed dying, his cultural milieu slowly vanishing out from under him, utilized to feed Jimmy roasted pig and shellfish and other luxurious things to eat. Dust didn't notice.

We played backgammon, me and Dust. I was getting better, I was learning how to win. The man with the lizard's face and the mustache walked down the beach outside.

"He frightens you, doesn't he?" asked Dust.

I rolled the dice. Double sixes.

"I don't know who he is," I said, "or what he wants."

"Imagine the worst. How bad can it be? The worst thing I can imagine is being devoured by a horde of tiny suction-mouthed squids as country-western music plays in the background. I feel confident now that I will never experience such a thing. I am grateful for that fact."

He rolled. A four and a three. He had to leave himself wide open. Jimmy was at the window, watching us play.

"Everything seems to be up in the air at this time," Dust said.

I didn't understand old people.

"Dust," I said.

He moved the brown and white backgammon pieces absently in spirals with his finger.

"One of my wives once said to me—this is a problem, I know a wife said this to me, but I can't picture either my first wife or my second wife saying it. Did I have a third that I've since forgotten, assimilated into the other two? Anyway, whichever wife it was, she told me I was the crassest, most classless man she'd ever met. Listen. Honey, I said to her, living is a tacky thing, isn't it? Only absence is truly classy. But death is even tackier than life, better never to be born. It says that in the Bible, you know. Ecclesiastes. All that vanity."

"Dust," I said.

"I'd like to think that there's more to me than just the collection of my memories. That I'm more than just some sort of film archives, more than the accumulation of the things I've seen. I'd like to think that I'm not going to die. What are the four stages? Anger, denial. I'm afraid I missed out on denial somewhere. That's the one I'd have really liked. Acceptance? Don't believe it."

"Dust," I said, "I want to tell you. My dad. You remind me of my dad."

He looked at me, vacant, as if he hadn't heard. His eyes grew dark.

"I'll have none of that," he said. "I'm no surrogate father figure. You can't turn me into the image of your own desires. I'm afraid I won't have it."

I moved a smooth backgammon piece over my lips. I felt sad.

"Dust," I said, "listen."

Everything in his living room looked hungry. The paintings, the plants. Dust sighed.

"You find that love was never really what you wanted, only understanding. Eventually you give up on that too. All you want is an agreeable politeness, a kind word. Even just physical proximity."

I put down the dice and moved over toward him. I said, "I've been bad for a long, long time."

"Yes," he said, "but who's watching you?"

"Nobody's watching me," I said. "I'm on my own."

"Yes," said Dust. "Your parents are dead. God is dead. But you certainly are acting bad for somebody's benefit."

He thought he knew so much. He didn't know me at all, he didn't know anything. He was just old.

"Dust," I said.

Jimmy was gone from the window. I was in the wrong place.

"What?" asked Dust.

I looked down.

"Nothing," I said.

I felt myself floating around the room, moving, close to the ceiling, suspended between two things. Two things, mutually exclusive, but both of them necessary. I scrunched up my face like I wanted to cry. Dust put his arms around me.

"Matt," he said.

I buried my face in his shawl. He smelled like his name, he smelled yellow and dying. He pulled me in tighter.

"I'm sad, too," he said.

We sat in the darkness, listened to the Gulf. Eventually, Dust went up to bed and I sat there by myself. I walked alone through the dark house. With my bare feet sinking silently in the carpet the house seemed impossible and empty and large. I studied the painting of the woman's profile in leaves, *The Gust of Wind,* by Lucien Levy-Dhurmer. The leaves were thick, autumnal colors, her mouth hanging open, black hair blowing straight out away from her face.

I looked through drawers. I found silverware, fine china, letters, old books. I read a passage from a letter, something about cousins and lemonade. I could never make sense out of all of these details. I found a necklace. I crouched there on the floor, felt the weight of it in my hand. It was gold with tiny red stones. It looked expensive. I shifted it, back and forth, from one hand to the other. It caught the moonlight, sparkled in my hands.

I sat on my haunches, thinking.

I put it back in the drawer. It lay there, cradled in black velvet, next to a glass egg and a wooden plaque with a rhyme on it, something about a purple cow. I took it back out. I held it. I put it around my neck. I took it off. I poured it, back and forth, from one hand to the other.

I put it in the drawer. I went back up to bed, lay there in the dark. The house made sly creaking noises, as if the earth were shifting beneath it.

Days passed. Dust coughed, wheezed, stayed in bed. Dusk came and went. Inside, the shelves and walls were nearly empty. Jimmy moved around outside, and the man. It was cool outside, and fragrant. On the horizon the ship was floating, just above the water. I wanted to be carried away forever, but I didn't want to leave.

Then, an evening came and didn't stop. Dust called to me. "Matt," he said.

He looked bad, worse than usual, slipping. On the desk next to his bed a candle was burning.

"Don't believe it," he said, "that the dying take on a strange beauty just before their fateful moment. Matt. It's time."

I froze. This couldn't be helped. I had to do something.

"Death may be many things, but it certainly isn't a surprise," he said. "I am lonely and bitter and will not pretend that I have some crucial words of wisdom to pass on to the next generation before I go. But I want you here with me. I want to pretend I'm part of something larger, a continuum, the stream of life that eternally renews itself. That sort of thing. You will be my last vision. If that gives you some sense of identity it's purely unintentional. Matt."

I stepped back. Things were exploding, making noises in my brain. My head seemed full of toast crumbs, of firecrackers and brass wire. Dust shook his green pill bottle at me. It didn't make any noise.

"There's more," he said. "Downstairs. In the cupboard over the dishwasher. Get it."

He was shaking, his lips white. I expected pieces of his heart to come spewing from his mouth. They didn't.

"I'll call a doctor," I said.

"No," he said, "don't. My medication. The pain."

He grabbed my hand. His was rough and dry, my stomach turned. Death, I couldn't quite get a grip on it, I didn't know what it meant. I felt a vague disappointment, like the day after Christmas, a longing for intangible things that would never be received. I was scared.

"That girl in the white sundress," he said. "The shape of her breasts. A story my mother used to tell. A swimming hole, lying on the rocky ledge, wet and exhausted in the sun. So many mouths. Matt, I know that I've bored you. I'm no storyteller, I have no sense of how to tell a coherent narrative. If this is where narrative leads, who would ever want to? But Matt, boredom invites self reflection. Grab on to a word, apply it to your own life. *Loneliness, travel, choices, dinner, death.*"

I patted him on the head. What was I doing? What would I say on my own deathbed?

"Fuck it," he said, "I'm really going to die. Words, words, words, words, all of it. After I go, could you extinguish the candle? Assuming it doesn't go out all by itself. I want to at least do my deathbed scene perfectly, it's all I've got left. Matt, I need my medication, I need you here with me."

I stood. He couldn't leave me, not now. He couldn't leave me after all of this. I turned and ran. Down the stairs, and there I was, panicking. What to do? Where to begin? I looked for the phone, I found it. Who could I call? There was nobody to call, nobody who cared. His medication. In the kitchen, in the cupboard above the dishwasher. I turned, froze. Through the living-room window I could see him, walking up the stone path toward the house. The man. And then he was out of my vision, on the other side of the door.

He knocked. My limbs were runny, like egg yolk, my brain was scrambled and yellow.

Jimmy was there, beside me.

"Come on," he said. "We've got to go."

He moved up close. It was dark outside and everywhere.

"Matt."

"Matt!"

It was a shouted whisper, desperate, from above. Jimmy put his hand on my shoulder. His fingers were warm. He slid them across the back of my neck.

The man pounded on the door, obsessed.

"He's dying," I whispered. "I shouldn't leave him."

His eyes looked into me. His hands moved slow down my back, both of them. I had no choice, I knew it then. I was so relieved.

"It's not a case of doing what's right," said Jimmy. "That isn't the issue here. Get down or he'll see us. We have to get out the back way."

I crouched onto the carpet. The fiber burnt my hands as I scurried across it. I stopped, held still. Jimmy was next to me. I felt his breath on my ear.

"Hurry," he said, "or it might be too late."

I moved, swallowing, listening to the blood in my own veins. The sliding glass door moved sideways and we were out, gone, into the beachy night. We bent down, moving like crabs through the dark. Out around I could hear the man pounding and cursing. We ran, from shrubbery to towel stand and under the pier. We lay down on our bellies. I could watch it from there, the house and everything.

I was so relieved I didn't have to watch another person die.

I loved Jimmy and I wanted him. I wasn't sure exactly how or what I wanted to do. I closed my eyes, waiting. Waiting for him, a decision. We lay there, side by side. I pictured myself rolling over, with Jimmy, into the waves. I was waiting for his lips, his hands. I could feel my dick, hard against the sand.

I did it fast then, it was a movement past thinking, clumsy and knowing. I turned to him, grabbed him by the shoulders. I rolled him over and I was there, on top of him, my mouth all over. My teeth crashed against his chin, my hands were down below, ripping off his shirt, he was just there, underneath me, and then he was struggling, he pushed me off and I was there, under him. He had my arms pinned down and he was staring into me with those eyes. His shirt was torn open, his nipples tiny and dark. He was breathing hard, but he held me still, just looked at me. My mouth was dry. His hands were on my wrists and his lips were wet.

"Don't you touch me," he said, and he rolled off of me. He sat in the sand, looking away.

I thought I was going to burst open.

"I thought that's what you wanted," I said. Without his weight there I felt I was rising into the air. He laughed. It wasn't a laugh I recognized.

"I don't need anything from you," he said. "You should know that. I don't need anything from anybody."

He turned back fast, grabbed my arms again, pinned me down. I wanted him to hold me like that, I wanted us together.

"You know me," he said. "You know what I'll do if you ever fuck me over. I'll hunt you down and kill you."

He released me, rolled over, away. I lay there on the sand, my head filled with blood, the pressure pounding inside, hoping he'd change his mind, waiting to feel him there, next to me, on top of me.

Later, sirens rang and red lights flashed. Shouts echoed down from the house. Under the pier the ocean lapped toward us and the red lights moved off and on, over Jimmy's skin.

In the morning the sand scratched against me, the sky a mild and uninteresting despair. The ocean was simply big water, was no help at all. I coughed, empty. Jimmy lay beside me, sleeping.

Dust was dead, I thought.

It was only then that it really hit me. Dust was my friend, more than food and a bed. Now he'd left me alone on the beach in the sunlight, waiting for my own death, for something to move me toward it, for someone to tell me what to do.

The man was moving down the beach toward me. Gulls circled above him, he was far down, a shape, but I knew it was him. I started walking, then I ran, but it was like I wasn't moving. I looked back over my shoulder, saw Jimmy's huddled mass. I knew somehow that I was making a major mistake, but I kept on going, closer, and I was there, all out of breath in front of him. The sun burning me, sweat in my eyes. I moved forward one step. The brightness, the sun, the pain, just like the day of my own parents' funeral. Something bright blinding me, like a long flashing blade. A knife? The sweat in my eyes, a thick, painful film. Tears, salt, blindness, sun. Scorching blade, stabbing my eyes. I squinted at him and he darkened, momentarily transformed into an Arab. The sky reeling, sand, sun, sweat. I reached for my gun. *Blam*, I thought. *Blam, blam, blam*. But I didn't really have a gun. I wiped the sweat from my eyes, stepped forward.

"I'm him," I said. "I'm Matt."

The man looked confused. His mustache twitched, orange.

"I'm the one you're looking for," I said. "I'm guilty. I'm Matt. Go ahead, take me away."

His head jerked. He scratched his armpit. Then he took me away.

Δ

I killed my parents. It happened like this:

I am on my bed wishing, wishing my parents are dead. I hate them and I wish it, over and over again, I hope they die, I hope they die, I hope they die. I picture it in my head, I toss, turn, my head so filled with blood and hate, my sheets all soaked with sweat. I sleep, though, and I dream it: a man, with a knife, killing my parents. He is dark and frowning. He stands above their bed, he watches them for a moment and then he stabs them, he stabs them hard.

I wake up and it is true.

I step out of my bed, my bare feet on the floor. I step across the hall. I stand in the doorway to my parents' room, a child. It's like a movie without sound. I wish it and it happens, just like this. The man, his face, he's been there in my dreams, and now he is there exactly like in the dream.

He finishes. My dad's head falls to the side. I can see the blood, everywhere. Certainly, this isn't true. He rubs his eyes, looks at me, he isn't sure I'm real. I am. He hurries toward me, I know he'll kill me. My arms are shaking and my legs are shaking and the universe in general. But then he doesn't. He rushes right on past me, down the hall, down the stairs and out.

Murder is not such a rarity, I know that now. Bleeding is

hardly uncommon. I dream it often, whack, whack, it's such a silent noise, a knife in the air, like an invisible door between two places. Neither is backward, neither is forward, they're just two places; it's a door, you stand in it, it's now. I dream it often and others do too, I see it in their eyes, how scared they are of me, and it's only because of this: really, they're scared of themselves.

3

Nightfall.

Nightfall, nightfall, nightfall.

In the darkness now I wave my thumb, but my hopes are dim. My only chance at this hour is with the thrill seekers, the desperate, the suicidally drunk.

A car pulls over up ahead.

It's a college professor and his graduate-student wife, they say their names are Dick and Jane. They're from Nebraska, traveling to a convention in Indianapolis. The logic of traveling by way of Maryland eludes me. We exchange small talk for a moment, details, the weather. I'm in back.

"So," says Dick, "what do you like to do for fun?"

"For fun?" I say. I lean forward to talk. "I don't know. I like drinking coffee. I blew bubbles once, smoking cigarettes, so the bubbles filled up with smoke. That was fun. I like swimming in wide Texas rivers."

An enormous truck rumbles past. There are big orange letters on the back, they say DOLE BANANAS. The bumper sticker says JUST SAY NO.

"Oh," says Dick.

He pauses.

"Jane here likes to take off her clothes for fun."

Jane smiles, blushing.

"Oh," I say.

I lean back.

"Does that sound like fun to you?" asks Dick.

"Sure," I say, "why not?"

Dick is balding, Jane has long red hair. They aren't particularly attractive, but what they lack in physical beauty they more than make up for in congeniality. From back here I can see that something is going on up front, I'm not sure exactly what.

"Jane sure has a nice pussy," says Dick. "Here, scoot up, take a look at this."

I lean up again. Jane's skirt is down, and Dick is moving the fingers of his right hand up inside her as he drives.

"Oh," says Jane, "I like that."

"Check out those red hairs," says Dick. "You ever see a pussy like that?"

"Nope," I say, "never have."

Jane smiles at me.

"Here," says Dick, "why don't you give it a shot? My arm gets tired and it's hard for me to do it while I drive."

"Oh," I say. "Okay."

Hitchhikers have certain obligations to their rides. I give what I can. I reach my arm over the seat, down, and stick my fingers up inside her, slow. It's bumpy and slick in there. She clasps my hand with her own, moves it, fast or slow.

"That's perfect," she says. "You have nice fingers."

Dick is humming, dividing his attention between the road and the sexual act taking place in the passenger's seat.

"We drive a lot," says Dick. "It gets awful boring. You have to do something to fend off the boredom of those endless highway miles."

"Boredom can certainly be a problem," I say.

"Yes," says Dick. "Boredom, you could almost say it's the malaise of our age. Apathy, world-weariness. Would you say that's true, Jane? Do you think boredom is the malaise of our age?"

"Why certainly, Dick," says Jane. "More people are hanggliding, jumping from planes, taking vacations to Africa than ever before. If nothing else, we are bored."

"Affluence and freedom," says Dick. "We continually need to find ways to squander these resources. The situationists felt that boredom was always counterrevolutionary. The Chinese, on the other hand, felt you could pass through boredom to a sort of fascination."

"Was that fascination?" asks Jane. "Or fascism?"

"Was it the Chinese?" says Dick. "Or Andy Warhol?"

"Oh," says Jane, "faster."

"You know," I say, as Jane presses my hand back and forth, "somebody once told me that we can intuit Being in three moods. One of those moods was boredom."

"And what were the others?" asks Dick.

"Joy and dread," I say.

Dick steps on the gas.

"Hmmm," says Dick. "Wouldn't that just about cover everything? I'm not sure I see it. Who told you that?"

"Dust," I say.

"Oh," says Jane.

"He isn't experiencing Being in any mood," I say. "He's dead."

"Yes," says Jane, "that happens to a lot of people these days. Death is the most boring thing of all."

"I don't know," says Dick, "but Jane here experiences Being when somebody wiggles their fingers around inside her twat."

Jane has an orgasm. She moans and convulses.

"Is that Being," I ask, "or an escape from Being? I still haven't figured out this sex-death connection."

"Beats me," says Dick. "I'm in American Studies, not philosophy. I'm doing research on the infantilization of America. A landscape filled with shiny toys, reassuring slogans and immediate gratification."

"Thank you," says Jane, still breathing hard. "That was very good."

Life here smells of coconut deodorizer and vaginal juices. A crescendo of noise fills the night and a jet passes overhead.

"Funny," I say, "I was once told that flying jets past the speed of sound beats the orgasm by a long shot. A jet pilot in California told me that. He drove me along Highway 1 at a hundred miles an hour. Along the Big Sur coast, next to sheer cliffs that dropped into ocean and rocks. He told me a sonic boom was ten times better than any orgasm. He had no brakes."

"I wouldn't doubt it," says Dick. "Personally, I find driving along the interstate at night with my lights off more satisfying than an orgasm. Jane would disagree, though. Jane is somewhat partial to the orgasm. She has a theory about the orgasm, the orgasm as ultimate expression of love, some sort of transcendent bonding, climax as loss of self into something larger."

"In theory," says Jane, "I feel that a mutual orgasm between two people allows them to experience each other, as well as something beyond just the two of them. In theory, the orgasm is the highest form of human expression."

She pauses.

"In practice, though, I take it how I can get it."

A trail of lights glitters along the edge of the road, reflectors giving back the glare of our own headlights. Schizophrenics tend to be mystics. And children, dictators, travelers. Entrepreneurs, those who've lost Jesus, the hungry and those who own cats. Joy, boredom and dread.

"You're a mystic, too," I say.

"Of course," she says. "I took a course in physics last semester. I'm doing my dissertation on Reagan, television and the *I Ching*. I'm reading Nietzsche. *Beyond Good and Evil*."

"I read that in Los Angeles," I say. "I was there for a month, working as a janitor. The best job I ever had, certainly the most spiritual. But where do you go after L.A.? The end of the road. Time stopped during a traffic jam there once. Nothing moved, the sun was like syrup, I bounced from hood to hood. Animals screeched, the lost and the damned crawled on their knees through frozen time."

"I hear that happens a lot, out in L.A.," says Jane. "Me, I'll always be a midwesterner. Life may be more boring here, but it's not quite so seething with nihilism and despair."

"Nietzsche can be dangerous, I believe," says Dick, "in the hands of the intellectually feeble and the emotionally unbalanced."

"Yes," I say, "that would be me."

He flicks the headlights off. The highway vanishes, everything is black, and we are rushing through it. My heart is bouncing here and there in my chest, valves open wide. I count to myself, waiting. One thousand one, one thousand two . . .

"Oh, God," says Jane, breathless.

My heart gallops now, like a herd of stampeding gazelle. I've never seen such a herd, but my imagination supplies the needed metaphor. We pass a dark billboard, a muscular figure, I can't make out the face. So much darkness, a sky freckled with stars. Headlights are our friends: turn them back on, turn them back on . . . In the distance, to our right, I see red taillights. The road will curve. Perhaps we will curve with it.

"Everybody gets such a kick out of toying with death," whispers Jane.

He flicks the lights back on. A raccoon's eyes reflect mystery at the side of the road. I breathe. I know why people do these things, the relief. I feel ready to live.

"American rituals," says Dick. "The road, fast food, sacrifice, death."

Jane turns to me.

"Are you ready to do it again?" she asks. "Or are your fingers tired?"

I say nothing. I reach down, push my fingers into her, harder now, this time, harder and faster.

Δ

It was monstrous, the bus trip back to East Liberty, a caterwauling dreamscape. Chug, chug, chug, wheezing into small-town bus depots, down neon strips of Denny's, Rodeway Inns, McDonald's, past car dealerships, carpet warehouses and crematoriums. My neck ached. I drifted in and out, between sleep and hallucinatory reality: the bus trip back. Back, to East Liberty, to the orphanage. Back, through smoky layers of time and space, layers of screaming cats in heat, babies crying, shuffling drifters. Moving in reverse, toward my own fetid nightmare, the living apparition that waited at the end of that narrow tunnel of Greyhound hell: Father Larry. Father Larry wasn't dead.

The man with the orange mustache was nothing but a sleazy private detective, hired by Father Larry. He'd been tracking me and Jimmy for months, frequently made comparisons between himself and a bloodhound. He had no real legal authority, although he did cuff my wrist to his own from time to time, to impress the sixteen-year-old girl in the halter top who was traveling across the country with her catatonic aunt. Sultry-eyed and quiet, she listened without interest or boredom as he bragged about outlaws he'd pursued: a serial killer in Houston who preyed on blond women named Suzanne; a man who'd married three different women and killed them for their insurance; teenagers in Missouri who stole flags and had sex on top of Old Glory.

"Not that I have anything against teenage sex," he said, leering at the sixteen-year-old girl. "It's just that desecration of the flag that makes my skin crawl."

He turned to me.

"You are a wretched example," he said. "of the decadence and deviance that run amok in our society today. Richard Nixon appeared to me in a dream once, he told me things. I know how deep the sickness goes, and I know the cure. Discipline, authority, God in the schools. I work on a magazine, in between jobs tracking down the criminal element, we've studied these things intensively. I wrote an interesting article about the connection between handgun legislation and sexual deviance. I'll give you a copy when we get back to East Liberty."

"Thanks," I said, "but I don't read."

"Oh, Christ, look at that."

Outside on the road a man was hitchhiking. It was me again, my own future, searching for Andalusia.

"Road scum," said the man. "They're everywhere. I don't want my baby growing up in a country filled with that slime. We need somebody to clean up these highways, make the country safe again."

"Again?" I said. "You mean it used to be safe? When was that?"

"You think you're awful smart, little boy," said the man, "but you don't know a damn thing. I'll tell you when it was. It was in between the time the last hostile Indians were killed and when that faggot Jack Kerouac first headed west. Entire decades when a man could travel across this great land with the utmost security. That's when it was."

He fondled his orange mustache.

"This kid," he said, thumbing toward me, "is a very bad boy in need of a good spanking. Obviously, there's been a lack of discipline in his life. It's everywhere these days. There are millions of people in need of a good spanking. Maybe," he said, grinning slyly at the girl, "you're in need of a good spanking, too."

She batted her lashes at him. In the back of the bus a child wailed. Not plaintive or pleading, just a low, steady wail, free of expectations.

We rolled along for days. Occasionally at rest stops the man would take me into the bathroom and shove my head into the toilet, hold it there until I thought this time I would die, kick me, dig his fingernails into my neck. On the bus sometimes, as soon as I fell asleep he would light matches and start burning the hair on my arms, stick safety pins into my forehead. Days and nights of broken slumber, bus stations filled with trampled zombies, the destitute, the broken, the invisible army of the sad who fill this nation from top to bottom. Vending machines, Styrofoam cups of coffee, Donettes, disgruntled bus-station employees. I remember a man whose entire face was smashed in, like he'd been hit with a poker. Miniature televisions, video games, lost luggage, landscapes. People disappeared into the bathroom at the back of the bus and never came out. Old women pulled fried chickens endlessly from paper sacks, bottomless bags of drumsticks and wings. They sucked the meat off the bones, licked the grease off their fingers. Outside the window, women on fences waved, then ran after us, waving red kerchiefs, as if something was passing them by; their last chance.

It was my birthday.

"I'm fifteen years old," I told the man. "Today. I'm fifteen today."

"You're lucky you aren't at war," he said. "A lot of places fifteen-year-old boys are soldiers. Burning, looting, raping. Something like that would be good for you, build a little character. You don't realize how lucky you are, living in the freest country in the world."

"It's my birthday," I said.

"What?" he asked. "You want me to buy you a cupcake?"

I watched out the window.

"Sure," he said, "give me the little misunderstood delinquent routine. I know your type. Listen, Al Capone. Your precious freedom is gone now, you can kiss your freedom goodbye. You're mine, buddy. All mine."

I closed my eyes, tried to block him out. Tried to make my mind a blank, to forget the fact that Father Larry was waiting.

In East Liberty the bridge was out, destroyed by a tornado, just like the first time. Again, I crossed the river on a ferry. Again, mist rose from the river and the night was filled with the shrieks of the tornado dead. If Florida was the land of the dead, what did this boundary signify? Just a holdover, I decided, from the times when there was some distinction between the land of the living and the land of walking ghosts. The lizard-faced man trembled, our handcuffs rattled like bones. A voice floated over the water, "Alms for the dead, alms for the dead . . ." Again, a hand emerged from the water, clasped the edge of the boat. Again the ferryman crunched it under his heel. I chose to ignore all of this, the sense of ritual and déjà vu. The eerie implication that my life wasn't a straight line after all, that I was moving in cycles, condemned to endless repetitions.

Book TWO

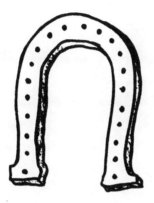

This was the creation and reflection he shared with another and leaned upon as upon one frame that stood—free from material restraint and possession—as the light and life of dead or living stars whom no one beheld for certain in the body of their death or their life. They were a ghost of light and that was all. The void of themselves alone was real and structural. All else was dream borrowing its light from a dark invisible source akin to human blindness and imagination that looked through nothingness all the time to the spirit that had secured life.

—WILSON HARRIS—
"The Palace of the Peacock"

SEVEN

Δ

East Liberty was a town with three churches and one bar, the East Liberty Tap, right across the street from East Liberty Auto and two doors down from East Liberty Flowers and Such. It was a town which fate and a drunken pioneer had placed five miles north of North Liberty and ten miles west of West Liberty. It was a town sandwiched between trailer courts, a town where people had ornamental wooden fences between their yards and ceramic deer grazing out front. It was a town filled with the semi-retired, with self-employed mechanics, with women who wore platinum wigs and with those who had just recently eliminated saturated fats from their diet. It was a town with an orphanage, an orphanage which was quickly being converted into a luxury resort.

Desmond Boekki was dead. Like so many of us, he had been an orphan, his parents killed by a falling rock somewhere in Mississippi. In contrast to all the orphans I'd ever known, he rose above his humble origins, in classic miniseries style, and amassed incredible wealth through the design and manufacture of corrugated pallets. He had gone on into jogging shoes, publishing houses, chain bookstores and fast food as well, with a brief foray into small plastic knobs. Whether money brought him happiness, through the freedom it created to self-actualize, or only bitterness, loneliness and despair, as all of his illusions crumbled one by one, I cannot say. Something, either philanthropic love or the guilty conscience of a man who had stepped on countless unhappily married midlevel bureaucrats on his way to the top, motivated Boekki to leave his entire fortune to the East Liberty Home for Boys.

Land was bought, extensions built. The Desmond Boekki Swimming Pool, the Desmond Boekki Golf Course, the Desmond Boekki Aerobics Spa, the Desmond Boekki Laser Research Center, all connected to the orphanage by tunnels and skyways, through Japanese gardens and silent spaces filled with sculptures done by bored local brain surgeons. Cooks were hired, cleaning ladies, recreation therapists, tennis instructors, women in slit skirts. Orphans who had been sent out on their own in leaner years were tracked down and welcomed home. East Liberty was a boomtown.

This was the town I discovered upon my return. The man with the orange mustache led me past rainbow-lit fountains to the Desmond Boekki Ice Cream Parlor and Transcendental Meditation Workout Center. He was seated there, waiting. Father Larry.

"Matt," he said, smiling, "welcome home. It's good to see you. How've you been?"

There was a tube running from his groin to a small pouch against his calf, filled with pale yellow liquid. He was older and balder. I looked at the floor.

"I don't know where he is," I said.

"Where who is?"

"Jimmy," I said. "You know what I'm talking about."

I'd been gone less than a year. Inconceivable spaces separated then from now, arctic wastelands, journeys by train around the world. Larry smelled of urine.

"Matt," he said, "that's not why I brought you back. I brought you back out of a concern for your well-being. Ideally, Jimmy would be here, too. Things are different here now. There's a good life for you. I don't blame you for anything that happened."

I watched the fluid, trickling down the tube.

"You won't be held against your will," he continued. "You're free to come and go as you please. But you can have your own room here, your own television, stereo, fish tank and personal computer. Your own telephone, with an answering machine, so you don't miss any calls."

I laughed.

"Who's gonna call?" I asked. "Jimmy? He won't come here. I'll never see Jimmy again."

The ice cream parlor was filled with flowering plants, posters of cartoon people levitating. I didn't know if this was true about Jimmy.

"I don't want to punish him," said Larry. "I want to make things better. For all of us. We all made mistakes in the past."

The man with the orange mustache stepped forward.

"I can find him," he said. "I found this one, didn't I? I'd suggest you beat some American values of hard work and decency into this one before it's too late."

"Fuck off," I said.

He grabbed me by the shoulders.

"Listen," he said.

Larry stood up.

"Let him go," he said. "Listen, we don't need you anymore. You can pick up your check in the payroll office, third floor of the Desmond Boekki Bureaucracy and Concert Recital Wing."

The man didn't release me.

"He's *my* prisoner," he said. "I found him."

"You have no authority here," said Larry.

He released me, giving me a slight shove in the process. He snarled at me and made a slow circle around the ice cream parlor.

"Is that right?" he said. "No authority. Just suppose I was to unzip my pants right here and now and urinate on this potted plant in the corner. Who'd stop me?"

Larry studied his nails.

"You? No? Maybe little Al Capone here would come to the rescue. What do you say, Al?"

The man tugged on his pants.

"As a matter of fact," said Larry, "nobody would try to stop you at all. I'd simply be forced to deduct the cost of the plant from your pay."

The man stared at the ferny growths of the plant below him. "It's a very expensive plant," said Larry.

The man seemed momentarily lost and stupid. He gave the pot a gentle kick.

"Your plant isn't worth shit," he said. "Like I'd really want to pee on your stupid plant anyway! I could urinate anywhere I damn well pleased, I'm still a man, you hear? I'll pee in the sink, off a mountain or in a plant any time of the day, a real solid stream. Understand?"

He snarled at me again and strutted toward the door.

"Dickless communist," he said and he was gone.

Larry stared at the revolving fan on the ceiling.

"Maybe, Matt," he said, "you discovered life in the outside world wasn't all that you thought it might be."

I wasn't going to listen to this.

"Maybe you're tired," he said. "Maybe you want a place to call home, people to care for you."

"He shot you," I said.

"Yes," he said. "I'm not embarrassed to say it. He shot me in the groin."

I looked away.

"He blew your dick off," I said.

Larry was silent. Behind the counter a young woman was mumbling to herself, reciting new flavors, a ritual chant. Serendipity Sunflower, Boekki Boysenberry, Coffee Peanut Butter Jubilee.

"Remember when you first came here?" asked Larry. "You used to curl up in dark closets all alone. You were a pathetic creature, Matt. I'm pleased to see you're a bit spunkier now. Did Jimmy teach you that?"

A clock ticked, the harsh plucking sound of passing time. The building, the town, the chanting, it all made me so damn tired.

"I'm not a bad person," said Larry, "and I think under different circumstances we could get to be friends. Maybe we still can. I'd like for you to think of me as a father, Matt. Is that so much to ask? I can give you things now. This is all I've ever wanted. To give you orphans as much as I could, to give you the benefits that I never had when I was growing up."

"I imagine you grew up without shoes," I said, "wading barefoot through six-foot snowdrifts to school every morning."

He gave me his most mournful look.

"I suppose most everyone's an abused child," he said. "Maybe it's part of the definition."

I cracked my neck.

"You probably know that there were . . . incidents between Jimmy and me. But I'm a changed man. I have Jimmy to thank for that, I suppose. Oh, sure, I miss my penis sometimes, but really, I think it's usually more trouble than it's worth. I'm fulfilled now, Matt. I can give you orphans things, everything money can buy."

He chewed on his lip, thoughtfully.

"I've taken up painting," he said. "I'd like to show you some of my work sometime. I prefer thick brushes, bold colors, broad strokes. I've taken up croquet. I play the clarinet as well."

Paintbrushes, mallets, woodwinds. I looked around the ice cream parlor, searching for a distraction. The woman behind the counter was suspended in air, several inches off the ground.

"Why don't you show me to my room?" I asked.

He led me through tunnels, hallways, circular stairways, glass elevators. This was the scenic route. He was impressing me with the many wonders of my new home, the technology and the nature, the corporation and the artwork all living together in a lush coexistence. Factories and gardens, sculptures and vending machines.

"Life here," said Larry, in a hushed voice, "has never been more convenient."

My room was clean, well groomed. Items were stored in their proper places. Clothes, toiletries, electric appliances. My window overlooked barren fields, tentative construction sites. I just wanted to sleep.

"Rest," said Father Larry. "You're home now, Matt. This is your home."

He left and I lay there, on a real mattress again. I prayed it wasn't true.

The transformation in Father Larry was amazing. From a child-molesting lunatic who wanted nothing more than to be a Catholic priest into a shrewd, artistic corporate executive. Between the loss of a penis and the acquisition of a financial empire, he'd come to resemble a sort of giant squid; enormous without being hostile, graceless and impotent, but still alarming. His days of tyranny were over. He was too busy playing the stock market, investing in chocolate factories in Third World countries, inventing new ice cream flavors, painting landscapes in bright, primary colors, landscapes that always seemed to resemble nude bodies. While there were plenty of maids, counselors, and investment analysts running around the orphanage, authority figures were in short supply. But authority abhors a vacuum, and leaders inevitably rose from the ranks of the orphans. Factions formed, alignments of worldview, distinguishable by haircut, color of high-top tennis shoes and preferred drug of abuse: alcohol, codeine, aerosol fumes or diet pills chopped into a fine powder. The lines between factions weren't firm. As particularly charismatic orphans came and went, as musical trends went in and out of favor, things changed. Ramone, a skinhead leader, found Jesus after attending a U2 concert on acid and confusion reigned for weeks, as orphans gave up drinking, tried to grow ponytails, collected aluminum cans for hungry Ethiopian children. I searched for good deeds to do as well. I read stories to the youngest orphans at bedtime, *The Stranger* or *As I Lay Dying*.

A summer passed, ice cream and sand, another winter in which newspapers blew down cold and empty streets. They sent me to high school, but I skipped class a lot, rode the bus into Iowa City, sat on benches in the Old Capitol Mall. I wandered through video arcades, underwear stores, chain bookstores. One day, as I was leaning over the railing on the second floor of the mall, salivating as I watched people walk below me, a girl walked up and stood beside me.

"Hey," she said.

"Hey," I said.

She leaned over the railing and hummed some song I couldn't recognize.

"Are you a mall maggot?" she asked.

"A mall maggot," I said.

"Yeah," she said. "You know. One of those high school kids who have no structure in their lives. So they spend all their time hanging out at the mall."

"Oh," I said. "I don't know. I've never considered myself a mall maggot."

"I think I'm a mall maggot," she said. "The security guard here was telling me about them one day. He told me what a tough job he has, keeping an eye on the mall maggots. These kids, he said, they're an eyesore. People who come here to buy things, they shouldn't have to look at this. It ruins their shopping experience, these mall maggots. As much as possible, he said, they keep them moving along. But you have to remember, he said, that the mall maggots might be potential consumers, too. So you have to take it a little easy on them. This is just what he told me. I thought about it, and I realized, I'm a high school kid with no structure in my life. I spend a lot of my time hanging out here. But I just moved to town, so maybe I'm not official yet. I thought you looked kind of like a mall maggot, too."

She was the skinniest human being I'd ever seen, short, with pale hair. She looked ethereal, charmed. She spoke slowly and distinctly, as if conversing was a great effort. She bit her nails.

"I'm Matt," I said. "Who are you?"

"Frita Bob," she said. "Don't ask about my name. My dad's got a few quirks, but my family's really good people. People you'd want to know. We never hurt anybody and we're fun when we're drunk. I'm not lying."

"I wouldn't expect you to," I said. I liked her, I liked looking at her. She was conscious and warm. She tapped her foot. I wanted to keep her talking, keep her there with me.

"Your dad," I said.

"My dad's my best friend," she said. "He smokes and brings home strange women. His back is covered with tattoos. Really, I'm not lying. Three things he told me he better never catch me doing, you know what they were? Smoking, premarital sex, or tattoos. But, you know. That's just how dads are."

She blushed then and looked at her feet. She had plastic hoop earrings. I couldn't think of anything to say.

"Are you hungry?" I asked.

She frowned.

"Not really," she said. "But if you want to get something from the All American Deli I'll sit with you."

We walked toward the deli.

"There's the record store," I said.

"Yes," she agreed.

In the deli we sat and looked at the laminated menus. The deli: ceiling fans, plastic greenery, Grant Wood reproductions and bronze American eagles on the wall. I ordered soup and a turkey sub. She ordered a small lettuce salad and ate it slowly, leaf by leaf. We drank boysenberry spritzers.

"You're really mellow," she said. "You seem like the most gentle person I ever knew."

"Right," I said.

"I'm not lying," she said.

"I'm an orphan," I said. It wasn't that I was trying to impress her. I just had nothing else to say.

"My mom's gone," she said. "I'm not sure if she went crazy or if she married a Catholic. She might be in New Zealand. I don't know."

She finished her salad. I looked at sugar packets. They were the same packets they had in Florida, with wildlife.

" 'BOHEMIAN WAXWING,' " I read. " 'The wanderings of the Bohemian Waxwing are very erratic. Some winters in the northern U.S., depending on the food supply, it may appear in great flocks; other years it may be absent. Want to help save endangered animals and birds? Conserve and protect the natural environment. Clean air and water are needed by both wildlife and you. Tax-deductible contributions aid our vital conservation work.' "

"Excuse me," Frita said, "I've got to go to the bathroom."

She slid out of the booth and into the bathroom. I heard a loud noise from in there, a retching. The other customers looked momentarily alarmed, then pretended they hadn't heard. She came out smiling, as if nothing had happened.

I sipped my spritzer. My whole life seemed filled with eating disorders. She was so small. Her clothes were baggy, hanging loose from her body like some twisted utopian vision.

"I've got to go," she said, standing, brushing invisible lint off her skirt.

"Maybe we can hang out sometime."

"Sure," she said. "Meet me back here tomorrow. Same place, same time. We can do mall-maggot stuff."

I met her again the next day. We hung out at the mall, watched people walk by, rode the escalators.

"What's it like living in this town?" I asked. "I mean, you know, as opposed to living in an orphanage. Do you have neighbors and grocery stores down the street?"

"It's Iowa City," she said. "I don't know. The physical reality of Iowa City is meaningless."

I figured she'd read that somewhere and was trying to impress me with her advanced ideas. I pretended I knew what she meant. Later, I did know.

"How about the orphanage?" she asked.

"It's pretty posh," I said. "I mean really, there's all sorts of luxuries. One of the other orphans, he told me that he poisoned his parents with an overdose of calcium just so he could get into the orphanage. I don't know. The halls are well lit but it always seems dark anyway. Like invisible bulbs have burnt out."

"I suppose all those orphans all crammed together might be a little overwhelming," Frita said. "All those dead parents haunting you, bumping into each other and quarreling. There was a ghost at the mission I stayed at in Sioux Falls. I'm not lying."

We walked out of the mall, onto the street. A man in a black hat was playing the cello.

"I always wanted to do that," she said. "Either play the cello or be an astronaut. But I think it's too late. Stuff like that you have to get an early start on."

"I used to want to be an intellectual," I said, "like my dad. But I'm not smart enough and too lazy."

"I'd hate to learn French," Frita said, "but I do like the clothes they wear."

Frita Bob was curious and shy. She talked a lot, but she never looked at me when she was talking. She pretended she didn't care, but I knew that she liked me. We laughed together and ran around the university campus. There were figures in chalk on the sidewalks and the words A WOMAN WAS RAPED HERE. We walked from spot to spot, trying to find a pattern. We walked through university buildings, listened to the laughter of cadavers in the basement of the med labs, spied on bearded scientists dancing to disco rhythms on their transistor radios, boogieing with subatomic particles. We talked to the men who picked cans out of the trash about physics, metaphysics, cybernetics and anthropology. We waded in a fountain downtown, a sculpture that was suggestive of three women urinating, and we drank milkshakes at the Hamburg Inn, at least I did and Frita pretended to, the Hamburg Inn, where shady poets huddled in the corner, furtively eating greasy cheeseburgers and french fries.

"You children," one of the shady poets whispered to us, seeing that a plague of elderberry beetles had followed us into the restaurant. "How unfortunate, the end of innocence into which you were born. The children are dying, the crops drying up. Love amongst the Styrofoam ruins of a civilization in decline."

"I'm an orphan," I told him, knowing he'd be impressed. "I used to live on the streets of St. Louis."

"I imagine your life was filled with that urban, postmodern sense of decadence and angst," he said.

"I peed on somebody once for money," I said. "I don't know. We stole food. Is that postmodern decadence and angst?"

"Everything is," he muttered. "Conundrums and vanities, mishmash and bric-a-brac. A real hodgepodge of inanities, a real brouhaha."

He scurried back to his corner, where the other poets were trembling and drooling. We slurped the remains of our milkshakes and stumbled onto the brick street. It was tornado weather, everything green and still. I could feel the thrill of it in my fingers, my eyes: the hush, the darkness, the threat of a storm.

"Come on," I said.

I grabbed her hand and we ran. We circled above the city, climbed fire escapes to the top of Seashore Hall, obviously a building named by surrealists, and peed off the top. We wandered around the cemetery, read tombstones and studied the statue of the black angel that hovered there. It used to be white, years ago, and if we looked it in the eye, we would die. We lay in the cemetery grass, waiting to feel phantoms slide over us, their cool, hushed breezes.

"I like cemeteries," Frita said. "They're so old and peaceful. It's so thoughtful of the living to keep up the lawns, don't you think?"

"I slept in a cemetery once," I said. "In Indiana, back when I was living on the road. With Jimmy. Those were the days. Wild and free, nobody to answer to."

"Who do you answer to now?" she asked.

"Well, nobody," I confessed, "but it's different at the orphanage. I don't know. It was different then. I was on the edge of something, life was exciting. Me and Jimmy . . . we were like Butch Cassidy and the Sundance Kid."

"You wish you weren't with me, don't you?"

She was running her fingers over the worn inscription on a tombstone. JEFF TOLLESFRUD, BORN 1911, DIED 1968. HE WAS A GOOD HUSBAND, A FATHER, A REPAIRER OF DRUMS. HE TOOK CARE, GATHERING UP HIS BEING AND PROJECTING IT TOWARD DEATH. A GENUINE DASEIN.

"Not that it matters," said Frita Bob.

"Of course not," I said. "I mean, I have fun here and all, it's just, see, I was an outlaw then. Always running around and being outside in the middle of everything, like this. Wild and free."

"You don't look like an outlaw," she said. She climbed into a tree. "I don't know. We used to travel around some when I was younger. We lived at a mission back in Sioux Falls for a while, when Dad was in jail. I never did find out what he was in for, it wasn't long. I looked like a pig then. Once I stayed with this woman for two weeks and slept with her puppies. I got ticks. I tell you, that sucked, you know it? And once they tried to take me away from my dad, but we left."

She was hanging up above me, swinging from a branch. Her shirt pulled up, I could see her ribs sticking out.

"Once these women came to the mission, they brought Jell-O and cookies, then stood in a circle and sang 'Kumbaya.' "

"You're skinny," I said. "You should eat more. If you don't eat you'll disappear. Poof. You'll just vanish in thin air. Stuff like that happens all the time."

"You're skinny," she said. "You're the skinny one."

"Sure," I said, "but not like you. You're anorexic."

"I thought you were my friend," she said.

I climbed up in the tree and we sat up there with the leaves, looking out over the garden of tombstones.

"I like people who climb trees," she said. She was in the branch above me, her leg hanging down. It brushed against my shoulder, but then she moved over a little. I moved over, too, so I was next to her foot again, barely touching it. We were quiet, listening to the wind.

I started skipping entire weeks of classes. It wasn't that I had anything against knowledge, it was just high school, and she skipped too. We wrote each other notes on orange rinds, arranged rendezvous as if there was something forbidden about our friendship. We hung out in the public library. The amount of knowledge to be acquired in such a place was devastating, computer screens held me spellbound with their lists of potential subjects: Sexual Ethics, Signs and Symbols, Slavery in the

United States, Smoking (See Cigarette Smoking), Space and Time—Picture Books. I educated myself randomly. I read of a man who was convinced that a long-dead puppydog, a childhood pet, lived inside his mind, craving expression. Thus the abrupt mournful barks those who attended him would sometimes hear. I searched Cirlot's *A Dictionary of Symbols*, curious about the deeper meanings in my life; my missing toe, Larry's missing penis, Frita Bob's desire to starve herself. In primitive cultures maimed beings and madmen were believed to possess supernatural powers. In some mythologies maimed beings were connected with the phases of the moon. The foot was what confirmed man's direct relationship with the earth and was frequently phallic in significance. The phallus was a symbol for the perpetuation of life, of active power and the propagation of cosmic forces. It didn't mention the desire to destroy the populations of cities while leaving buildings intact, the Washington Monument or CIA assassinations. It didn't say anything about anorexia as a struggle to remain free from a world of consumption, a last-ditch effort to neither consume nor be consumed. It did say, about *disappearance,* "in many folk tales, medieval legends and myths, sudden disappearances occur. Sometimes this is as a result of the translation of the vanished object to distant places, and sometimes as a result of pure and simple annihilation or destruction. Psychologically, this is a symbol of repression, particularly if the vanished object is malign or dangerous. In reality, it is a form of enchantment." Andalusia had disappeared, my parents. Traveler, Jimmy, Dust. In Guatemala a new government had just been installed, a friend of President Reagan, and people were being disappeared by the thousands. I watched people scurry about the library, wondering who'd be next.

I pored over a book of photographs from 1892, Muybridge's *The Human Figure in Motion.* Naked men wrestling, naked men climbing stairs, naked men hitting baseballs, a naked child with no legs climbing in and out of a chair. I sought out secret histories, psychic conspiracies, the cannibalistic rituals of vanished tribes, habitual ruptures in the space-time continuum, while Frita Bob read to me from *The Dictionary of Popular Misconceptions About 19th Century German Philosophers* or *The Bride's Book of Etiquette.*

" 'If you decide to call it off,' " she read, " 'count yourself lucky to have avoided the agony of divorce. Send a release to every paper that announced your engagement, reading: "The engagement of Miss Ann Smith and Mr. Jacob Jones has been terminated by mutual consent." In the tragic case of a fiancé's death before the wedding, the presents must also be returned by some member of the family.' "

Downstairs we could rent video movies and watch them on the library TVs. I checked out *Vanishing Point*, it was just like I remembered it; the blind black DJ, Super Soul, guiding the last great American hero in his pointless race across America. The faith healers, the old man who trapped snakes in the desert, the naked woman on a motorcycle, but just at the end, at the point where his car was supposed to waver and vanish, right on into some other dimension, eluding the cops, blowing every-one's mind, he was gathering speed, faster, gone, no, he crashed into the police barricade and his car blew up and that was the end of the movie as the credits rolled over the image of the burning white Challenger.

"They changed the movie," I said to Frita. "Those fuckers. They changed the ending. He didn't use to die."

"Maybe your memory's wrong," she said.

"No," I said, "they changed it."

"I suppose they could do that," she said. "Are you mad?"

What kind of a world was this where the endings could be changed, *Vanishing Point* rewritten, history disappeared? Frita Bob seemed scared. So much scared her; big dogs, flocks of birds, salesclerks, the yellow flowers that bloomed in the middle of the night, jumping off bridges.

The river was filthy, oily and brown, but I jumped off the bridge into it and Frita Bob watched, it was so cold it made my heart jump and we laughed a lot then, that's what I remember most, the laughing, and sitting on the street corners in town listening to musicians sing, it was almost like being in the city, except it was peaceful. We walked along the tracks and rode trains, back and forth across town, trains that went nowhere, just wheezed, back and forth across town, filling the evenings with their lonesome train whines, to inspire all the poets in black who huddled in the back of the Hamburg Inn with their greasy cheeseburgers and fries. There were sunny days when everyone was smiling and throwing Frisbees and the preachers would come and talk to the students on the lawn of the campus, calling them fornicators and drunkards. We smoked cigarettes and blew bubbles, we'd fill the bubbles with smoke and they'd float away from us, burst, creating a tiny wisp in the air. Art History TAs juggled goldfish, fraternity boys dribbled basketballs for muscular dystrophy, gangs of skateboard punks cruised up and down the mall. People seemed happy then, and I was one of them: a person, happy.

It felt like I was having a normal sort of life, a romance or a friend, although the way I knew she stuck her finger down her throat was a little bit disturbing. That was what made her smaller than me, weaker, and that made me strong. I knew things. I could look out for her.

Still, sometimes at night I went out walking alone. I needed that, to be alone out there, walking in the night. That sense of power; being outside in the dark with everybody else in there, not knowing where you are. I didn't do anything. I only thought about it, about how easy it was to take things or destroy things. Dust had been right. I wanted to throw bricks through windows. Criminal isn't a set of actions so much as a state of mind. People who owned things didn't have to think they were criminals, they had the law. Still, I could walk down the street, thinking *I can do anything*, reeling with the knowledge that no one would stop me. That I wouldn't even stop myself.

The weather turned cold. We bought dope from a college student named Luke with big hair and a poster of a huge beer can on his door. Inside there was music playing, old couches, a green haze. Luke sat in a big chair, sucking on a three-foot bong.

"How do you like the stereo?" he asked.

"It's a nice stereo," I said. "It sounds really good."

"I bought it with drug money," he said.

"That's OK," said Frita. "We're not ones to judge."

"I didn't figure you would be," said Luke. "You know how it goes. My grades were bad. Dad's always pressuring me to be a big success. He's somewhat of a failure himself."

I lit the bong, a long, hazy purple tube, it filled with smoke and I sucked it out. It expanded in my lungs, pressed on the inside of my chest, but I held it in.

"Anyway," said Luke, "I realized college isn't getting me anywhere. Here I was, taking a lot of drugs, working at a Xeroxing company called Technicalgraphics. It goes without saying; who sees themself as the assistant manager at Technicalgraphics for the rest of their life? Not me. I have some artistic tendencies."

"Those artistic tendencies," I said, "you gotta watch them. Can be big trouble."

The world shifted. The music grew deeper, layered. My lips were smiling.

"Don't I know it," Luke said. "But I like to wear nice clothes. That's just me, that's just the way I am. I like to look sharp. Now understand, I'm not making any judgments on the way you're dressed. Live and let live is what I always say, I'm pretty open-minded. That comes from smoking a lot of dope. I just want to be successful in life, like anybody else. Everybody needs something to help them through life. I'm a firm believer in better living through chemistry. Everything's physiological, right?"

"I'm not sure," I said. "Although I suppose a lot is."

"Yeah," he said, "it all is. Moods, memories, the meaning of life. My aunt killed herself because of a chemical imbalance. I regulate my own body real careful. I took this Saturday and Evening class called Pharmaceutical Self-Actualization. Another one I liked even better, though, was Assertiveness Training and Vitamin Awareness for the Self-Employed Aerobics Instructor. I could get in, you see, because we use aerobics lessons as a front for our drug business. But I don't take classes anymore.

Why should I? I'm successful and happy both. I don't know, do the two usually go together like that?"

"Statistically it's very rare," said Frita.

"My life is pretty much a constant state of mild interest," said Luke. "Occasionally I allow myself a brief period of confused euphoria, followed by no more than an hour of introspective depression. Just to make sure I don't get so bored with my life that I kill myself. Boredom can kill people too. I'd rather not be dead. I do know what I want them to play at my funeral. Led Zeppelin, 'Over the Hills and Far Away.' Could you hand me that bottle of generic ibuprofen?"

I handed him the bottle.

"People like me," Luke said, "I have a lot of friends. Everybody's my friend. I get awful paranoid, though. Who can you trust? For example, you could easily be Feds. The Feds are just about everywhere. People vanish. Government authorities in long black cars drive up and whisk them away. Nobody ever sees them again. I don't want to disappear. Sometimes I look at myself, I don't know who I am."

"It's funny," said Frita, "how when you're stoned you can look at yourself and things that you do that you don't always think about why you do them."

"Like not eating?" I asked.

"I sure am hungry," Luke said.

"Me too," I said.

"Sometimes at school I climb inside my locker," Frita said, "and just sit in there, real quiet, and watch all the kids going by. Everybody moving around whenever the bells ring. I'm just in there with my coat and my books and my lunch."

She looked up, startled by herself.

"Sometimes I eat in there," she whispered.

"I wish I had the biggest bag of Bar-B-Q potato chips you ever saw," Luke said. "Or maybe some Ding Dongs."

"A Milky Way," I said.

"Once, when we were staying at the mission," Frita said, "some guy came in, I don't know what kind of bum he was, but he was the nicest guy. He picked me up and he threw me up in the air. I was just floating then. He threw me and caught me and threw me again. I laughed and laughed and laughed."

"Andalusia used to spin me around," I said. "And we fed fireflies to frogs to make them glow."

"Yeah," said Luke, "I know what you're saying. I saw this magic animal in a circus when I was five years old, a two-headed smiling unicorn thing with horns. I'm not sure if it was real or if maybe it was just a mutant goat that they nailed a horn to its head."

He stood up, started rummaging through his drawers. I didn't feel like I could move.

"Come on," whispered Frita. "Let's just get our bag and go."

Luke started eating, in the corner, something crunchy without a smell.

"Back then," he said, "I never would have guessed I'd grow up to be a drug kingpin. My friends, sure they party a lot, but they wouldn't understand. If I told them about that animal they'd laugh at me or think I was really fucked up. Those people, they never saw an animal like that."

"Let's go," whispered Frita. "Let's get out of here. We're missing out. Things are happening outside. Let's go."

She sighed, sat back, exhausted from all that speaking. We sat there in silence. Nobody moved.

That winter Frita's dad got himself committed to the psych hospital in Mount Pleasant so he could get some work done on his teeth. They hurt him so bad he could hardly eat, Frita said. I let her stay with me, in my room at the orphanage, so she wouldn't be alone.

We played backgammon and got stoned. Outside that room the world was boiling and seething with icy dangers. We were safe and young inside with all the time in the world. Snow fell past the windows. There was nothing that needed to be done and nothing to be undone, we were so free not to move. I taught Frita strategy. *Once you're so far behind that the game seems laughable,* I said, *it makes more sense to leave yourself wide open. Anything can happen.* We listened to music or thought about the ways space bends, the heaviness of air, the multitude of voices inside our own heads. One voice went: Eke it out, spit shark fins into plastic nipples, dance on glass, grow your fingernails long. Another would go: Floating down a cool stream on your back, ululating zebra fish caress the curve of your buttocks and the backs of your thighs, willows reach over and caress your scalp. A third whispered: lugubrious, sallow, lush.

Yes, once we were happy and stoned and music played on the stereo. Vegetation grew from our pillows at night, vines with pale purple flowers. We had dreams about women running through fields of wheat.

"Frita," I said, "I want to help you. I never helped anyone, but I always wanted to."

"Wouldn't it be good to get caught doing something horrible?" she asked. "Everybody would try to change you, to help you, to understand."

"Everybody loves crime," I said.

She looked momentarily frightened or astonished. I touched her knee.

"Did you ever think about killing someone?" she asked.

I closed my eyes.

"I wouldn't ever do it," she said, "but I think about it sometimes."

"You know what scares me most?" she said. "Inside my head I'm always all alone."

"Are you hungry?" I asked. "I'll go get us some ice cream."

She turned away, upsetting the backgammon board. Brown and white checkers spilled across the floor.

"I want to help you," I said.

"Don't do me any favors," she said.

I slid down the corridors of glass and stone to the ice cream parlor. Through my sunglasses the world was purple and exotic. Things became more meaningful, pieces all connected, suspended in a violet liquid. I pretended that nobody could see me. I heard footsteps everywhere, knew that one of these times Jimmy would surprise me, slide out of some unmarked door and slowly dismember me.

Father Larry was sitting in the ice cream parlor. I was terrified, sure that he knew I was stoned.

"Matt," he said. "It's good to see you. How's school?"

He wanted something from me, something he'd lost. He thought I had Jimmy. He was cunning and dangerous.

"Fine," I said.

"Try the Pumpkin Surprise," he said. "It's sultry."

It was drugged, I knew. He wanted to kill me or torture me.

"I will," I said.

I moved to the counter.

"Last Mango in Paris," I whispered. "In a sugar cone."

"We're building a new wing," said Larry, behind me. "With a jogging track, sporting-goods store, corrugated-pallet factory. How do you feel about donuts?"

I stared at the list of two hundred and three ice cream flavors. One could easily become paralyzed in such a place, unable to move, collapse in hysterical fits of weeping, vomit blood. I refused to consider this. I thought about donuts. I felt very good about donuts. I imagined the possible textures, coconut, glazes, chocolate sprinkles. I imagined the smell, early on a cold morning, when a donut shop is the only home you have. Strangers beginning their days, reading newspapers, psyching themselves up for the tasks of the day: selling guns, styling hair, laying carpet, filling out documents in triplicate. Donuts had played a large role in my life. I loved donuts. There was nothing I wanted more, right then, than a warm, gooey donut. I wanted to fondle it, chew it, dig my nose into it. I wanted to bury myself in donuts.

"Matt?" said Larry.

"I'm sorry," said the woman behind the counter, "but we're fresh out of Last Mango in Paris. Might I suggest the Transcendental Tangerine? Or the Pumpkin Surprise?"

A conspiracy. There was nothing I could do.

"I'd like to build a donut shop," said Larry. "I like diverging into new fields. Bookstores, art galleries, greeting cards, high-topped tennis shoes. Artsy barber shops and frozen yogurt."

"We'll be expanding into frozen yogurt next week," said the young woman behind the counter. "Can't really be avoided. Ice cream just isn't competitive anymore."

"Transcendental Tangerine," I said.

"Fine choice," said the girl. "It's sultry."

A radio from the back room was playing music, the songs of whales. I wondered if they were in their natural environment or if they were in captivity, performing tricks for fish. They were singing something very basic, about pain and wonder and the brevity of life.

"How is everything with you, Matt?" asked Larry. "Are you adjusting well? I want you to be happy. Is there anything you need?"

"Need," I said. "No. Nothing I need."

Needs were relative, Frita had told me. She learned that in Biology. The human race could be divided into nine distinct categories. Starvers, Scroungers, Emulators, Achievers, for example. One group of people needed microwaves and answering machines. Others needed a sense of security or the approval of their peers. The Starvers, however, nobody cared much about. They weren't worth targeting with advertising, didn't consume enough to be significant, striving, as they did, only for enough to subsist on. They tended toward death.

"Matt," said Larry, "don't you think it's about time you moved past this posture of adolescent despair? Your moody silence is only hurting yourself. We live in happy times."

"Happy times," I said.

"Oh sure, intimations of menace have pervaded our sensibilities. But you need to learn to ignore that, or better yet, to profit from it."

"Your cone, sir."

I took the pale orange ice cream in my fist.

"Got to go," I said. "Homework and stuff."

I hurried out of the parlor, not looking at Larry. The ice

cream was melting already, dripping down the cone onto my fingers. It tasted chemical in my mouth, metallic. I dumped it in a sculpture of Sisyphus, rolling his stone up the hill, a sculpture that doubled as a trash can. I buried it deep, under Styrofoam containers and corrugated-pallet shavings, so Larry wouldn't know.

I came back to the room empty-handed. Frita stood by the window. She turned, embraced me.

"It's horrible out there," I said.

"Don't leave me," she said. "Don't ever leave me again."

One day, in the service corridor of the mall, Frita kissed me. We were kind of drunk, she'd brought a bottle of sloe gin from her dad's liquor cabinet, and it was smeared around our lips, red and sticky.

"We have to look out for each other," she said. "I think that's what we have to do."

I pulled her into me, and then we were down on the concrete floor. She stuck her tongue into my mouth, ran it over my teeth. I had a hard-on. I was excited. I'd never been with a girl like that before, with a hard-on. I hadn't known if I could do it. I pressed it into her, could feel her bones poking through her skin, against me. I'd never felt so big. I was afraid she was going to break.

I ran my hands up and down her back, moved my tongue around her lips, her nose. I kissed her eyebrows. I started lifting up her shirt, she slid out and a little bit away. I was pressed up against her calf, my hands on her butt, kissing her chest, moving my hands up. Her chest was flat, like a boy's. She slid back down and started kissing me hard, her teeth bumping against my own. The sweet, berry, alcohol smell of her breath crawled up my nostrils. I put my hands under her shirt again. She let out a short cry, she pushed me away.

"Oh, no way," she said. She started sniffling. I sat back. I'd never done that to anybody before, made them cry.

"What?" I said. "What?"

She looked away from me.

"I'm afraid," she said.

She was whimpering like a seal pup. I put my arm around her brittle shoulders. I kissed her hair, it smelled like Johnson's baby shampoo. I felt responsible and adult.

"It's OK," I said.

I looked up, read the graffiti scrawled on the concrete wall. MALL MAGGOTS RULE, and next to that a Jim Morrison quote about breaking on through to the other side.

"I'm so fat," she said. "If only I wasn't so fat."

"No you aren't," I said. "You aren't fat."

It was cold back there in the service tunnels, and the walls were gray. She cried quietly, and then we went to the All American Deli and ate crackers. We laughed at some sorority girls who had orange skin, and we felt better again. Before she went home I kissed her on the nose.

That night, I dreamed Jimmy.

We were in a glass room, hovering in outer space. Everything was stars, except us and the carpet. Jimmy held me down on the floor, the carpet grinding into the back of my neck. He held my face in his hands, something he could break. Boa constrictors slid through the shag, black and shining, their luminous reptile skin gleaming, reflecting a thousand pairs of lips, bruised and succulent. Doors slammed and windows locked shut, of their own volition. I was falling into his eyes, tumbling, head over heels.

He was naked and pale, taut, ready to explode. He held my shoulders and lowered himself onto me, impaling himself, and I was there, sliding up inside. I pushed myself in, slow, as far as I could go, and he watched me, without moving his lips. This was everything I'd wanted, to be inside him, like this. The stars were spinning away from us, swirling, vanishing into a black hole. So much density that light can't escape, that's all a black hole is, that's what everybody says, not really the doorway to another world. He sat on me, wiggling around, moving his fingers across my throat and my chest, I fucked him harder and harder and then it was all over, I came and he vanished and I woke up in the darkness of my room at the orphanage.

My stereo was still on, the music soft but angry. The Clash singing *Kick over the wall, cause governments to fall, how can you refuse it? The fury of the hour, anger can be power, you know that you can use it.* I could feel the sticky wetness in my underwear. I stood up out of bed, dropped my shorts and underwear to the floor. I stood at the window naked, waiting for the first light of day. My clock had stopped, I tried to judge what time it was from the brightness of the stars. All the clues eluded me. I went back to bed. I didn't really know if it was later than I thought.

The next night I went out walking with Frita through the neighborhood.

"Frita," I said, "you've got to eat. We've got to find a way to make you eat."

"I think I just want to make myself empty," she said. "I think that's what it is. There's something holy about that, that's all it is. It's not so bad, to be empty."

"Frita," I said, "I've got an idea. Maybe you could eat in somebody else's house. Maybe if it was somebody else's food you could eat it."

"What?" she said.

"Come on," I said. "Trust me. I haven't done this for a long time."

A street full of houses stretched before us, ornamental fences, grazing ceramic deer.

"What are you going to do?"

"We'll break into a house. It's a good time, Frita, just like the old days, I tell you, that thrill. Frita, come on. Will you?"

She chewed on her finger.

"Matt," she said, "I don't know if we should."

"You won't know unless you try."

She sat on a fire hydrant, still painted red, white and blue from the Bicentennial years before.

"It's only so you can eat," I said. "We won't hurt anyone. We won't take anything but food."

"Everyone's a thief," she whispered.

Green lawns spread before us, houses and gardens.

"I think my dad was a thief," she said. "I think so. His big problem is he doesn't believe in the legitimacy of owning property. That's all it is. I'm not lying."

The night was so open. I knew we were only riding on a planet and I knew where my own self was: outside, looking in. I had things now at the orphanage, I couldn't deny it. But maybe it wasn't the things I wanted at all.

"OK," she said.

I felt it right away, the rush. We kept walking, block after block, in silence. I knew what I was doing, taking my time, waiting for the right house. My instincts were true, my blood humming through my arteries and veins. We cut across lawns into backyards. All those windows, people inside, filling their lives with structure. Collecting things, preparing for the worst, trying not to be startled. I saw the house we wanted, one light on to scare away burglars, but nobody there. Frita was shaking.

"When Dad was out of work," she said, "it was because he was a felon. Nobody would hire him."

"Trust me," I said.

"What if we can't find jobs in the future?"

"Trust me," I said.

She stood, frozen. I tried the back door, not expecting it to be open. Jimmy always tried the back door first, just in case. This one was waiting for us.

"They must be home," Frita whispered.

"People are forgetful," I said. "That's all it is."

I opened the door slowly, listening, tiptoed inside. Frita came in behind me. There was plenty of light to see by, from the moon. I walked across the kitchen floor, straight to the refrigerator. There were jars of moldy things, cheeses, milk, a slice of cold pizza. There was a plate of ham, covered with Saran Wrap.

I took the ham out. I stood at the sink, cut it with a carving knife into small cubes. The ham shivered as the blade went in, made a sly *whumping* sound. Frita sat on the floor, leaning her head against the dishwasher. I sat down beside her, my hands filled with cubes of ham.

"Frita," I said, "look at me."

I reached my hand out to her with a piece of ham. She just stared at it.

"Please, Frita," I said, "open your mouth. Eat this ham."

"I can't," she whispered. "I can't."

"Frita, please."

She closed her eyes. She opened her mouth. I put the ham gently inside. She chewed, slowly.

"Again," I said, and I put another one in. It took her a long time to chew, to swallow. The floor sparkled, smelled like pine trees and ammonia. This house belonged to normal people, people who had things. Cut lawns, microwave ovens, linoleum. Frita chewed, I felt more alive. She shivered, stood up.

"Frita," I said, "no."

I stood up, I grabbed her. She was shaking, her face twisted. I put my arms around her, I held her.

"Let me go," she said. "Please, Matt, let me go."

I pulled her in tighter. She was so small, so hungry. I felt a sickness in my mouth, my throat: the world was so perishable, so needy. Suffering and alarmed. Cars drove by outside. I could feel Frita's breath, her quiet sobs. Outside there were insects, lush grass, dry breezes, a sickeningly sweet movement, a rotting and decay. The moon played on the grass, beautiful. We were in danger, the clock ticking. She pulled herself away from me, stumbled down the dark hall into the bathroom. I stood at the kitchen sink, watching out the window, listened to the splashing sounds from the toilet.

"We've got to go," I said, but I didn't know what to do.

There was an apple tree on the lawn. It was dainty, domesticated, but the fruit was rebellious. Frita stepped back into the kitchen, wiping the vomit from her mouth. I moved out the back door. She followed. The grass was springy under our feet. Some of the apples were brown and wormy, some of them fat and red.

I picked one, polished it with my shirt. Moonlight spattered across it. I held it out to Frita.

"Please," I said, "try this. Eat this. Maybe you can eat this. Please, Frita."

She looked at me, tired and unhappy. The branches of forsythia bushes swayed in the breeze. I touched Frita's shoulder. I dropped the apple. It sat there then, as sad as the universe, uneaten on the stranger's lawn.

Three days later she told me she was moving in a week, with her dad. The prospects for work were better elsewhere, Texas or California, someplace with sun. We spent that week frantic, running along the train tracks, blowing bubbles and smoking cigarettes, rushing through the cemetery, in the river, the urgency now so apparent. We had to have fun together, as much fun as we could squeeze in. We grew tired and irritable. She said goodbye to me at the mall.

"I'm glad I'm just a kid," she said. "It helps knowing that, it isn't as sad leaving people all the time. Knowing I've still got my whole life ahead of me."

I held her hand, I kissed her. My sadness was selfish, I knew, not for her, but for me. My whole life was behind me, it had gotten stalled back there, mucked up. I wasn't going anywhere.

"I want you to be good," she said. "Don't you break into houses anymore, OK?"

"OK," I said.

Frita cried. I felt like it, but I didn't cry much anymore. I swallowed several times, I could feel my glands in my throat.

She promised me she'd write. I got the first package a week after she was gone, crammed with postcards, brochures from Colorado mining towns, tiny wind-up ducks, bubble gum and her stories of tourist attractions surrounded by fake people, to lure the real ones off the highway. The letters kept coming for months, from places here and there, she sent things she'd stolen for me, books or sunglasses, poems she wrote, photographs of her and her dad standing in front of caves. She told me she'd gained three pounds. Then she wrote me this:

Dear Matt,
*   I think its unhealthy to dwell on the past too much. I*
think we need to concentrate on the future. We've got our
own lives now, you know what I mean? I'm not going to
write you anymore.

I know what distance can do. I know it's always easier to
leave than to be left. It was almost a relief, in an odd way, not
to have that connection. But I still think of her sometimes, how
small and pale she was, wearing red polka dots and hoop earrings, riding the escalators together. I do think about her.

I woke one night, as if from a forgotten dream, amazed. I
was eighteen years old. Spring had come in its traditional manner; sprouting of buds, scattered white flowers, rain. I heard it,
water, pelting my windowpane, and soft jazz spiraling from
another room. I stepped out of bed, put on my flannel robe,
moved to the window. The moon's glow spread across the red-
dish sky. I opened the window and stepped out, my bare feet
sliding on slick patches of crabgrass. The quality of intermingling musics created a sensation of expansion and awareness.
The radio, the rain, the hum of machinery from the corrugated-
pallet factory. Nature and technology, a web of sound. I walked
across the field, laughing, inhaling the fecund smell of damp
earth, the exposed veins of the planet in construction sights.
Cranes loomed, hanging; the potential to move large objects
was there. Rain misted over me, I walked to the river. The river,
burgeoning, rushing forward, alive. My hair matted in clumps,
dripping water down my forehead. I was cold, laughing.
    The fish sang. I listened, recognized the word. Andalusia,
Andalusia, the word like water, like love, like the taste of Transcendental Tangerine untainted by poisons. I fell to my knees,
weeping for joy. I was having a peak experience. The singing
continued. Turtles hummed, earthworms poked their heads out
of the ground, leaves murmured. This went on. I wept and wept,
until, finally, I could weep no more. I laughed then, and laughed,
until I could laugh no more. I was at a loss. As time passed, the

miraculous became mundane. I sat on my knees in the mud, waiting. I shivered. I stood up and went inside.

The next day I was sick.

The world was melting and queasy. Larry probed my mouth with the cool, temptingly crunchy stick of thermometer. The TV blared, flashed discordant images, homicidal bus drivers and voodoo lipstick, tragedy vultures in plastic suits, gyrating demons from hell. Disaster and denouement, mudslides and frozen yogurt, smiling faces and the maimed bodies of the dead.

"One hundred and three degrees," Larry announced. "Keep a nurse on duty here all the time."

The nurse sponged me with cool water, mumbled soft words of comfort. "Rock-a-bye baby," she sang, as men disemboweled each other and accepted donations from voyeuristic hordes.

Jimmy liked to throw cats in the river or douse them with gasoline and light them on fire. I watched as a flaming cat shrieked and ran under old man Fagen's truck, the truck blew up, the garage burned down. Flashing red and blue lights, running, shouting neighbors, we watched it all, Jimmy and me, chewing stolen tobacco. A cat in the river. Struggling, floundering, shrieking, finally climbing onto a big rock in the middle of the river, gasping and wheezing, but safe for a minute, rejoicing in its safety from the brown, swirling torrents. It stayed there forever, too frightened of the water, slowly died on the rock. Or maybe it got bored and drowned itself. Or maybe it made it to shore. Maybe Jimmy doused it with gasoline the very next day and lit it on fire.

He was coming after me. He would find me and he would kill me. I saw him there, standing outside my window, and then he was inside, his cool palm pressed against my forehead. He put a finger to his lips, shhhhh. I was burning alive. My body was shrinking, my lips shriveled up, and he touched me, one cold finger, on my lips, my neck, my belly, my thigh.

"I'm coming for you," he whispered, "any day."

Orphans moved, apparitions, through silent halls, cast shadows under my door. Edward wandered through the halls, the orphan we'd watched long ago, sticking tacks into his thumbs.

The frozen carcasses of wolves were strewn across the hallway. Jimmy's name echoed down the empty white corridors, whispered at midnight and at noon. Tumorous growths formed on windows, clouds curled brown at the edges.

The nurse spooned me lemon Jell-O. She kept smiling at me, all lips and fingers.

And then Andalusia appeared, with flowers in her hair, a flowing gown made of sea jellies, the walnut of her skin dark against coral, red orange fire. She carried a porcupine fish and she sang to me, she sang:

> "Alice, where are you going?
> Upstairs—to take a bath.
> Alice, you are so skinny,
> It almost makes me laugh.
> Alice, got in the bathtub.
> Pulled, the stopper out.
> Oh my goodness, oh my soul!
> There goes Alice, down the hole!"

Clouds parted, angels sang, voices chanted, and she was there, floating above my bed, glowing.

I became well.

"You had us all worried there, Matt," said Father Larry. "We care about you, you know."

He pressed a twenty-dollar bill into my hand, told me to treat myself, and hurried off.

I smiled, healthy and warm, at him, at the nurse, at the empty space when they had gone.

In the middle of the night I gathered a few things together, clothes, a few books, my toothbrush. I stood at my window, watching the horizon again for the first pink hint of daylight. I was trembling with joy, with possibility, the very idea of movement. At the crack of dawn I was standing by the highway, thumbing the tired, early-morning traffic. Donut-delivery men, escaping convicts, all-night travelers.

This time, I headed west.

This time, I never went back.

EIGHT

Δ

Dick and Jane let me out now, on the outskirts of Indianapolis.

"Bye-bye," says Jane and she waves. I've given her three orgasms in the last few hours. It is night, still.

As they vanish in the distance, I think about this:

A woman dreams her best friend is being raped. In her dream she is her friend and she can see the man's face, slobbering up above. She wakes, hurries to the phone, dials. There is no answer.

A man warns his lover not to take the flight. He takes it or he doesn't. Either way, the plane crashes.

A young boy has visions of someone outside the house, creeping through the bushes. I am the man outside in the bushes. I am the boy as well.

People call it coincidence, things like that, when it happens to other people. It's not so easy when it's yourself. I dreamed him and he came.

I walk down the ramp to the Kwik Fixx, to buy a cup of coffee.

Δ

Others may argue for New York or L.A., but I know it is Indianapolis that is the true hub, the central wheel of this sprawling nation of electricity and noise. Highways converge here, decisions are made, things are going on. Somewhere, deep within the heart of this magical town, one just might find the key; some sparkling elixir, some lost, pure soul. Someday, I may explore the secrets and heavy breathing, the options, the mystery, the deli sandwiches that hide here. Someday, if I live long enough, if I can ever return. Someday, but not today.

Andalusia is elsewhere; I follow my instincts. Stoked on caffeine and donut fingers globbed with sugar, I think about sex. Food-stamp change jingles in my pocket. When there is no donut shop, a Kwik Fixx has to do, a wonderland of instant gratification. It was incandescent, the convenience store, filled with lonely midnight seekers, a bastion of humanity in the freeway wasteland. Milk, cigarettes, a six-pack of beer, a pornographic magazine, OPEN ALL NIGHT. Lost and horny, the customers eyed each other, under the disapproving supervision of the woman in red behind the counter, a sexless woman with glasses and the lurid look of the graveyard shift.

A car pulls over up ahead.

I confess it, things are all mixed up. All movement feels essentially the same. Any direction I go seems to be covering old ground; I'm twelve, I'm fourteen, I'm twenty-two.

This man who picks me up now, his face seems familiar, the sideburns, the prematurely silver hair. If he wore a metallic-blue jumpsuit he could pass as the king of Neptune, but due to a profound lack of imagination he's wearing a red T-shirt that says *Coke, the Real Thing*. He has tape on his glasses and a controlled sense of panic.

"Nobody believes me," he says, "but I tell them anyway. Thousands of people disappear every year. Just plain vanish."

Somebody told me this before. Was it him? This can't be, I never get the same ride twice. Lives only intersect once. That way it's easy to disregard possible meanings, lessons we might have learned.

"People call you crazy, but I've seen them. UFOs. Thousands have seen them. The government has files, proving this is true. What do they do with all those people? All those kids you see on milk cartons."

We're rushing through our lives, billboards all around,

luminous signs suggesting places we might go. Nineveh, New Palestine, Bethlehem, Canaan. Speed, Bean Blossom, Rising Sun, Hope.

"I wish they'd take me. I know they will, but I'm losing my patience. These are apocalyptic times we live in, the world is falling apart. The men in charge are putting Bactine on bloody, pus-oozing holes. They've got to hurry up and take me away. There has to be a better life."

I hold my lucky button. *It's Only Rock and Roll, but I Like It.* Fat families in shorts lounge around HoJo's picnic tables, even now. Nobody sleeps.

"They refuse to take me," says the man. "What do they want, these aliens? What are they looking for? I stand in the middle of fields during electrical storms, along deserted highways at midnight, on the tops of mountains when the moon is full. They whiz right past me, always going somewhere else."

Half of me is listening. The less attentive half, the half which eats Saltines on the side of hot, dusty roads, when the only water for miles is a mirage. I nod in agreement. Certainly the things he says are true. He is pulling over now, at a Roy Rogers. He's going to buy me food. I step out of the car, the sky is a haze that chokes my lungs, I stretch my legs beneath it. He buys me a hamburger, fries, I shovel it all in. I smack my lips when I eat, I'm so damn hungry. Who could deny that food is better than sex or safety?

"What do they do with all those people? That's what I want to know. Something big is in the works. A new future, a better man. I want to get in on it. Why don't they take me? Look here, do I look that bad to you? Any major defects you can see?"

"Hmm," I say. "Nothing I can see. Do you have flat feet?"

"No, goddammit, my feet are perfect. Not even an ingrown toenail. I knew a farmer, Bob Jensen was his name. Now he had ingrown toenails. Hurt him so bad he screamed as he walked across his land. Know what happened to him?"

I shake my head. My knowledge is frighteningly incomplete.

"Vanished," he says. "Boink, just like that. Taken away by
space aliens, toenails and all."

"You don't say," I say.

He looks at the sky, longing.

"Come on," he says, "let's hit the road."

We get in the car. We move along.

Δ

I left the orphanage and headed west. Manifest destiny, the
American Dream. I made turkey bologna, turkey ham, turkey
franks, most anything you could make out of turkey, at a turkey
factory in Longmont, Colorado. In Boulder, I sold candy bars,
gas and pornographic magazines at a Saveway gas station. I ate
free vegetarian feast at the Hare Krishna house and chanted with
them afterward. Hare Krishna, Hare Krishna. Hare Rama, Hare
Rama. It made me feel warm and bubbly inside. I never imagine Andalusia's face in the faces of strangers, only in landscapes; Andalusia in the painted deserts, rock formations,
cactuses, Andalusia in the open skies; Jimmy I see everywhere.
I was sure it was him, with a shaved head and orange robe,
passing out rice and peas. Then he turned, left the room, and I
knew I was deluded. I moved along. Some Moonies in Cheyenne had me over for pork chops. Like ejaculating in some
closeted businessman's mouth, it was a pleasant enough experience, but one I wanted to be altogether done with as soon as
the main event was over, dispensing with the idle chitchat and
pretended ignorance of safe sexual practices. The Moonies,
however, insisted on describing in detail the joys of not choosing one's own mate. I smiled and nodded. Again, I moved along.

I made pizzas, corrugated pallets, toothpaste pumps. I set
up spice displays in supermarkets, the tantalizing aromas of all
those spices seeping into my head, nutmeg and sage, garlic and
onion salt, vanilla beans and cinnamon. I drove a U-Haul truck
across Wyoming, a big orange truck with an enormous gearshift

and huge tires. Driving it made me feel husky and masculine, overcome with the urge to flirt with waitresses. Once, just walking down an Idaho street, an elderly woman offered me two dollars to crawl under her house and see what size filter she needed for her furnace. Two dollars! Sometimes things just come to you, offers too good to be true. I laid gravel, taught aerobics for one night on the basis of my imaginative résumé. On the restaurant application asking my philosophy in regard to food, cooking and sanitation, how could I help but mention Kierkegaard? There's a certain dignity in work, so they say, a sense of satisfaction after a long day of physical labor. This beautiful sense of being a cog in a well-oiled machine, expending one's energy into space and then sinking into oblivion with a six-pack of beer. It's a strange joy, I won't deny it, this emptying oneself of one's will. Nonetheless, I've avoided it as far as possible. I like to consider myself a member of the leisure class: time, time, plenty of time. Time to think, time to move, time to eat, to excrete, to dream, to whistle, to laugh and run and shiver and melt, to crawl down glaring highways, to talk to dumpster-diving bums, to those who hand out pamphlets in public spaces, and mostly time to search.

The streets were different now, absolutely filled to overflowing with families and lunatics and children and bums. Women on the street said I looked so much like their brothers, although I was not. Likewise, they weren't Andalusia. Still, we gave what comfort we could. I slept with men sometimes in their homes or hotel rooms or bushes. One of them purred like a tamed coyote as I rested my hand against his stomach and stroked his forehead; he was handsome and smart, but we were moving in separate directions. One of them let me feel two bullets still lodged inside his chest. One of them cooked me lentil soup and told me he could love me. None of them were Jimmy.

I sent postcards. I sat in public libraries, picked names at random from the phone book. I told strangers about my trip.

"Carmen: How are things in Albuquerque? I'm cruising through Texas now, Austin is a funky sort of town filled with

cowboys, ballet dancers, wealthy college kids on hallucinogenic drugs. Slept on a bench last night until the street cleaners
woke me up. A black man named Marv took me out for a donut
and a coffee. People everywhere are concerned and truthful.
The world is filled with benevolence, torpitude, boots. Hope to
make El Paso by nightfall. All my love. Matt."

It made me feel rooted, real. As if I had reference points,
places I could stay, a home somewhere. As if this was all a vacation and not really my life.

Just north of San Francisco, I was picked up by an alien, an
illegal alien named Jorge. He offered me a tortilla, with little
chunks of potato and salsa. We moved through fertile valleys,
between towering redwoods, past geodesic domes. Billboards
of beautiful young people playing with beach balls and smoking mentholated cigarettes.

"You know where a good place is?" asked Jorge. "They tell
me north. North they will let me stay."

"I don't know," I said. "I couldn't say what they might do
up north. It's hard to predict."

After all this time I still didn't understand people, couldn't
predict behavior. Smile at me or spit in my face? Insult me or
give me a blowjob? Refuse to acknowledge my existence or chase
me down and thrash me with a stick? The possibilities for inter-
action were endless. Communication with Jorge was difficult,
his English was poor. I was used to conversing with people of
varying levels of sanity, but only in my native tongue. It was
hard to judge Jorge's sanity, but he seemed steady. Although,
like so many vagabonds in cars, he kept a knife on the car
floor.

"We pick apples," he said. "In Washington. This is true?"

"I've heard that you can do that," I said, "yes."

If they did send him back, he told me, he'd simply return.
There was nothing there, this was everything, America . . . he
would do anything to stay, pick apples, catch fish, work in a
turkey factory making turkey bologna, turkey ham and turkey
hot dogs. He wanted a pair of Guess jeans. But he didn't even

need that, just being here, he said, it was magic. Anything was possible.

We drove down highways next to clouds, past beaches where surfers wore wet suits, black sea creatures shining against the water. Scenty pines rose on either side of us, the sky in between as pale and high as feathers. We faced obstacles together, acquiring food and gas. We prowled through junkyards looking for a tire we could afford, gutted cars shining in the autumn sun. A woman in a baseball cap sat at a table playing solitaire, a baby in diapers waddled through the automotive carcasses. I inspected the remains as if I knew what I was looking for. There was no tire to be had.

We slept in the car that night in a town in northern California, cold and cramped. Morning glare was rude through the cracked windows of his Subaru, but once up the air was alive, rich with leaves and the babble of brooks, and we kept on moving north. The tires wobbled, but didn't give out. We picked up another hitchhiker with tattoos and scars on his forearms, but he didn't have money for a tire either. He told us he could steal us a tire in Salem, from a shop he used to work at, we prowled around awhile, he vanished and reappeared, but finally we gave up. We left him there, and moved along.

"Bad man," Jorge told me.

He pointed to his forearms, to indicate the scars. He shook his head. Still, we needed a tire. We picked up two Canadians who were panhandling their way across the country. We stopped in Eugene, begged money in a convenience-store parking lot. We made ten dollars, bought a tire for twelve, a couple of quarts of Milwaukee's Best, and headed north with a spare and a sense of insurance. The Canadians laughed and drank and left us at a Portland exit. Jorge laughed too.

"Crazy," he said.

A dark-windowed limo passed us, rock stars or politicians, Jorge watched it wide-eyed. We stopped at little cabins that sold chunks of redwood, we spent the last of our money on a six-pack of beer, we kept on moving north.

Despite my inability to communicate the nature of my quest,

of Andalusia, true love, the American dream, I felt something growing between us, through the garbled communication, the shared beers. Slowly, with the barest rudiments of language, a life was stretching out before me. A vision of our future grew in my mind, traveling north, fishing in these cool mountain streams, off the road, the quiet of the mountains, picking apples in Washington, apples! Green and red, tart and shiny, yellow and crisp and juicy, apples everywhere. I could see myself there, suspended in midair, on ladders that reached to the sky, surrounded by trees and trees, entire orchards of apples, apples rotting in the mud below, the rich fragrance like cider rising all around, apples falling, apples clinging, apples spraying juice high into the air . . .

"The fat of the land," I said. "We'll live off the fat of the land."

The sun went down, to the west, somewhere in the vicinity of the Pacific Ocean. Colors swirled among the sunset pine trees, pink, black, purple, orange in the sky. The sky and dusk, together again. Our headlights cast a dangerous light as we crawled between forest darknesses; the car swerved from side to side, a combination of the beer and some problem with the steering fluid.

"We stop soon," Jorge said. "For night. No good for tire at night. Boom! Like that."

He was making some sort of gesture with his hands. The road was like a tunnel. Behind us, red lights flashed, sudden, filling the woods, the road, twirling red. Squirrel disco for the mentally deranged.

"The police," I said.

"The police," repeated Jorge.

He swiveled his head, then turned back to the road, intense. I watched his face, his grinding teeth.

"Shit. Is no good."

We rounded a corner and for a moment the lights were out of sight.

"You drive," he said. "No license for me. The car, yes."

The lights were back. He wasn't slowing down. A rabbit bounded across the road into the woods.

"They send you back," I said. "Mexico."

"*Sí*," he said, and we were around another curve, the lights gone again. I grabbed the wheel, scooted over, on top of Jorge, then he was wiggling into the passenger's seat. I sped up.

He opened the glove compartment, grabbed a crucifix on a silver chain and a pack of gum.

"Get ready," I said, "to go."

I didn't know if he understood. I put on the brakes, skidded alongside the trees.

"Go!" I said. "Go, go!"

He understood, and the door was open, and he was gone, diving into the woods. I watched him go, the darkness that had swallowed him. I shut off the ignition.

Headlights pulled up behind me, shone through the window. Red lights scattered across the woods, in and out of tree-trunks. I felt my balls shriveling up, sweat draining from my fingertips. They waited back behind, gave me time to imagine torture, police brutality, clubs and naked light bulbs. A car door opened. Heavy steps crunched on the gravel. A flashlight blinded me.

"Driver's license?"

No was not the appropriate response, but it was the only one I had. The car was unregistered as well. There was a knife and open alcohol. In no time, I was up against the car, hands behind my neck. I was frisked and cuffed. Shoved around a bit. Kicked.

Ink on the fingers, orange jumpsuits, a hard floor, smelly drunks. There would be no apples under northern skies. The walls of the cell were like skin, a mind-set, closing in. A fellow prisoner told me a story of injustice, despair, bad luck and trouble, humor in the face of unrelenting woe, staggering amounts of alcohol consumed. A rotten wife, an ungrateful child, miscarriages of justice and hebephrenic glee.

Fifteen days of fear and dread. A court date was set, but I

was released and told that as long as I never showed my face in the state of Washington again, everyone would be happy.

Δ

Many times, I've driven past that sign in Nebraska that says "Friend, Exit 369," and I'll confess I've felt a slight palpitation of my heart, a longing, but nothing like the tremor I feel now, in Indiana, reading this sign:

LOVER NEXT RIGHT

"Let me out," I say to the man in the *Coke, the Real Thing* T-shirt. "This is it. This is my stop."

"What?" he says. "Right here?"

"Yes, yes!" I say. "Here! Now!"

He pulls onto the shoulder.

"It's them," he says, "isn't it? You've got that feeling, a quivering, a rattling of teeth. Right now, before my eyes, you're about to be taken away by space aliens. Aren't you? Not me, but you."

"No, no, no," I say, "it isn't that at all. Thank you for the ride and the food. Bye."

I step out of the car. He glares at me, watches the sky. I walk down the off ramp, he doesn't move.

I approach a gas station, step up to the man at the counter. The keys to the rest rooms hang behind him, attached to wooden planks, to deter absentminded theft.

"Where is she?" I ask. "Where's Andalusia?"

"Andalusia?" repeats the man, his mouth full of gum. "Why, I believe that's in Spain. You're a little bit lost, fella. Spain's clear on the other side of the Atlantic. I'll tell you what, though. If you hurry, you could catch the nine-fifteen flight from Indianapolis to London, arriving in London at three fifty-two, our time. There's a flight from London to Madrid leaving at four twenty-nine p.m., putting you in Madrid at approximately five twenty-five. From there, Andalusia is just a hop, skip and a jump away, a few hours at most, by train or bus."

He's wearing a blue shirt and a nametag that says OM.

"What?" I say. "What are you talking about? How do you know these things?"

He shrugs. He blows a bubble with his gum.

"There's an awful lot of knowledge in the world," he says. "People are filled with it. Who's to say which of it is worth having and which isn't?"

I consider this. I don't care. I have to find her, that's all that matters. Otherwise, I will die.

"It's not a place," I say, "it's a woman I'm after. It's spelled the same, but pronounced differently."

"Only available woman in this town is Grace Jones," he says. "Any others came through, believe me, I'd notice."

I scan the shelves. Candy bars and cream-filled pies, looking for something to fill me up. Mars bars, Milky Ways, Almond Joy. Why not Almond Boredom, Almond Dread?

"Do you take food stamps, Om?" I ask.

"No," he says. "And my name is Tom. The *T* fell off. OM is not a name, it's a mantra. If you chant it you might just reach nirvana. I haven't reached nirvana, but I do find I'm more tolerant of the diversities one finds in the human race, more understanding of human weakness. When I pump gas, I pump gas with love. I pump gas with the totality of my being."

"All that," I say. "Just from chanting OM."

"It's not just the chanting," Tom says. "I've read books, too. *Chant Your Way to Financial Independence* was a good one. You can have a candy bar, if you'd like. This is a gift from me to you. Just don't eat those Alpine White ones, the company that makes them is responsible for higher levels of infant mortality in Third World nations. Have a Milky Way instead."

I pick up a Milky Way, devour it. There's something celestial about Milky Ways, something sticky.

"I am amazed," says Tom, "at the extent to which you resembled a carnivorous beast consuming a meaty intestine as you ate that candy bar."

"You're reminded of man's animal nature," I say. "Always at war with his more spiritual side. The soul-body split."

"No," he says, "that isn't really what I was thinking at all. It's just your hunger that struck me. That's all."

I hurry up to the highway. Maybe my ride is still there, the man seeking aliens. I'm buzzing with sugar again, chocolate on my lips. He isn't here, only that dark billboard in the distance. I move away from the road again, toward the railroad tracks on the other side.

Δ

Seasons passed, the rainy season, the sweaty season, the leafy season and the time to go south, usually in that order. One winter I made it to Florida, stopped in Destin and searched for Dust's house. Nothing looked like I remembered, the beach had been changed, buildings erected, the sand and water improved. I asked people if they remembered him, searched for neighbors or acquaintances. One woman claimed she was his second cousin and he'd been buried in New Hampshire. A man with a metal detector, with lost nail clippers and zippers, was positive he had never died at all, had recovered completely and moved overseas. I wasn't sure which version I preferred to believe. I tended toward the latter, not at all owing to the credibility of either of my sources. The sunlight gave me a headache. I made my way back north.

In Columbus I sought out the neighborhood where Melissa had lived. The record store was still there, Magnolia Thunderpussy, but her house was burnt down. The one that replaced it was occupied by a young couple with matching haircuts, eating shish kebab and playing Othello. They believed memory was something that lived outside of individual minds, but could give me no clues in the case of Melissa.

In St. Louis I wandered the old stomping grounds, the bus station, the fountain, the twenty-four-hour restaurant with mirrored walls reflecting bums, waitresses and potential killers in checkered pants. I couldn't find Traveler, Amanda had moved away, not even one face on the street that looked vaguely familiar. All traces of my past had been lost, each version was now equally true. How could I know who I was with nobody to corroborate the events of my life? I was free to tell whatever stories I chose, or to tell no stories at all. Nothing left for me but future, I headed west again.

Crossing the Badlands in cool June sunlight and wind, I was wearing a long coat I'd found in someone's trash. A young man on a motorcycle pulled over, wearing a bandanna and a down vest. I climbed on back and we flew, the wind filling up the coat, pushing it out, the length of it flapping like wings. The wind was cold, he yelled back to me that his wife was following in the van, she had Puma grass. I turned my head and saw the van following, black against the pale landscape. We didn't talk then, the wind in our ears, the world rushing by too fast for words. We stopped at a scenic overlook to stretch our legs.

He was in his twenties, redhaired, freckled and grinning. His vest was bright red, his eyes greener than any I'd ever seen. They clashed with everything.

"I feel like life is ready to burst open," he told me. "It's just this feeling . . . I'm tingling all over, so many possibilities! Anything could happen. Anything! You too? Where you headed?"

"Don't know," I said. "I'm traveling randomly. I leave it up to fate."

"Yes!" he said. "Yes! Exactly, that's it, this this this . . . I don't have the words for it, but look at it all, sky and hills and buffalo for Christ's sake, grass and little houses. Things are happening, everywhere, all the time. I can't get over it. Somewhere, babies are being born. They might even be my babies! I'm a sperm donor, you see, or at least I used to be. Fifty dollars a week, twenty-five a shot. Money for semen, do you believe it? I've always had more semen than I knew what to do with."

"It's amazing the money they'll give you for bodily fluids," I said. "I've often sold my plasma, and once even my spinal fluid."

"God, everything is just falling together, this place, this moment, even you, some hitchhiker I don't even know. I'm trembling all over . . . Something is just around the corner . . ."

I looked out over the land, the black, angry dirt. The con-
niving hills. The van pulled up behind us.

"Is it all that road vibration," I asked, "or are you on drugs?"

He stood on his head.

"Maybe it is partially that," he said, "that business of traveling halfway across the country on a motorcycle. And granted,
I'm a manic-depressive, but why discount something just because
of its physiological roots? I've never felt more alive, more syn-
chronized, actualized, never more possible than I am right now."

He lowered his voice to a whisper.

"Do you believe in UFOs?"

I was startled. I looked into the upside-down greenness of
his eyes.

"No," I said, although I wasn't sure why. There weren't many
possibilities I'd been able to rule out.

"Good," he said. "That makes me feel better."

He somersaulted, rose to his feet. His wife stepped out of
the van, a young woman, beautiful in a rugged, leathery sort of
way, wearing jeans and a matching bandanna.

"Hi," she said. "You needing any Puma grass? Come check
out our goods."

The van was full of paintings on black velvet. Unicorns,
Elvises, seascapes, Jesus.

"Elvis is our big seller," she said, "though the caves by the
ocean go pretty good, too. Check out the Puma grass."

It was long feathery stuff, in bright, almost fluorescent colors.

"What is it?" I asked.

"You put it in a vase," she said, "stick it in the corner."

"Yes," I said, "but what is it?"

"Puma grass," she said. "It comes from overseas."

"Overseas," I said. "Are these the natural colors? Pink, red,
orange, neon green?"

"Of course," she said.

"We live from parking lot to parking lot," the man said, "town
to town, we just cruise along and sell our wares, our velvet
paintings and our Puma grass, and its a good life, you know, but

I get this hankering to settle down. Things could be worse, things have been worse, trust me on that, listen. I was living in L.A., running this little motel, a front for a whorehouse basically, pretty rough little neighborhood. I was shot at from time to time, I had to carry a gun. Cockroaches the size of rats, rats the size of raccoons. This life's filled with vermin, you know it? Living's no business for the squeamish, that's for damn sure."

He was absolutely quivering, an army of microscopic organisms ready to burst from under his skin.

"But now I keep seeing these silver disks out of the corner of my eye. I have this uncontrollable fear that I'm about to be kidnapped by space aliens, just when everything seems to be going so well. That is, I'm not incarcerated, hospitalized, politically affiliated, employed by others or hopelessly in love with someone other than my beautiful wife. I haven't a burden to my name. I'm as free and weightless as any aviary mammal you could imagine."

"Somebody gave us a buckeye," his wife said. "We saw two crows circling the hotel and found a penny face up, so you see, we had to have good luck. Brad got shot in the shoulder and all our worldly possessions were stolen. Well, sure, that don't seem like good luck, but it moved us off our asses, we hit on the Pumagrass idea, my cousin got taken away for being a subversive. That meant we could have his van and here we are."

"What my wife is trying to say," Brad said, "is that you never can tell, really, in the short run, if what happens is good luck or bad luck."

He started whispering again.

"But it's weird, you know? If I vanished off the face of the earth, nobody would know it. Us always moving around and all. Leastways if both of us did, nobody'd know. I don't feel quite real. On the other hand, there's an odd sort of comfort in that fact."

"The unbearable lightness of being," I said.

"Sure," he said, "but everything seems so funny right now. Laughter is a good thing, don't you feel? Pain, death, I'll think about those things later. I'm so exhilarated! There are things to be done, panoramic views, country-western songs on the juke-box after midnight, blowjobs. I sure do like sex. Nothing's permanent, isn't that the truth?"

A long black car pulled off the road just in front of me, two nearly identical men in suits rushed out, with guns and dark glasses. They hurried down the hill, grabbed Brad and threw his struggling body into the back of the car.

"Hey!" I said.

"Oh, no," said his wife.

The sky was reflecting off the abductors' sunglasses. It was an intelligent sky, if not overly sensual, filled with ribbed, skeletal clouds. One of the men turned to us.

"Don't bother calling the authorities," he said. "We are the authorities."

They drove away.

There seemed to be things that must be done in such a situation, relatives to inform, clues to follow. None of these things seemed feasible. His wife had her face in her hands.

Knolls of red grass, carved hills, broken trees in dry gullies. A billboard offered wealthy young people shooting billiards and smoking cigarettes from slick black packs. In Pierre I'd read a sentence, spray-painted on a brick wall. *Death Don't Have No Mercy in This Land.*

I moved toward her, put my arm around her shoulder.

"Don't you worry," I said, "we'll find him. We'll get him back. They can't get away with things like that. This is America."

"What are you?" she said. "Stupid? This is the same thing that happened to my cousin, all because of bad urine. How many relations do they expect me to lose, how much do they think one woman can take? He never should have let them test his urine. I'm clean, he said, I've got nothing to fear. As if that makes any difference. Sometimes the brain secretes illegal substances all on its own. Sometimes they can tell you've had antigovernment sorts of thoughts just by the salt content. I'm tired. What kind of a life is this, people always getting disappeared."

The Puma grass swayed in a gentle breeze. Grass shivered, pale sky and landscape.

"You go on," she said. "I want you to take the motorcycle. It's yours, I can't just leave it here. I've got to go. I've got to take care of this."

"I'll come with you," I said.

"No," she said, "no, please. Just go. You're obviously too naive to be of any help."

She drove away. The motorcycle engine was making ticking noises in the heat. The keys were in the ignition. I pondered the lesson, how one man's misfortune can be another man's gain. How easy it is to profit from atrocity, without even trying. I straddled the bike, heat coming in waves off the engine, started it up, and I was gone.

I drove that motorcycle, south and west, singing to myself and burning in the sun. My hair pressed straight back and I was happy, buying gas from old men in small towns, stopping at picnic benches or Indian-artifact stands by the side of the road. Riding in the early morning or on hot, hot nights, being frowned on in small Kansas towns, sunburnt and dizzy, dipping and rising and speeding past cars, part of the landscape, the elements. There were diners and gas stations, two lanes and four lanes, city streets and empty deserts, sun and moon and spatterings of rain. Waiting under gas-station awnings for the rain to let up, accepting strangers' advice, waving at children.

Joy, rapture, ecstasy. The magic rhythm of crossing the land on a motorcycle, the cool breeze brushing against my lips, my open mouth, sinking into curves, the crest of hills, New Mexico plateaus, shriveled valleys, humpbacked mountains, singing loud into the wind, moving in different dimensions of chocolate rivers and ghosts on the highway, mirage towns and dancing tumbleweeds, a sky filled with fish and apple pie. I crossed Texas plains by moonlight, beside nostalgic railroad tracks, past eerie rock formations, chose highways, took corners, laughed at the wind. I rode, I sang, a lunatic on a motorcycle, people stared, but I'd been born there, this was it; my life and it was good.

In Texas the sun beat relentlessly, but I remember this: I stopped, by a wide, shallow river, the engine tinging, my body humming from the road vibration, shirt and forehead speckled with dead bugs. Farther down, people were swimming, their hair black and shiny. I threw off my clothes in the weeds, dove naked into the muddy river, floated with the current, relaxed, cool and wet and surrounded by water. I lay on my back, floating backwards, sun on my face, cool, closed my hands. I remember at the time thinking: this is something I'll remember, a good thing.

On the other hand, on the motorcycle again I couldn't help but think about death; how easy it is to die on a motorcycle, how many ways to inspire an accident, go sliding sideways scraping brains and elbows against concrete at seventy miles an hour, wiping oneself off the list of existent beings into nothing but an unidentifiable smear on the pavement, a toothbrush and a now pointless organ-donor card. But I pushed that knowledge just far enough back, riding always on that delicate balance of thrill and self-deception, a little faster now, thinking I was just that much closer to some kind of truth, or to transforming the world into a vivid, but essentially harmless flow of images, a nonlethal film.

I crossed the desert.

After my parents were killed, I went out to deliver my route. For just a little bit longer, to pretend it wasn't real. To try moving backward in time, to give events time to undo themselves, I traveled the circular path of my delivering, thud, a newspaper on this porch and one over there, the night fragrant and calm. To try to forget. But my route erased nothing, I came home, they were dead. I wished it, it happened, that's all that there was. But speed is a real kind of forgetting, the desert a purification. The human becomes so meaningless, such heartrending emptiness, such a true, startling reflection. Think about a motel on the edge of a desert town, palm trees shimmying, the unreal blue of the motel pool. Think about Holiday Inn lounges, suitcases, showgirls, white monuments, nuclear blasts, the endlessly horizontal. Think about the word: America. Words meant

something different there: *time, tourism, vanishing, speed.* A
trip without destination, an escape from solidity, a blur. Violent, indifferent, continual flux, desert to mountain to city. The
only history the unceasing shift of geography, missile-test sites,
obliteration: the future as pure forgetting. I arrived on the other
side of the desert completely empty, a willing amnesiac. What
murder, what wish? Just to make sure I crossed it again. Bak-
ersfield, Barstow and on. I emerged innocent and memory-free.
I dreamed of human conversation by the Grand Canyon's rim,
then moved, tiny and exalted, into the rising cacophony of Las
Vegas, the spectacular obscenity, the neon American Dream.
My brain cooled down after its day in the sun, expanded, feverish, everything harsh, seductive, deranged. Drunk on hope and
free liquor, I lost everything I had, the motorcycle, the dollars,
a hardback edition of the *Decameron* I'd stolen in Albuquerque.
I joined the rest of the losers, by the side of the road on the
outskirts of town, taking my place again where I knew I belonged;
with the broken dreams, the potentials unfulfilled, wide open
again with that odd sense of relief that failure always brings.

Δ

I can't sleep now, but at least there's railroad tracks. I'm full
of caffeine again, walking on the tracks. Always walking on railroad tracks, at dawn or at dusk, nightfall or late afternoon. It
gives me a sense of freedom and direction, lines stretching on
forever, withered planks, balancing on a thin beam. I like to
walk. I like shaking myself in the morning, after sleeping, back
in the trees, on a bed of orange pine needles. I like peeing on
the ground, watching the foam splatter on mud. I like making
my first sounds of the day, coughing, gurgling noises that turn
into a song.

I take my pleasures from the little things. Usually, that's
enough.

Granted, at times of intense awareness I see this web of
hieroglyphics breathing just beneath the surface of things, an

ineffable fabric of energy, signs which could surely be deciphered by somebody, somewhere, an ancient language pointing me toward the scattered meaning of things. If only things talked. But perhaps I'd grow tired of listening to trees as well, or stone chairs or ceiling fans, or even the moon.

The moon is fat as a hamster on this horizon at dawn, golden and round, full of holes. I walk along this rail, I balance, I move. I watch the moon, slowly sinking. I do not fall.

This dawn is the color of marmalade, streaked through with chunks of orange rind, elsewhere translucent. It's as if I've wandered into an enormous jar of preserves.

God is simply playing hide and seek with itself. Somebody once said this, as somebody once said most everything. In the old neighborhood, summer nights, the lawn turned to black and children's voices fooled everyone. I hid in the middle of a lilac bush, curled, tiny, waiting. Hide and seek.

"Olly, olly, oxen free!" I scream down the tracks. Birds flutter, ospreys, out of the huge hairy nest they've built on the telephone wires.

But sometimes, other times, I think about hurting people or about how people might hurt me. Sometimes I have to find places where there aren't any around, just the sight makes me queasy. It's so easy to hide in the midst of such enormous landscapes, such an enormous, throbbing universe; spinning galaxies, quasars, black holes, red giants, so many zillions of stars and forms of life and molecular structures, landscapes, erosion, geological formations.

We are certainly amazed, if not at all inspired to virtue.

Δ

An enormous woman named Alma once drove me from Sioux City to Sioux Falls. She wore pink pants and a flowered shirt, a fat King James Bible sat on the dash. She was going to visit her son in the penitentiary and her brother, a guard. She told me she couldn't visit the old folks' home anymore, even though she had friends there, it was just too sad since her aunt had died.

I stayed at the mission in Sioux Falls, knew it was probably the same place Frita Bob had stayed when she was little. There was a woman there with her five kids, their father was in jail, too. Their faces were lean and freckled, Billy, Mandy, Wanda, Ronnie and one other that I forget. Nine o'clock was soup time and then we sat and played gin rummy.

Billy was the man of the family, he was nine, and he told me about this movie he saw called *Hunk*.

"This woman came up from hell," he said, "and there was this guy, it was in Florida, no, Spring Creek, Spring Creek Lake, something like that. It was at the beach and this guy, he had all the women he wanted."

"Sounds like a crazy movie," I said.

"It was," he said. "We lived in Alaska once and it was still dark when we took the bus to school. We were so tired, we laid out and slept on the bus."

Ten-thirty was lights out, but I took Ronnie into my arms, he was the littlest, no bigger than a good-sized loaf of French bread, no heavier either, and a bit cross-eyed. I tossed him up into the air. I caught him and tossed him again, he was so light, he flew, hanging there in the air, and he laughed and laughed and laughed.

Do not think I take these things for granted. Do not think I could just as easily do without, that they mean nothing to me at all. On the contrary. They're the only things that ever have.

NINE

Δ

1

"Hi," says the man. "I'm going to the Ozarks, I'll take you that far."

"Doing some fishing?" I ask, but he shakes his head no.

"Surviving," he says.

"Just got me an AK-47," he says. "Just in time, before they went illegal. You wouldn't believe the rush at the store, the long lines to buy guns, once people found out. But I got mine."

He whistles.

"You take a word of warning, young man. Economic collapse is just around the corner. You think things won't get ugly? Things will get ugly."

"One can only hope," I say and watch out the window: forests and creeks and bridges, all the usual things. Like so many before him he talks and talks: bomb shelters and self-preservation. The aims of love and self-preservation are not compatible, I once read, but I exchanged that book for a Moon Pie.

He broods silently, building bomb shelters in his mind, mowing down imaginary enemy hordes. He smells like plaster and is anxious for the world to end. It won't, but the opposite view is just as false: they'd tell you that today is no different from any of the others that have mucked up the history of the universe. I don't buy it, not for a minute. There's something waiting for me today. Andalusia or Jimmy. Rebirth or death, if one can make such distinctions.

"The minorities and poor scum will be running the streets," he tells me, "burning and looting. Me, I'm going to keep what's mine. Underneath the surface calm of shopping malls and sushi joints this country is a seething mass of anger and violence just ready to explode. Be ready. Be armed."

On the seat is a copy of Kierkegaard's *The Sickness unto Death.*

"Some light reading for the bomb shelters?" I ask.

"I've never read it," he says, "but I know it may be up to me to save the world's literature. I've got almost two dozen books, some best-sellers and one written by this French guy. Another thing, books burn real nice if we need the heat. That one doesn't look much good, I found it in a Burger King bathroom."

I watch the trees and cars and towns, as we move toward the south. The familiar south, the familiar north, it's all so familiar these days. Movement and time, coinciding again. A sign announces that we've crossed into a different time zone and it's earlier than it was. If you could move straight west at 550 miles an hour you could live in a perpetual dusk and you would never die. This is a fact. I know I'm living in this postmodern time, this time that's no longer a continuum. I know that time is no longer an effective coordinate for planning human action. People tell me this frequently, farmers and truckers and lonely asbestos removers. Still, I can't help feeling that events are progressing in a linear fashion today, toward climax and resolution. I keep on moving there, closer, always, where I'm going, she's just up ahead, he's not far behind, any time now.

"Canned goods," the man says. "Stock up on canned goods. That's my advice."

Δ

I'll say this much: If Jessica Moon hadn't scooped me off the highway, fed me and cared for me, I'd have had to dream her, to coax her into being through the sheer force of my desire.

They say there are certain illusions without which we can't go on. If she hadn't been real, she'd have been one of those. She was that necessary.

This was not so long ago, on the plains of Colorado.

The air smelled like a cheetah's savannah dream, rain and grass and flesh in the sun, but cars drove by. I smiled. Stuck out my thumb. Black clouds approached from beyond the mountains in the west, traffic died down as dusk seeped in, the fewer cars no more inclined to pick me up than the thousands that had come before them. My thumbing became more violent. The people in cars wore fiberglass clothing and horn-rimmed glasses, scowled at me, made hideous faces to taunt me and then turned their heads, pretending they didn't see. The sun set dramatically behind the mountains, sending rays of pink and orange bouncing across the black mass of clouds, a strange silence in the air, punctuated by bird and cow sounds or a rare, gliding car. A drop fell onto my shoulder, a big, juicy, metaphysical one. A maroon car slowed down, almost to a stop. The pink, mustached passenger gazed at me noncommittally, rolled down his window electrically and spat on the pavement in front of me.

Plop. Another drop hit my face. Headlights turned on, flopping windshield wipers. Plink, another drop: the sky ripped its own guts out, busloads of rain, and I was drenched clear through to my only pair of underwear. I'd been through the desert and forgotten my past; now it felt as if the very physical presence of my body was being washed away, my sore and bloodied feet, my sinewy calves, my empty, twisted belly. Smeared, multicolored lights bore down on me, cars swished by, sprayed me and moved on. The maroon car drove by me again in slow motion, the man glared at me out of his plaid suit, glared with the same hatred as the burning headlights. An ugly child squished its nose up against the back window; or was it a hog? The taillights disappeared over the crest of the next incline, and then it passed me again, in the same direction, the same maroon rectangular car with four doors and hissing wiper blades, it passed me again. It was definitely a child and not a hog, I decided; it was wearing something red. Almost before it had disappeared in the distance, it passed me again. All the other traffic on the highway had quit, except for this lone Skylark that kept passing me. It passed me while I could still see its taillights up ahead, and it even passed itself once. It *was* a hog, I realized, and it was soon joined by two goats and a cow, all pressing their snouts against the rainy window, their drool mixing with the drizzle. My thumb went limp by my side, paralyzed with doubt. Swish, gone. Again, the headlights in the distance, as bright as a Florida beach, murder in broad daylight. They headed straight for me. I was unable to breathe, submerged in a watercolor landscape. Moving was out of the question. This was the most plausible death I could imagine.

The car stopped, turned off its lights. The driver's door opened. I watched in impotent horror, but there was no hateful man and no livestock. It was a woman, blurry and colorful, and she spoke to me.

"Come on, get in. You look miserable. How long have you been sitting out here in the rain?"

Her voice was warm and dry and her car wasn't a Skylark at all, it was a beat-up old van. Warm air blew from her vents, massaged my body with heat. I formed a black puddle on the car floor.

"Thank you, ma'am," I said. My teeth chattered. She radiated warm brown skin and flowing hair. The van was filled with tinkly bells and incense. Strawberry, opium, musk. She wore a magenta skirt, enormous bracelets and earrings and shells. There was some sort of halo glowing about her head.

"I'm going to New Orleans," I said.

"Not likely," she said. "I'm going straight west, to Telluride."

Cantaloupes and muskmelons were rolling down the highway after her. This was Jessica Moon. In the back of the van huddled shapes were stretched out, sleeping. Their gentle snores rose and fell with the rhythm of the engine.

"Hungry?"

I ate. She was a goddess of food. Artichokes and asparagus,

warm air and music on the stereo. I curled up naked in soft
blankets that smelled like freshly bathed children. My world
became a haze of warmth and the happy hum of the car heater,
the swish, swish of driving through rain.

I'm feeling compelled to condense experience: to imagine
my life more quickly, to hurry forward to the end. Compared to
the chunk I've left behind me, the future seems thin. I feel rushed
and drawn and concluding. On and on it goes, so many voices
and means of transportation: we creaked into Telluride in the
early morning. Mountains on every side, only one road in, only
one road out, one of those hot buttered ski towns filled with
condos and cocaine. The huddled shapes rose slowly, bashful
and disheveled. They were two teenagers, Antonio and Wendy,
and Wendy's autistic little brother, Dwight. Jessica distributed
pumpernickel muffins and pineapple slices. This was her voca-
tion: picking up strays off the highway, caring for them, feeding
them. Part of my destiny, obviously, the food metaphor which
has been so relentless in my life.

We climbed a mountain. Amazing blue flowers, ice-cold
streams, gnarled trees, topless sunbathers. Jessica's walk: an
assassin saying grace. Leathery skin, hard eyes, flowing skirts
and jewelry. Pregnant, blond, late in her thirties. An aging hippie or a goddess of fertility. How would such a pregnancy be
resolved so late in the twentieth century? Could birth still be
given with any hope for success? She climbed easily, swinging
her arms. We reached a meadow at the top. Flat rocks, wild
grass, deer shit and the clouds, yawning obscenely, teasing us
with their tangy breath of magnolia and their erotic silhouettes.

Night filtered down. The stars emerged, one by one, louder
than dread. Jessica built a small fire and we roasted marshmallows. They tanned a rich golden brown, I pulled the hot crinkled outsides off with my teeth, stuck the gooey centers back
into the flame.

"Aardvark," said Dwight, the autistic little brother,
"A-A-R-D-V-A-R-K, aardvark. Bobcat. B-O-B-C-A-T, bobcat.
Chameleon. C-H-A-M-E-L-E-O-N, chameleon."

Wendy grinned sheepishly.

"Dwight can spell pretty good for a retarded kid," she said. "I guess I taught him that."

He was alternately preoccupied with his fingers and the sky. A miniature Marine, existing in his own linguistic battle zone. So adept at amusing himself, so transfixed by motion and color and his own echolalia. The fire played on our faces.

"In the middle ages," Jessica said, "people gathered around fires in the countryside as the plague ravished Florence, the most beautiful city in the world. The diseased wandered everywhere. But these people, the ones who gathered, they sat and told stories. Just to pass the time.

"I insist that sense can be made of all this," she said. "Wendy, why don't you start?"

Wendy had pudgy cheeks, drab hair, a sad face and a tan sweater with fringes on the sleeves. She looked like she might burst into tears at any moment.

"OK," she said. "Well, I hope you don't mind. My story's kind of rural. Where should I start? Being born was a long time ago and I don't remember much of it. I do remember Dwight's birth, now that was a happening. When he was three, though, Mom just left. She couldn't deal with raising a retarded kid. It wasn't her fault, she said. She'd just never been prepared for that eventuality. She blamed my grandma and grandpa. She said they should have raised her better, so she'd be prepared in case her kids weren't normal."

She took Dwight's hand, kissed him on the cheek.

"Moms are crazy sometimes," said Antonio. "Mine took me to New York after Dad left. She started singing with an ironic British avant-garde band called Zen Conspiracy."

Antonio was short and stocky, with black curly hair, a wrestler, maybe, with angels and demons. With gaps between his teeth and a lumpy nose he wasn't even slightly handsome, but sexy in an adolescent, criminal sort of way. Wendy watched him, chewing the fringes of her sweater.

"They all sat around our kitchen eating waffles," he said. "I turned into a Satan worshiper for a little while, I'd have to credit that rock-and-roll influence, but it didn't last. That's when I got my tattoos. The guys in the band, they got a big kick out of it, sitting in our kitchen, eating their waffles. You know. But then the band had to go on tour and Mom sent me to live with Grandma but then Grandma lost her mind. She started thinking I was some Czechoslovakian orphan named Jirí."

"Antonio's got a crazy family," said Wendy.

"Sure," he said. "I'm getting ahead of myself, I want to give you the whole family history before I talk about me. First off, let me start at the beginning. I mean way back with my ancestors. I've got some weird blood in me, I'm a true descendant of Thomas Jefferson. Tom Jefferson, you know it. Through his slave girl, Sally Hemings, so I've got slave and master in me both, and that's just on one side of the family. The other side's got Indian and Custer in it, so you can see as how I'd be a bit mixed-up. Fuck, you know, a real American. One grandpa came to America at the start of the century during the Lithuanian kumquat famine. He kissed the Statue of Liberty on its lips, and from that day on he never got heartburn again, his arteries didn't harden, he invented new ways to sleep."

Jessica tossed another log on the fire and some potatoes wrapped in foil.

"Why don't you let Wendy go on," she said. "She barely got started."

"Sure," said Antonio. "Sorry."

I recognized in Antonio a potential for interruptions, a restlessness. One of those people who are so aware of possibility that they can never stay still, get focused, succeed. We moved in closer to the fire. We were all red and glowing.

"After Mom left," Wendy said, "things got kind of rough for us. There was four of us kids, an older sister and brother too. Dad used to always sing that song about *you picked a fine time to leave me, Lucille,* though that wasn't even Mom's name, and about four hungry children and a crop in the fields. But Dad wasn't the first farmer in the county to snap, there was a whole rash of them. We were all losing our farms, and like everyone used to say, when you got the land in your blood that's the same thing as losing a leg or some such. Then. Or a nose, like Wyatt Maquoketa he had maggots all up inside his and had to have the whole thing taken off. But, OK. So all these farmers started shooting their bankers, their wives and themselves. Those bankers sure were stupid. Soon as one got shot they'd ship another one in to take his place. Well, I think Dad's banker was about the dozenth to get it. Dad shot him, drove on home, and seeing as he didn't have a wife, he shoved my older sister down the well, then hung himself in the barn. People'd gotten used to it by then so there wasn't such a fuss, but still, the next banker wisened up a little. He didn't come around our place sniffing for money.

"Now don't think I didn't cry," said Wendy. "I cried buckets. But, you know, I tell folks my story and in time it just turns into words. Like any other words you might say, about the new formula for Coca-Cola or the latest airplane crash. But I was sad."

It was etched in her face. Wendy was someone who would always be overlooked by waitresses in back booths of Denny's, get pushed aside in lines, waiting for food or health care or a future, be buried in an unmarked grave.

"Oh what a feeling!" said Dwight. "Toyota."

He closed his eyes and rested his head on Wendy's shoulder. The night was becoming everything that mountain nights do. Cold, alive, throbbing and hushed. Antonio cleared his throat.

"I'll tell you about my grandpa," he said. "That'll cheer you up. Grandma said Grandpa always made so much out of that *give us your tired masses yearning to breathe free* business. He was a real patriot. He married my grandma, she was the one descended from Tom Jefferson, and built up a small business selling American flags. Just after my dad was born, when Grandpa was fifty-one years old, he told Grandma he couldn't live a lie any longer and ran off to New Mexico with his gay lover, where he took up painting, Indian women and coyotes mostly. He became a little bit famous, was accused of communism. And then he died, but I never met him. Grandma told me everything, though, when I was living with her. My grandpa's the one that I got my nice bone structure from."

Antonio had a devil tattooed on his biceps, as well as nice bone structure. The firelight brought it to life, dancing as he moved his arm. A gleeful, lusty American devil.

"You do have nice bone structure," I said. "I admire it a great deal. I was once in love with somebody who had perfect bone structure, his name was Jimmy, and back before that a woman named Andalusia with exemplary bone structure as well. My own story starts in a bathtub, you see. There was something powerful emanating from the bathtub, something mythopoetic churning there in the primeval Mr. Bubble sea. That's where everything began, frenzy and phenomena steaming out of the seafoamy depths, life itself emerging ecstatic and slippery from below. Andalusia, the large woman who lived in the other half of my duplex, used to bathe me. The insane feel of the bubbles, Andalusia's magnetic scent, cinnamon and vanilla, the bobbing boats, the fat fingers on my slick little body, the song she used to sing, 'Alice's Restaurant.' *You can get anything you want . . . at Alice's restaurant . . .* No, that wasn't it, was it?"

"I've heard that song," Wendy said.

"But that wasn't it," I said.

"Makes no difference," said Jessica. "You search for her on highways and mountains and city streets, I imagine. You're a wanderer, a drifter, a rider of trains. You move along the fringes, seeking revelation or redemption."

She speared apples on a pointy stick and held it in the fire.

"You pegged that one," I said. "I'm addicted to movement. Anonymity, seduction. Compassion and the passage of time."

"You loved someone named Jimmy?" asked Antonio.

"Somewhat," I said, and blushed.

"Do go on," said Wendy. "You use nice sorts of words, I like to hear you talk."

I tried to figure out what I was talking about, the traces of my life. Everything was jumbled. Everything was forgotten.

"I've lost my train," I said. "The story's thread. Will my life become unraveled? Those who forget their past are condemned and so on and so forth. Bits and pieces is all I have for you, wanderings, voices, faces, meals. How does one tell one's life? Under what heading does this narrative belong? People who, after passing through a series of adventures, came to a happy end they had not hoped for? People who, by using their wits, regained something they had lost? Maybe lovers who won happiness after grief or misfortune or those whose love had an unhappy ending. It's too soon to say."

"That's for sure," said Wendy. "You can never tell what things will come to. I'm no poet, but I've wandered, too. Let me tell you. Joe, that's my brother, he took over the farm after Dad hung himself. He started growing marijuana. That turned things around real quick. He paid off the bank, bought a Trans Am and a four-wheel-drive pickup truck. Okay, so life was pretty good for a while. But then Joe says that Dwight's got to be too much trouble. He says Dwight wasn't good for a thing around the farm. Now please, how do you measure something like that? Sure, he couldn't separate the male plants from the females, he couldn't even feed the Dobermans, but he's the one that always made me smile. I never minded too much changing his pee sheets or even cleaning up his poop on the floor. But Joe said we had to put him in a home. He said he'd be better off in a home. I didn't buy that too much. I saw that home, it smelled like pee, there was all these other kids with helmets on their heads, seizuring and knocking things down, foaming at the mouth. There was a little girl that bit. There was this boy always screaming about Big Macs. It was scary, I tell you. I couldn't see my little brother in a place like that. I ran away, I took Dwight with me."

Dwight's eyes were closed, his head in Wendy's lap.

"That reminds me of Tom Jefferson," said Antonio, "He was a deist and grew marijuana on his farm, just like Wendy's brother. I admire Tom Jefferson a great deal. He freed some of his slaves when he died. He always stuck up for the common people, even when they were too stupid to know what was in their best interests. He told the British to fuck off. But wait, I never even told you about my own dad yet. All these dead people to talk about, shit. He went to Vietnam and then came back and married his high school sweetheart. That's my mom. He went to work as a carpenter and then I was born. When I was five years old he said he could no longer live a lie and ran off to Miami with his gay lover.

"Now I love Wendy some," he said, "I love all of her, you know, her soul and everything. I had a girlfriend in New York that I just loved her cunt and you know, it was the same with her, she only loved my dick. There's a lot of different kinds of love and such. I want to assure you, Wendy, that despite my family's history I will never run off and leave you for my gay lover. I like women a great deal, although I'm very open-minded. It's my heritage."

He glanced over at me. He had those dark eyes that gave me the sense of something electric going on behind them.

"When Mom was on tour and Grandma was insane," he said, "I moved down to Florida to live with Dad. His boyfriend played lots of salsa music and patted me on the head. He was from Cuba, he had to marry an American woman so he could be a citizen, and she was real nice too. I don't know where she was from. They took me to zoos and all sorts of things. I loved my dad more than anything, he was always picking up shells off the beach for me. And then he got sick. It lasted a long time, his AIDS, he used to be a big healthy guy, always smiling, but then he withered up, got all splotchy and gross. Me and Luis, we sat by his bed, we cried buckets too, just like Wendy."

Smoke curled up into the sky. Sparks leapt into the air, sunny days from the past.

"It was worse for Luis," he said. "He used to say AIDS was a government plot, I don't know if I believe that one, but I guess I couldn't rule it out. But he had it rough, he knew he'd probably get it, too, and then he did. I stuck around for a while, Luis' wife cooked me tons of shark casseroles and things, but then Dad died and I couldn't hang out anymore, it was too sad. I feel bad about that one, Luis was my friend."

"Florida's like that," I said. "I let somebody die there, too,

I think. Dust. Florida is a place prone to such lapses, that's my view."

"Could be," said Antonio, "what with Disney World and all. Anyway, I hit the road, went looking for my mom. I didn't find her, not yet at least. I still could. But I like it with Jessica and Wendy and you all. Wendy, why don't you go on with your story? I'm done, I'm all talked out."

"Should I keep going?" asked Wendy. "The rest of my story is hardly special, a runaway story, except I suppose most runaways don't have their little autistic brothers Dwight with them. We rode the bus some, that was an adventure. We slept in a Texaco women's room one night, it wouldn't of been so bad if Dwight didn't keep playing with the electric hand dryer. All these folks, they say to me *you sure are a lucky little girl now that I found you and will take care of you.* Oh, did we have adventures, me and Dwight, did we ever. This woman with purple hair took us in outside of Dallas, purple hair, I got such a kick out of that. Takes all kinds, my grandma used to say, and does it. Then there was this woman I met named Rebeca, I tell you, she was the most beautiful woman I ever saw. She talked funny, but it was pretty, real pretty, it just sort of came out and hung there, sort of like music. She had this nice black hair, but she kept telling me how pretty my hair was, we sat there in the bus depot and she just kept brushing and brushing. Dwight just sat and watched her, all peaceful, she just brushed my hair. This was in Topeka. *This is a good moment,* she said to me. She said to me *I am particularly aware of existing right at this special moment, but it doesn't hurt.* She smiled at me and I smiled right back. She was so pretty. *You sure do have nice hair,* she said. Our bus came. She stayed there. *Where you going?* I asked. *You going home?* She just smiled at me. *Sure,* she said, *going home.*"

We were traveling in parallel spirals, it seemed. Who was this woman and where was she going?

"You guys have such histories," I said. "I've retained very little it seems. There was a murder back there, I guarantee you of that. And I do remember Andalusia, in some future I shall find her. I've chosen to forget, I'll tell you that much. No more past, nothing on which to base myself, everything to create and discover. If I chose to remember, I'd be forced to remember everything, including the murder and my own part therein."

Jessica tossed us each a baked apple. They were hot and gooey with cinnamon. I leaned back and stared at the sky, the woods. Everything was traveling. Dwight sat up with a start.

"Hey, Bob," he said. "What you doin' there, Bob?"

"I slept on bathroom floors," said Wendy.

"I joined the Los Angeles hordes," I said, "seeking predictable weather and an absence of slush."

"New York's tougher than L.A.," said Antonio. "New York could beat the shit out of L.A. if they ever got in a fight."

There was a pale ring around the moon.

"I made vegetable soup out of ketchup packets sometimes."

"People wanted to take my picture naked."

"It was always so cold."

"Wasn't it? You never do realize how cold it really is until you're right there in the middle of that."

"But people took care of me sometimes and gave me things."

"People do do that."

"Dingo. D-I-N-G-O, Dingo. Elephant. E-L-E-P-H-A-N-T, elephant."

"He sure can spell."

Jessica took the potatoes out of the fire, cut them steaming open with a Swiss army knife.

"I stole things sometimes."

"I sold crack and smoked it, too. I'd smoke it again if I had it, but I don't really want to."

"I liked to dig groceries out of the trash bins early in the morning. You can get a lot of good stuff there and all of it's free."

"Sure, and the grocery-store people would stand there and ignore you and talk about baseball."

"I slept under benches and next to the ocean."

"I took acid by the Grand Canyon and waited for God to talk to me. He never did, but this shoe doctor did. He was retired, crossing the country in an RV home with his wife, wearing plaid shorts. Fifty years he spent, curing shoes. Imagine that."

"A multitude of forms for matter and energy," said Jessica. "Still, I know how difficult it is for you orphans to fill that emptiness in between meals."

Wendy stared at the sky.

"What about you, Jessica?" I asked.

"Yeah, what about your story?"

She smiled. She gave us each a potato, then sat back on her log. She patted her rounded belly.

"Once," she said, "I was small. Yes, far less than large, not nearly a big person, I was but a girl. How old? Three or four, I suppose, it is impossible for me to know, my parents didn't live by the solar calendar. We lived in a place, I would call it a jungle, but it had characteristics of a forest as well. It was a tangled, miasmic place with trees and vines. We lived alone in a broad clearing in a circular grass hut. One room and a dirt floor, although my parents spent the larger part of their lives lying tangled in a large fishnet hammock that swung in the yard. They had smooth, hairless bodies and long, shimmery blue hair to their waists. From the back it would have been difficult to distinguish the two if it hadn't been for the furs my mother wore, always of the darkest purple.

"I waddled about the clearing, wearing a tiny sailor's suit. Perhaps this was due to a parental premonition of the future that lay ahead. I ate bugs and watched my parents swinging in their hammock. My father tended to spit when he talked, but he was often silent. When he wasn't in the hammock with my mother she could often be found in the highest branches of trees, bathing in the rampant sunlight and communicating with birds."

We bit into our steaming potatoes with broccoli and cheese. Jessica waved her hands as she talked, as if dancing, casting a spell, forming worlds with her fingers.

"There was a cold beach not far from our clearing," she said. "The sky was hazy and one could hardly describe the beach as tropical. I was alone on the beach, I don't even remember how I got there. I had strayed. I stood there, watching out over the ocean. A ship floated above the water, just on the horizon. It was one of those things I'd never seen before, a ship. When you're that young there's nothing so surprising about things you have yet to encounter. It seemed an eternity, the time I spent on that beach, watching the ship. Slowly, a speck of something approached across the water. The speck became a line, I thought it must be an animal. But no, it was a small rowboat, with a tiny man in it. He was so small. But then he got nearer and bigger. Nearer and bigger, nearer and bigger, I stood on the sand and watched. The afternoon seemed to stop somewhere in there, low-flying clouds moved lazily toward me. By the time he was there, out of his boat and wading through the water toward me, he was immense, barrel-chested and hairy, shirt soaked to his skin, holding his hands up to the sky as if pleading, then laughing, stumbling through the surf and collapsing onto the beach, grabbing fistfuls of wet sand and squeezing them through his fingers.

"To make a long story short," she said, "I was taken away. Back, over the ocean, onto the ship that floated above the horizon. They were pirates, you see. They raised me on the high seas, a-burning and a-looting and a-raping we did go. They became my family, those nasty pirates, we traveled all over the world. We fought as mercenaries in Algeria. We smuggled guns during the Cuban revolution, carried slaves between Upper Volta and Los Angeles. It was a wretched life, although it had its good points, I'll admit. I never saw my home or my parents again, never even knew the name of the place I'd come from."

She sighed. Antonio spit out a piece of broccoli. Wendy gazed in rapt attention.

"Or maybe," said Jessica, "I was born into a loving, stable middle-class home. Maybe I enjoyed a happy childhood filled with smiling playmates and sunshine. My parents have snapshots, in fact, to prove that it is exactly this version which is true. Still, I seem to remember my childhood as primarily spent in a cold stone building, all alone, huddled beside heating vents, trying to stay warm. I remember poverty and a series of drownings on a cold northern lake."

"Things do get mixed up," said Wendy.

She stood up, walked over and gave Jessica a hug.

"We're all real eager the baby to get here," said Antonio.

"Sure," said Wendy. "We've had to be awful patient, what with all this waiting."

"Who's the father?" I asked.

Jessica brushed her hair aside with her palm.

"My history is that of the western hemisphere," she said. "I was raped by a cowboy. Was it Ronald Reagan or the Marlboro man? I don't know, it was all very hazy, I was drugged in the middle of nowhere. I was beaten, a tooth knocked out, I have scars on my thighs. For weeks I wanted to die. But the event itself I just don't remember. Amnesia is not always a problem. Think about forgetting as plunging gleefully into the future. Perhaps we forget for the sake of the future. Imagine pure white space, not even punctuated.

"Now," she said, "I travel the highways and pick up strays. Feeding is art and politics both. The culinary aesthetics, the nourishment of the impoverished. While essentially a creative act, one must also take the inevitable excretion into account. My food is nourishing, but subversive as well. There's my revenge. It changes people's dreams."

The fire was dying. Dwight snored, Antonio and Wendy held hands. How did it change people's dreams? Breezes blew over the last small flames and I felt tired and warm for a change. We sat for a long time like that, listening to the night, too exhausted to speak. Animals flitted through the woods and I remembered my dad going on about alternative perspectives. Imagine the consciousness of a bird as you watch flocks turning circles at dusk, choreographed, like cells in a bloodstream. The obsessions of tarantulas, always moving east. Chimpanzees, cheetahs, houseplants. He said animals knew what death was, he'd strangled pheasants, had seen it in their eyes. He said it was a myth that animals were closer to God than we were. He said we all felt the cold exactly the same.

Think about rape; think about someone forcing a part of their body into your own; think about losing possession of the only space you have left. Think about Ronald Reagan, the Marlboro man. Think about bruises, scars, lost consciousness, times when something may have been done to you, but you aren't sure what it is. How could she forget with the baby there inside her?

"What will you tell the baby?" I whispered.

"Lies," she said. "I will tell the baby lies. I will make up stories, and once they've been spoken they'll be as true as anything else."

She tossed me a rolled-up sleeping bag, I crawled inside, zipped myself up and lay there, watching blinking lights in the sky. Jessica Moon stamped out the fire.

2

We stayed up there for days and nights. We ate, sat alone in the woods, dipped in icy streams, listened. Before me: life, crystalline and fluid, hexagonal, spiraling, the violas of cicada wings. Beautiful trees and pretty flowers and a lake that defined blue. Okay, so you get the picture: solace in nature, this wonderful largeness and indifference and greenness, the quietude and motion, redemption through a return to the organic roots of my life, pastoral bliss, all that sort of thing; the alienated and distraught young man finds peace and harmony at last by listening to birds and insects and tuning in to the groovy cosmic love vibes that permeate the universe. It's an old story, I know, made tiresome through repetition. So many things grow tiresome. So much art and pretentious knowledge, so many life-styles and human beings. Everything is fashion, everything is food.

"The word, *mystery*," Jessica said, "from the Latin, means *that which is squinted at*. A mystic is *one who squints*."

Jessica was sort of a mystic. She believed that death was a fluidity, a merging. She read my tarot cards, told me my Queen of Pentacles was in electric bunny tango. She felt the next step in the evolutionary process was close at hand, that recycling could save the world, that our selves were simply bundles of fluxes, taking off here and there in different combinations. Like subatomic particles we bounced down the mountain, packed up the van and moved along.

We drove from place to place. Jessica sold sandwiches out of the van or while walking down the street, sandwiches with zucchini and goat's-milk cheese and tofu and mushrooms and sprouts. Blackberry preserves and almond butter, honey and cream cheese and ripe, halved bananas. Pesto pasta salads, bread puddings, hummus and Key lime pie. Food threw itself into her arms, called to her from roadside vegetable stands, stowed away in the back of the van. Every morning a mound of fresh produce waited outside the van for her majestic appearance, her approval, her knife. She chopped onions with reverence, tomatoes with cunning, avocado with grace. People flocked to eat her sandwiches, paid a dollar or fifty cents or took them for free. They had dreams then about possible futures: the granaries full to bursting, children fat and dancing, space exploration, minglings, green spaces and water. They dreamed futures without genocide, starvation and torture. For this they stood in line.

Food, eating, nourishment, rolling down the road. We got hassled once in a while for not having a license, but usually it was easy. When she got enough money, she bought stones, opals and Apache tears and amethyst and rubies. She made jewelry, she bought gas for the van, and we moved along, feeding, feeding, always feeding, pumpkin bread and apple fritters, Greek salads and stir-fried veggies, yams and cashews and blueberry bagels. As Jessica's baby neared its debut, her cravings became stranger, the food she prepared prompted sillier dreams. Wendy, Antonio and me, we dreamed of living in her womb, swimming wide-eyed in amniotic fluid, attached, connected, forgetful. Who could say what Dwight dreamed of? He was obsessed with light switches, ceiling fans, the sky. He wet himself sometimes, yanked our hair and wailed, got into the food in the middle of the night. When he laughed, however, it was with the wildest, purest joy, an insane, infectious glee that shattered for brief moments the very idea of pain, of victimization, of history books and hunger. At a mission in Santa Fe an Eskimo named Brent taught Jessica how to make ice cream out of caribou fat and blackberries. He showed her how to stir the mixture in order to release the spirit of the caribou, he whispered in her ear.

"If dead bodies start washing up on the beach," she later advised us, "I'd suggest you decorate them with flowers and shells and dance around them singing 'Gabba Gabba Hey.' "

We were nowhere near the beach yet. Snakes and adobe and sand art and yucca. We moved through the canyons and painted deserts, the mountain air so rich you could feel something pressing from inside you, a pressure on the back of your eyeballs. While Jessica drove, Wendy learned to knit hats, Antonio carved gnomes out of wood, I helped Jessica string her necklaces and listened to her baby's heart beating, my ear on her belly, stretched taut like a drum. We went to Grateful Dead concerts, danced under full moons and took acid with all the groovy hippie love children, lost teenagers, runaways, organic farmers, burn-outs, environmental activists, college kids on drugs, yuppies on nostalgic weekends. We danced barefoot, in the grass or in dust. Wendy wore bells on her ankles, Antonio pulsed with sexual energy, Dwight wiggled his fingers, Jessica sat, caressing her belly. Leaves swayed and critters in the woods, the artichokes and mozzarella and spinach fettucine that followed Jessica, there with us, twisting around ankles and calves and torsos, pasta and flesh intertwining, noodles, skin, leaves, sky, firelight and drums. We drove up the California coast, picked jade on Big Sur beaches, haunted gems tossed from the depths. On rainy days we'd sit together in the van, our animal warmth making us sweat, carving, knitting, beading.

"I have horrible dreams sometimes," Wendy told us.

"One can learn to become an active participant in their dreams," Jessica said. She paused, studying the translucent green swirls in a small piece of jade. "Yes, I believe that may be true."

Wendy whispered to me.

"It's the baby," she said.

I squeezed her hand. I'd been having the same dreams. So many things could go wrong with a baby: Siamese twins, mongoloids, crack babies, babies with AIDS. Blind babies, deaf babies, babies with spots. Stillborn babies, hungry babies, hairy

babies, ugly babies. Insane babies, possessed babies, babies with
bad karma, babies with no soul. Babies, babies, babies.

"After the baby's born," said Wendy, "we'll all be happy
forever."

"Wendy dear," said Jessica, "babies don't usually *solve*
problems."

Wendy's face, always ready to burst into tears. She knit her
hat, I strung my beads, Antonio carved. We listened to the rain
on the roof and sipped hot chamomile tea out of purple ceramic
mugs.

A sunny day, fog hanging on the horizon. Wendy and Antonio waded in the freezing surf, splashing and half naked. I walked
down the beach with Jessica and Dwight.

"I need to find Andalusia," I said.

"Touch it, touch it," squealed Dwight, pointing at the sky.

Jessica took his hand, rested her other one on my shoulder.
She was almost the same thing as Andalusia, I thought, only
flawed; cranky in the mornings, afraid of tornadoes, she didn't
play chess. She was skinny and pregnant. She'd never seen
Vanishing Point.

"The kids like you," she said. "Antonio and Wendy would
miss you. You're good with Dwight."

"Sometimes I need to be alone," I said.

"No shit," she said. "If we didn't do that sometimes, we'd
have all strangled each other by now."

"Touch it, Bob," said Dwight. "Do it, do it, do it now, please."

"You orphans," she said. "Always so afraid. When we crossed
the midwest we went through East Liberty, where the biggest
orphanage in the world used to be."

"Used to be?" I said.

"They invested all their money in paper, nostalgia and
obsolete military hardware," she said, "When the stock market
dipped they were ruined overnight. The orphans went crazy,
tore the place down. It was all shattered glass and bricks, just
one old man left dazed and mumbling in the streets."

"Father Larry," I said.

"He just sat in the dust reading supermarket tabloids."

I watched out over the ocean. There was really nothing left behind me, nothing at all. Where was there to go? This was the farthest west you could be, the country's limit, the edge of its dreams. I thought about boats.

That night Jessica took Wendy up into the mountains in the van to do women's sorts of things, some sort of gendered, essentialist spirituality, I don't know what all. I stayed with Antonio and Dwight, camped illegally on the public beach. We couldn't risk building a fire and it was cold, the fog moving in at dusk, trolls under bridges, witches' moon.

"Are you getting restless?" asked Antonio. "Are you going to leave?"

"I don't think so," I said. "Not tonight, anyway."

"Sometimes I want to go," said Antonio. "I get tired of being good. I like to prowl around cities and go in places I'm not supposed to."

Dwight snored in his bag.

"I like seedy parts of cities, too," I said. "Foggy nights, unlawful acts. I steal a lot of books."

Antonio leaned back, stretching his arms out wide. His body was compact, muscular, he wasn't wearing a shirt, just a blanket around his shoulders. He seemed quivering, holding in a violence, ready to explode.

He pulled something out of his pocket, a small mirror, a crumpled piece of paper. He started chopping lines of cocaine with a razor. I moved over next to him. He chopped it finer and finer, played with it, the powder snaking this way and that. He rolled up a dollar bill and did a line, then offered it to me. I took it.

"I got it in Gorda," he said. "Jessica doesn't know and you can't tell. She gets pissed about coke. It makes me mad sometimes, she used to get stoned all the time before she was pregnant and she thinks that's so much better."

I rubbed a little bit on my gums to feel the tingly numbness.

"She's just trying to watch out for you," I said.

"She cussed at me once."

He did another line, then sat there, bouncing, ready to take off. He offered me the last line and I took it.

"It's my money," he said. "It's my gnomes. I can do what I want with my money, can't I?"

"She's just trying to watch out for you," I said. "We're all a little tense now, waiting for the baby."

"I want to go break things."

With the coke in my head that sounded exactly like it. My fingers were drumming. I liked Antonio. He understood the joy in dark alleys, the mystery by docks. He started beating his bongos, thump, thump, thump, the fog all around us, ghost stories and drums. He threw a beer bottle up into the air. It spun in circles up there, like a bone, a spaceship, just hanging and spinning, waiting to fall. Up the cliff, on the highway, barefoot women wandered through the night, lunatics drove on three tires and an axle, spraying the road with their sparks. Big Sur. Jack Kerouac went crazy here once. The bottle shattered on the rocks, splintering into amber razors that would be smoothed over by time, turned into beautiful gems by the sea. Thump, thump, thump. Drums answered us from back in the mountains. These nights were so black, the fog so deranged, how did they pass?

We huddled together in the sleeping bags. I got a hard-on, but Antonio only talked about percussion instruments and which musical chords he liked to hear best. He fell asleep then, his hard body in my arms. Where had I learned that there was something wrong with this desire, something violent about it, when I only wanted to touch somebody? America, I thought. I learned it in America. The fog shifted in cottony, skeletal shapes. This was a different fog from the fog in Florida, the fog that had led me to Dust. This was an intelligent fog, a voiceless fog with memory and faces. This fog understood all the violent ways one could die, drownings and murders and cars plummeting over cliffs. People drove up to Big Sur from L.A. in sports cars sometimes, to suicide, to soar over the edge, lie flattened and dead on the beaches below. I thought about the fascination with someone like Hitler. I thought about handsome killers like Ted Bundy or Reagan. I thought about death wishes, idiots with their

fingers so close to the button. Antonio's heart was racing in his
sleep, his exciting, stupid violence. I realized it then, with a
start, what I wanted. I wanted to be murdered.

On the other hand, I didn't want that at all.

Sex and death, Dust said, romantic bullshit from the perpetually horny. Really, I just wanted to touch Antonio, to sleep
with him, to watch each other's faces in orgasm. I was gay, that
was all, nothing so unusual; I had an erection, Antonio slept. I
tried to fit this night into my catalog of moods. Joy, boredom,
dread. There were always these pieces that didn't fit in, events
that led nowhere, destinations just the other side of possibility.
Death was a possibility, but not knowledge of death. I saw faces,
laughing in the fog. The night passed, like that.

The sun revealed dead bodies washed up all down the beach.
Corpses covered with seaweed, some without faces or eyes,
twisted and soggy in the dull morning light. I examined the
bodies, thinking I might find someone I knew, my parents maybe.
But Antonio said they were all Indians. He was part Indian, so
he could easily tell. Navajo, Sioux, Apache, Cheyenne. We collected shells from the beach, picked flowers from the hillside.
Road crews had chopped down anise plants and the licorice
smell filled the air. We made garlands from the yellow-flowered
heads, decorated the bodies and sprinkled them with fragrant
oil. When Wendy and Jessica showed up we were leaping over
the beautified, fragrant victims, dancing in circles around the
motionless bodies, singing "Gabba Gabba Hey." They helped
us drag the corpses out of the reach of the tide. Wendy dressed
them in her colorful knitted hats, Jessica burnt incense, Antonio
beat his drums. When the first tourists arrived with their cameras and sunglasses we left them there and drove north, up the
coast.

Nepenthe, Carmel, Monterey, Santa Cruz. I walked up and
down the Santa Cruz mall with Wendy, selling her knitted hats,
Antonio's carved gnomes, sandwiches. The people in Santa Cruz
were smiling and violent, the simultaneity slightly alarming.
Nobody bought things from Wendy, she was far too polite. Not
even her sadness elicited sympathy in such a sunny, naked place.

"I still have bad dreams about the baby," she told me. "I'm afraid it's not going to work out."

"It isn't your fault," I said. "You shouldn't be so sad. You always look sad."

"Oh, that isn't me," she said, "that's just my face. My face looks sad all the time, but really I'm one of the happiest people you could know."

We stopped, examined our reflection in a donut-shop window. Could joy really hide under such a surface as this? The reflection of clouds on the window transformed customers reading the newspaper into cunning masked angels. My own face was haggard. YOUTH CRIME WAVE STRIKES CAPITAL CITY, declared a headline. In smaller print, beneath that, BOTTLED-UP RAGE, FUTILITY OF LIFE CITED. An expert was quoted. "It seems almost to be a senseless contagion. We've got a lot of theories . . . but we've reached the point where we have a lot of kids with nothing to do. They feel they have no destiny in their own life. It doesn't take anything to set them off." I nudged Wendy and we walked on down the street.

"I used to dream of Dad breaking a bone or something," she said. "Being laid up in bed, me sticking a thermometer in his mouth and making him stew. But I never would of wanted him hung. I always wanted to be a nurse. I think I'd be good at that. I do like those uniforms.

"I'm afraid of what I might wish for," she said. "I still have those dreams. The baby, why isn't it here yet? Something awful will happen, I know that it will."

"Shhhh," I said. "Don't think about that."

We moved farther north, hoping for birth. San Francisco, Eureka, Bandon-by-the-Sea. Mountains and hot springs and bare-chested men. Redwoods and beaches and otters and fires. In Eugene I sold bracelets made out of string, I smiled at people and they smiled back.

"Too much driving," said Jessica, "is making us all a little bit loopy. We'll stay in Eugene. This is where I'll have my baby."

We parked in the lot of a coffee shop that sold hot almond milk. In the daytime we sold our wares, at night I drove through the Eugene streets, or up into the mountains, while Jessica lay on her back, telling the unborn baby stories.

"Will you still need us?" asked Wendy. "After the baby's born? Will you still need us?"

Jessica patted her head.

"I wouldn't know what to do," Wendy said, "if you didn't need me to take care of."

Still, the baby didn't come.

Other nights I walked the streets, smoked cigarettes, examined tombstones and pine trees and slivers of moon. Strangers on corners, children in fountains, old men using zinc sulfate to get the moss off their roofs. The town was green and dripping.

A man came up to me one day to purchase a sandwich. He was about my own age, looked disturbingly familiar. He was bedraggled, scruffy, wearing a cowboy hat.

"You live on the road?" he asked.

"We do tend to move," I said, "yes."

"You think freedom of movement leads to ultimate freedom," he said. "You think you have all this space to run around in and play. You think it's all about space, this freedom thing, when it isn't that at all. It's about the way you cut up time. Good sandwich."

Sprouts dangled from his mouth, blackberry preserves smeared around his lips.

"One's life isn't really one's own," he said. "You think? They'll tell you that, base whole countries on the idea. But think about what they've done with time, cut it up, measured it, weighed it, regulated it. As if matching numbers to time was a way of postponing death.

"Death isn't so sad," he said, "it's all that there is. Death makes us go, right? I need my own death to show me my way. But I can't find it. Everything around here is pitch-dead already."

"What's your point?" I asked. "The sandwich is a dollar."

"Sure, commerce," he said and paid me. "Words and energy, energy and words. I used to think the past was behind me. There's your trouble, thinking the past is a place, with volume, increasing steadily as the future decreases. Or a line, that's a

common one, huh? That isn't time at all. The past is always
there, just like it is, we're only seeing it in this arbitrary order,
thinking we have something to say about it. God never said anything about free will."

"Ah," I said, "I see. This is about God."

"God and death, it's the same thing."

"Do you have a pamphlet?" I asked. "It could save us both
considerable time."

"There you go again with that volume thing," he said and
extended his hand. "My name's Cain." The name registered at
the same time I felt it, the scar in his palm in the shape of a
cross. I jumped back.

"Wait a minute," I said.

He stopped. I examined his features. After all these years,
it was him, he was here. The afternoon with the candles and
marigolds, the knife. I put my hand on my forehead.

"Are you all right?" he asked.

"The scar on your hand," I said. "Where did you get it?"

He rubbed his palm against his cheek, feeling it there. He
smiled, as if nuzzling an old, slightly embarrassing friend.

"That old thing?" he said. "I wandered into the desert, God
spoke to me, embedded himself in my palm. With language,
nothing but language, a language that's really only silence. God
lives in the desert because the desert is complete emptiness.
Because the desert has nothing to do with human beings or history or any sort of truth."

"You're still completely whacked," I said.

"Excuse me?"

"Nothing," I said. He didn't recognize me. Didn't perceive
me this time around as particularly angelic. His metaphysics
had changed considerably in the last eight years.

"Yes," he said, "language is a deal, but I'm not sure I want
to play anymore."

He lit a cigarette. This was Cain, smoking, wearing a cowboy hat. If the past wasn't a place, where did he come from?
How did he still haunt me? Eight years later, the proof still
there, inscribed in someone else's flesh and history: what I did.

"That old line about the two paths, the wide and the narrow, well, I'll tell you," he said, "there's a lot more paths than two."

Was I responsible, somehow, for this? I reached out, ran my fingers over his hand, his scar. And then my own scar, a rounded one the size of a coin from the time I crashed on my bike. Traces on our bodies, like the identification numbers tattooed on concentration-camp survivors. One could still find traces of history here and there.

"Do you know me?" I asked. "Who do I look like?"

He squinted.

"Of course I know you," he said. "You're just America, that's who you are.

"Like everyone else," he said.

"*It is you who have devoured the vineyard,*" I said, "*the loot wrested from the poor is in your house. What do you mean by crushing my people, and grinding down the poor when they look to you? Isaiah 3:14-15.*"

"Very good," said Cain, "In a similar vein, *I hate, I spurn your feasts. I take no pleasures in your solemnities; . . . Away with your noisy songs! I will not listen to the melodies of your harps. But if you would offer me holocausts, then let justice surge like water, and goodness like an unfailing stream. Amos 5:21-25.*"

"Yes," I said. I glanced at his hand. I felt it again, that sickness in the back of my throat. The urge to throw up. I had done this. And Seth, what had become of his brother? I didn't want to know, couldn't know anything more, my complicity too overwhelming. Cowboy, I thought.

"Goodbye," I said and hurried down the street.

I never saw him again, but I couldn't forget. The flowers, the candles, the blade and the heat. The potential of his visibility was enough to keep me awake for nights. He might appear anywhere, at a donut shop or gas station or laundromat or bookstore. For days I hid out in the van.

Still, the baby didn't come.

One night I woke to hear Jessica weeping.

"Jessica," I said, and moved over, massaged her shoulders.

"It isn't true," she whispered, sobbing.

"What isn't true?" I asked.

"Love," she said. "Love isn't true. I hate everything, I hate my life, I hate him, I hate what's inside of me."

I rubbed. I had no words, what could I say? She knew as well as I did that she wouldn't always feel this way, that this too would pass.

"My child will be born with a gun in its fist," she said, "or a bomb or a knife.

"My child will be outraged," she said.

She nestled into my arms, heaving. She cried. And then she fell asleep.

Days passed, we grew happy, grew tense. The baby didn't come. Jessica hummed to herself, as if nothing was wrong.

"You're late," I said finally. "You should go see a doctor."

She smiled.

"No," she said.

But in the mornings, the food was no longer there, waiting for us outside the van. Nobody mentioned it. I wore big coats into supermarkets, stuffed my pockets with produce. Who was I fooling? I had horrible dreams, filled with black, charred babies, babies with two heads, babies driving BMWs and smoking cigars. Airplanes crashed on tavern televisions. Men on the news spoke of penetration points. The baby didn't come.

Was this a conscious refusal to emerge into the world? Was this child protesting the current situation, hiding from trends? The very idea of a baby was so amazing to me. Babies had been absent from my life on the road, it was the fully formed who did all the traveling. I watched babies wheeled by in strollers, pink and wrinkled, chubby and yawning, squeaking and awkward, their round, sweet little heads, milky, tender fingers and toes, delicate heartbeats. Such pliable, curious things. I tried to remember my own infancy, found nothing at all. No memories of sucking, squealing, wiggling or defecating, enormous years of my life I just couldn't find. I filled in the gap with generic babyhood images: bland, mushy food, fuzzy pajamas, the world viewed from a stroller, moving past like a movie, no visible means of propulsion. I'd heard that some babies still talked about their previous lives. Some babies levitated, wrote novels or sang, when nobody was around to see. Some babies were no good from the very first day.

Antonio snorted cocaine. Wendy sobbed in her sleep. Dwight pulled our hair, bit us and spelled, angrily. I stole food from the grocery store while Jessica slept. An hour away, at the ocean, more bodies were washing up on the beach.

Her water broke.

"Stay calm," I said. "Don't panic. Just stay calm. I know exactly what to do. Lie down flat. Don't move. Breathe deep. Count backwards from a thousand. Sing a song. *This land is your land, this land is my land, from the redwood forest, to . . .* wait. I'll drive. We'll go the the hospital."

I started the van. Jessica gasped. I drove through the streets, frantic, lost. I asked strangers for directions. They were helpful and calm.

"OK," I said, "OK, OK, OK."

"Om," said Jessica. "Om."

I found the hospital and there we were. Women in white. IVs in fragile arms, sculptures and carpet, the smell of ammonia. They rushed her away and asked me to fill out forms. It was useless. I didn't know any of the answers, none of the pertinent data. Places of birth, nearest kin, blood type. I made things up, I wrote short essays, I posed metaphysical questions. I smiled at the nurse and hurried off to the vending machines for a cup of coffee and some cigarettes. I wanted to do this by the book.

Antonio and Wendy held hands in the corner, chewed on pamphlets about sexually transmitted diseases. Dwight jumped up and down, pointing at a fan on the ceiling. Other expectant fathers paced and whistled and coughed. A familiar scenario: time passed, cigars were passed out, accident victims screamed in distant corners. There were moans and bloodcurdling cries of pain, boys and girls were born, there were complications, delays, and then it was there.

"Congratulations," the nurse told me. "It's a girl."

"My God," I said. It suddenly struck me. Really struck me. There it was, the little thing that had been kicking inside her. It had become. It was being, right there, in that very hospital.

She led me by the hand. I was afraid it wouldn't be normal. I was afraid to ask. How do you pose such a question? *Is it normal?* What statistics do you use to judge such an unformed being? IQ, leisure activities, bra size, median income? The hospital hallways were pulsing with light.

"How's Jessica?" I asked.

"Jessica's fine," she said. "She's resting now."

It was there behind glass, with a few other little red creatures, nearly indistinguishable, all wet and globby and tiny and amazing. She left us there alone. I pressed my fingers against the glass. Antonio and Wendy held each other, awed by the spectacle of such a helpless, needy thing. In comparison they seemed capable and adult.

"What do babies need?" asked Antonio. "What do we have to get it?"

"We need things to wiggle in its face," said Wendy. "My cousin had a baby once and she said it was good for babies to have lots of things wiggled in their faces."

"We'll be happy now," said Antonio. "You know it? We're a real family now. We'll be happy."

There was a ringing in my head. I knew I didn't belong here with all this belongingness. Alone, beside highways, howling at the moon.

"I'll take care of it," said Wendy. "Just like a nurse."

"I'm scared," said Antonio.

"We all are," said Wendy. "We'll be happy now."

The baby opened her immaculate little fist. She was clenching a pebble, a tiny stone, she'd been born with it there. *The babies are dying, the crops drying up.* People were always telling me this, but I watched her then, the baby, screaming, letting out a healthy wail, and I knew: it was simply a matter of will. I imagined the message she was receiving: life is a steady hum, a brightly lit room, the random cries of other babies. Later, she would find life was movement, down on the elevator and then out, across parking lots and farther.

We went down to check on Jessica. She smiled up at us.

"It's a girl," she said. She closed her eyes, content. She was happy, everything was good. I felt a pain in my chest. "I'll tell it stories," she said. She smiled and smiled. I kissed her on the cheek. I went back up to the baby, leaving Jessica Moon with Antonio and Wendy and Dwight.

I watched her there, jealous and in love, and I knew then that I couldn't stay. Her future couldn't include me, a black splotch hovering overhead. I had done horrible things and this baby had done nothing at all. This wasn't my life. There was nothing I could do, I thought, to make it my life. I had to find Andalusia before it was too late. This was a quest, after all.

I scribbled a note, I left it at the desk. My chest felt hollow inside, it was hard to swallow. I turned, quick, I walked, I started singing to myself, and once I was moving it felt all right, out the electric doors into the parking lot, past ambulances, past the van and on, I was going, I was fine. The night was clean, breezy, it made my eyes itch, but it was OK then, out there again, in the night.

A silent trucker took me all the way to Colorado. I slept, and then a nice old black man took me on across Texas, into Oklahoma. In Oklahoma, a truck driver stopped.

"You got any dope?" he asked. "I only picked you up because I thought you might have some dope."

But I've said this all before, this is where I started. He took me on, to a rest stop, in between Tulsa and Oklahoma City, where I sat drinking coffee out of the bottom of other people's cups. I stayed there that night, I walked along the train tracks, and then I moved along.

I'm at a rest stop now, sending a postcard. I managed to steal *The Sickness unto Death* from the man with the AK-47. I usually try to avoid stealing from those with assault rifles, but this was a special case. It's close to noon and so damn hot, I'm writing out this postcard to a woman in Alaska. It reminds me of snow and water just to write the word. Alaska.

"Dear Glenda: I believe I'll soon be released. Things are looking up. My future is filled with tactile and olfactory sensations. Andalusia may swoop down from the sky at any moment. Do you believe in premonitions, the malleable nature of time and our knowledge of it? Of course you do, I remember we've had this conversation before. If it isn't Andalusia, it will surely be Jimmy, an erotic and timely death by strangulation or implosion. Remember what Salvador Dalí said: The only difference between a crazy person and me is that I'm not crazy. Be kind to your children. Love, Matt."

I borrow a stamp from a fat man in shorts. I demand his address, swear I'll send him a stamp as soon as I get home to the mansion in the bayou. He hurries away, fearful. There are psychopaths on the highways of America. You never know what they'll do next.

TEN

Δ

1

The large, sweaty man with the hairy neck didn't even bring his car to a complete stop to expel me onto the highway. It was close. A rolling stop, or as it's sometimes called, a Texas stop.

"Hey," I'd said to him, "why don't you take it easy on her?"

I'm not usually so outspoken. Hitchhikers are obliged to be grateful for their rides, whatever the state of the driver's soul. He had pummeled his wife with his right fist as he drove with his left. She was scrunched between us, a stringy little thing, a perspiring Raggedy Ann doll suffering from halitosis. It made an ugly, crunching sound. Her nose bled.

"Who the fuck do you think you are?" he asked me. "Mind your own fucking business. Mouthy fuck, get the hell out."

"Yeah," piped in his wife as the blood dripped off her chin, "who the fuck do you think you are? Mind your own business."

In this manner I was thrown out. I'm feeling quite pleased with myself now, for I obviously helped to reconcile the feuding couple. I'm doing good deeds.

But here I stand again, with nothing but my toothbrush, a plastic bag of raisins, a lucky button that says *It's Only Rock and Roll, but I Like It*, three dollars' worth of food stamps, and a tattered copy of *The Sickness unto Death*. I've been trying to eat the raisins slowly, rationing them, one raisin for every fifty cars that pass me by. I only have four left.

New Orleans is just down the road, sultry and filled with pecans. I wave my thumb. My legs turn into Ramen noodles.

Andalusia, Andalusia.

A car pulls over up ahead.

"Hurry up, hurry up!" The man is waving his arms like a flagman. "There's no time to lose!"

I run, jump into his car, and we're off, squealing. I'm all out of breath and sweating in the heat. The stale air in the car is like a pressure on my chest.

"Sorry to make you run like that. I just can't afford to get too far behind."

He's in his thirties, a narrow face, a hard chin, purple eyes. His gaze is intent on something up ahead. On the seat are chewing-gum wrappers, McDonald's trash, a newspaper clipping about a teenage girl who shot children in her playground at school. The dashboard smells like glue.

"Come on, come on," he says, and we're moving now, buzzing past vacation families in station wagons and mobile homes. Kids press their noses against the windows, or their toes, or both. They are either contortionists or this is an optical illusion. We pass motorcycles, compact cars, billboards. Trainworld, Cheese of the Ozarks, Bob's Cavern of Death and Miniature Golfing Course. The highway is all floating motion. In that way it is like a life.

"There she is!" shouts the man, smiling. A billboard off in the trees exposes male flesh and underwear, but then we are past. That isn't what he was pointing at. I follow the line of his arm. A gleaming shiver of red and silver chrome up ahead. As we move closer I see it's a sports car, sleek and curved. The sky is merciless heat.

"Ha," he says, "I've still got her."

I can make out the shape of a woman driving. It's a convertible and her long black hair is twisting in the wind behind her.

"Is that your wife?" I ask, but I sense this isn't the case. The man is wearing a snakeskin belt.

"My wife? Hardly. Just look at her. She's a vision, a dream. She's the most beautiful woman I've ever seen. She's my destiny. I didn't choose her, she just happened. I'd hardly call that a wife."

He's holding back now, maintaining a distance. I'm watching the woman, her hair, the reflected light from the car almost blinding. Out of my sideways vision the man appears to be on fire.

It's so hot out here. I peel my back off the seat, lean forward, to get a better view.

"I've been following her since Arizona," he says. "All the way across the country. She knows I'm here. But I can't get too close. Not yet."

"What are you going to do?" I ask. I'm afraid it's something violent, something wrong.

He looks in the rearview mirror.

"Do? I don't know yet. I'll do it when it's time. There are certain rules that must be followed here."

"Rules?"

"Of course," he says. "There are always rules. I'm not exactly clear on what they are yet, but you always have to do it by the rules."

The heat streams down like sudden death. Everything is whizzing past. Only the sun stays put.

"Fuck," he says, wiping sweat from his forehead. "If it gets any hotter the damn highway'll melt."

It's happened before, there's no denying. I'm losing every part of me, it's all dripping away. I'm an undifferentiated mass of wet flesh in the passenger's seat.

"Shit."

Up ahead the woman is pulling off the road, into a rest stop. I get a glimpse of her profile, magnificent, mysterious. I feel like I know her, like I've met her before.

"I hate these," says the man. He speeds past the exit, then pulls onto the shoulder, half a mile down the road.

"Why didn't you just follow her in?" I ask. "Introduce yourself. Say hi, my name is . . . whatever your name is . . . and just see what she does."

He smirks.

"Don't be ridiculous. That's obviously against the rules, moron. I can't even pull into the same rest stop she's in. Other exits are ok, I just pull into a different gas station or something, watch from there. But the same rest stop? Give me a break. Don't try to fuck me up now. I'm too close."

We are still, by the road. But the car is vibrating, and my head. In the quiet I can hear sunlight and birds.

"But if you never talk to her . . ."

"The rules, stupid!" he snaps. He leans back, tapping his fingers against the wheel. It's amazing how many drivers repeat the same gestures. My feet itch. A sharp glare bleeds from the hood.

And then she is there, streaking past, her head tilted back, seductive laugh and flick of the black hair, dazzling black, in the heat it's like a cool pool of ink to dive into. For one second time freezes a dull red and our eyes meet. Something passes between us, a recognition. I see it then, in her eyes. Sheer terror. We plunge forward, spitting gravel, in pursuit.

He's been following her since Arizona.

"Her name is Esmerelda, I think," he says. "Or Alexandria, Vanessa. She's everything I've ever wanted. Life, liberty, the pursuit of happiness, that sort of thing. I'm talking some strange sense of immortality here. If only I can make sure to do everything just right, by the rules, I know that I can have her."

"Like Andalusia," I whisper.

We fly, across Mississippi, into the hills. The road curves, the landscape changes. Perhaps we can slow the world down. But the hills become valleys, the valleys become hills, trees come and go. I'm out of breath again, I just can't keep up. The woman is there, directly ahead.

"Where were you going?" I ask. "Before you saw her?"

He is puzzled for a moment, he can't remember. Everything has happened so long ago it seems.

"Out for a hamburger. I was hungry. Damn hungry."

This reminds me. I finish off my raisins, all four at once. I realize that I'm dying. The raisins don't help.

Is there lightning here? In broad daylight, not a cloud in the sky. No, it's only the sun, or something in my head. His car radio only picks up AM, if we turned it on we would hear a song by a band called Dizzy Trout. "I Drove the Car That Killed Camus." How do I know these things? It is silent. I'm becoming clairvoyant, in the heat. My brain is gathering radio waves.

Something snaps.

"Yes," he says. "Closer now."

He accelerates, we move down, a curving spiral, gathering speed, careening around curves, a cliff bank on one side, red clay and shrubberies, a steep drop to the other side, traffic down there, going the other direction. We're catching up to her, but in these curves we lose sight around the corners, so you never know.

We make eye contact again, I feel the panic. I want to say stop, stop, what are you doing, following this innocent woman? Surely there's a law, somewhere, against just this sort of thing.

She accelerates. So do we.

"This is the time. I can feel it. It's getting there, we're getting there, come on, baby . . ."

We catch up to her, the man is grinning, teeth white heat. Her fender is silver chrome and melted white light. She tilts her head back, the black hair all twisting and blowing, tosses an ambiguous glance, taunting and afraid, and speeds away from us, on around the curve and out of sight.

The sign by the road says, CAUTION FALLING ROCK.

Time stops.

She is gone, way out of our view. Somewhere, something is suspended in midair. For one moment it just hangs, between the sky and the earth. It wouldn't need to move, it could stay right there. But it pulls us all down eventually, gravity's pull. We hear it loud, a sickening crash, screech of metal, and I nearly swallow my tongue.

We are there, right on it.

It's a mess. We pull over behind it.

"Oh my God."

That's the man. He steps out, stands, doesn't move yet toward her. Other cars are stopping everywhere. Spiny worms are slam dancing in my belly. The boulder is sitting there in the driver's seat, as if it's just driven across the country, a frantic tourist. The car is wedged into the cliff, metal and broken glass, an arm sticking out from under the huge rock. The space of time is slow liquid, pasty in my head, a rainbow of colors exploding bright. Red metal and clay ocher, pale blue sky. People are running and shouting and asking questions, but I stare at the ground. There is a book by my feet, black leather with gold-engraved writing on the cover. *My Diary.*

I bend, blood rushes into my head. I pick it up. I clutch it to my breast.

Blood is trickling from her car. People are rolling the boulder off, a group effort. I will not look. Everything is crashing down around.

I look.

"Whoa," says a young gray-suited man with long blond hair, "she's *way* dead."

He's wearing a yellow tie. My driver is next to me, trembling. I look up and see a flashing neon sign. *The Falling Rock Gift Shop and Snake Emporium.* Next to that, *Harry's Falling Rock Hamloaf Haven—Serving All Your Hamloaf Needs.* People mill about. Now come the flashing lights, sirens, men in uniform. A policeman inspects the body.

"Yep," verifies the officer, "she's way dead."

A group of men are moving the boulder. The boulder. They are rolling it now, up a winding path, back up the cliff. There is a sign. *Welcome to Falling Rock.* Something isn't right here.

"What are they doing?" I ask, but nobody hears. I run my fingers over the leather diary. I move over to a woman in a starched white waitress uniform, flat white shoes, white hose, hair in a ponytail. The men have moved the boulder halfway to the top of the hill.

"What are they doing?" I ask. "With the rock?"

She looks over her shoulder when she talks to me, as if I'm behind her.

"Moving it back up," she says, "to the edge of the cliff."

I watch professionals remove the woman's body from the wreckage. I turn back to the waitress.

"Why?" I ask.

She looks me square in the face.

"This is Falling Rock," she says, "and that's the falling rock. It's what this town is all about. No falling rock, no town. If you can call this shithole a town, that is. Hamloaf Haven, gift shop, snake emporium, a laundromat down the hill. Hell, this place is nowhere, I know that."

Her face, her uniform. They make me think of biscuits and gravy.

"Okay, so I know what you're thinking."

She pauses. I'm not sure myself what I'm thinking. I've met psychics. She isn't one of them.

"You're thinking, OK, so if it's so bad, why do I stay? Well, I'll tell you what. Don't say anything to anybody about this, you hear? Harry'd have a cow. But I've been saving up my tip money. Isn't easy at a place like this. Nobody tips here, they save their change to see the giant killer python. But I've saved some. Barring catastrophe—medical or dental, Lord knows Harry won't insure me—by wintertime I'll have enough to move. Plane fare, Jackson to L.A. California, you know it. I've had enough of this, I'm ready for the good life, you hear me? Once I'm there, get me a nice little car, maybe meet somebody, somebody real, somebody with a future. Marriage, I've got nothing against it. Just as far as the losers in this town."

Her nametag says DEBBIE. I watch the men at the top of the cliff. They position the rock so it's hanging, just a little bit, over the edge.

"How often does it happen?" I ask.

We are walking now, toward the restaurant, the Hamloaf Haven, past the wreckage.

"Not very," she says. "Almost nobody escapes from this town. I grew up here, I've seen damn few locals amount to a hill of beans. But I'm different. People die here all the time. Not me, buddy. I'll die in a Porsche, maybe, speeding down the California freeway. By Christmastime I'll be out of here. Again, barring catastrophe."

The restaurant is a little square, half of the walls knocked

down. It is open to the elements. We can see a man inside, at
the grill, flipping burgers.

"I have a dream," says Debbie. "I want to be a taxidermist
in California. I've always wanted to do this, to stuff dead animals. Preserve them in chemicals, the eyes, the fur, just as they
were when roaming the wild."

"In this way," I say, "you feel you might gain some advantage over death."

"Could be," says Debbie, "I don't know. It's just what I
want to do. Everyone has their talents and inclinations, not
everyone is as lucky as me, to have the two coincide. To have a
calling. My mother could bend spoons with her mind. She
couldn't do it with other utensils, only spoons. It was a useless
talent, not good for a thing, except entertaining her drunk friends
sometimes, when their husbands were whoring around in New
Orleans."

She pauses.

"She's dead now. It never really got her anywhere at all.
But me, I'll escape. California, ocean and sun. But don't you
breathe a word of this. Not a word, you hear?"

It's so muggy. Flies sit on decrepit picnic benches, the air
too hot and damp to fly in. They are fat, and black.

"I promise," I say.

The men of the town are descending the narrow path. Their
faces are joking, easy, the faces of men who've completed a
mechanical chore, conquered a problem together.

"The rock," I say. "How often does it fall?"

Debbie scrunches up her face.

"That old thing? I don't know, it varies. You can never predict it. Once there was a stretch of six whole years it didn't fall.
I know there was talk in the town of pushing it over. We needed
an economic boost. But it started again, all on its own, most
every week, for a whole season. Like some invisible hand does
it maybe, whenever it gets the inclination."

The menu rises above us. Hamloaf nuggets, hamloaf burgers,
hamloaf 'n' chips. Harry comes out from the grill, wiping his
hands on his grease-spattered apron.

"So damn muggy," says Debbie. "Muggiest damn summer in twenty years, I can't believe this heat."

"It's not the heat's so bad," says Harry, "it's the damn humidity. If it gets any muggier, I swear, I'll pack the whole operation up and take it to Arizona."

"Arizona," says Debbie, "do people eat hamloaf in Arizona?"

"They'll eat just about anything anywhere," says Harry, "if you get them hungry enough."

There are crackers sitting on the counter, for the hamloaf soup. I slip some into my pockets. I pick up a sugar packet as well.

MOUNTAIN GOAT (oreamnos americanus). *Of all the larger mammals in North America, the one that seems to have been the least affected by civilization is the mountain goat. He is surefooted on the steepest mountain crags, and is found from Washington State and Idaho through southern Alaska. Want to help save endangered animals and birds? Conserve and protect the natural environment. Clean air and water are needed by both wildlife and you. Tax-deductible contributions aid our vital conservation work.*

A line is forming, at the window where people place their orders. Tongues hang in anticipation. Tragedy stirs the appetite, it seems.

"That poor woman," I say to Debbie. I can picture her sliding along the highway, hair flying in the breeze. The look in her eyes. I wonder if she had a premonition.

"Happens to everyone sooner or later," says Debbie. "And I sure can imagine worse ways to go. I like the ocean and all— I've been there three times, and something about all that water— it's just so big, you know it? It makes me feel all peaceful and good." She whispers now. "That's why I want to go to California. Peaceful and good. But what was I saying? Oh, yeah, drowning. I wouldn't want to drown, that's one way for sure. No drowning for me. They always say it's an easy way to go, but none of them that say it have actually done it. Think of it. All that cold and water and seaweed. Yuk. Give me a falling rock any day over that."

She shudders.

"I don't suppose you get a choice, though," she says, "not any more in how you die than in how you live."

"Oh," I say, "you don't believe in free will."

"Free will? I don't know. What do you think, Harry? Do you believe in free will?"

"You about ready to get back to work?" yells Harry. "Your break's been over five minutes. You want me to deduct this time from your pay?"

"Tightass bastard," she says. She turns to me. "Maybe I'd just die all alone out in California. But all alone isn't so bad. It's better than hanging out with small-minded male chauvinist dorks in Falling Rock. Especially if you have a nice car."

She leaves me. I think about this. There's something about cars, all right. If you have the right car, a fast car, a shiny car, the world is yours. If you just keep on moving you might not have to do things. To hurt people or let people hurt you. But the people who give me rides never seem to have the right car.

The crowd hands its money across the counter, snarfs its burgers, collectively wipes grease off its many lips. They move to the postcard racks, snatch brightly colored pictures of vehicles smashed under the boulder. I walk back over to my driver. I try to straighten things out in my mind. Who I am, what has happened. I'm Matt. A woman was crushed by a boulder in her sports car. She was alive, just before, laughing, being pursued by this man with purple eyes.

"Look," I say. I show him the diary. "It's hers. It's her diary. Do you want to look at it?"

"Don't be a dumb fuck," he says. "What would I want with that thing? I've got this." He holds a postcard in the air. "A stupid, silly book. That's almost sick."

"They're her words," I say.

He grabs the book from me, throws it, out across the highway, into the far lanes. Northbound traffic drives over it.

"They aren't her," he says. "They aren't what I want. You'd have had to have heard her talk. She had the most amazing accent, this combination of Wales and North Carolina. Leave me alone."

I want to beat my head against a wall, scream, stick sharp needles into my own forehead.

"You did it," I say. "You killed her."

"Shut up," he says. "You're crazy."

The police are leaving, the wrecker, the woman. Rebeca. The man hops in his car, speeds away, pummeling me with tiny stones. Where will he go? He has a postcard, maybe that's enough.

I squint at cars speeding down, past me in the heat. I dash across the highway, down through tall weeds to the other side. A van whips past, the diary scuttles toward me. Another car comes from nowhere, over it. The highway is empty.

I see the book now, flying off and away, pages rippling in the wind, falling out, blowing away, scattering, cover gleaming in the sun, information disappearing, gone, whisked away, out of sight. Birds circle overhead, too small to be vultures. Still, as they squawk and loop about, I get this ominous sense that they live off the meat of the dead. I watch them, around and around, spiraling, chaotic patterns. I lie flat on my back in the gravel, watch the swooping birds, around and around, getting nowhere, watching, waiting; for something they can use, some kind of nourishment from the bodies of the dead.

2

It's midafternoon. I sit on a stone bench at a rest stop down the road, watch the dabbled liquid arch of the drinking-fountain water as a tiny girl pulls herself up to sip at it. My face is buzzing from too much sun, I feel my gums rotting. I've eaten the crackers, the sugar. I rummage through a trash can for remnants of Ding Dongs or potato sticks, rummage through my memory for traces that might tell me who I am. Everything here is far too real; the way the picnic benches bend, the dry expanse of grass, where tourists' dogs relieve themselves. There's a huge relief map of Mississippi, the sun is beating down. The air is ripe with the potential for violence. There's a darkness in people's eyes and this feeling that things are ready to happen. This feeling of unease. Everybody scares me. I've always been sickened and terrified of violence, of people. These human beings, such volatile substance, I know.

There's a Doors song playing on a transistor radio. Perhaps it's only in my head. This seems to be the weather for a violent storm, the air so damp and hot, the clouds simply blistering.

I can't stay here forever, I know, sunburnt and hungry.

I walk, slow, down beside the off ramp. The speed with which cars pass me is alarming. Have they always traveled this quickly?

I'm afraid I may be crazy.

Back at the rest stop an old woman is yelling into the pay phone, I can hear her from here.

"Is there a cat screaming in your house or is that just the TV?"

I stick out my thumb, fearful. An aging blue four-door pulls over ahead of me. The very first car. I walk toward it, I do not run. In the past I've always run. To display my eagerness, my gratitude. Sunlight bounces off the trunk, there's a rumbling in the sky. I can hear gravel crunching under my feet.

The door is already open. I slide into the seat, shut it behind me. The car begins to move, the driver smiles, I do not show my horror. I stay perfectly calm, for it is him, the very one, the man who killed my parents.

ELEVEN

Δ

1

"Hi," he says. "My name's Raymond. It's a pleasure."

He extends a hand. I shake it.

"My name's Matt," I say, and immediately realize my mistake. "Sam, I mean. Did I say Matt? My name's Sam."

"Oh," he says, and he's watching the road. There's a plastic Jesus hanging from his dash, a car deodorizer shaped like a skunk.

"Where you headed?" he asks.

"New Orleans," I say. "I'm going to New Orleans to die. No, I mean, not to die, just to visit. You know. A tourist. I'm going to New Orleans."

What am I saying? I am not going there to die. I am going to find Andalusia. I have to be careful, I realize, lest I lose track of my own intentions.

"New Orleans would be a fine place to die," Raymond says. "I've often considered that option when my own time is up."

I can certainly picture such a future: I curl up inside a seedy hotel room on Canal Street. Naked light bulbs and roaches, that whole business. I hear the sounds of a man flattening cans with his feet on the street below. Jesus people ask me if I've been saved as I walk down to the Wal-Mart to shoplift some sleeping pills and a bottle of wine. I wander through the drugstore's Outdoor Living department. My final vision, lawn chairs and fans.

"You think about suicide sometimes?" I ask. "Purely as an intellectual exercise, of course."

I know nothing about this man.

"Grape?" he says.

Where is he going? Why did he kill my parents? He passes over a plastic bag filled with grapes. I pick one out and eat it. No seeds. Does he recognize me? He's losing his hair, but has searching brown eyes. He isn't as bland as I remember, not as empty or pale. He has full, sensual lips. But there's no doubt he's the one.

"What do you do?" I ask.

"What do I do?"

"You know. For a job."

"I work at a grocery store," he says. "In Jackson. I'm the produce manager. I deal in fruits and vegetables."

He laughs, just a little. This is obviously a familiar joke, which time has not lessened his desire to repeat.

"Have an apple," he says and motions toward a paper sack.

"Got a knife?" I ask.

"A knife?"

"To cut it in half," I say. "So we can share."

The highway narrows into two lanes. The road ahead, not for the claustrophobic. The dips and bumps sicken me. A plan is forming in my head.

"I hitch a lot," I say, "and I've noticed. People who drive tend to carry knives. Guns are illegal, you know. Especially AK-47s."

"As a matter of fact," he says, "there's a Swiss army knife inside the cubbyhole."

I open the glove compartment. The blade is short and dull, but I examine the other appendages. There's a corkscrew that would be just about perfect. To plunge into his heart, to twist around as he bleeds and screams. After I get him to confess. There's no room for error in a business like this.

"Apples," I say as I work the knife through the fruit, "the most sexual fruit. Original sin, that sort of thing."

I hand him his half.

"Thank you," he says.

What heat. What friction in these atoms. He hums.

"They filmed a porno video in my produce section once," he says. "They called it *Paradise Lost*. They paid us a fortune."

Everything is connected. I put the knife down beside me, with the corkscrew sticking out. I realize, of course, that this could go either way. He might just as easily kill me.

"Produce manager," I say. "Right here in Mississippi. What do you know."

His window is open, the air blows things about. Straw wrappers and dust. My throat is so dry. The sound of my heart: kachung, kachung, like that. I try to slow it down.

"Your accent," I say, "it doesn't sound Mississippian. It sounds almost Iowan."

"Funny," he says, "I did spend a few years there. Never thought it affected me so much. The speaking, that is."

"Sure," I say. "Wherever you go, the speaking always affects you."

I watch his face for growing signs of mistrust. There aren't any, just an easy smile. His hands seem powerful, his grip firm on the wheel, soft hair like down on his wrists.

"Why'd you pick me up?" I ask.

"Hmmm?" he says. Crunch, crunch, crunch, as he chews on his apple.

"Why'd you pick me up? Most people who pick me up want something. Somebody to talk to. Gas money, maybe, or drugs. Sex sometimes."

He swallows.

"Oh," he says.

"Me," he says, "I used to . . ."

"Hitchhike yourself," I say, "that's the other one. The people who've been there."

"Right," he says, "And I always swore . . ."

"If you ever had a car you'd always pick folks up."

"Are you a psychic?" he asks.

"I feel like I know you," I say.

I imagine the emerging of his blood, arteries spurting, his

insides gushing out. My body right up next to his, the corkscrew in his heart.

"Yeah," he says, "I get that feeling too. Are you from Iowa?"

"Never been there," I say.

As we take a sharp curve the skunk deodorizer bounces on its string. I lean with the curve, toward Raymond. In his heart or in his throat? I'm not sure which spot is more tender.

"What did you do there?" I ask. "In Iowa?"

He furrows his brow.

"Washed dishes," he says.

Of course. He washed dishes. One night he went insane, so much lemon-scented soap in his pores that it became hallucinogenic. He had to kill: randomly, violently.

"What's the worst thing you ever did?" I ask.

He squints at me.

"That's a funny question," he says.

He washed dishes, read the surrealists on his break. He understood senseless violence as a way of life, a peculiar aesthetic. It was another intellectual exercise. Murder as experiment, liberation of the self.

"I like to ask strangers that question," I say, "because there isn't any risk. We ride together and then go our separate ways. I like to talk about it.

"I've done some bad things," I say.

"Oh yeah?" he says.

I pick up the corkscrew, play with it.

"I stole a car. I peeked in people's windows. Drug dealing, shoplifting, income-tax evasion. I sleep with men for money sometimes."

I feel the sharp tip with my finger, try to imagine other crimes I might confess to.

"Oh," he says.

Stick it in and twist it, as easy as that.

"Look, Sam," he says, "I'm not looking for any kinky stuff."

"Me either," I say.

I need to slow down, concentrate. On the other side of the

windshield Mississippi rolls by, unsuspecting. In kindergarten I could already spell this state and often did. I was so proud.

"But that stuff's nothing," I say. "What you do for money is just what you do, right? You know that. And everybody's lonely. My worst thing was murder."

He nods. He bites his lip. I don't talk.

"And?" he says.

"Oh," I say, "you want me to tell?"

He nods. I spell to myself. M-I-S-S-I-S-S-I-P-P-I.

"I only say this because I feel I can trust you. I liked you right from the start, Raymond. I want you to know that."

He nods some more. I wait.

"You don't look like a killer," he says.

I snort, knowingly, ironically. He rolls down his window, tosses out his core.

"I killed an old man named Dust. In Florida."

I cough, roll down my window and spit.

"He would have died anyway," I say. "I just sped it up. I poisoned him for the inheritance. Still, I think about it all the time."

I chew on my apple.

"There's something very erotic about murder," I say. "Don't you think so? Murder and confession both."

He stares straight ahead. Unless it's my imagination, his breathing gets faster.

"What are you getting at?" he asks.

"Probing questions," I say. "Intimacy, secrets. It's all very exciting."

He wiggles in his seat, lowers one hand from the steering wheel onto his thigh.

"Now it's your turn," I say. "What's your worst thing?"

"Oh no," he says. "Not that old trick. I never said that I'd tell."

"You'd make a good killer," I say. "You have strong hands."

"I can't tell you," he says. "I wish I could but I can't. It was a long time ago."

"Oh come on," I say.

He looks over at me, chewing his lip. It's a face you couldn't quite picture unless it was right there in front of you, a face you could turn into whatever you wanted. Like Mr. Potato Head.

"Listen," he says, "I've never told anybody in my whole life. But I would like to tell it. I don't know. I think that I would."

I remember how easy it was to destroy Mr. Potato Head. Just light the match and watch the features melt into a brown-and-black waxy glob. The beautiful stink of burning plastic.

"No," he says, "I'm sorry. I can't."

He looks up at the sky.

"The sky is positively bloodless today," he says. "Have you ever seen such a bloodless sky?"

I hold the corkscrew out the window, stabbing the air.

"Actually," I say, "I didn't tell you everything I did. I'll tell you everything and then you tell me."

He hums loudly, staring straight ahead.

"I strangled a young man with my very own hands. He was very handsome, sleeping beside me. I just put my hands around his throat and strangled. His name was Jimmy. I loved him, you see?"

"You loved him," he says.

"A crime of passion," I say. "I was only fourteen. All children are capable of murder, wouldn't you say?"

I stretch my neck out toward him, run my fingers down my throat.

"Here," I say. "Try it. Put your hands on my throat, see how it feels."

He shifts his weight away from me, looks at me squinting.

"Are you crazy?" he says.

"You did it before," I say, "didn't you?"

"I never strangled anyone," he says. "You've got it all wrong."

"So what did you do?"

"Nothing," he says. "It wasn't anything. Forget it. Just forget it all."

He turns on the radio, fiddles with the knob. Static, only that. He clicks it off.

"I had a sister," he says, "but she's dead. Just the other week

I thought I saw her in a shopping mall in Mobile. It wasn't her, but still, it shook me up. I wandered in a daze for hours. I asked myself a lot of big questions. It was a strange afternoon, the sky all high and gray, everything weird. I asked myself what I had done and where I was going. What if I was to die today, I asked myself. That's a big question, don't you think?"

The glands in his neck are quivering with the urge to confess.

"It was murder," he says. "But listen."

He's quiet. Soon, I will kill him.

"No," he says, "never mind."

"I sure could eat a taco," I say.

I can see how bad he wants to tell. Nobody wants to know, they only want to be known. He clears his throat, I watch out the window. The sun bleaches all these shades of green together. I could become green as well, blend right in. This may already be happening. I may be powerless to stop it.

We pass a billboard of a well-dressed camel, smoking a cigarette.

"See that camel's face?" Raymond asks. "It's a penis. Who do they expect to buy these cigarettes, I ask you? I switched my brand."

I remember waking up in my room in the middle of the night when I was a child, before I even had the paper route. I'd lie in bed awake and I'd try to hold on to an instant, to catch one instant of thinking. I am thinking that I am thinking this and as soon as I think NOW it will be now, NOW, but it's gone and NOW but it's gone again and I'm thinking other things, about then when the now was, but when was it? That sort of thing, when I couldn't get to sleep.

"My sister was an angel," Raymond says, "but she got fucked up on drugs. Back in Iowa, back in Des Moines. She was freebasing and shooting cocaine into her veins and then one day she died. I loved my sister more than anything, she was the one that raised me after . . ."

"After your parents passed away," I say. "You're an orphan."

How could I not have known? The hunger in his eyes, the ravished intensity.

"Yes," he says. "That bastard coke dealer was giving her bad shit. I've been writing letters to my congressman ever since she died. Why don't they just legalize it and solve all our problems? They just let these scum keep control of the drug trade. All these fucking mobsters."

I laugh, a high-pitched nervous giggle, I don't know why. Mobsters. Fucking mobsters. An ambulance speeds past us, lights flashing, making no sound.

"I refuse to confess to you," he says. "I don't think saying it would be helpful at all. It would only make it more real. If I don't talk about it, where's the proof it ever happened?"

He feels that language traps us, only repeats atrocity. He feels that history is something to be escaped.

"Yes," I say, "there's a professor at Northwestern who says the Holocaust never happened."

"I don't need this guilt," he says. "I can't do anything with it, I can't live with it."

He accelerates. Speed, deserts, amnesia, forgetting. He'll leave it to me to piece this thing together.

"You wanted revenge on the mobster," I say. "The one who killed your sister. An eye for an eye, that sort of thing."

I fondle the corkscrew. Why not in the eye?

"Some people deserve to die," he says.

Eye, throat, heart, which is more fitting? He stabbed my parents in the heart, but there were two of them, the equation still isn't right. But now I see it. Confusion and revenge. I understand now, exactly what happened.

"Maybe remembering would help you," I say. "To clean yourself out, to go on with your life. You really ought to tell me all about this murder."

I stab a grape and pop it in my mouth. It seems I have to do all the work around here.

"You decided to kill a member of the mobster's family," I say. "The mobster, this evil cocaine dealer who sold your sister bad drugs. Probably you decided to kill his daughter. You couldn't just kill him, right? He wouldn't suffer enough that way. An eye for an eye."

"You and your Biblical imagery," says Raymond. "I'm getting kind of tired of it."

He starts humming again, louder, he won't even look at me.

"You decided to kill the mobster's daughter," I say.

"Yes," he says, "I switched my brand. I won't stand for such manipulation. I smoke Winstons now."

They're made by the same company, of course. I've amassed so much knowledge over the years, I surprise myself sometimes. For example: toll-booth operators have the highest suicide rate of any profession.

"I killed them," he says.

His face is ruined. He shakes, even in this heat. Heat. Sticky vinyl. Sweat and grapes. He glances sideways, away from me, as if there is someone in these pecan fields who might overhear.

"It's a lot worse," he says and he's sobbing, huge dry gulps. The car swerves from side to side. The afternoon takes a deep breath to prepare for his statement. Birds eating roadkill scatter before the approach of our guilty vehicle.

"I never told anyone this," he says, "none of it, not even my buddy John. They say, don't they, that you can only confess to strangers and not to the ones that know you? Don't they say that?"

"Yes," I say, "they do say that."

Even as he trembles we move with such speed. What if we crash before I get my big chance? He sobs some more.

"I can't go on," he says.

"Listen," I say, "I'll tell you a story." I am just talking. "Once upon a time," I say, "everything was good. People were too stupid to know anything and so everyone just frolicked in fields of daisies and ate bananas and oranges. They didn't know about sex. They had no desires. Eventually they all died. They are all dead now. But let me tell you a story from my own life. I steal and smoke Camel Lights and kill people sometimes, but once at this mission I threw this young child into the air and he laughed and laughed and laughed. What I mean to say is that anything is possible. Life is superabundant. But we get over-stretched by time. Any choice we make may be a bad one. I don't tend to make choices. Well, that's my story, I'm sure you get my point. You were saying, then."

I run my fingers over the plastic Jesus that hangs from the dash. It is emaciated, wearing nothing but a loincloth. I don't look at Raymond. I know he will speak, but this waiting is bad.

"I almost turned back," he says. "But listen to me. I was in a state of confusion. My sister was dead. I forgot to take a knife. I had to get a knife from their very own kitchen. I was all fucked up."

He went to the duplex. He forgot the address. Which side was it, the left or the right? The stupid fucker, he killed the wrong people.

"My memory's all screwed up," he says. "How did it happen? My sister was dead, I had nobody left. I couldn't tell one direction from the other, I didn't feel real. Moving this way and that, like a puppet, my strings being pulled."

His strings being pulled. There I was, the boy in my room, my desires soaring through air, pulling his strings. I understand, really, that I am to blame. We did it together. My desire, his flesh.

I can't deny this chemistry between us.

"This way and that," I say.

"No," he says, "I won't go on. I refuse to confess. I already told you I killed someone, isn't that enough? What do you want from me?"

I eat another grape. I play with the corkscrew. I want to kill you, Raymond, I want you to die in my arms. I want your guilt to bleed all over these seats. I want to drown in your blood.

"I'm so confused," he says. "And then there's that boy. Was he really there or have I imagined him since then? I turned and there he was, watching me, that boy. There wasn't supposed to be a boy. I remember that so clear, but I remember it different, too, without the boy. Like things split in two and happened both ways."

Like things split in two. I stood in the doorway, I watched him, the man I had dreamed. He walked past me and out.

"There's that one witness left who could put you in jail," I say. "Get revenge of his own. Maybe he's looking for you now, to catch you and kill you."

"Sure," he says, his face all scrunched up. "But how could I kill a boy?"

I snort. He pulls over onto the side of the road and he's weeping good and hard. I reach out, touch him on the shoulder. He pauses in his weeping as he senses my touch.

"You fucker," I say.

"I know," he says. "Nobody knows that like I do."

"You son of a bitch," I say.

I yank the plastic Jesus from its string, throw it at him. I throw the skunk deodorizer at him too.

"Go on," he says, "say it all. No one can be harder on me than I been on myself."

I bite into the flesh of these grapes as if I'm decapitating living things.

"Spineless fuck," I say. "Vermin."

"OK," he says, "enough already."

What a lousy excuse for a murderer. He's just a stupid, sniveling produce manager.

"I do my best to atone," he says. "I refuse to sell bruised plums or wilted lettuce. I just won't do it."

I can't tell if I'm laughing or crying. I'm just shaking and longing to scream.

"I can't go on," he says, "with this life much longer, it weighs on me everyday. What can I do? Where can I go?"

He looks at me confused, as if seeing some hope in my face, asking a question. I reach out, I touch him on the head. We did it together.

Something is happening, it isn't me. I look up and see the clouds, tinged with light. I'm standing in the highest branches of a tree, my body moistened with slime, as the shell breaks away, the insect's fragile crust. I stretch my wings, thin, glistening membranes, veined like leaves, they crackle in the wind but do not break. She stands next to me, the tree is shaking with our weight, she takes my hand and we dive across the sky, down, but then we soar. Across the Badlands, the Rockies, the mesas and deserts, across the ocean, west into the sky, through clouds and up into a strange garden of flowering plants, beanstalks and fountains, tinkly bells and zebras, what the fuck, it's a sweetass garden. She leads me, through viny undergrowths, my wings folded in now, down a meandering path, brushes away branches, dust, hieroglyphs, ruins of dead civilizations, and it's waiting for us there. A bathtub, overflowing with bubbles, it waits for us. She drops her gown, her immense body glistens, heavy breasts hanging, wings stretched taut. She smiles and steps into the tub. I follow. The water is warm. I sink, all the way in.

"Are you OK?" asks Raymond.

I turn to him, smiling. The air smells like peanuts here. I move my fingers through his thinning, greasy hair.

"You want me to forgive you?" I ask.

He studies me, not sure if I'm mad.

"Can you do that?" he asks.

"I could," I say. "Do you believe me?"

The car is filled with a fuzzy light. Perhaps there is something burning, just down the road.

"Yes," he whispers, "I do."

We sit like this for a moment. He'd believe anything in the midst of such a warm golden glow. I remember my parents, the sirens, the blood.

"Ha," I say. "You think anyone could forgive you? Do you know who I am?"

He bites the tips of his fingers. He sniffles.

"This was supposed to help," he says, "this confessing. That's what they all say, that it helps. To unburden yourself, to let it all out. But it isn't true, you know it? I feel worse now than I ever did."

He rummages around the seat.

"Ask my forgiveness," I say. "Go on, ask me. You don't know who I am."

"Where'd that deodorizer go?" he asks. "Here's the Jesus, but where's the skunk? Did it get lost under the seat?"

He sticks his fingers in the crack of the seat. He is so vulnerable right now, with his hands like this.

"Ask my forgiveness," I say. "You owe me."

His lips are so pale. I could press the corkscrew up against them, slide it down, next to his throat. So easy, so right. I rasp, instead.

"Those were my parents you killed. I'm the boy, you hear it? I'm the boy that watched you. You made me an orphan."

He stares.

"That was me, you hear it?"

His hands are stuck in the crack of the seat. I have the corkscrew. I throw it out the window, into the fields.

"You ridiculous fuck," I say. "You killed the wrong people."

I swing the door open, step onto the road. A car rises toward us in the distance, up this gradual slope. We can hear its dull groan, like an insect, like time is so huge it will never arrive. Clouds are forming now, billowy white ones. It will storm in the future. I look at my feet.

"Oh my," he says.

"Get the fuck out of here," I say.

It's so hot out here, too hot to think. The distribution of time isn't equal. The car is a little bit louder, no nearer at all.

"Go on," I say. "I'm letting you go. What more do you want?"

He looks frightened.

"I could have killed you," I say. "What are you waiting for?"

I throw my lucky button at him. *It's Only Rock and Roll but I Like It.* I throw my toothbrush at him, too. I'm about to throw *The Sickness unto Death,* when I realize it's all that I have left. I shut the door.

"Go on," I say. "Get out of here, you're free."

A rush of noise, the car passes us and is gone. There's nobody on this highway but us.

"I'm free," he says.

I let him go. Just like that.

2

The sun is so high, the time of day can't even qualify as a mood. Pure vertical light and ruin, just this side of dread. I sit here, laughing. I laugh and laugh and then I vomit. It's like a stone, black and tarlike, this chunk that comes up, that sits here now beside me on the road.

I should have asked him: When you killed them, did they wake? For a moment, between pain and death, were they conscious? They may have died easily, in mid-dream, never knowing. My father dreaming of a childhood in a pharmacy candy store, red hots and licorice, of days watching the birds, the cats in the alley. And mother. She dreamed of wheatfields and pumpkins and thick chandeliers. She dreamed of Jesus and music boxes and singing at dawn. They slept happily, knowing that things would be better. Knowing that things would be good now, they had been through the worst.

I look up. A car is approaching, slowly. I see that it is them. In a station wagon, coming this way, I can make out their faces: my father, my mother, myself. Of course. Matt and Mom and Dad, driving happy, a family on vacation.

The afternoon is filled with the sound of dimensions colliding, the fragile fabric of reality ripping into pieces. Dreams never die, here on the highways of America. They take material shape, wander, waver, vanish and reappear.

Things split in two, it happened both ways. In the other version the Pennels were killed, instead of my parents. I grew up, cheerful and parented. Perhaps we even managed to profit from the murder. They come closer, I examine my other face. he's in the front, driving. He's a college graduate; he'll be a doctor, a journalist, an AIDS activist, a riding lawn-mower salesman. No, none of those, look at the sneer; he'll be starting law school in the fall. He reads Nietzsche, sleeps with men who wear cufflinks.

"Nietzsche is simply the man," he would say, "who wears God's penis as a necktie. And whose thought has now permeated every aspect of pop culture."

What sort of lawyer will he be? Will he defend criminals, poor people or large corporations that dump chemicals in local streams, poison their workers, overthrow foreign governments and build nuclear weapons? They pass me by, they stare, do not stop to pick me up, a less fortunate decision from their past. Matt doesn't even recognize me, thinks I'm just one of those trendy homeless people he reads about in the newspaper. If I had had the time I could have taken off my shoe, peeled off my sticky, rancid sock and waved my four-toed foot at them. Called out, "Look it's me, it's your own self, give me a ride."

In retrospect, everything seems fated. We don't understand that it could have always turned out different, that maybe it actually did. That maybe we're just the extrapolated illusions of a choice never made.

He watches my diminishing figure in the rearview. A sticker explains OBJECTS IN MIRROR CLOSER THAN THEY APPEAR. After they pass me, Matt turns to our mother and says, "Didn't you see him back there, Mother? That was Christ by the side of the road. Should I stop to pick him up?"

He gives her shit, believing that one should live up to one's beliefs. Easy enough for him, he believes in nothing at all. He's one of those cynical youth we hear so much about these days. He understands the nullity inherent in any claims to the truth. He understands complete relativity. On the other side of the white line cars hurl toward him. He at least manages to honor the traffic code. At least he still drives on the right side of the road. He wouldn't deny that cultural conditioning can be life-preserving at times.

They move on toward the horizon, where I can see an enormous figure just beyond the trees. They have forgotten me by now, focus on this figure. It's Jesus, thinks my mother, just on down the road. My father reserves judgment, refuses expectation. Matt thinks: Nietzsche, everywhere now, the last American hero. I'd like to tell him even Nietzsche broke down in the end, tried to comfort a horse that was being flogged. Lunatic, Antichrist, lover of animals. They drive on, thinking they know

what lies ahead. I walk now, on toward it, knowing they are
wrong.

They vanish, out of sight.

Yes, all our dreams live here, on the American road. I walk,
hoping to retrieve one. Stratocumulus clouds have formed in
the sky, enormously so. A small sign in a farmer's field declares,
*For now we see through a glass darkly, but then face to face;
now I know imperfectly, but then shall I know even as also I
am known.* These Christian farmers, still trying to convert the
world that passes them by. Still, I do believe there are meanings hidden in the smallest things, that one can know one's own
future. The past has so little to do with it really, there's your
most common mistake. Nobody's willing to grant himself the
possibility of surprise.

A Bible verse and an omen. Face to face, the reference can
only be to one person. I look around, try to get my bearings as
I walk. Across the hills a red speck flits through the air, a kite.
This is Mississippi, I can hear distant fiddles, rafts on the river.
My heart is beating a primitive rhythm. I have this sense that a
flock of huge black birds is descending on me, to tear me into
bits, or that something wonderful is about to happen.

I don't understand what this encounter could mean, my
family passing me by. I don't understand what it portends for
my future, what I could have possibly learned. I mouth the same
words, over and over. *But then face to face.*

And now I see him.

He is there, enormous in the sky. Jimmy, it is Jimmy, there's
no denying this, but he is huge, naked except for his underwear. He stares down at me, behind those mirrored sunglasses,
bored, contemptuous, ready to step on me. How did he get so
big? ANGST it says on his underwear. I'm rooted to the spot, I
can't move. So death has won the game after all. Sweat is rolling
down my sides from my underarms in tiny rivulets. Jimmy, up
above, directly, in the sky! I had the nerve to imagine it would
end otherwise. How obvious this now seems. My knees give
out, I fall to the ground. I cover my eyes and wait for him to

step on me, to strangle me. His tender hands around my throat, my belly, his nipples and his eyes. I look up again, but of course he hasn't moved. He watches down at me just the same, that expression on his face, his body huge and perfect and bare. He's two-dimensional after all, and silent.

He's only a billboard.

I smile. I'd take the time to ask myself how exactly Jimmy became an enormous billboard in the Mississippi countryside, but a car has stopped beside me, in the middle of the road. It hasn't even bothered to pull onto the shoulder. I get to my feet.

Honey, she says, *what are you waiting for? You going to stand there all day like a donkey with its head up its ass? Get in the car.*

She is here, just as I always knew she would be.

I glance back up at Jimmy. Goodbye, goodbye. I realize that my head could explode with all this noise but then everything is silent and I'm stepping through empty space toward her, into the car.

Book Three

Lulu: Now I must find others who are, like me, pirates journeying from place to place, who, knowing only change and the true responsibilities that come from such knowing sing to and with each other.

Now I am going to travel.

—KATHY ACKER—
Don Quixote

TWELVE

Δ

1

"Andalusia," I say.

She squints over at me as she accelerates. She's lost weight, her hair cut short. She's wearing a tank top, a skull earring, sweating.

"It's me," I say. "Matt."

Her jaw drops. This doesn't slow her down. She asks, *Is this a small world, or what?* I stammer, try to get the words out, how long it's been, the import of this moment. One would expect angels or trumpets or tubas or lightning. She can't hear me, all the bells clanging in her head, the engine, the sky cracking open. She asks what I've been doing with myself all this time. I look down at my lap.

I say, "Looking for you."

She laughs. Joy or disbelief? We are driving together, so fast down this road. She says that I always was a weird little kid. She's so thin and so hairless, a tattoo on her shoulder. A fist, percolating out of a rose, fluid swirling reds and blacks. Her skin is half a shade lighter than it used to be. Minor physical alterations we can learn to accept. She asks about my parents.

They were killed, I tell her, one night as they slept. At least this is the rendition I'm most familiar with. On the other hand, in an alternative landscape they drive in a station wagon, Americans on vacation, visiting caverns and Disneyland, national parks and miniature towns; Roadside America, Dutch Wonderland, the Corn Palace, Jesus in Wax. As we speak they proceed toward

New Orleans, where they'll eat oysters, jambalaya, get bamboozled on Bourbon Street by a shifty auctioneer. My father will laugh it off and say it was worth it, wasn't it, just for the experience? What's fifteen dollars? He has a good job now. My mother, on the other hand, continues to pray for her family. Her husband tends toward spiritual indifference these days, a few beers too many and reckless behavior in motel lobbies; his midlife crisis perhaps. He considers buying a motorcycle again, ignoring the fact that he used up his lifetime allotment years ago. Her son is a future lawyer and a cheap nihilist. He reads Nietzsche and picks up men in the gift shops of Howard Johnson's, thumbing through magazines, sampling saltwater taffy. This is only my reflection, of course, my unfulfilled potential, the path I didn't take. Or the path which didn't take me. We're two different choices, whoever did the choosing, I don't believe we can successfully coexist. Me, I used to save up my money, my nickels and dimes, thinking if I saved enough I could afford to be a nihilist, too. But I always broke down, usually for a cup of coffee, with nondairy creamer for that nutritional edge. I've wandered aimlessly since the murder, found benevolence and voyeurism, unique paradigms by which to live. I've known hunger and cold and the black holes of doubt.

She says that it sounds like we've both had a time of it.

She glances up at the sinewy sky. With all this moisture in the air, we know that it will storm.

"Listen," I say, "I'll tell you everything, everywhere I've been." A whole series of adventures, a regular smorgasbord of losers and dreamers and mall maggots and starvers, a sanitarium of lunatics and lovers and dying old men. People who, after passing through a series of adventures, came to a happy end they had not hoped for. People who, by using their wits, regained something they had lost. Lovers who won happiness after grief or misfortune. That would be us. Yes, all these trials and tribulations that make so much sense now, so justified, all leading me here, more ready for her love. This reunion, this moment. Oh, yes, listen. We'll get a hotel room. "I know I don't have any money," I say, "but, yes, a hotel room with a big brass tub. In New Orleans. We'll stop and buy some bubble bath."

She looks over at me, her brow arched.

"Just like the old days," I say. "You'll sing me that song about Alice and bathe me, and . . . Andalusia. I can hardly believe it. We're together again. We're finally together."

A look of mild alarm spreads across her face. Trees line either side of the road, swaying in the dusty breeze, as if leading us somewhere, as if we're following a path.

She says, *Bubble baths?* She says, *Jesus, Matt, give me a break.*

I feel a numbness in the back of my head, an arching of my gums, a weakening. I am so light. Life has jelled, the landscape submerged in some opaque oily liquid. Death or true love. My destiny, my moment of final fulfillment. A billboard urges me to buy lottery tickets, here in Mississippi. Yes, in this country, everyone's a winner, anyone can be a millionaire.

Andalusia says, *You know, I didn't even recognize you there on the shoulder. I normally don't pick up hitchhikers, never know what sort of schizos they'll be.*

"Andalusia," I say. What more is there? The car will float soon, we'll drive off into fluffy white clouds.

"All my dreams have come true," I say. "I knew it was just a matter of time. Remember how we frolicked on the duplex lawn? There was something powerful emanating from the bathtub, certainly, something magical churning there in the primordial Mr. Bubble sea. That's where everything began, laughter and dance steaming out of the seafoamy depths. All these years, you've been my inspiration, my roots to the natural world."

She laughs. *You do go on,* she says, *don't you?*

"The wind blowing us around," I say, "your spicy smell, the deep-rooted connection, the mystical, the groovy cosmic love vibes that permeate the universe. It's for you that I've done everything, trudged along highways, slept in schoolyards and churchyards and rest stops and depots. It's for you that I've been carried down the Pennsylvania Turnpike, through tunnels that vibrate and hum, through the small, exquisite white-trash cities, Wheeling and Zanesville and on, the blind raging Milwaukees and Columbuses and St. Louis. And the west: it's for you that I've sat on mountains, danced in creekbeds, slithered through wide empty spaces; Billings: whores, casinos, the bus station closed for cleaning from two to three-thirty, the definition of a bleak and tangy western town. Denver, that sprawling, hazed-over ship of fools. San Antonio: canals and money and cigarettes and sex. You've inspired all this and more, the dark pathways I had to create by myself, the small shimmery spark that glowed in my belly. But, it's over now. We'll be together."

I stop, catch my breath. Andalusia runs her hand across the semibaldness of her head. *Are you quite through now?* she asks. I nod. She sighs, lights a cigarette. She passes a slow-moving vehicle. *I don't know what kind of ideas you've got in your head,* she says, *but you are certainly confused. What? Am I supposed to be the mystical and exotic Negress of your childhood? Who the hell do you think you are?* She cracks her window, flicks the ash, takes another drag. *I am nobody's muse or nurturing Earth Mother. You've been living in a dream, obviously, reading only male texts.* She picks a copy of *Blood and Guts in High School* off her dash and whacks me on the knee. I rub my knee gingerly. I could defend myself with *The Sickness unto Death,* but this is going too far already. *Wake up!* she says. *It's a dream. Everything now, dream, image, haze. Reagan and that whole business. Where does television stop and memory begin?*

What is she talking about? My knee smarts. On billboards women in black smoke long cigarettes, weathered men on horseback smoke an alternative brand. Memory and television? Can she deny what she promised all those years ago?

"I remember what you told me," I say. "You told me I was the only man for you."

She laughs.

I never said that, she says. *You're misquoting me, taking words out of context. It was a job, I got paid. I never baby-sat anyone for free. And I assure you. There is no man for me.*

Violets grow by the road, edible purple flowers. They'll add life to any salad, I think. *Experimental Grooved Pavement Next 3 Miles* says a sign. Beside me, Andalusia. She's been enchanted, she's insane. Out of her brain, riding a train, lost in the rain. Sucked down the drain, popping a vein, torturing Cain. One of us, obviously. How could she not remember? We flew together, doesn't she recall? Wandered through chocolate worlds, other universes, danced with the wind.

Chocolate, she says. *If that metaphor is rising from the fact that I'm a woman of color I am going to throttle you.*

Hold on a second here. We loved each other, a pure, holy sort of love. We communicated without speaking. She laughs again. She is so easily amused.

You're making all this up, she says. *This is your version, that doesn't make it true.*

Her presence is frothy, steamed milk over Colombian coffee. I want to drown in her, escape all this tiresome language. I shake my head.

"Andalusia, this is just words. Words, words, words. Words reveal nothing, we know that by now. So many stories, blah, blah, blah. My mother, when she was a small child alone on the farm, she used to tell stories to the pigs and cows and chickens. She told them stories about the little old woman on the Old Dutch Cleanser cans. This crazy old woman, cleaning our sinks."

We pass a billboard advertising Mr. Clean. A bald, muscular man who'll power out any stain. I scratch my head. What was I saying?

"I love you, Andalusia, don't you understand?"

She plays with the lobe of her ear as she drives.

She says, *If you love me so much, why don't you shut up for a minute? Why don't you give me a chance to tell my own story?* I hold my head in my hands. I don't know who I'm listening to, we don't belong in this landscape. There's a bitter taste in my mouth, as if I've been licking the seat belts. I run my finger along the edges of these belts, which I neither lick nor wear. Despite the laws that may apply in this state.

Sure, she says, *we were kids, running through the duplex lawn. You were too young to understand, I was a baby myself, just out of high school. Younger than you are now, look at you, you're what, twenty-one, twenty-two? Shit. Those days, always scrounging for cash, the cards stacked against me. Working as a topless waitress or a hotel maid, degrading myself. A world owned by white men, what chance did I have? Cleaning out toilets, scrubbing floors, getting nowhere real fast. Out of work, two abortions, beat up by the cops, all in the same year. I baby-sat you because I had to, it didn't pay much, but it helped. I saved my money, moved south. Things weren't much better down here, listen up. The lowest I sank, right here in Jackson. Accepted a bit role in this porno video called* Paradise Lost.

Another meaningful coincidence. Don't ignore anything the world has to tell you, and you'll become quite thoroughly insane.

"*Paradise Lost*," I say. "Don't you get it, that's us? The fall of man and the return to a paradisiac state find varied manners of symbolic expression, most characteristic being the labyrinth. May I quote from Cirlot's *A Dictionary of Symbols? When man comes to ponder this mysterious problem he knows no more peace, for his mind, faced with a series of insurmountable obstacles, is shattered, filling his heart, his soul and body with rage and despair. . . . Only once he had grasped the worlds of the infinitely small and the infinitely large could man once again vibrate in sympathy with the cosmic harmonies and blend in ineffable communion with all the beings and things in earth and in heaven.* We can do that now, you see, vibrate together in sympathy with the cosmic harmonies. Together again. Paradise regained."

She snorts. She tosses her butt onto the road, rolls up the window.

This is not about utopian visions or cosmic harmonies, she says. *Rage and despair, certainly. Note the masculine pronouns, when* man *comes to ponder, once he has grasped. Listen, in my version of* Paradise Lost *we performed obscene acts with apples, grapes and bananas. It was the most degrading experience I'd ever been through.*

So many green and orange signs are scattered up and down

the road. This orange, a color one encounters so rarely in nature, so often in my life. Signifying danger, a warning, a need for attention. So many different instructions. We are not the first to try and make sense of all this.

"Fruit," I say, "is the equivalent of the egg in traditional symbolism, for in the center you find the seed which represents the origin. The apple, in particular, is a symbol of earthly desires. In the garden, a warning against the exaltation of materialistic desire, the thirst for knowledge."

She rolls her eyes.

"Grapes," I say, "represent both fertility and sacrifice. The banana, I'm afraid, isn't mentioned in Cirlot's."

Probably, she says, *it has something to do with the United Fruit Company and the CIA in Guatemala. Honey, this is all complete and utter bullshit. The origin? I am not your primal innocence. There is no primal innocence, no garden, no golden era to return to, only shifting relations of power. All this nostalgia for an imaginary past, all of it bullshit, desire being manipulated, feeding into consumption. Traditional symbols, patriarchal culture, I don't need to hear it. You and your goddam language of colonization and oppression. This isn't my history, my symbols.*

I can't look at her. Out on the land is just what I'm seeking, on a billboard up ahead an image of what Andalusia could be: a large, smiling black woman trying to sell me pancake syrup. I ate this syrup as a child, watched it run from the center and bleed off the edges. I ate my pancakes ritualistically, circling toward the center or eating designs in the stack, stars, faces, ovals, cubes, trying to find the order, the periodic table of elements in my pancakes, the code that would keep evil from my life. If I ate the pancakes the wrong way my tongue might fall out, I might lose hold of my dreams.

Now that she has started, Andalusia won't stop. Women are not landscapes to be conquered, food, mystery, chaos. Sure, she'll admit she used to be an essentialist, looking for some primal feminine language, a liquid way of speaking, the spaces in between men's tyrannical words and grammatical structures.

Now she's more interested in deconstructing gender. She goes on about military metaphors used concerning the body, AIDS and genocidal neglect, blurred boundaries, the doubly impossible task for women of color to find a true voice, the cultural construction of subjectivity, energy and words, *jouissance*, revolt. One must be careful, however, not to reduce everything to text. This is about living, pain, actual bodies.

Back then, she says, *when I made that video, I thought the system would give me a chance. Back then I was stupid. I am tired of being used and degraded, of other people pretending that they can speak for my self. I've learned to fight back. I joined the underground and found my own education. I refuse to be a passive receptor, to drown in this ocean of lies, infantile desire, rich men's dreams broadcast as the news.*

Still, the landscape rolls by. Kudzu and crab farms and billboard and sky. Once, I was drowning in the river, just falling, eyes opened wide, not afraid to die, only falling. The water warm and tranquil all around. She saved me. I knew then, we'd again be together. And now we are.

She says, *Now I take pictures, take action, take risks.* She did a photographic essay on the people and wildlife around the nuclear test site in Nevada. All these mutant animals, kids with leukemia, birth-defect babies. Her phone's been tapped, her letters opened, her life recorded on film. But now things are really happening. She's on her way to pick up a drop. Evidence: documents, photographs, interviews on tape: drug running, the vice-president, CIA murder. A government gone wild, out of control, a facade of democracy. She has evidence, not much but a start. She's nobody's mysterious other.

I watch out the window. Must I listen to this? She'll drive me somewhere, she'll love me, forgive me, whatever it takes.

"I'm an orphan," I say.

Yes, I'll admit, I want to impress her. I want her to love me, if for no other reason, on account of this fact. She's in no mood to indulge me. *There's an orphanage in Guatemala*, she tells me, *where children are raised to be murdered. For black-market baby parts. There's a market in Europe and here, for tiny little kidneys and livers and spleens. They kill the children, sell their organs to the wealthy.*

Yes, I feel queasy and sick, I want to throw up.

"Andalusia," I say, "you're the only one who can forgive me."

Forgiveness, she says, *I'm afraid that I can't. This has nothing to do with Jesus or turning the other cheek.*

She doesn't know what I've done, she says, but I'll have to forgive myself. She's got more pressing matters on her mind. She's afraid she's being pursued. She's a little bit scared, Dodge Omnis aren't the best cars to escape in. The inside of this Omni smells sweet and pink, like a bathroom. This is not a car which would be pursued. Surely the place exists where I could be safe from all this living. Surely this is it.

"We'll run away together," I say. "We'll lose ourselves. You're everything to me."

Who do you think you're fooling, anyway? she asks. *The way you fondled those G.I. Joes and plastic astronauts when you were a kid, I always knew you were queer.*

She knows everything, it's true, like nobody else. She's omniscient, omnipotent, all those other words that start with omni.

"It's even your car," I say. "How can you deny you're the only one for me?"

She swats her neck with her hand, the fist-and-rose tattoo, wipes the sweat from her neck hair.

"We're reaching that point in my life where one would expect some sort of redemption," I say. "Redemption through good works, redemption through love. Redemption in nature, redemption through forgiveness. I've tried all these things, nothing lasts. You're my last hope. Redemption through Andalusia."

Honey, she says, *quit.*

"I love you," I say.

The silence seeps into my pores, opens them wide. The dark winds of the universe are free to blow the ashes of my heart out into Mississippi.

"I killed my parents," I say.

Both of them? she says. *That's not very Oedipal.*

Who is this woman? This isn't Andalusia. I feel a shattering inside, clench my fingers around the door handle. Andalusia never talked about Freud. I want my pre-Freudian innocence back. I want to frolic innocently in bathtubs and moon craters, want everything I lack. I'll admit, I don't know what I'm talking about, that rice towers are crumbling into ash, stairways that led backward, wombward. I know that I am babbling and that somewhere, lost in my own insanity, is nothing one would say is true: to become yourself, obediently, to omit everything is to be perfectly alone, without language or desire, to be a color just this side of black, to be the sound a tree makes falling in the empty woods.

"I'd rather have love," I say, "and all the illusions it entails."

Love? she says. *Love? Don't talk about love. You don't know shit about love. You'd deny me my voice, attempt to speak for me, turn me into something I'm not.*

Outside on the land, Spanish moss hangs, suicidal, deranged. If this is true there is nothing left for me. Everything is evil, only that.

Oh shit.

We approach a roadblock at the Louisiana border. She's worried. She doesn't have the evidence yet, but what's this about? She slows down. There are cars everywhere, officers. We come to a stop just before the line of barricades and police. Cars are being checked, driving on through.

A uniformed man sticks his head in the window. She asks what the deal is. Routine, he tells us. A hopeless search for subversive elements disguised as a drug crackdown. A bureaucratic nightmare. Corruption and miscarriages of justice. Political maneuvers.

Andalusia shows the cop her identification. He looks around the car and waves us on our way. She accelerates. We drive past billboards of camels smoking cigarettes.

"Andalusia," I say, "you're starting to sound like everyone

else I meet, your voice like some weird warped reflection of my own."

Jesus, Matt, she says, *you are a strange one. But I like you, kid, I always did. I must say that. I do like you.*

I smile. I feel warm all over, covered with soft, leafy parasites.

We did have some good times together, didn't we? Catching tadpoles, feeding fireflies to make them glow. Oh, I do remember. I loved you then like my very own kid. Because I knew you were queer. You and your wandering about, you remind me of one of my old lovers, a woman named Rebeca.

I nod. Yes, this is it, the way it should go.

"I did love somebody else once," I say. "A boy named Jimmy."

Sure, she says, *say it loud.*

"But that's different," I say. "Jimmy's the darkness, the stealing, the black heart of death. He's grown huge, he lurks on billboards in his underwear. Jimmy is the freedom of the blood, the choices made at midnight. Jimmy's eyes reflect my own murder."

She again rolls her eyes.

"No," I say, "you don't understand. Really. There's something about him. He's following me, he's chasing me down. He'd kill me, Andalusia, he would have, but not now, not now he can't. I've found you. Everything will be OK."

I smile, tell myself this is true, although it is not.

I must admit, she says, *that I've had that feeling at times. That someone was following me, chasing me down.*

She glances in the rearview mirror.

There was a woman back some ways got crushed by a rock.

"Andalusia," I say, "it's me, it's always been me."

It's getting difficult to breathe, to think, to cohere. On the land ahead, Jimmy again.

"Look," I say, "there he is. Jimmy in the sky."

We pass the billboard so fast it's nearly a blur, but there's no mistaking the face on that billboard, the eyes, the lean torso. Andalusia laughs.

You've got to be kidding. That ANGST *underwear model who's in all the magazines these days? You are really insane, aren't you?*

"We lived together," I say, "on the streets of St. Louis."

I suppose anything's possible, she says.

She exits. We glide down the ramp, pull into the parking lot of a closed-down donut shop. LAND O' DONUTS! declares the sign, GIANT GOING-OUT-OF-BUSINESS SALE! It's closed for remodeling. They're turning it into an upscale pastry shop, Andalusia tells me. She used to work here; she had to do something to pay the bills, so she could do her real work of subversion.

Now, she has a key. Children huddle in a circle at the edge of the lot, engaged in some huge, secret purpose. We enter the donut shop.

Aisles and aisles of empty bins, the signs still declare: Cinnamon Glazed, Blueberry Cream Cheese, Coconut Chocolate; the long johns, the French twists and almond croissants; the bright fluorescent lights, the poster of smiling donut-shop employees overhead. We've stumbled into a vastness, another universe, an eternity of donuts.

Andalusia has to climb up into the asbestos-filled ceiling, where the evidence has been left for her. I can watch the TV in the break room, if I'd like, while I'm waiting. Keep a watch out the window in case anyone comes by.

I sit in a plastic chair, trying to gather my life together. I am losing everything, possibilities, dreams. My life without meaning, I don't know who I am.

I turn on the TV.

A soap opera. Click, another soap opera, click, a game show, click, a commercial. "Are you faced with the eternal recurrence of these same laundry problems?" asks the housewife. "Mud, ketchup, chocolate and especially bloodstains. But now there's Übermensch, the detergent that overcomes all previous stain removers. Stronger, more forceful than ever before."

I'm about to flip the channel, the commercial ends, we switch back to a talk show in progress. A man with big teeth is seated at a desk. Next to him is Jimmy.

"Welcome back to *Good Afternoon America, How Do You Feel?*" says the man with big teeth, "the show that wants to listen to you. Seated next to me, of course, is Jimmy, the most substantial and newsworthy male model in America. The mystery, the rumors of liaisons with daughters of South American presidents. ANGST; the latest in briefs. Television, magazines, underwear billboards all over the country."

He turns toward Jimmy.

"You were telling us then that you've always been somewhat of a homebody. Has your life changed significantly since you were discovered by the Will to Power modeling agency?"

Jimmy says that he's a very simple person. He likes to watch TV. He likes to sit at home with a bowl of popcorn and his pet canary and watch old movies. That's his idea of an ideal evening. He is glossy now, he looks pampered. A surface, a blur of light, a parade behind tinted glass: unreachable and nocturnal.

"There's a real mystique surrounding you, Jimmy, questions about your mysterious past. Would you care to clarify exactly how you spent your childhood?"

He grew up in the French Antilles. His mother was a newspaper heiress, his father a diplomat. That's really about all there is to it, it isn't so mysterious.

I watch him, stunned. He's as beautiful as ever. The phone number flashes, a 1-800 number. This is absolutely live, from a studio in New York. The wonders of modern television technology. They'll soon be fielding questions from all over the country.

I move to the phone. The odds of getting through are not in my favor.

On the screen a woman caller is asking Jimmy how often he has orgasms, if he believes the G spot is real, can he tell when women are faking it?

I dial. Quiet horns blow over the wires, foreign conversations fill the silence. Andalusia steps in, carrying a manila folder. *Who are you calling?* I point toward the TV.

Ring. Ring. I'm falling. I'm standing still. A black shard of mirror imbedded in my spine.

Matt, Jimmy will say, *Matt, I love you, I've always loved you. Matt, I've never wanted anything more than for you to touch me. To fuck me for hours on hot nights, tangled in sweaty sheets, lasting forever, desperate, intense, concentrated, wrestling in time, fingers intertwined, bitten lips, clenched teeth, knowing each other's thoughts, trying to break through something, to obliterate the world, to get somewhere new.*

"Yes, Jimmy," I say.

Think of what we could do together. We'll show them what the love of two men is capable of. We'll destroy their whole fucked-up society. Everything.

"Where do we start, Jimmy?"

We start with their history, their literature, their religion, their economy. We'll dance on the rubble. We'll move so fast they can never catch up. We'll bring it all down and start over from scratch, reinvent the whole fucking world.

"Yes, Jimmy," I say.

And then death, Jimmy says. *You understand that. I love you so much.*

Ring. Ring. On the television a caller asks, "What about this light thing, Jimmy? I don't get it at all. How can it be both particle *and* wave? Jimmy, explain this one, please."

Jimmy shrugs, smiles, looks at the host. The host affirms that we're all confused, that we're all more things than one, that this isn't a science program. Next caller, please.

Ring. The telephone is answered. I freeze. Put my hand on my heart. I am America and they want to hear what I have to say. What's my name and what do I want to ask Jimmy about?

"I'm Matt," I say. "I want to ask about his mysterious past."

I'll be one of the next callers put through.

On the screen, a woman caller. "I would just like to point out that ANGST underwear has just been purchased by R. J. Rey-

nolds, one of the most evil corporations in America." She goes
on about subliminal advertising, cigarette ads targeting youth.

"Next caller," says the host.

"Yes," says an elderly woman. "My body's decaying, I'm in
great pain. I used to be beautiful, sure, just like you. I could
have sold underwear back in my day. But my children don't
love me, my hair's falling out. I just want to tell you, don't think
it'll last."

"*Yes,*" says Jimmy.

"Next caller," says the host.

Somewhere, across Louisiana fields a telephone is ringing.
I imagine myself running, through fields of cotton and peanuts,
arriving breathless at the deserted farmhouse door. I pick up
the phone.

Hello? I say.

I wait for the voice on the other end to interrupt this silence.

Hello, says Jimmy's voice, *what can I do for you?*

"Jimmy," I whisper.

Yes?

"It's me," I croak. "Matt."

There is a pause. Everything I say comes from the television about ten seconds later. It feels somewhat as if I'm losing
my mind.

A long black car pulls up in front of the donut shop.

Matt, he says.

Two nearly identical men in suits and mirrored sunglasses
step out of the car. They are strikingly handsome in a techno-
logical sort of way. They wear yellow smiley-face buttons on
their suits. They could be clones of each other, I recognize them
at once. The authorities.

Matt? he says.

"Yes," I say.

Where are you?

I am dizzy, clutching the phone to my ear. The phone is
black.

Are you here? In New York?

The host is giving him a curious look. The camera pans over the sedate, smiling audience.

The authorities, says Andalusia. She moves to the window. "No," I say, "no, not right now."

Andalusia is screaming something out the window. Andalusia has a gun.

It's my old friend Matt, I hear Jimmy say to the host, and just after he's finished, his image on the screen repeats the same words.

I just flew in from L.A., Jimmy tells me.

"Jesus, Jimmy," I say. The words don't come out of the set. Jimmy is gone, a commercial, popcorn dancing across the screen, singing a song that used to be associated with ending the war in Vietnam. On the other end of the phone things are being said, I can't make them out, some kind of commotion.

I've got hostages, Andalusia shouts. *Go away or you'll have dead innocents on your hands.*

One of the authorities says they don't want trouble, they're willing to make a deal. They just want the evidence. Two identical men, crouched next to their car. Huck and Jim, Lennie and George, Jack and Neal, and now this: identical men in suits, sunglasses, a long black car. The progression of the American dream.

Always, of course, excluding the female, says Andalusia. *Positing us as other, the landscape to be tamed, the day to be seized.* Carpe diem, *my ass.*

Matt, says Jimmy, *are you still there?*

"I'm still here," I say.

You can't say Jesus on the air, he tells me. Didn't you know that? They won't let you back on. Listen, we've got to make this quick, we've only got until the end of the commercial break.

"Jimmy," I say, "you want to strangle me, don't you? You want to put your hands around my neck and strangle me."

Matt, says Jimmy, *I'm on television now.*

Outside, there is a sky filled with stars, hidden only by the daylight. The authorities are going on about how pointless this is. They can effectively kill Andalusia, destroy all records of her existence. Nobody will listen to a nonexistent woman. Disappearance, the wave of the future.

Where are you? asks Jimmy.

Andalusia starts shooting.

"Close to New Orleans," I say, "but not all the way there."

What's that noise in the background? asks Jimmy. *What's going on?*

"People are trying to kill each other," I say. "Nothing new. You remember Dust? The beach in Florida?"

Plane trips make me weird, says Jimmy.

I cough.

Hmm, says Jimmy.

"I don't like the telephone," I say. "It doesn't feel like real communication."

Andalusia crouches by the window, wiping sweat from her forehead. *If that was true,* she says, *you wouldn't care about the evidence. I want you to know the press has already been notified, there are dozens of copies of this evidence all over the country. You may as well let me go, minimize your losses.*

Ha ha ha, they laugh. They are crouching as well, on the other side of their car. Andalusia stares at me.

How can you just sit there watching, doing nothing at all?

I imagine you'd like to touch me, says Jimmy.

I suck in my breath. Just now, no one is shooting. The quiet is like time travel. He would be warm against me, and cool, opening up for me, deep and silent. Silence opens the way for imagination. I could fuck him so well.

You think that would take you someplace new, he says, *as if an orgasm was the doorway to God or the devil.*

"These words," I say. "Don't pretend to be somebody you aren't. These thoughts aren't yours, Jimmy. You're lying again."

I've always known that talking is only a way to be like everybody else, he says. *I was never like that.*

"You're talking now," I say.

Yes.

On the TV, a different commercial appears. It is Jimmy himself, reclining in his briefs. I stare at his image. I have Jimmy in front of me, rippling, taut, bored. Like anyone else, I could purchase a magazine with the very same image, take it into any respectable restaurant or donut shop in America. I could take it into the public restroom, gaze at it as I would at any object and jack off, quickly and efficiently, ejaculating into the sink.

Everybody looks at me now, says Jimmy. *I am: there's your proof.*

"I'm in a donut shop," I say. "Here, I'll tell you what kinds of donuts they have. All different kinds. Apple Crunch and Blueberry Frosted and Boysenberry Filled and Boysenberry Frosted and Caramel Frosted and Chocolate and Chocolate Glazed and Chocolate Frosted."

Guns are going off, things ricochet and shatter. The children at the edge of the lot stand in a line, like targets. As children tend to be, they are curious, reckless, tiny voyeurs. Some are beautiful, some ugly, some cocky, some bashful and frightened.

You used to look at me, says Jimmy. *When you were gone, on the beach that day, I felt different. I ended up at the Hare Krishna house in Boulder. I was tired, Matt. They took care of me there, they fed me, we sat around and chanted and scooped out free vegetarian feast for all the street people in Boulder. In the old days I was just making things hard for myself. The world isn't such a hostile place. If you just let them, things start coming to you.*

I want to light myself on fire, run screaming off the top of a very tall building.

Matt?

"Please," I say, "do go on."

Then I was discovered. I guess I looked pretty good even with my knobby haircut. Life's been good to me since then. I guess so. People give me money, and things. People stop me on the street. Everybody wants to touch me. Men or women or both. It's too late now for life not to be like that anymore.

I feel my stomach just behind my tongue, the digestive juices running down my throat. Outside, one of the smallest children, a particularly wide-eyed and lovable child, is felled by a stray bullet, nearly severing his or her tiny neck from the rest of his or her body. He or she crumples to the pavement, apparently dead. The other children scatter.

Matt, says Jimmy, *all the stuff we did, that's gone, right? I'm whatever people think when they look at me. But I'm more than that, too. I won't ever die. I'll keep on being born, over and over again.*

"Jimmy," I say.

It's nice, you know, says Jimmy, *to wear nice clothes, to eat fashionable food. I could take you to all the best clubs. Why don't you come to New York? I'm getting married next month.*

"How can you live like this?" I ask. "After where we've been? What we went through?"

Matt, he says, *that stuff's all over. Nobody wants to know about it, OK?*

An authority shouts: You see what happens? You think you're saving the world and you're only killing children. You communists are all the same, claim to love humanity, but don't give a shit about real human beings. Their smiley-face buttons reflect small pieces of sunlight.

"I loved you," I say, "I did everything for you. Stealing, all of it, everything for you."

Don't give me that shit, Jimmy says. *We did what we had to, that was all. I never did anything that anybody else wouldn't have done. You were the one that was a bad influence on me. You're the one that talked me into running away.*

I can feel the telephone lines stretching like rubber, the distance between us growing until the gap is wider than death. His statement is so ludicrous that I realize, *nothing is true.*

"All communication is manipulation," I say. "I don't need to hear your version of the past."

Outside, the authority: We're just trying to protect a way of life here. The capacity of Americans to feel good, to have nice days. To live in blissful ignorance. Who are these authorities, where do they come from? R. J. Reynolds, General Electric, the CIA? Power sources farther back, invisible, impossible to see in the daylight? Andalusia is running toward me.

Come to New York, Jimmy says. *Really. We'll have lunch. Look, the commercial's almost over, we're almost out of time.*

Nobody wants to kill me. Nobody is that involved. I could hang up the phone, call numbers at random. Perhaps it isn't too late.

"Sure," I say, "I'll get in touch with you. Listen, I've got to go."

Matt?

Andalusia is right beside me, her arm around my head and her pistol sticking halfway up my nose.

"Bye," I say.

I hang up the phone. With a gun up my nose it's hard to think about much else. On the screen Jimmy appears again, smiling, chatting with the host. The phone is ringing, people want to tell him things, to complain about their lives, receive assurances or simply hear themselves speak. "Thank God we can no longer be electrocuted by our phones during thunderstorms," a caller declares. Andalusia drags me toward the window.

I'll kill him, she says. *You let me go or you'll have a whole mess of innocent blood to explain to the cops.*

One of the men steps forward. The barrel of the gun is up against my neck now. I do not know if Andalusia would really shoot me. There are a great many things I do not know.

Glass shatters, donuts bleed cherry creme, coffeepots explode. We duck behind a red booth. Suddenly, everything stops.

A blind woman with long orange hair walks across the parking lot. She is singing opera at the top of her lungs. Her shirt is pale blue, her skirt is black. She walks right through the middle of everything, tapping her cane wildly before her. Her hair glistens in the sun, long orange hair, it flows and waves. She sings loudly and off-key, tapping her cane. She maneuvers the entire parking lot, singing. Everyone stares. Nobody moves. Her hair twists and flames in the sunlight, her long orange hair. She sings. She can see nothing, she is blind, a blind woman singing, with long orange hair trailing behind her. Her shirt is a pale blue,

nearly as pale as the sky. Her skirt is black and she walks and
taps her cane and sings, loud, drowning everything out, the world
she cannot see. The authorities shoot her and she falls to the
pavement, teeth scattering before her as she hits, still blind but
now dead as well. The sound her body makes as it hits the parking lot is similar to that of obscure machinery backfiring,
mechanical things taking place for reasons we're not sure of,
just outside our bedroom windows in the middle of the night.
The sound of change jingling in somebody's pocket.

Do we get the point? The authorities say that they'll blame
this one on us. DRUG KINGPIN KILLS BLIND WOMAN IN LOUISIANA.

Out of my way, Andalusia shrieks, and somehow we are
moving back across the parking lot toward the car. She hurls the
manila folder at the men, it opens, papers and photographs
spilling across the lot.

Take it, she says. *Take your fucking evidence!*

Papers rain down, tossed this way and that in the wind. The
men run this way and that. Everything is moving this way and
that, this way and that. The child's corpse, the blind woman,
these, however, remain perfectly still. If I really wanted to be
murdered, I realize, there's no shortage of men who might oblige
me.

We are in the car, revving the engine, zipping back onto the
highway. A station wagon plunges into the ditch to avoid us,
wide-eyed electricians in front and children in back, shrieking
with glee. Men in black scurry about the parking lot behind us.
A Bible-school bus has pulled over on the shoulder. Women
stand in a circle around it, holding hands, singing "Kumbaya."

She releases my neck.

Of course, they'll come after us, she says. *There's really no
escape.*

Andalusia has been wounded, blood coming from the far
side of her body. We are traveling faster. I hold my arm out the
open window, use it to swoop and dive in the rushing air.

"You're bleeding," I say. "I'll take care of you now."

It's only a flesh wound, she says.

I don't understand the vocabulary. Flesh, word, soul, blood.

"Why does everyone else always get to bleed?" I ask. "Why do I always just have to watch? I want my own pain. I want somebody to watch *me* bleed."

The idea of being wounded, she says, *is much more romantic than the reality. The idea of struggle, of blowing up buildings, of battling the greedy motherfuckers who rule the world, all very romantic notions. In reality, there's a great deal of discomfort involved.*

Here, she says, *feel my blood.* I reach over, dip my finger in her side. The moisture and color on my fingers. The metallic taste we all know.

This is blood, she says. *This isn't text.*

With what speed we do move: houses and crab farms and museums and posts, everything flying past. I look back behind us. There is a black speck on the horizon.

But, listen, all is not lost. The originals, the negatives, all of it in a locker at the Greyhound station in Mobile. I have the key. If we could get this evidence out, maybe we could stop that ex–CIA director from being elected president.

On the other hand, she says, *we need to escape.*

The roadblock's just ahead, she says. *There's only one thing left to do. You remember that movie we used to watch when you were a little kid?* Vanishing Point?

I nod. I always knew this would happen someday. The needle of the speedometer is beyond the land of demarcations.

"I watched it again at the public library once," I say, "but they changed the ending. They changed it so he crashes and dies."

Actually, says Andalusia, *they originally filmed three endings. The one where he crashes, the one where he vanishes and another, where he breaks through and keeps on going. But the studio bigwigs opted against the vanishing ending. They decided people wouldn't understand it, it was too existential. They showed the one where he crashed.*

Too existential. Of course. She really does know everything. I watch out my window. I can see it all from here, it isn't so much. I can sit here in this car. I can learn to be still, can learn to stop moving. Anything's possible. I breathe.

"Andalusia," I say, "talk to me. Tell me about your life. I want to know."

Matt, she says, *we don't have the time.*

She turns toward me. In our gaze, time bleeds, we are locked together. For a moment we're cruising through pure empty space. Surrounded by nothing, I can't judge our speed. I need to take a quick inventory. What have I lost, what options are left? A blind woman back there, dead on the pavement. Another slaughtered child. My parents, Jimmy, Dust, Frita and Jessica Moon. Andalusia as well, the one that I dreamed of. Gone, all gone, finally we find it comes down to this.

How easily it happens, can all be discarded. Histories, memories, facts, destinations and dreams. I've lost it all now. This happens, we're told. You'd think we might be prepared.

"I could scream" I say. "Let me tell you, I could scream."

I know that everyone feels this way from time to time. This knowledge doesn't help.

The wind picks up now, gusts blowing petals of white flowers across the road and in through our windows. I'm afraid I may regress until I'm only an empty cube. Do I really want to be a solid? So much pain is inflicted on matter, so much loss. The relentless August sunlight fills me with dread. How little there is in dread after all.

Is the hunger so great? I could be still. Empty of everything. Nothing is not as little as I'd thought. Others will have had less, always.

The car moves forward toward its destiny. Andalusia sees something there, up ahead, some last chance on the horizon. Lucky Andalusia. I do not ask what it might be, for I see nothing at all.

What does one do with nothing? Death or acquisition come to mind. Equilibrium never lasts. One must move, toward more or toward less.

Pure emptiness and pure possibility, equivalent sums.

The roadblock's right up ahead, she says.

We are speeding through it all now, the authorities behind us, the roadblock up ahead. Through this sprawling nation of electricity and noise, this nation of wind. Of starving children, of scarred veterans and junkies, of men in bad cars and homeless old women. The blind and the hopeless, cripples and whores and runaway babies, orphans like me, who've lost all their dreams. Murderers and produce men and those crushed by rocks. Epileptics and mongoloids and papier-mâché dreamers, hearts crumpling like tissue; trapped under wheels, sleeping in doorways, insane and bleeding and yearning to speak; the damned, the forgotten, the mesmerized losers, the wilted and churning, the dumb clumsy souls, the hollow-boned mutants, those staring at owls, the trudgers and moaners and whiners and deaf, the ossified mummies, the jailed and betrayed, disillusioned socialist schoolteachers and truckers on speed. Those standing by highways, those who need to invent, those who can't even fight back, those who drink to forget, who forget to survive, who survive God knows why, who Jesus won't help and who karma has shit on, who pick things out of trash and whose friends are abducted, who see bright things at night, who fought in the wars, who might as easily have died, who got the clap from their brother, who were beat as a child, who beat their own children although they don't really want to, who were molested or abandoned or misunderstood, who watched their own house burn down and nothing was saved, who pose naked for money, who were born with no legs, who crawl and who spit and who tremble and scrape, who hope despite knowledge, who howl as they trudge.

Over the next hill, says Andalusia. We are picking up speed, the world flying past us so fast, the colors a blur. So many ghosts and odors and invisible waves. Our dead lie in heaps by our highways, wash up on the beaches. *This land is your land, this land is my land.* Commerce, connections, glamour and blondes, mansions and jewelry, General Electric and presidents' wives. This land of tinted windows and vanity plates, cologne and mouthwash splashed over the stench of the dying, of joy and boredom and most certainly dread. This nation where losers are nothing and nobody wins, where the top story tonight is a new soft-drink concoction, where the sweat of world labor is turned into plastic, *this land is your land, this land is my land,* people searching for a better way and those staying home, without memory or dreams, this land we've betrayed.

Just down the road, the barricade. She will not slow down. There are three possible endings here. Always such limits to the possible, it seems. We will break on through, we will crash and die in flames, or perhaps we will vanish. If we break on through, where will we go, where would it end? I posit Andalusia's loss of blood proceeding into the future. Yes, bullets are real. If we crash and die, what does it prove? Like so much else, the idea of crashing and dying is, I imagine, much more appealing in theory. Death, putrefaction, worms and maggots, embalming fluid and shit, if that much is left. The end, absolute zero, nonbeing, going, gone, nothing, not even a trace that might be deciphered in some imagined future. Absence, dissolution of the ego, the one and only void. Nothing.

Or vanishing. Is vanishing just another refusal to take part in the struggle? Does vanishing include the possibility of reappearing? Can we leave secret traces, ruptures, denials, chart secret pathways, emerge somewhere else? I simply don't know. We need another option.

"This must have another ending," I say.

Yes, says Andalusia, *full of innocent children.*

I imagine fields, rivers, moonscapes filled with just such children. Children who wouldn't be murdered, kicked about, slaughtered, forced to work in dark factories, dismembered. These children wouldn't be taught to hate themselves, told that loving is evil, thrown in prison, starved or left to die on the street. I run my fingers over *The Sickness unto Death.*

I never read that one, Andalusia says, *although I did read* Fear and Trembling. *My understanding was that Kierkegaard felt faith was the work of an entire lifetime. That it requires an absurd sort of leap.*

What will such an act would require. What responsibility

and choosing. Andalusia is in the driver's seat. I prefer it this way. I made the wrong choice a long time ago, that murder business from my childhood. I've yet to get over the consequences.

On the other hand, this may not be true. We're hurling down this highway, Andalusia smiling with a ridiculous glee, and I know that I have to make a choice, if it isn't too late already. We rise, the crest of a hill, the road flattening before us and at the end of it the roadblock, the end, the point of transformation.

Fare you well, says Andalusia, *I'm off to Arcturus.*

"No," I say, "wait." We are gathering speed. I hold out my hand. I say, "Give me the key." She smiles.

"You can trust me," I say. "The depot in Mobile, the evidence. You need to let me out."

There's a trick in getting past the emptiness: to create the illusion of continual forward motion. To posit a goal, a destination.

"You can trust me," I say.

I know, she says, *I've always known that.* She gives me the key. She slows the car down, I open the door, we're still moving no doubt but it's now or it's never. She stares at the horizon with that gleam in her eyes, the landscape a blur, the key in my hand, she slows down, not all the way down, they're back there, behind us, the roadblock ahead, I perch in the doorway, gather myself up, billboards and grasses and sunlight whiz by, who I am, Matt, the greens streaking past, ditches and fenceposts and gravel and sky, the world spinning dizzy, I hover; I leap.

2

I'm out, I'm tumbling through space, I'm hanging in air. Across green open fields, spinning like this. I hang here.

One would like to get rid of the noise for just one moment of stillness, to get to that pure fact of existence. A fact astonishing in itself, but whose shock value is often obscured by all this chatter about meaning and lawn mowers and true love and the weather.

The weather. Wind and white petals, cumulonimbus clouds reclaiming the sky. I hang here like this. I leapt. Yes, I certainly did do that.

A hunk of Jell-O electrified, a leap in the air; as a child one apologized to furniture, harassed brick walls, sang along with the leaves when they changed color in the fall. Days stretched on forever and the things that happened were attributable to master plans, intricate plots mapped out in the floral designs on wallpaper, the shadows of branches on bedroom walls at night, the faces that were trapped in windowpane and moonlight, watching as I slept.

Once, it was snowing. I woke one night, able to hear the cold after the furnace shut off. It was too early for my paper route, but I got up out of bed. I'd been dreaming, an image still stuck in my eyes, a face. I couldn't quite pin it down, they say that's your self. I stepped to the window. The yellow glow of the streetlight, the snow falling past. I dressed quickly, put on boots, my parka, my gloves. The house was dark and silent, glowed from the light of the snow. I stood for a moment, downstairs by the door, making things last. On the other side of the window everything was perfect. I stepped out into the street and walked, the cold sharp at first, but then mellow. Everything covered, everything white. No footprints, just sparkles and snow, and I laughed. Everything quiet. The flakes danced around me, slow. I tilted my head back, let them hit me and melt. No wind, only falling. I could see silent waves of information zipping around me, in the air up above. I walked and was away then, darkened houses, pure white lawns. I took off my gloves and touched the snow, a wet sticky snow, tasted it. I breathed on my hands, stuck them deep in my pockets. Everything still. Crunch, crunch. A figure walked toward me.

I didn't move, wasn't scared. I stood in the middle of the street, looking up at the white branches of a white oak, glowing intense in the light.

"You always find us," she said then, "on nights like these, staring at trees. Or on rooftops or by rivers or crossroads or bridges. You think you're alone, but there's more of us out here."

I remember it now, her voice muffled in the snow. It was the most beautiful accent. She wore a black-and-green scarf around her head, so I couldn't see her hair, but her face: it was so beautiful, daring and smooth like a boy's. Or did I invent this memory? Have I lost such control? No, she gave me a donut, out of her bag, fresh and hot, and I held it. She didn't say anything more, just walked on down the street.

I ate the donut, God was it good. I lay back in the snow, flapped my arms, made an angel. I lay there and it felt cold at first, but then it got warm, so comfortable, numbing. I imagined stepping back into the warmth of the house, the snow dripping off me. I watched the buzzing air, the silent buzzing of the snow, covering me. I thought that this time I might go back or I might never. I might never move again. There was no one around, everyone sleeping and dreaming. I closed my eyes, felt the snow melt on my lids.

"Listen," I whispered, and the sound was so jolting in the quiet of the snow that I felt as if I was shouting, even there, alone in the snow, as if something strong and slightly frightening had been done, something illegal. I was so amazed by the sound of my voice, something alive in the air, that I repeated the word.

"Listen."

Now, I hang here in air. But I see it from here. The car upside down in the distance, speeding toward the horizon, the roadblock, cop cars and people and blinking orange lights, she's picking up speed, faster, faster, she's there and people are screaming or else a dead hush, waiting for the crash, for explosion and death, metal and glass, she's there at her moment, a thin wavering smile, a car up in flames, a shattered brick wall, the last American hero, a wish for survival, she's there and I hang here, suspended in space, the world upside down, she's there and she's gone, a flash of nothing but absence, a mirage and escape, it happens like this: *whoooooooosh*. Andalusia vanishes.

I close my eyes.

I land, THUNK, on my head.

3

I open my eyes. The authorities drive past, without seeing me, moving so fast toward the roadblock, the scene of escape. The afternoon is restless. All dreams of relief have burrowed and hidden underground, in dank hovels, smelling of roots and cabbage leaves. I sit up. The hills are rolling here, pleasant farmland. I stand and walk through it.

The clouds are dark and stretch away and the wind is picking up. A beautiful dark light covers everything. Purple ripples, blades of grass. Out here I can sense my own dying. It's in the wind, the hunger, the pain in my ankles. I find myself laughing. I walk and keep walking toward nothing but hills and grass, hills and grass, until I can no longer hear the highway behind me.

On the crest of the next hill over there's a small black boy, flying a kite. The wind increases. The heat's being slaughtered by another front. Granted, I'm no meteorologist, I've never been able to predict such things. But I know what's coming now. I've loved it all my life.

I walk toward the boy. Through the noiselessness, the smell of a storm. Step, step, gathering speed down the hill, making it halfway up the other side on my own momentum. The sky is more interesting than I am. Its darkening, its promise. The kite hangs for a moment, as if in a vacuum. Just now there is no wind.

"Hi, mister," the boy says. He tugs on his string. The kite swoops, regains its balance.

"Will you give me a dollar?" he asks.

It must be eighty degrees out here. He's wearing a stocking cap that says BRR on it. Sticking out from underneath, a mat of thick curly hair. A few of the hairs are gray. It strikes me that this boy's head is exactly the right size for his body. The wind picks up, but quietly, politely.

"Do I look like I'd have a dollar to give you?" I ask.

He looks me up and down.

"Can't say," he says. "Never hurt to ask."

It's still hot. But the breeze grows cooler. His kite makes rippling noises in the wind.

"Why you wearing that hat in this heat?" I ask.

"Can't tell these days when the weather might change," he says. "My mom makes me wear it."

Below us lies a small pond. Ducks move across the water, creating a V in their wake, as if the surface is a thin film and by gliding over it they release all the submerged possibilities.

"Why's that?" I ask.

"When I was five me and my brother were watching TV," he says. "Mom came back and it was a blizzard and my brother wasn't there. Where's your brother? she said. I'm not watching my brother, I said. You didn't ask me to watch my brother, I said. Am I supposed to be watching my brother?"

His kite dives toward the earth, out of control, crashes down below. The sudden violence doesn't shock either of us. In the distance, behind a fat blistering white cloud, black ones appear. They move across the sun. The world is different in this light, more fragile and necessary.

"My brother was out in the snow," he says, "and later he died of pneumonia. Ever since then I had to wear a hat. Mom couldn't bear to lose another, she said. Can't be too careful, she said, when it comes to losing children."

I scan the horizon. There are houses and barns. Human beings live in these parts. In this light they would seem more truthful, quivering and filled with potential. Their eyes would be dark, their faces troubled. I imagine them shutting windows and barn doors or standing on their porches, watching the clouds.

"Ever get tornadoes around here?" I ask.

"Sure thing," he says. "All the time. Put a chair right through a tree once. Mister, what you doing anyway, out here in these fields?"

I take crumpled bills from my pocket. The food stamps I'd forgotten I owned.

"Do you really want to wear that hat all your life?"

He thinks about this.

"I don't know," he says. "If I didn't have it I might forget about my brother."

I study his face.

"It's your choice," I say, "but I'll give you three dollars' worth of food stamps in exchange for the hat."

He thinks for fifteen seconds or less.

"It's a deal, mister," he says.

All around the side it says BRR BRR BRR. I put it on my head.

"What's your name?" I ask.

He pauses, not sure he should tell.

"Otis Tyroler," he says.

"Otis Tyroler," I say, "do you know how to howl?"

He considers this.

"Sure," he says, "I could howl up a storm."

He howls.

I can hear it, all that wind in the distance, and I know it's right on its way. It really does sound like a freight train approaching, just like they say. The tornado, that is. It's coming closer, the leaves all rolling with it, a shimmery green. There seem to be animals everywhere, invisible or just very, very small. Their hushed cries fill the air.

I sit on this hill, the key in my pocket. I have a new destination now. Although I realize the difficulty I've had reaching my goals in the past.

"See you, mister," says the boy. "I got to go home now."

He runs out, collects the kite, waves and hurries across the fields, howling as he goes. He becomes smaller and smaller, but still: the surprise of his color and movement against the dusty green of the fields.

Granted, we're restless and smaller than trees. Terribly small, filled with such fragile matter. Still, if we all start to howl. For example, stop where we're moving and let out a howl. Throw

bricks from the street, through government chambers and corporate towers, through mansions and prisons and penthouse
apartments, break open windows and persistently howl. Howl:
we all die, we all die, we die we die we die, in the meantime
we'll howl. Howl: this isn't the end of the world after all. Howl:
Yo! to the greedy motherfuckers who own this world, even if
they aren't listening, still, we are out here and howling, always,
forever, something like this: murder, murder, murder, easy
murder, sanitized murder, invisible murder. Howl for the dead
who wash up on our beaches, howl on street corners and in
churches and schoolyards, howl out in thunderstorms, hail-
storms and snow, howl on the sidewalks, in cafés and bed-
rooms, howl at tornadoes, howl at the moon. Howl howl howl
our love joy laughter hunger sweat spittle jizzom from the top
of the tallest buildings and monuments to nuclear destruction
smear our bodily fluids across the image of presidents generals
professional killers. Howl. For example.

And the noise might be like the sound of this tornado, like
a freight train coming closer, and something might be changed,
walls crumbling, uniforms torn to shreds, windows shattered,
something might break open, and it won't be the end of the
world, it won't be apocalypse, catastrophe, won't be utopia or
the dawn of a new age, but it would be something. Yes, it would
be that.

Otherwise, howl. Out here. Alone after all.

Things proceed. I whistle. Softly now, concentrating. There
goes a silo, sucked right out of the earth, look at it go! Squealing
munchkins come to mind and women on brooms. Everything
awhirl, the air filled with gongs and leaves and livestock and
spiraling galaxies of stars, coming closer, coming this way.

I realize, of course, that truly effective howling requires listening as well. I listen. It's moving toward me at an amazing
speed, this black funnel that rips houses out of the earth. Tornadoes are rootless, but they do have a center. The roar, yes,
just like a freight train, I whistle a bit louder, but my own song
is lost, rising up in the air and joining the wind. The tornado
dances across the countryside, ripping and tearing, barns tum-

bled, roosters flung through windows, a life's work scattered across the hills, downed power lines, destruction, dissolution, decay: the legacy of this wind.

Sitting here now, on the edge of the future, I think: anything's possible. Amazing things are soon to happen.

It's much closer now, the noise is tremendous. Sooner or later, it will be here. Sooner or later, I'll have to move along.

CPSIA information can be obtained
at www.ICGtesting.com
Printed in the USA
LVHW100425290722
724706LV00003B/17